PRAISE FOR
THE TENTH GIRL

"FARING'S EXQUISITE PROSE weaves a tale that is
both seductively eerie and wildly original.
I've never read anything like it."

—APRIL GENEVIEVE TUCHOLKE,
author of *The Boneless Mercies*

"Layered and challenging, and full to bursting with
intelligence, while at the same time EXUBERANTLY BIZARRE,
like it's having the best time on its own and
daring you to join in."

—RORY POWER,
New York Times–bestselling author of *Wilder Girls*

"This book envelops the reader with sweeping beauty
and tingling mystery from the very first page."

—NOVA REN SUMA,
New York Times–bestselling author of *The Walls Around Us*

'The story delivers NUMEROUS TWISTS AND TURNS, each
a deliriously unreal blow . . . . [A] wholly original tale."

—KIRKUS REVIEWS

★ "GOTHIC THRILLER MEETS SCIENCE FICTION in this
enthralling labyrinth of a story that is as deeply emotional
as it is entirely unpredictable. Faring is brilliant."

—BCCB,
starred review

THE
TENTH
GIRL

THE
TENTH GIRL

SARA FARING

{Imprint}
MAKE YOUR MARK

NEW YORK

SQUARE
FISH

An imprint of Macmillan Publishing Group, LLC
120 Broadway, New York, NY 10271
fiercereads.com

Square Fish and the Square Fish logo are trademarks of Macmillan and
are used by Imprint under license from Macmillan.

Our books may be purchased in bulk for promotional, educational, or business use. Please
contact your local bookseller or the Macmillan Corporate and Premium Sales Department at
(800) 221-7945 ext. 5442 or by email at MacmillanSpecialMarkets@macmillan.com.

Library of Congress Cataloging-in-Publication Data

Names: Faring, Sara, author.
Title: The tenth girl / Sara Faring.
Description: First edition. | New York : Imprint, 2019. | Summary: In 1978,
   to avoid becoming a desaparecido like her mother, eighteen-year-old Mavi
   takes a teaching job at Vaccaro School, an isolated finishing school in
   Patagonia, rumored to be haunted.
Identifiers: ISBN 978-1-250-62082-8 (paperback) | ISBN 9781250304513 (eBook)
Subjects: | CYAC: Schools—Fiction. | Supernatural—Fiction. | Missing
   children—Fiction. | Mystery and detective stories. | Patagonia (Argentina
   and Chile)—Fiction.
Classification: LCC PZ7.1.F3673 Ten 2019 | DDC [Fic]—dc23
LC record available at https://lccn.loc.gov/2019002534

Our books may be purchased in bulk for promotional, educational, or business use.
Please contact your local bookseller or the Macmillan Corporate and Premium
Sales Department at (800) 221-7945 ext. 5442 or by email at
MacmillanSpecialMarkets@macmillan.com.

[Imprint]
MAKE YOUR MARK

@ImprintReads
Originally published in the United States by Imprint
First Square Fish edition, 2020
Book designed by Elynn Cohen
Imprint Logo designed by Amanda Spielman
Square Fish logo designed by Filomena Tuosto

1   3   5   7   9   10   8   6   4   2

01000011 01101000 01100101 00100000 01100010 01101111 01101100 01110101 01100100
01101111 00100001 00100000 01000101 01101100 00100000 01101101 01100001 01110100
01110010 01101001 01100001 01110010 01100011 01100001 01100100 01101111 00100000
01110011 01100101 00100000 01100101 01101110 01100011 01100001 01110010 01100111
01100001 01110010 11100001 00100000 01100100 01101100 01101100 00100000 01100001
01110100 01101111 01110010 01110010 01100001 01101110 01110100 01100101 00100000
01110001 01110101 01100101 00100000 01110010 01101111 01100010 01100101 00100000
01100101 01110011 01110100 01100101 00100000 01101100 01101001 01100010 01110010
01101111 00101110

To EAF and WOF,
who never once hesitated to
give me more books than I could carry

PROLOGUE

Do not be fooled:
territorial spirits inhabit our earthly flesh
as we move through this brightly painted world.
And long after our flesh rots,
the spirits remain, playing in the muck.
Only the gods are free of them,
watching from beyond the ice,
in their forgotten houses of cloud.

—ZAPUCHE TRIBE TEACHING

At the very southern tip of South America, where fields of ice meet mountains of salt, a finishing school for girls existed on a lone shelf of rock. The school wasn't *always* a school—no, it was once a grand country home, built for a wealthy family fleeing unnamed bloodshed in Europe. No one quite understood how this family tunneled vaulted cottages into sheer Argentine stone, but after their escape from the old country, nothing was impossible for the De Vaccaro family. As the stories go, their clan relished life atop their cliff, at least for a time. Their matriarch, Domenica De Vaccaro, was a cheerful woman with strong hands the size of a giant's, who ate a dozen eggs each day for breakfast—raw—and instructed her sons to *walk off* their troubles and pains. And walk off the sons did—to the City of Good Airs. The remaining De Vaccaro house shrunk to nearly nothing, but Domenica knew how to manage a problem as trivial as loneliness. She recruited girls from other rootless families abroad and offered them a rich education from her perch over the ice.

The first class comprised only ten girls, one of whom was Domenica's own young daughter. She taught them herself. But in time, the classes and the faculty both grew. A president's daughter attended. A tyrant's. An exiled artist's, and the daughter of the minister who exiled him. Such was the will of Domenica De Vaccaro—any gap could be bridged: political, moral, and otherwise. Experts visited from far and wide to take in the Patagonian air and teach lessons ranging from the practical (arithmetic) to the mystical (curing illness with candlelit vigils). The reputation of the school soared, and Domenica soon handpicked her ten pupils per year from the stacks of handwritten letters that reached her ice-locked home, as if flown there on desperate paper wings. They were happy, her pupils, and the precocious little things went on to explore all corners of the globe, enriched with a level of experience few outsiders could understand. Surely, said the Buenos Aires society pages, there was something in the meltwater.

One day, tragedy befell the historically fortunate De Vaccaro family, as tragedy is wont to do. A mysterious illness swept through the house and school, an illness that could not be cured, much less described to those who did not feel its chill in their own bones. The local Zapuche tribe—from which many of the staff hailed—whispered that unhappy spirits from across the world had flocked there to help their tribe seize back the cliff. They called these spirits *los Otros*, or *the Others*, a name that may be known to you. In time, the house was emptied out—barren, but never soulless.

Sixty years later, an intrepid group of teachers, led by De Vaccaro descendants, ventured out to that remote edge of the world. They returned to the house and reopened the school.

We find ourselves there, on the ice at the shore.

Welcome to Vaccaro School.

I

MAVI: ARGENTINA, MARCH 1978

The boat wove around dozens of fat, fake-looking icebergs parked in the aquamarine depths to reach this solitary dock. Three hours on the lake, and I never glimpsed another person but the captain, a ruddy-faced, early-emphysema case. After hour one, I was grateful when the massive ice shelf appeared. Its milky-blue shell looks like a cloud formation drawn by a five-year-old—at least from afar. Close up, cracks form black veins in the ice. Black slices that are five times the length of the boat, above the surface alone. Acid worms through my stomach: If I slipped down one of these crevasses, I think I would reappear on a different plane of existence. A Patagonian Alice, lost to Wonderland.

Glacial water gurgles behind me as the captain idles the boat. He crosses his arms, and tattooed mermaid's breasts bulge on his wrist.

Argentina, home of the 1978 FIFA World Cup, reads his pristine sky-blue shirt. A proud proclamation from a country plunged into a state of terror.

"We're here?" I ask, uneasy, studying the worn planks of the dock, broken wooden teeth. I can't see a single building, and overgrown bushes conceal any path up the stony hill.

The captain grunts—the most he's managed besides a series of coughs and belches since we left Punta Bandera—and eases back into his pleather seat, crinkling open his empty bag of ham-flavored chips to funnel spare crumbs down his gullet. I know my cues. I step off the boat, wood creaking. He doesn't even glance back as he pulls away. At least I can rest assured he hasn't taken me out here to rob me and leave me for dead. Silver linings . . . I take a breath, one breath, of the crisp air, painfully fresh compared with the Buenos Aires smog I sucked up only yesterday. There's already a chill damp enough to penetrate the warmest of coats—my ratty one won't stand a chance as winter nears.

You shouldn't be here, the wind whispers, curving around to caress the base of my skull. Because good Catholic girls aren't meant to run away into the wild, much less alone. Or so I've heard. Faraway, savage mountains, crumbling rock faces, and lonesome ice peaks—that's all there is to this inhuman landscape. I rebutton my coat, stiffen my shoulders. I tamp down my nerves—hoping to fool even myself—but I feel it stronger than ever now, that citrusy ache that fills you before beginning a brand-new chapter of life. New-school jitters, sort of. I'm five years old again, every cell alive to the thrilling or wretched twists I might face ahead.

I shoulder my half-empty bag. I was told the house would have everything I could possibly need—the kind of blanket assertion that concerns and delights. Would they have those miniaturized complimentary chocolates fancy hotels leave on down pillows? Or provide a stiff cot and a Bible to rest my head on? Who does Vaccaro School think I am, and who does it want me to be? Does it know me as the daughter of a wild-haired rebel, or as the daughter of a buttoned-up professor? I wonder, for the millionth time, if I'll be as natural a teacher as my mother was, even though I am young enough to still be in school myself: I'm eighteen, despite feeling a decade older. I wonder if the others here will accept me, even though I've had no chance to soften the edges my godmother always clucked about, with no small dose of affection. I wonder if I'll be able to hide what I must in order to fit in. All I'm carrying with me is the little clothing I thought to be Vaccaro School–appropriate (prim and boring but patched of most holes), my first-ever curriculum plan (embarrassing and incomplete, yet earnest—sure to be thrown away), and toiletries (a toothbrush with graying bristles, a leaking bottle of face cream). It's hardly enough to make do in the wilderness, unless pumas enjoy Lancôme. So I hurry down the dock, locate a set of stone steps tucked into the hill like an afterthought, and climb toward what I hope is Vaccaro School.

The steps are never-ending: the kind you'd expect to find billy goats prancing up, jaunty little grins on their slit-pupiled faces. I wish I had legs that slim and toned; ten flights in, I'd even accept the tufty beard in exchange for them. I swear that the mottled gray slabs beneath me are identical, too, never changing no matter how far I climb—it's as if some god, somewhere, personally curated every molecule on this rock face during an obsessive-compulsive fit. When I collapse on my bag to catch my breath, the geometric pattern of rock stretches above me into an uphill infinity, the trek a warped Sisyphean task. Lord help me.

And that's when I turn: Behind me is a sheer drop, some three hundred meters down to ice. If I were to slip down the stones, I might slide all the way off the steppe and the earth. A familiar ache of loneliness cuts through me like a boning knife. *I came here to escape*, I remind myself. Posing as a twentysomething to teach here was the only way to protect myself from the men who took my mother. If I didn't feel lonely, I couldn't have fled far enough. But visual reminders like this of the bald fact we live and die alone are few and far between, and they hit me on a primal level. I only hope my mother doesn't— didn't—feel this way in the black oblivion of her cell.

Adrenaline powering me, I push on, and a single chimney materializes behind a copse of brushy-topped araucaria trees as if on command. I see the pitched roofs of hill structures, too, some meters up the steps—medieval-looking and all too incongruous. I pass stone cottages built into the mountain, shuttered. It's difficult to see where one cottage ends and the next begins: They're precariously stacked shoeboxes in the home of a hoarder, uneven layer teetering atop uneven layer, defying my layman's impression of the rules of architecture. The rusted handles of the heavy doors rattle but don't give.

Something in the atmosphere is wrong here, a something I can't articulate—I only feel a discomfort in the hollow of my chest, the same one that tells you you are *not* alone when you want to be, or that you are *entirely* alone when you shouldn't be. But the stones feel solid to me, rasping beneath my feet; the air tastes herbal in my mouth; the sweat smells tangy on my skin . . . The thought crosses my mind that I'm ascending a staircase to a misanthropic, colonial vampire who feeds on young Zapuche women's blood.

The trek, all in all, takes nearly an hour—an hour of woozy stumbling through thickening cloud cover. The fog engulfs the buildings and the path ahead of me, making it impossible to plot a course; I trip a dozen times and curse everyone possible. Mist or sweat soaks through my shirt under my coat, the only crisp white number I own. I briefly consider resting again on my bag so that I don't liquefy into a puddle before Carmela De Vaccaro, but I'm too spooked to sleep when I can't see a meter in front of my own nose.

When I reach into my bag's depths for a clean scarf to mop

myself up, a mottled cloth flag ruffles out of the haze, its pole affixed to the most imposing stone structure I've ever seen. The building is a swollen version of the cottages, its facade crusty and burned. Diseased, leaking pus-like grout at the window seams. Malformed gargoyles hang off ledges irregularly shaped to resemble clouds, intricate swirling carvings adorning their edges. It's grand, wholly European in style, and a touch dilapidated—visibly rich in a history that those who live inside likely want to forget. Bloodred baroque curtains block the second-floor windowpanes, and the unmoving, thickening mist obscures those closer to the sky.

The flag alone ripples with life: On it shimmers a fierce, sword-wielding woman dressed in a yolk-yellow cloak, emerging from a cloud. Lord, I could kiss her: It's the De Vaccaro crest, recognizable from the cover of the brochure. I drop my bag and punch the air. Staggering up the building's front steps, I feel my shoulders relax, and I'm able, for the first time, to fill my lungs to the brim with air.

But the door is an iron wall as impenetrable as a bank vault, and the door knocker is shaped like an unsmiling woman's head—she's understandably upset, I suppose, that visitors will slam her head for all eternity. I paste a jagged fake smile on my face and knock with her. Then knock again. Politely.

"Hello?"

The flag flaps above me, the golden warrior, in her impractical getup, watching. I circle round and find no other entrance, no other stair. Not even a ground-floor window.

Panic creeps up on me, slowly, steadily, from its hiding place on the stones, and latches onto me with its greedy, sucking mouth.

My calls swell into shouts. I pound on the damned door until my palms bruise. Throat scratching, I look for a hidden snack in my bag, sustenance I did not have the wherewithal to pack. I eye the cream— read the ingredients list. *Shea butter*, I think hungrily. Madly.

I chuck pebbles at the various windows as the gargoyles chuckle at me; they know I'm a runner with nowhere to run to, pitiful prey.

It's the truth: I've nowhere else to go, even if the boat captain returned to the dock by magic. My safe havens only exist in memory, and my memory's poor, a winding montage of half-repressed sights and smells, pulled from a life I feel no ownership of. But I better kill that thought. If I think about my past too long, my mind unravels.

I sit and shut my eyes for a minute, only a minute while I mentally regroup, and a tingling warmth spreads through me, a bone-melting exhaustion. I sit, splayed across the steps like an old drunk, a look not all that different from my recent setup in Buenos Aires.

I never intended to strand myself in the Patagonian wilderness.

"Between you and me, Mavi, my dear," said a mustachioed principal on my thirteenth failed interview, grasping at my knee with a limp fish of a hand that made me gag, "someone would have to *die* around here for a role to free up. Unions, you know."

The realization made me consider murder, or at the very least, a nunnery and the associated Catholic-school jobs. But the truth was, there were jobs; there were simply no jobs for me. More than one staff member at every school guessed (correctly) that I might be lying about my age and that the English-language teaching degree a family friend had procured for me was fake. But most important, they knew about my mother.

They knew the rumors about her helping—or indoctrinating— the bright-eyed, radical strangers she called my cousins; they knew the government had taken her away for this; they knew I might be taken next and they would be punished for associating with her kin. As a country, we've learned one harsh fact over the past few years: When the military government takes people to prison, they rarely, if ever, appear again. That's why we call them *los desaparecidos*—the disappeared. Those who vanished, with no explanation at all. And if you speak too loudly about the missing, if you venture to ask what has become of them, you risk becoming one of them yourself.

As for me, I was a living, breathing reminder of my disappeared mother—my confused grief and rootlessness palpable. My presence alone frightened my peers and even the otherwise fearless head nuns at school. So I dropped out and lived with my godmother, deciding I had a better chance at safety and anonymity while working in a new neighborhood. I waitressed for tips while trying to find a better opportunity. Nothing came. The pizza place cut shifts. The banks froze accounts. The cash I had was the cash I had on hand: hardly more than a handful of valueless currency. I had no passport and no hope of getting one. I was trapped in my country, the only country I'd ever known. Hoping for a better day that never came, then hoping to keep hoping.

I learned they were coming for me, too, when my godmother told me, wringing an old rag in her hands like a chicken that needed killing, that men in uniform had dropped by asking about me. She loved me, she said, but as with many people she loved, our time together must be over, sooner than she wished. They'd killed my mother in prison, she was sure of it, and if they found me, they would kill me and her both.

"The angels will protect you," she said, kissing me and slipping me a wad of bills. Then it was time to go.

So of course I was elated to receive an offer to teach English at a school through an old and loyal colleague of my mother's, the same guardian angel who furnished me with my fake degree, a man we called Tío Adolfo, our Angel of Peace. The offer was from Vaccaro School, in Patagonia, of all places. The end of the earth. He pressed the glossy brochure into my hands like a ticket to paradise. Vaccaro School had once been a finishing school of historical significance, long abandoned and recently reopened by the De Vaccaro widow, the sole owner of Argentina's second-largest cement company, after the death of her husband. Its reopening would signal a return to more civilized, old-fashioned values—the school would be free of any and all modern technologies, and the privacy of her students (the wealthiest girls in Argentina) was paramount. *She needs new teachers, and she won't ask where you come from, much less question your age*, Tío Adolfo had said. *Besides, you're precocious—you always have been. And she's connected—old money, but at a remove from the military government. Follow her rules, and she will protect you, if it comes to that*. We both knew what he meant.

The brochure photos were striking, showing proud stone structures built into a hill, as well as images of what I assumed were the interiors of those buildings: gleaming, modern, asylum-white classrooms, better than American hospitals in the movies. A dream come true. A way out. Carmela De Vaccaro, a striking platinum blonde who looked like a Norse god crossbred with a Lithuanian model, with rows and rows of teeth she flaunted painfully in every photo, was hoping to find a *young and innovative teacher with an experimental edge* to teach English to her class of twelve-to-thirteen-year-olds. *I know English!* I thought cheerfully. The offer was room and board plus a generous lump sum after the successful completion of the nine-month term. The only catch being that you were stuck in the middle of nowhere for nine months—which was no catch at all, at least for me. It was perfect.

Well, there's another drawback, Tío Adolfo had clarified, clearing his throat, *but you'll think it silly*. Vaccaro School was thought to be haunted.

It was built on land seized from the territorial Zapuche tribe by De Vaccaro ancestors in the nineteenth century. He explained at length, with the wariness befitting an academic speaking about the unsubstantiated and vaguely paranormal, that the Zapuche enacted bloody rituals every time their land fell under threat. It was said that a Zapuche shaman cursed European farmers who had cleared a Zapuche forest to create farmland in the 1800s. Some of the farmers went mad shortly thereafter, shrieking that ravenous ghosts were sucking their skulls dry, before gruesome deaths. The farmland was abandoned. Even though few Zapuche remained in the area, none of the teachers Tío Adolfo knew would set foot on Zapuche land, much less Vaccaro School, because it was rumored that the last crop of Vaccaro teachers floated away in rough-hewn coffins some sixty years ago, the victims of what was likely another savage Zapuche curse. *Were any of this true*, he'd added, *the curses shouldn't touch you because of your Indigenous blood.*

I found this argument dubious, seeing as I had never learned specifics about my father's tribal roots beyond how they shaded my skin. Regardless, the rumors of these supposed ghosts and their mystical mumbo jumbo didn't matter to me. A haunted house sounded whimsical and sweet after witnessing the government's loaded threats and the raw violence on both sides—the world wasn't a child's game. The stories were surely propaganda to subjugate the Zapuche, anyway, so they would not reclaim their land.

My isolation in the Patagonian outback couldn't come soon enough. In the last few weeks before going to Vaccaro School, I left my godmother's apartment, claiming I had a safe place to stay. I meant to stay with Tío Adolfo, but when I visited the university to find him, they informed me he was no longer employed there. I sat on the school steps, considering my vanishing options, until a nervous clerk pulled me into a quiet office to whisper into my ear that after giving another impassioned speech condemning terrorism on the right and the left, my dear Tío Adolfo—the Angel of Peace—simply hadn't returned to work.

Wishing to protect my godmother, I slept in a Catholic homeless shelter run by angels (until I felt I was imposing, taking the bed of someone needier with older, weaker flesh and bone), and in an old gallery of shops, my head pressed up against glass separating me from luxury shoes and bags—glossy leather bits and bobs that cost as much as my godmother's rent. In the mornings, I was woken up by a security guard who toed me with his orthopedic shoe before telling me to beat it.

I convinced myself during those nights that Vaccaro School would be more than a place to hide—on the surface, it might be your typical finishing school for rich girls, teaching classes on crossing their legs the right way and understanding the rules of polo and the like. Bizarre classes for the bizarre rich, unlike anything I'd ever known. But I told myself it would be the first place in my life where I would *excel*. And I would earn the right to root myself someplace good and wholesome by following the rules, working hard, and possessing the very, very, very best of attitudes.

Dripping. Dripping on my cheek, coupled with the stench of tobacco and sweat. It's arguably the least pleasant way to be thrown from a reverie excluding actual pain, in a moment of extreme thirst and dishevelment. I groan and clap a hand over the slime, my mouth dry as cotton. The dripping smells less of sweat and more of . . . I look skyward, expecting a bird, and see the face of a man—not much more than a boy—with his lips pursed. Dumbfounded, I stumble to my leaden feet. He peeks from a window above me, smirking, wiping his mouth, before dipping back into the building.

I recognize the smell of the goop. The viscosity of it.

He spat on me.

He spat on me! A swell of anger rushes through my neck like a flurry of poisoned quills. I skid down the hill to peer into the upper windows. All but one remain shut.

"I know you're there!"

Anger overpowers the nerves: its blessing. I wipe my cheek until there's no trace of glop and rush the door, slamming my hands against the metal facade.

"Forgot the password?" someone calls from above. Male. Smug. The same face peeks out: unfortunately a handsome face, well-chiseled like the gargoyles, though with infinitely more intimidating proportions. Too bad the devilish face houses a brain with a silly child's sense of humor. He fingers the lit cigarette like it's a missile to be launched.

"Did you spit on me?" I ask. My blood sugar is far too low for this nonsense, shea butter be damned. "I've been left outside for hours and you spit on me?" The quake in my voice irritates me as much as the whininess, but I hold firm.

He smirks again. He's not remotely perturbed. In fact, he flicks his cigarette into the air, ashing on me fragrantly. I clench my teeth: They say teachers should be patient, but I haven't truly begun to teach. And he's not a student.

"How's this for a password, you bastard?" I say, and as my hands move into a once-obscene symbol that's lost too much of its power lately, the doors before me groan open.

I freeze. I squint at the threshold to make any sense of what's beyond the door because it's impossibly dark inside. The scent of must overpowers, too. Must and clove with a hint of spoiled legumes. There's a shadow within the shadows—a woman the size of a skeletal giant. She strides out in a floor-length caftan of sorts, and she towers over me. I wonder if she's hiding a smaller human being beneath the tent—it would be a grotesque but stupendous magic trick.

Her face is bare and drawn but grand, despite the beadiest eyes I've ever seen; her hair is pulled back so tightly I fear a giant black plunger is sucking out the back of her scalp. She clears her throat, with a long look at my impolite gesture. My hands, with minds of their own, pull away to feel at my hairline, and her nostrils flare.

"Miss Quercia, I presume? You are late."

I smile sheepishly, as one is wont to do. I can feel my armpits sweating again, as if they haven't already done their fair share on the climb. She crooks a finger at me to scurry behind her. I'm not much of a scurrier, but I don't think she'll be satisfied by anything else.

"There must have been a misunderstanding with timing," I say, pitching myself into the darkness and slicking back my hair. I'm obsequious all of a sudden, nervous and squirrelly. I've made a fool of myself on my first day. I've lost my temper. I risk losing everyone's good impression of my good attitude. And my hands are filthy and sticky, which means the rest of me must look it, too. "I've my lesson plan all written up for tomorrow's classes, and I look forward to discussing it with Madame De Vaccaro—"

"What possessed you to climb the property with your luggage?" she asks as we press on into the darkness, ignoring me and the fact that one understuffed bag doesn't make for luggage. We've entered a cloud of fetid tobacco smoke. But for her huge form before me, I would be blind, unable to perceive the depths around me. I expected a grand entrance hall, and while the ceiling heights are magnificent, the narrow corridors bend and curve, it seems, or else I'm still woozy from my climb; I don't see a single corner, and I've already lost sight of the entrance.

I splutter. "Necessity?"

"A member of the staff was waiting for you all afternoon by the gondola off the second dock. You look dreadful." Less an insult than an observation. I bite my tongue until I taste metal and watch her bun bounce in the darkness.

"There is no time for you to change out of your street clothes, so you shall have to go without supper," she says, as if it's obvious. I look down at my damp coat and once-crisp white shirt with a hint of sadness. "I am Ms. Morency to you. De facto head of administrative staff."

And in that elaborate title, I've learned half of what I need to know about her. "A pleasure."

She doesn't reply. But I hear a rustling, a sighing, and I strain to listen, to see. Words, spoken in a foreign language? To my ears, the voices come from cracks in the ceiling. I rub at my eyes, as if that will help. It must be a draft.

"It will also be too late to see the mistress tonight. You must remain in your room in the evenings. One is not safe alone in the house at night."

"Sorry?" I ask, clutching my bag closer. The air is rank now, the smell of spoiled food intensifying into a presence as physical as Morency herself. "Why not?"

"But in the morning," she continues, ignoring me, "*in the morning*, when you are permitted to move about the house freely, and you do see the mistress, you would be wise to hold your tongue around her." I assume she means Carmela De Vaccaro. "And to keep your hands to yourself."

Clearly she witnessed my display outside. "Oh well. There was a boy, he—"

"Oh, Miss Quercia," she says, dripping disdain, "isn't there always, with girls like you?"

I stumble in the darkness behind her, grateful not to have her eyes on me. I slip off my coat, but it feels as stuffy as before.

We pass another bend, and pockets of dim light spill from old-fashioned gilded sconces lining the halls. The burgundy Persian carpet is rich, deep, bog-like; my feet sink in with each step. I must be trailing dust and dirt and God knows what. The walls are covered in a fabric I would imagine is called damask even though I've no idea what that is; its texture and pattern remind me of a turbulent sky before a downpour. Dark, grandiose paintings of overcast landscapes hang in burnished golden frames along the walls. Expensive, hand-carved furniture dots the hall, the miniature sort that creaks with disdain and threatens to break the second someone gets comfortable. I glimpse inside an open doorway on the left after Morency hurries past: The figure of a man stands by an unlit fireplace in a sitting room. He leans over the fire as if warming his hands on the dead coals.

A flash of gray, a winged creature with bristly antennae, dances past my face. The moth brushes my cheek, giving me a sick chill. I rush after Morency, not so eager to be left behind in this lavish maze for neurotic moles.

"This is nothing like the brochure," I hear whispered. As I'm stifling a chuckle, I realize I must have said the words aloud.

She makes the smallest of noises: perhaps a laugh. A cough. A groan. Perhaps her shoe squeaked. Doubtful. Whatever it is, it's suppressed. We reach a cramped back staircase, and another man appears at the top of the flight. Try as I might, I can't make out many of his features in the near darkness. He has a thick neck, broad as a tree trunk, and his skin is as dark as tobacco—smells of it, too. He nods and grunts at Morency, or so I think, and I expect her to introduce us. I nearly wave at him, but a shiver goes through me when I see no sheen to his eyes; they are, if anything, empty black holes reflecting the flattest of glimmers, like the bottom of a well. I look down, face hot, and as he passes, he contorts himself toward the wall to avoid skimming me, the rest of his face hidden in the shadows. His thickly veined hand trembles.

Once free of him, I breathe in, out. More musk, plus that underlying fetidness. My throat itches, and I ascend, expecting a hallway as claustrophobic as the stairs.

Yet the second floor is as richly adorned and magnificent in scale as the first, with many doorways marked by polished, antique golden numbers lining the hall. We arrive in front of room 7, its gilt numeral askew so that it resembles a drunken, upside-down *V* or a prostrate stick man. I can't resist shifting it into the proper position. Ms. Morency's right eyebrow darts upward, and I grin, though I shouldn't. Of course, the *7* collapses when I release it, and so does my smile.

"Your room, Miss Quercia. Please treat it as you would your own." She appraises me, her eyes lingering on the sweat stains blooming from vulgar spots. "Better than your own." I have a feeling she is thinking to herself: *I can't imagine what sort of hovel you came from.*

The floor of that sales gallery in Recoleta, I want to tell her, with a saucy wink. *Like the other rats, and yet, I was hired by your mistress.* We stand in front of the door with a good meter between us. She looks profoundly disappointed, while still carefully tending her haughty uninterest. A difficult expression to master, especially for another commoner—it must require prolonged exposure to the discontented rich, like the cad upstairs. She draws a key from a fold in her caftan with slender, bony fingers, knuckles double the size of mine.

"Where is everyone?" I ask, squeaking. She glares at me with pencil points for pupils. She's intimidating when she's not reduced to a bun bobbing above my head in the darkness.

"I already told you that we were at dinner." She dangles the key. "We attend dinner together at the same time every night, and we return to our quarters together at the same time every night. There is a system here in the evenings, and you've interrupted us all. Do not expect to flourish here with that kind of behavior. You are a long way from the uncivilized streets of Buenos Aires. You are a long way from anyone who cares for you and tolerates your flaws. Do bear that in mind."

And with that, she drops the key into my hand, turns on her heel, and glides back the way she came, an apparition in all black.

A long way from anyone who cares for me and tolerates my flaws. As if there's a dossier of people meeting that description.

"You would be well-advised to lock the door behind you, if you wish to survive this place," she sends back, her morbid warning echoing down the hall.

The hollow in my chest fills with a choking sort of glue. It's not fear, exactly: It's that I've never frustrated someone so much immediately—in fact, I've never been so despised by a stranger at all, outside of President Videla's uniformed goons. I wonder if she dislikes everyone here or if my tardiness set her off. I can't help but feel as if there's a trait integral to me that disappointed her. As if she caught a whiff of my smell and determined I'm the most odious one here.

You shouldn't be here, I hear whispered again, by a draft, a vengeful ghost, or—the truest source—my traitorous brain. But where is someone like me meant to be?

I drop my bag on the floor and rest my forehead against the door. Morency's mention of dinner reminded me that I'm half-starved, and the lack of an invitation hangs heavy in the air, but I'm too tired to defy her and properly make an enemy. Perhaps if I go hungry, I'll be forgiven. *Morency*. I find myself wishing I had raced up and undid her bun, because I'm certain she would unravel.

I fiddle with the lock and open the door into the damp dark, hoping for the very best.

"Let's do this," I whisper to myself, as if my mother or another guardian angel stands alongside me, watching with a gentle smile.

2

ANGEL: 2020-0

The knife cut too-hot treads, and now I'm here.

I'm here, I'm here, I'm here, I'm here, I'm here . . .

I feel the mantra like a heartbeat, its rhythm giving me new life.

Here won't be heaven, but it'll be close enough. Because if *here* means anything, it's *not that fucking hell*, and that's all that matters now.

I open my eyes.

I'm somewhere pitch-black and splintery-looking. No land, no sky, no water to acquaint myself. I freeze, my imagination blooming with all the unholy mistakes this place could be, this cheap wood box, this airless cavity—

Something glimmers in the darkness, and I freak, half expecting a sub-sandwich-size rat to nibble on my toes. *Welcome to the brave new world, Angel. You're what's for dinner.* But no, it's not a radioactive pest that's glowing: It's me.

I'm out-of-body. I'm floating. I can't feel my fingers, my toes, but if I squint, I can see their outline, their crystalline shimmer piercing the muggy dark. It hits me at once, like a shiver up the spine: This is a ghostly reprieve. My old hands, with their chewed-up nails and wonky knuckles, my knobby knees that always cracked, my asthmatic lungs that couldn't manage a half mile, my skin swollen with constellations of pus: They're all long gone.

The feeling spreads back into all parts of me gradually, like I'm warming up beside an invisible fire after a spell in the cold. I push my starry arms into the wood guts of the closet walls, and there's no resistance. I go on and on, the asbestos stuffing no more than a cloud. It's magical. Frightening, for someone who should be immune to fear.

I'm glittery Casper, my new flesh made of crystal webbing.

I'm fairy floss, spirited far, far away from the ol' USA's unfortunate present.

I'm fucking free.

I churn myself through the walls and into a small, empty bedroom. Unremarkable, except it's entirely painted in light apricot (one of Mama's favorite colors). *Aha,* I think to myself. RGB color code 253, 213, 177. *I got it, Mama. Gorgeous.* I squeeze through a door marked *7* to find myself in . . . a hall.

The house is unreal, as Charon said. Sconces made of real burnished gold, looking like specially wrapped expensive chocolates; the rugs look lush, mattress-deep; and the ceiling heights . . . ! I sound like Mama when she'd peruse the real estate pages for houses we couldn't afford. *Angel,* she'd say, *look at this one with the marble kitchen island! And a flipping disposal!*

Mama. I feel that pang at the back of my throat, unavoidable even now, I guess.

Am I still Mama's Angel in this new world, or am I something else entirely?

My first name, the monstrosity that is Angel, is more commonish than people think. Mama named me Angel because she said I was born blessed, with a lucky star over my head. I told her once that's not how angels work, and she said, "*Cállate*." I shortened Angel to El when I didn't feel like the meaning behind it was true anymore—after I wrecked my life beyond repair, and—

A man lopes past me in the hall, built like a pro tennis player, his hairy forearm brushing the air where my abs would be, if they had ever existed—yet I don't feel a thing. He has superpale skin, so stark that his thick shoe-polish-colored hair stands out crisp like dog fur on a purebred husky. Ice-blue eyes, the disconcerting kind you find on one of those huskies, or, better yet, a whitewalker. Cheekbones the writer of a teen magazine listicle could cut herself on.

I'll be real: He's what my brain-dead half sister, Liese, would call a *phenomenal catch, like,* Bachelor-*worthy*, before even speaking two words to him. But his angular face scares me. It's cruel in its symmetry, if that makes any sense at all—like the God that made him perfected his glossy exterior as if to make up for skimping on a bargain-basement interior. I knew one too many people like that.

"Oh God, I'm so sorry," I say, flustered by our closeness. Force of habit. Despite all my colossal screwups, despite being *here*, I'm unfailingly polite in person, *always* blushing at strangers, no matter the savage thoughts in my head. And it infuriates me now more than ever. The dude stops, as if he's heard a whisper, but after a second— after a haughty grimace, the kind of expression you see on people who demand managers when coffee isn't scalding hot—he stoops to pick up a sheet of paper on the carpet that I hadn't seen. It reads: *Yesi's Lesson Plan*, followed by carefully printed notes in a beautiful cursive hand.

"Peasants," he says to himself, crumpling the sheet into a ball. Bitterness pinches his face, and boredom deadens it immediately. He keeps moving, walking with the sort of swagger you have if you've known only great comfort in your life. One comfort being the absolute and total certainty that you're important. If they made hazard signs for assholes, this guy would be the poster child, and I would be the hoodlum scratching x's into his eyes.

I could do almost anything next. And yet, I follow him. A part of me wants to scare the shit out of him if only I could figure out how. We go down the steps at the end of the corridor, through a stone hallway, up a carpeted stairway, and into a royal-blue bedroom with a jaw-dropping vista.

And I recognize it.

It's the Patagonia of my dreams, ripped straight from one of those bizarro Nat Geo specials they used to screen in middle school— fields of windblown wildflowers unfurling before silvery peaks, their blooms like stars studding the night sky. A shock of blue-white glacier rising from the depths, the kind intrepid explorers probably crunch across with snowshoes or crampons or whatever it is they wear (the closest I got to that kind of equipment was passing a ripped guy in a Patagonia vest on the Third Street Promenade once). It's a thousand times more vivid than anything I could have ever imagined—my dreams remade in Technicolor. I stumble a little on nothing but air, feeling an invisible knot in my invisible throat as my breath is taken. *Argentina.* As a kid, I watched Mama wordlessly paint this view dozens of times, dabbing in each layer with deference, a respect I now understand. Leo DiCaprio would lose his mind, seeing these glaciers before global warming melted them. Ice—great sheets of pale blue, jagged and milky against an indigo sky. Snowy mountains in the distance, peaks puncturing the haze, and enormous hunchbacked cumulonimbus clouds billowing in to meet them. Impossibly majestic—it brings the Zapuche stories I heard as a kid to life, each and every one of them set here.

So I'm *here*, I think, for the umpteenth time.

The whitewalker cracks a window and lights a hand-rolled cigarette, coolly observing the expanse. He leans forward, angling for a view of the steps, and I follow.

There's a girl down below.

She's a little bit older than me, I think. Nineteen, twenty. She has softly curled brown hair that falls to her waist in a curtain, framing a nut-brown face. She climbs up the hill of stones below us, wiping sweat from her brow, with a look of total determination on her face, like she's that fierce Patagonian explorer I imagined. But when she glimpses the house, she breaks into a goofy grin, ditches her bag, and punches her fists into the air, like she couldn't care less if anyone's watching. It disarms me, makes me smile for the first time in a while, at no one at all. *Hmm.*

The whitewalker watches her like he's a cat and she's the mouse he plans on batting around until she's good and bloodied. *Peasants,* I hear echoed in my head.

"Stop it," I say, snapping at him. He doesn't hear me.

As she approaches the door, she evens out her shirt and hair, composing herself again—the picture of decorum. I know immediately that she's a teacher, but I wonder what she teaches since she's so young. She knocks politely once. She waits a beat, folding and refolding her hands, and knocks again.

No one answers her—I would, if my crystal hands could get purchase on the doorknob. She flits about the steps, craning her neck to see into windows. She hasn't seen the whitewalker yet, for whatever reason. He takes long drags from his cigarette and sneers at her, and I want to smack him across the head. I jab him on the shoulder instead—my finger darts into the squeegee-flesh of his muscle with practically zero resistance—and all he does is shiver. But that minuscule movement of his sends a jolt through me. *So you can feel me.* But can he hear me?

"Answer the door, fool," I hiss.

He doesn't. He licks his lip, pulls out a book titled *Tropic of Cancer*, and languorously turns the pages, without a single look at the words. He tears out a sheet of the book to roll a cigarette. I punch at him repeatedly, but the magic that had him noticing my touch before has worn off. Minutes pass as I creatively try to shock him and scare him to no avail, but my fingers do dive deeper into his flesh, and I wonder if I could wedge myself into his overtoned body. Call out to her through him. As I'm hovering around his shoulders to try, he opens the window, and leans over the edge.

Outside, the girl's slumped on the steps, eyes closed, chin in hands. She must be so exhausted from the trek up, and now she's been abandoned on the steps as the darkening clouds encroach upon the house. About to get soaked.

Somewhere inside the house, a bell rings—a pleasurable rolling tickle. Whitewalker registers the noise before looking down at the girl again. He's smoking a new cigarette; he leans forward and ashes its flaming butt on the girl. He grins so maliciously at her that I expect horns to sprout from his head, and then he pitches the entire damn cigarette at her.

It lands near her back, ash end scorching the stone. Inches from the ends of her hair, which blow closer with the breeze. What a game—singe the new girl. Not even I would try this kind of crap on my worst days. Seething, I launch myself out the window, like a knight in crystalline armor, intent upon helping her, God knows why. Her fist-pumping, maybe.

I land gracefully beside her, Olympic gymnast–status. I swear she smells like sweet bakery bread—the first scent I can kind of pick up on. I stop myself from savoring it (creepy) and tap her on the shoulder.

"Wake up," I whisper. Again, God knows why.

She shakes me off, as if roused by a fly.

"Oh, come on. Wake *up*."

I hover a hand over her cheek to slap her awake. But that's when I pause.

When she's still, her eyes shut, the hard edge melts from her features. She's gentle-looking and delicate, like a fawn, with eyelashes to match and a dusting of freckles. As my hand meets her flushed skin, she slaps a hand over mine, through mine, and I feel her clasping the area between palm and wrist, that delicate spot that sends a tremor through me when touched.

She opens her eyes, catching mine for a moment. My invisible pair. It's as if, in that gummy layer between sleep and full consciousness, she can see me, the pained and desperate and lonely and lost me. And if the harshness of the whitewalker's expression scared me, the tenderness of hers is . . . soothing.

Shit.

I know that she can't see me. But I still fall back, self-conscious. And she cranes her neck up, up toward the window I jumped from a moment ago.

"I know you're there!" she shouts at the window, coming to her feet, all that intensity rushing back.

Whitewalker pokes his head out. "Forgot the password?" he asks.

"Oh, seriously, shut up," I say to no one. And I thought I couldn't hate him more. He watches her with a churlish grin, the kind that the dangerous Casanova would flash the ingenue in Mama's telenovelas before claiming he loved her. *Do you hear this asshole?* Mama would say, grabbing my hand and cackling. *Don't fall for his BS, Maria Eugenia. Don't do it. He's hollow. Let him become a bad memory, girl.*

"Did you spit on me?" she asks. Spit? Did she think my touch was *him* spitting on her? I cross my crystal arms.

The pink in her cheeks ripens to red. At first, I think she finds the dickhead attractive, because she looks at him the way my sister, Liese, looked at her meathead husband (He-who-must-not-be-named) before he impregnated her with his demon seed. But her jaw sets.

"How's this for a password, you bastard?" she says, flipping him off. I laugh out loud. If only I'd done the same to every idiot I'd met, instead of cursing them in my head and babbling *Oh, wow, sorry for existing* aloud. It's less than ideal timing for her gesture, though, because the door before us opens, and I swear those black clouds scoot in and settle overhead as a scowling specter of a woman appears in the frame.

The girl stumbles to her feet, blood draining from her face. But she composes herself quickly, looking unruffled as can be, if a little paler. I feel an alien swell of pride and admiration. I follow her into the house and help her with her bag as best as I can because I can tell she's beat, and the scary woman deposits her by a door marked with the numeral 7. The same door I came through upon my arrival. Fate. She takes a deep breath, a hopeful smile wavering on her face.

"Let's do this," she whispers to herself as she opens the door and flips a switch, flooding the room with light. Another whiff of bakery bread—it's the smell of the crispy-flaky facturas Mama would sometimes bake at home for breakfast, plus a hint of caramel flan. *You better inhale these before I do*, she would say. *They give me life.*

I stop.

Not because I'm worried the girl will *see* me in the light (ha), nor because I'm super concerned about her privacy. (I grew up with a Latin mom and siblings who wouldn't leave me alone, and I have far too few boundaries, okay?)

I stop because a vibrant flicker of excitement—of joy I thought lost to me forever—interrupts my thoughts. So sharp and bright and sweet I could cry.

It whispers that there could be a story waiting for me here in Patagonia.

It whispers that this girl could be in it.

Let's do this.

Snap out of it, Angel. To have thoughts like this now is traitorous, cruel, wrong.

But I can't help that I have a sick history of tending to my weird fantasies like rose beds, fantasies that feel too rooted in something real. Sometimes, in the glow I felt after Mama told me bedtime stories, I imagined my Argentine relatives—the ones I never met, the ones I couldn't be sure existed, the ones Mama must have left behind— chattering around me like protective fairies, gently teasing me, asking me to get off my ass and help with the cooking, laughing together. I could *feel* our bond, our closeness, a loyalty that would never wither and die, even though none of it was real. These stories I told myself kept me going through the dark spots. At least for a while.

I shudder, waiting for the feeling to pass. She shuts the door behind her, and I don't follow her inside.

Angel. Get Charon's warning through your thick-ass skull.

Charon explicitly told me not to become attached to anyone here. Because I'm not like them, no matter what I believe. They can't see me; they can't know me. Our kinship is all in my head—it's even more intangible than I am.

Charon is my unwilling asshole of a spirit-mentor, the Snape to my Harry, if I was a loser who thought that way (I am—don't tell Charon). I met him in the cloud house, a halfway house for spirits built by a cheeky Zapuche god with too much time on his hands and tucked in the sky above the ice.

The first time I saw Charon, I was a little put off, to be honest, because he looked like the worst kind of crackhead bum—the sort of guy Liese wrinkles her nose at on street corners—slumped on his cloud chair inside the cloud house, his lumpy potbelly draped with a stained tank top (it looks like a soiled bandage, but he treats it like a Christmas tree decoration), a scraggly, pube-like beard, and two rodenty-gray eyes that either scrunch up to judge or widen with mania. He caught me staring at him even though I was a crystal blur, and he set down his runny cheesesteak. He stood, ranting in a booming voice as his "unique" form of introduction, spittle and juices running down his chin:

There Charon stands, who rules the dreary coast,
A sordid god: Down from his hairy chin
A length of beard descends, uncombed, unclean;
His eyes, like hollow furnaces on fire;
A girdle, foul with grease, binds his obscene attire.

I know now that he meant to freak me out, but I couldn't stop staring at the legitimate clown-car crash of his performance.

"I can tell you're watching me, scumdog millionaire," he said, in more of a bark than anything else. "You're not invisible to me." He ripped into his cheesesteak with gray teeth. I didn't ask him where he got it, nor if I could taste it, even though I wanted to (I know, gross).

"Uh, who are you?" I asked aloud, before wondering if he could hear me. "And why can I see you?"

"I'm fucking Charon. For fuck's sake." He's got a mouth on him. "I'm your spirit guide. Like the boatman across the river Styx." He sighed. "Little turd hasn't read the classics."

"I played a Greek mythology RPG once," I said.

"Let me guess. You played as . . ." He trailed off, squinting at me, and I felt self-conscious, wondering how much of me he could see.

"Hercules or Athena, depending on my mood." Obvious hero choices, maybe, but I was scrawny and vulnerable once upon a time, so it was a pleasure to play someone strong, someone fierce.

"Ya don't say." He narrowed his eyes further and sucked his teeth with disdain—yet we've been semifriends ever since. He's sort of a godlike presence, I would say. I mean, he's definitely *not* God. He's just uninterested and blasé and weird, and above it all, he carefully tends to his perverted sense of humor. And that's how Catholic God acted toward me a lot of the time. Charon doesn't leave the cloud house, but he is a treasure trove of information (practical and metaphysical) as juicy as his cheesesteaks. Even if he's not the most eloquent.

"It's going to be sick in the house," he told me that day.

"Um, yeah," I said, being meek and bland as always, with a decent lacquering of sarcasm that a stranger wouldn't notice. "Sounds sick."

"Show some respect," Charon said, seeing right through me. "You being here and not in your own personal hell is all thanks to the Zapuche tribe. One of their goddamn shamans, to be specific." He fought a lecherous grin, as if the shaman was an ex-lover whose warm skin he could still feel. "Now listen to me, kid. And listen good. Time is circular to the Zapuche—like a stream their spirits can dip into anywhere. It's a gorgeous concept, isn't it? Anyway, stop me if you know all of this"—but really don't stop me, his eyes were telling me—"but this shaman, she cursed this pocket of land seized from the tribe by European colonizers during her lifetime, turning this spot into a frothy rapid, churning together the Other Place and their ruined world over and over and over again. So besides the average Zapuche spirits roaming around this place, there are Others from all ages, too—drawn here like bees to honey, like moths to a flame, like cockroaches to sweet, steaming piles of garbage. Dip in, dip out, dip in, dip out, but only as an Other, and only in this one stretch of

30

metaphysically spumy stream—the only stretch left to Others. *That is sick.*"

"I think you're mixing metaphors," I said, even though I was devouring his every word. I knew I was lucky to be here—that it was an alternative to my personal hell.

He looked down his nose at me. "Did you even listen to a single word I said, you cockroach?"

Later I would know that calling me an insect was his way of expressing paternal affection. I am the pretty little cockroach Charon never had.

After I leave the nut-brown girl in her room, I shimmy through doors and walls to find more activity and end up in a room with a thirty-foot table, covered in outrageous, steaming platters of food and intricately etched crystal pitchers of drink. A feast unlike any I've seen outside of illustrations of grandiose royal gatherings in history books. At least twenty sit at their places:

A tall, icy-blond woman at the head, rearranging her silverware with a precision belying her distress, which is tangible in the air around her. The specter who answered the door to her right, sucking in all air and heat and light. Whitewalker, frowning with boredom and guzzling great quantities of a beverage as deep and rich as wine. Beside him, a series of young girls, chattering among themselves, glistening and gleaming with too-perfect youth, like life-size Bratz dolls. One twirls her braids, staring into space. Another secretly carves an initial into the wood of the table by her leg. A couple press gloss to their lips and pout for invisible boys. There are ten little girls, if you include a tiny girl with pale ringlets, seated away from them, who seems to wither before them, not quite here, not quite there. She looks no different from the little girls farther down the table, except for this studied unease of hers.

A man with short, curly white hair and a faraway smile scribbles into a pad. A woman with cat-eye glasses twitches her nose, pupils darting from face to face. A second, wrinklier woman squirrels food into her napkin, then cracks her knuckles on the table to draw attention away from her lap. As if anyone would care if a fist's worth of food disappeared from the overwhelming spread. Last, a flat-faced man with a neck the width of a fire hose snorts to himself. And there, an empty space. The new girl's space.

They're finishing their meal. They shovel food into their faces, as if they're learning how to consume the slabs of meat. Even though their chewing is nasty, watching them makes me miss eating. I used to cook a lot with Mama, making a mess as we whipped up the sweet corn empanadas and gnocchi and milanesas she ate in her youth in Argentina. That food fed some part of her soul that I never came to know, hide it as she did.

I grasp at an empanada in front of the uneasy Shirley Temple look-alike for kicks, and the pastry moves a millimeter or so, to my surprise. The girl startles. I wave a hand before her, and she squints at the faint glow. Maybe I'm imagining her reaction. But I feel a weird little kick in my chest, like a leprechaun's giggling his ass off. I laugh to let it out, and she shoots up, her chair scraping against the stone floor.

Everyone at the table looks at her, at us, and at the icy-blond woman at the head of the table. The specter smolders, and not in the sexy, Liese-approved whitewalker way.

"Whatever is the matter, Yesi?" says the icy-blond woman. "You haven't been excused."

"Right," Yesi answers. "A bit of a cramp in my leg. That's all. I'm sorry, Madame De Vaccaro."

"Please sit."

With a crooked smile, Yesi obeys. Her hardened face tells me she's much older than I thought.

Within minutes, Madame De Vaccaro dabs at her mouth with the corner of a napkin and rises from the table. The little girls and the whitewalker follow her in one direction. The others follow the specter in a loose congregation back toward what must be the staff quarters. I wait for Yesi. I follow her down a hallway, toward her room. She makes a wrong turn, separating from the pack, and stops in the dark, blinking at the bare walls with clouded eyes, lost and blind.

"I'm Yesi," she whispers, caressing the face of an invisible person. "I know you're there."

"You do?" I ask. I remember: She must be Yesi of the crumpled lesson plan. Another teacher.

"I know you're there," she repeats, her fingers curling closed. I can't tell if she can hear me. She trembles. A vein forms a ridge on her forehead. "Please. Won't you talk to me?"

And though I should be relieved to be sensed—even thrilled—I only bubble with an acidic rage, hot and thick in my invisible belly.

A teacher shouldn't be trying to make friends with us, just as I shouldn't be making friends with them. It'll make life more difficult for her. For everyone.

She should be locking herself in her room and praying. She should be guzzling bleach. She should be jumping from the roof onto the ice.

The Others like me don't even remember what good is. The Others want to suck the joy from the lives of the usurper-innocents, to instill fear and suspicion, to breed weakness and mistrust.

Sure, maybe some of them are like pixies, wreaking innocent, small-potatoes havoc. But some are the kind of soulless creature that likes to watch live-feeds of thirteen-year-old girls hanging themselves to feel something. And they think they're owed a cosmic hall pass

33

here, as if something of theirs was taken from them in the past, as Zapuche holy land was taken from its tribe.

"You should go," I say to her. "You should hide." I shudder, watching the vein pulse near her scalp. "Stop talking to us."

She doesn't respond. As I float off, she stands in silence, waiting for an answer that will never come. Attempting to quiet her quaking forearms with unsteady hands. Despite her fear, she looks as innocent and trusting as Mama in her hospital bed, nodding yes at the doctor telling her she might squeeze out a few more weeks if she followed his painful instructions. I feel sympathy for her, this stranger. I feel guilt for not helping her.

I look at my own crystal hands as I float. I thought that I would be free here. I thought I could distract myself with pathetic stabs at humor, with random bursts of activity, and with that old friend *anger*, if all else failed. And truth be told, my familiar pain does feel lighter, more diaphanous, as if it's threaded loosely through me instead of a weighty, suffocating chain around my neck.

But the guilt hasn't dissipated like the rest of that physical crap. It seems to be growing. Now it's tumorous, enormous, the size of a little boy clinging to an ankle. *Why did you do what you did, Angel?* Monster. Imbecile. Waste of space, even when hardly anything is left of you.

I stop in the hallway outside room 7 and flit up through the skylight. It's inky-dark outside, and there are so many stars—dozens of them carpeting the sky.

Angel. Am I blessed to have been spirited to this place, when all I wanted was to be a body, sealed in a coffin, soul fogging up the lid like steam until it dissipates?

I watch Patagonia's constellations for a sign—finding nothing. You'd think a damn lucky star could guide you instead of winking all self-satisfied over your head.

3

MAVI: ARGENTINA, MARCH 1978

The bedroom light blinds me like a flashbulb, so my first impression of my new domain is the smell of mothballs, with a spine-tingling top note of antiseptic. My eyes adjust: The walls are painted in the palest of oranges—the color of the moon on nights when it hangs low in the sky. The room is small—the size of a postage stamp—and spartan. It's also windowless. Yes, windowless. It'll be a minor miracle if I wake up in the morning. I also have a bed that looks like a mere sliver of a single, sagging but neatly made, a minuscule dresser, and a chair fit for an elf.

Three mismatched doors break up the blank apricot walls. The hall door through which I entered, a door that opens into a shared bathroom (I try the other room's knob to no avail), and a closet door.

That's what it looks like, at least—the door itself is jammed and smaller than the others, as if built for a sneaking goblin.

Nothing in here would set the average heart aflutter.

But: It's my room! All mine!

I fall across the bed and grip the sheets in hand—*so* soft, if paper-thin. And I'm grateful. Absurdly grateful to be given a chance in this extraordinary (in the most literal sense of the word) place. It's a stroke of luck to be granted entry into this privileged world of ancient stone and fine carpeting, even if I will be an outsider in street clothes at first. Here, I am not shapeless, unwanted, a coward drifting through life—I am a young woman in my room. A decent adult, not a ghostly little reminder of my mother's tragic end. I have been given the chance to own a real life, such a rare thing, and all I must do is abide by the house rules until time scrubs my past clean.

I move toward the dresser and open the top drawer to unpack my little clothing: It's empty, but for—ah, yes—an old Bible, the one touch of personality, if you can call the most popular religious text in Argentina such a thing. The inside cover is inscribed with the name *Marguerite* in looping script, plus the year *1918*. A shiver works its way up my spine, and I slam the cover shut. My name, Mavi, stands for Margarita Victoria. It's possible nothing's been changed in this room since Marguerite lived and died—that I'm her new incarnation. I check beneath the dingy orange floral bed skirt to make sure she isn't still holed up there, and breathe a sigh of relief when I see the bare baseboards.

I try the jammed closet again next, kicking at it until the knob rattles and turns. I recoil: Inside, there is a cramped, dark, dust-filled hole that reeks of decay, with a faint whiff of urine. I feel for a light switch along the wall, and a splinter nips me, lodging itself into the meat of my hand.

Cursing, I suck it out, and that's when I get the feeling I'm being watched. Something lurks in the corner. Something malicious, wheezing in the dark.

I tremble and slam the door closed. I don't need the closet; I've never owned enough clothes to fill the dollhouse-size dresser. I only wish the closet door had a keyhole and a key with which I could lock it shut for good.

I take an irresponsibly lengthy hot shower in the fully functioning bathroom (thank Marguerite's God, it has a skylight!), wondering if I'll be surprised by a sour-faced resident of Vaccaro School—real or imagined—barging through the connecting door. Once I'm warmed through, I drop back onto the bed. I try to fall asleep—I really, really do—but as the minutes pass, I could eat my own arm I'm so hungry, and my mind won't slow. Soon, I'm shivering beneath the thin blanket on the bed.

I've no choice but to defy Morency and venture out into the house at night to forage for food. Locate a pantry. A bowl of dried-out sweets in a foyer. Something better than Bible leather to chew on. I throw my lumpy winter coat on over my pajamas, as if to look more civil, and creep out of my room and into the dark of the hall.

The corridor is as dead as before. Musty, too, as if bowls of mothballs have been set out as potpourri. Too quiet. I'm overwhelmed by the feeling that a group of teachers, clownishly giggling and watching from behind their keyholes with port in hand, will leap out at any moment to either greet me or threaten to scalp me in the style of the old locals unless I spill my secrets. Tiptoeing down the hallway, I try doors as a matter of curiosity—hesitantly—and they are all locked. I turn up the collar of my coat. The cold is the damp kind, the kind that seeps into my joints if I stand still, as if the air hopes to curl its way around the delicate skin of my neck and sicken me.

I will give Morency this: The house unsettles at night. I hear nothing behind the doors, only the softest creaking and whistling as the house rests. Drafty old beast. A part of me dreads wandering farther—*one is not safe alone in the house at night*—but the starving part beats the cautious part down.

I climb down the stairs and find two routes to choose from—the winding maze with damask wallpaper leading back toward the front door, reeking of clove and tobacco, to the left—and a second, low-vaulted stone hallway I hadn't noticed earlier, to the right, glowing faintly under a hidden source of moonlight. I take the latter, always susceptible to scratching the itch of my own curiosity. The softest scrape of my shoe's soles on stone echoes here: The house can feel me in its belly.

The hallway extends in darkness for some time—at least sixty miserable footsteps, during which I watch my back every couple of seconds, my own ragged breath spooking me. It's frigid and bare but for lines of golden sconces modeled after gaucho heads, hanging from the walls as if the men were put in pillories. Every face is unique: one toothless, grinning in his wide-brimmed hat, another bearded and scowling, and one winking lecherously with eyes of amber.

Only my mother would have appreciated the impossible layout of this house—if she could get past its colonial lavishness. Throughout my adolescence, we had young women and men in and out of our tiny apartment, staying in a hidden room behind a cupboard; lanky, sweating, keen strangers who patted me on the head and back and arm, desperate for human contact, while I waited on pins and needles for my mother to tuck me into bed. Sometimes I would eavesdrop on their conversations in the kitchen until I fell asleep; when they spent nights inside the cupboard, they told me in the morning it was a secret game. Of course, they were guerrillas, the lot of them. As I grew older, I came to understand that many were my mother's own students, awed by the powerful light of her idealism, as I was. I met only one who was afraid, and that was likely because he was too intelligent for his own good; a young college student, Manuel, who came from a nice middle-class family and proudly told me at dinner that he had a magic tooth. I racked my brain to guess what he meant, and late that night, I decided to ask him. As I crept toward the cupboard, I heard someone sobbing in the bathroom. Not my mother, no. A boy's cries. When I knocked quietly on the door, Manuel opened it, bright-eyed, as if nothing had happened, only the reflections of tear trails, a piglet's pinkness to his cheeks, and the faintest quiver in his smile. My mother found us there in her nightgown. She hustled me off to bed with a stern look, before ushering Manuel to the kitchen. I listened at the kitchen door, hearing nothing of their exchange except these words of his: *I never thought this life would be so lonely.*

Only this year, I learned that his false tooth was filled with cyanide. When the military arrived at his aunt's doorstep some months after his stay with us to take him into custody, he bit down on the tooth in the middle of a family dinner, the poison leaking down his throat.

We could all stand to share his courage, my mother had said, re-telling the story, aglow with a sick cousin of pride. *He will always be remembered.* It was the first time her moral certainty didn't inspire me: Instead, it chilled me to the bone. It chilled me almost as much knowing I would disappoint her in not sharing it, too—questioning coward that I was. Hers is a certainty about the world I crave but refuse to feel blindly. Hers is a certainty that I could have used in Buenos Aires and that I could use now in this otherworldly place, but I've never felt more removed from it.

I press through one more door, this time on my left, expecting another claustrophobic stretch. But this time I've broken into a room that is vast and grand. It must be a ballroom: It's full of slipcovered furniture, looking like elegant black-robed guests whispering and conspiring in tight social circles. The soaring ceilings dizzy me after tunneling here. I stagger across the veined and patterned marble floor, passing fading murals of eerie pastoral scenes painted on the walls, silvery sconces shaped like clouds, friezes with a storm theme. Lit by that same hidden moon, yet the room also lacks a single window. The air, despite this, is frigid—my breath clouds before me. On the wall, a placid shepherd girl with a milky complexion sits below a slavering, red-faced, Indigenous demon in a charcoal cloud. Poor things, fixed in place and doomed to their narrow definitions for eternity, or until this detestable mural is painted over by some saintly creature.

A draft kicks up, brushing the slipcover skirts around, and I half expect furious heads to turn in my direction. I hear a peal of laughter, falling water, and whispers, building in desperation. Teeth chattering, I spin around to find the source, curiously out of breath, and bump into a covered chest, rebounding off. I curse in the darkness, but the words have no weight to them. I'll have a bruise the size of an apple on my hip.

Somewhere, another muted cackle. Something creeps nearby, flitting in between the pale folds of the covered furniture. *Hungry*, I think I hear it murmur, thumping on the walls, scampering around on the ground behind that one chair, dragging something heavy behind it, like a bad leg . . . I swear I smell a roast, too. A fatty roast with crispy bits, like the asados of my youth. Could it be a student, playing a joke? A mountain animal that snuck in through an open door? For me, at least, there is nothing worse than questioning my senses, because they are what remains to position me in the world when all other points of reference disappear. I shudder and run forward, knees weak, and I see, at last, the palest flicker of light down another arched stone hall. The broadening specks of gold—they are my salvation.

More strained and mournful whispers seep from the walls, the ceiling. An acoustic trick. I turn to glimpse the origin, possessed, while still running. And I slam into something, hard. Pain tears through my side. Falling to the stone floor, I see a face. Pale. Devilish.

"Oh," comes a groan. From where, I'm not certain. Perhaps it was me, again. *Oh.*

I find myself looking at a girl, a girl with hair so pale that her scalp disappears into her skin, who looks a little younger than me, rubbing at her forehead and standing above me in the dark. Small as a doll with consumption—the ideal owner of the furniture set in my room.

"Lord Almighty. I thought you were a creature," I say, hands coming to that soft space between clavicle and throat to steady my breath. "A ghost or something."

"If only," the blonde says. Her voice is deeper than I would have expected. Raspier.

I scrutinize her: She looks Swedish at best. Like a sickly pageant girl at worst. It's a kindly face, to be sure. Verging on delicately gaunt.

"What fun." She nods in the direction of the footsteps and wags a sliver of an eyebrow, a thread of silver in the dark. "We've been discovered."

She pulls me to my feet with teensy hands, her fingers cool and slick as marble. We dart through another doorway to the left, into a closet full of coats and wintry odds and ends, the first evidence of contemporary human life I've seen since leaving my room. I close the door behind us, and we're forced to huddle together in a pool of thick wool worked full of dust, as if all the nastiness that should be outside has been piled in here. I half choke on a scarf and throw the weave away from my face before falling forward in the open space at the back of the closet. It's huge. She eases herself onto the floor and crosses her dainty legs, two toothpick spindles, before lighting a flashlight the size of a pen beneath her chin, lighting up the craggy bags under her pale eyes, the elfin, upturned nose with a smattering of freckles.

"Who's out there?" I ask. "Was that you whispering?"

"Whispering? Oh, sure. Nothing helps me get to sleep like whispering sweet lullabies to myself in abandoned ballrooms." Her lady apple cheeks rise in a smile. She's dimpled, for goodness' sake. Dimpled. "You shouldn't be here, you know." Dimpled with an attitude. She has a rich, almost masculine forties film star's drawl. It makes me forget that she's young like me.

"I was lost," I snap back.

"I gathered. No explanation needed," she says, winking. "I have a minor passion for rule breaking, myself. But you shouldn't be in the ballroom now because Morency is on your scent."

She's right, of course: My stalker must be Morency. I peel more wool threads from my tongue, a torturous reminder of my hunger.

"She doesn't trust newcomers," she adds, scratching the dainty tip of her nose. "She won't like that you're out of your room. Not that the ghosts care."

I pause, and she grins wickedly, uplit in stark patches by her flashlight. "A joke. Remember? You thought I was a ghost. Goodness gracious."

I hesitate to offer a polite laugh: I've trapped myself in a closet, hiding out from an administrator. It's deeply incriminating. Deeply pathetic. I straighten my coat and appear more official—to ignore the fact we are packed into this outerwear like stray hangers. "So who are you?"

"Frighteningly adept at small talk, are we?" A dark chuckle. "I'm Yesi."

I raise a brow. "Yesi?" It isn't a name I've heard.

"A rare breed, but yes, a Yesi is flesh and blood," she says. "Mostly." She extends one hand: It's pearly, even in the dark, and so tiny I know I could break its fingers. "Yesi is my name. Short for something impossibly bland, which I'd rather not reveal. I teach creative writing. I'm an author. Aspiring, if we're getting technical. My book's almost complete—"

Footsteps outside. My eyes bulge, and her mouth slides shut as she clicks off the flashlight. We are pitched in darkness.

The footsteps slow. An arctic draft flows through the cracks in the closet doorframe. The footsteps stop. My heartbeat quickens to an audible pace—Yesi's, too. We wait, trying not to breathe. We are clasping hands, I realize—my left and her right. I urge my stomach not to make a noise; it graciously remains mute. The footsteps recede, by the grace of God. I'm exhaling, rising to my feet, when Yesi pulls me down again. She brings a single finger to her lips.

There comes a voice, so garbled as to seem inhuman. The sound is guttural, animal—the utterance of a creature with no human face at night, a black blur in the place of humanly protuberances. And I hear the clearing of a gullet. I clutch Yesi's hand in mine, though it's not much comfort, smooth and icy as it is. There's the sound of cracking joints beyond the door, and a chill works its way up my neck with each pop. I wonder if the creature is devouring a rat, skeleton and all, or unfurling its own spine to its full size.

"Miss Quercia," it speaks coolly. "Are you out of bed?"

I feel as if my lungs might burst from holding my breath.

"You must return to bed," it continues, more crisply than before. I know it is the voice of Morency, but it sounds alien. I look over at Yesi, whose mouth has set into a thin line. *What happens here at night?* I want to ask her. But we remain silent. Morency raps fiercely on the door, and terror seizes my guts. Were it not for Yesi's smooth hand—

"I will be forced, of course, to inform Madame De Vaccaro."

The banality of this threat causes my shoulders to relax a hair, even as I hug my knees into my chest more tightly, even as I expect Morency to pull us from the closet and thwack my knuckles rosy with a ruler. See, though the supernatural is outside my realm of

experience, the rule-abiding, administrative Morency can be managed. After all, from the logical perspective of a teacher, I can't see
what I've done that is so unforgivably wrong. I can't. Rooms aren't
cells. Teachers, much less de facto heads of staff, are not monsters. But
they are human, and they must be fed, and if they are deprived of food,
they will sneak out in their highly unattractive pajamas. I bite my lip.
Long seconds of silence pass. The closet door remains mercifully shut.
We hear nothing more, except the embarrassing thump of my overactive heart. It seems that Morency incarnate has drifted off.

"Is she always this charming?" I whisper to Yesi, my hands still
quivering.

"Oh, always." She clicks on the flashlight and grins. "The true
specter of Vaccaro School."

"What happened to her?" I ask. "She sounded off. Wrong."

"Wrong? Ol' Morenc? The word cannot be applied to her. Per
her."

I'm not sure how to express my fear. After all, if Yesi won't admit
to finding Morency's visit as unsettling as I did—mind you, I haven't
forgotten her death grip—then I don't think I can explain it. And
yet . . . "She sounded like she'd regressed back to some kind of demonic form," I say. "On account of my low blood sugar." I try for a
smile.

"Ha. So what are *you*, by the way?" She pokes a finger at my coat.
"Flesh and blood, or something more exciting?"

She's skilled at shaking Morency off—cavalier, even. Enough so
that I relax myself. That's the calming effect of another's presence,
especially that of a champion at hiding fear. Those I know who hide
their fear best do so because they're trying to hide it from themselves,
knowing it could corrupt some piece of them if acknowledged.

"I'm Mavi. English-language teacher. From Buenos Aires."

"English!" she says, standing up between coats, pressing them aside. "Lucky you. I never learned. Not well, at least. You must be good to come here and teach the little ones."

She offers me a hand. I pull myself up, used to the feel of her skin now, and open the closet door a few centimeters to peek through the crack. Emptiness. A milky glow fills the hall, as if emanating from a secret skylight. I shut it once more.

"I've been here my whole life. In Argentina, I mean. Sometimes I feel as if I don't know anything at all," she adds. "Beyond the stories from foreign books I've crammed into my brain. Fiction can seem more vivid than life sometimes, no? Fun fact about me—my memory's awful, so don't hate me if I forget what we've exchanged here tonight by the morning. My grandmother always tells me that jealous spirits must borrow my memories at night and forget to put them back. I've tried to write down every little bit of magic I've experienced in this house since I arrived to retrain myself, though. So far so bad."

"How long have you been here?"

"Oh, only a few days."

"First job?" I ask.

An impish smile forms on her face. "No, no, I've been teaching forever."

She could be a teen herself. She could be lying about her age, like me. If I hadn't heard her speak at length, I would have still believed as much. She watches the expression of doubt flitting over my face and chuckles.

"I started right out of school," she explains. "I barely looked older than the girls I taught. Like you. You can imagine how that went over in Buenos Aires." She waits a beat, eyes distant, as if recalling one of the memories she claims are so rare, before letting the flashlight drop from her face, illuminating a back corner of the closet. "I nearly bit off my lips to stop my eyes from tearing up in front of them. Baby

45

monsters. I was weaker then, greener, as you can imagine, susceptible to fantasies of changing girls' lives for the better with my overactive imagination. That same imagination made me an irresistible target." I hear a chuckle. She's wearing a mint child-size robe with pajamas dotted in pink clumps like roses underneath—another late-night sneaker. "The demon children dipped locks of my hair in red ink one day, hid a frog in my desk another. Poor thing. I didn't find it until a month later, when the room stunk of old fish and I was thoroughly convinced I had some kind of unmentionable infection." I can hear the vulnerability in her voice. For all her toughness, she also likes to overshare. But why? To rob these memories of their power? To come off as quirky and genuine and self-aware? Whatever it is, it makes me uncomfortable.

"But that can't be why you left," I say. "It's BA."

"No, no, of course not." She chuckles and swings the flashlight back to herself. "You're right. I came here for an adventure, of course."

And she smiles at me, a small, genuine smile, the kind you give when you meet someone you're 99 percent certain will be a great friend someday, so I feel inclined to smile back. She feels familiar to me now. She's nice, as nice as can be, with her rainbow of sleepwear and her miniature hands and feet. And I'm desperate for a friend at Vaccaro School. Of course, I can't help but wonder what secrets she's hiding.

"So you like it here so far?" I ask as casually as I can manage.

"I do. Granted, classes haven't begun. But I haven't missed the city at all. Vaccaro School pulls you in and hugs you close. You must acclimatize to its quirks, of course. But in no time at all, you'll embrace it back." She brushes lint from her pale green lapel.

"To be honest, I'm glad for a fresh start." I bite my lip.

"A fresh start?" She laughs again, a tinkling in my ear. "What exactly are you leaving behind?"

There begins the trail of crumbs, dropped carelessly for the amateur psychoanalyst to pick up. I could kick myself for falling into the oversharing trap. I hesitate a beat too long.

But she kindly waves it away and clicks off her flashlight. "Don't answer that. It's only that there's nothing fresh about Vaccaro School. It's as old and gnarled and troubled as a place can get. Though I suppose it isn't impossible. The family had their own fresh start, building the house onto a forgotten rock in the middle of nowhere, right? Just don't let Morency catch you wandering again, or you'll land yourself in hot water, then boiled to a nice lobster red." She nudges past me in the pitch-darkness. "Let's get out of here, all right?" She peeps her head out of the closet and pulls me after her.

That spooky crystal light filters through the hall, and the cold nips at my ears again. I raise the collar of my coat. "Boiling water sounds nice right about now." My voice, hardly more than a whisper, carries down the long stone hallway. I drop it even lower. "You'll have to share your Morency-avoidance techniques."

"Gladly. First off, you need to take advantage of her anxiety toward the house and everyone inside—she's as superstitious and suspicious as they come. When I asked her about the history of the house, she told me not to speak another word of its past on school premises. As if I'd summon a demon from its depths. And it took me three days to convince her I wasn't here to seduce the paltry ranks of male staff after she caught me asking one hunchbacked kitchen worker for a cup of hot water. I think I'm well on my way to convincing her of my complete and total purity now, though. Just have one more potato sack to refashion into austere schoolmarm garb before I've a complete set for the semester."

I can't help but chuckle, even though I'm half-scared out of my wits that her rambling will call someone out of the recesses of the house. It is as silent as a church on the night of a *fútbol* match. Mention of male staff makes me want to ask about the man leaning out the window. But I refrain. "Yesi, why exactly don't they want us to wander around the house at night?" I whisper.

"I'm not sure yet," she replies. "I'm trying to figure out why, myself. It's a bit spooky at night, I'll give it that. But isn't it kind of beautiful to experience primal fear? To feel your pulse quicken because a pile of well-laid stones catch shadows and carry sound in unusual ways? How often are we so bored and anesthetized by our routines—in our safe surroundings—that we lose all sense of what's magical about our existence?"

I can't say I've felt anesthetized by my routine as of late, but she looks at me and half grins, retying the robe's amber sash. There's a compulsive precision to her movements that I'm only noticing now; she fusses with the robe like it's an outfit on a beloved first infant. "I know I sound a bit melodramatic. We are perfectly safe. But I was always curious about what it would be like to live in a haunted house, and this is the closest I'll get. If you can survive living in a haunted house, I think, you can come to know all the oddest little nooks in yourself."

A conclusion that would only spring to the mind of a writer. I, for one, have no plans to explore those dark nooks.

"So you do or don't think the house is haunted?"

"It's all in people's heads, is what I mean. What we all fear is our perceptions being incorrect, even though they're subjective, anyway—hallucinating, and so on. But I like to imagine that at least the family's quarters are legitimately haunted. For the fun of it, if nothing else. *The De Vaccaros.* They do sound like an aristocratic vampire cult, don't they?"

Yes. "We're in the family's quarters?" I rub my arms, sporting goose pimples I can feel beneath the pajamas and coat. I could've sworn I only wandered five minutes. I look around and see more stone hallways arcing out from the closet door, leading God knows where.

"Well, they're just upstairs. But they're all interconnected, the hill buildings," she says. "Here's the real horror-story fodder: The family almost died out here, sixty years ago." She pauses for effect, pale eyes glittering. "And the staff were lost, too. I had to *dig* for this information because obviously no one would volunteer the details. Apparently, some sort of plague struck the household—bubonic, I heard, though the locals attributed the illnesses to *territorial ghosts*"— she rolls her eyes at me—"and rumor has it that only two members of the De Vaccaro family escaped in full health in 1918. Two! And no records tell how many perished, nor how many poor Indigenous locals went with them. That's why she—Carmela, one of the pair's descendants—had to hire most of us from the city. Because none of the locals would set foot here, even though it's been decades."

So Tío Adolfo was right. I try to make out some evidence of the family or its tragedy here. By my imperfect vision, we're only in another old stone hallway, damp and empty. No wet bacterial splotches on the walls. No black mold. No five-fingered bloodstains. Perhaps the furniture in the ghostly ballroom holds traces of the unlucky people who once lived here, but they'll stay slipcovered tonight. Every night, most likely. What happened sixty years before has no bearing on us now. And truth be told, next to Yesi, I feel removed from the tragedy. I feel titillated and warm and fuzzy inside, as if I'm bundled on a sofa watching a low-budget horror film.

But my stomach growls again, a hostile sound in the dark.

"If I don't eat, I don't think I'll make it back up to my room," I say.

She smiles again, this time with teeth—a neat row of Chiclets. "I know just the thing for that condition," she says, taking my hand and leading me beyond. She bobs and weaves, looping around to the right and down a long corridor, until we reach a pantry, smelling of dried foods, and with both hands, she pulls open a nondescript drawer overfilled with jars and jars of cereals and cookies and candy.

"Meals are fantastic here, by the way," she says, sliding out a tube of chocolate disks. "Morency will have them change the recipes to her favorite gruel if we let on how much we like everything, though, so don't say a word. And don't tell the girls about this secret reserve. It will be gone within the day."

"Starvation or diabetes for me, looks like," I say, shoving sweets into my pockets and into my mouth. They melt on my tongue. Pure ecstasy. How long has it been since I've eaten chocolate? "How are the girls? You've met them?"

"I've met them," she says, placing a stack of chocolate disks on her tongue. "Mariella, Gisella, Diana, Luciana," she lists, slurring as her mouth can barely close around the chocolate in her mouth, "Silvina, Michelle, Sara, Christina, Isabella . . ." She swallows. "Sweet girls. Truly. Of course, some of them can be a bit difficult at times—you'll soon get to know Mariella, the ringleader—but they're all bright. *Special*. You know."

I don't. But I smile back anyway.

"So few girls?" I had known I was teaching a small group of twelve- and thirteen-year-olds. But I had expected there to be other classes, other students. Looking around the empty halls now, I'm not sure why.

"Well, yes. It's a pioneering class. Carmela must have explained as much. She views this semester as an experiment in teaching—to see if the Vaccaro School model is viable. If Vaccaro School can even be brought back to life. And if she fails, at least the girls will have a unique experience on their perfect résumés. Having the Vaccaro School pedigree used to be huge in international circles, apparently." She raises a brow with a sly grin.

I watch Yesi's pale curls bob as we walk and wonder if she's as rootless as I am, as anxious to settle in. If she's hiding, too. We cut through a large dining room with a bare rectangular table that resembles the chopped and shaped core of a poor thousand-year-old tree, and a patio, before arriving back in the first stone hallway. I smell the same fetidness from before. Perhaps there is something rotting in this house and I am too unobservant to notice yet—too foolish to trust my instincts. The rooms and halls are quiet, but we peek around each corner dutifully. Not a single sign of life. We hurry up the staff stairs, with Yesi drawing a finger to her lips when we pass room 1. She pauses in front of room 6, chocolate smeared across her chin. She dabs at the stain with a finger.

"This is me," she whispers, pulling out a key.

"I'm seven," I say. It almost seems preordained.

"Yes, I thought so," she says. "The empty spot at dinner, the locked room, and all." She opens the door. Her room is far less barren than mine, and it's painted baby blue. She's also pinned a shimmery blue scarf to the wall—as if she cut a swatch out of the sky and created her own window. "I'm elated that I'm not sharing a bathroom with a swamp thing that only creeps out at night. Imagine the mess."

"I'm still a swamp thing," I say, pausing before my door. "I came by the admissions entrance this afternoon, and no one answered for hours. So I sort of fell asleep, covered in sweat and grime and who knows what else. That's why I missed dinner, in case you thought I had a better reason."

She frowns. "Nobody heard anything. It's a soundproof maze in here, you'll find. In any case, we're the youngest by at least a decade, besides the chickies. Maybe that's why none of the others heard. No excuse for myself, though." She kicks off her slippers, prim little blue mules with bows I hadn't noticed until now. "You'll like the teachers, by the way. The others. Mole is the science teacher, and Lamb, the math teacher, and—"

51

"Those are their names?"

"Oh no," she says, chuckling. "I gave them nicknames to keep them straight when I first arrived, and they stuck. Mole is the science teacher and resident nurse; she has glasses and a twitchy, pointy nose, and she's a complete snoop but hilarious in her way, and Lamb— well, Lamb is the cutest little old man you've ever seen, with tufts of white fur on his head and the sweetest disposition, always rambling on about imaginary numbers—" She looks at me and seems to re- member herself. "Well. Aren't I just the embarrassing grandmother everyone's ready to ship off to the old-age home?"

I smile back, belly full of sugar. I have to admit she is growing on me. Lightness and whimsy and charm: She'll make the dreamiest partner in crime.

"I need to sleep before classes in the morning," she says as we part ways. "Otherwise, I'll feel like my brain is leaking out of my ears. But I think we'll be fast friends, Swamp Thing."

"Yesi?" I ask, struck by a nagging thought.

She turns back. "Yes?"

"What's your book about?" I ask. "You said you were writing a book."

"It's a ghost story, of course," she says, showing that row of tiny, even teeth. In the light, her hair is painted silver—she isn't blond at all. And she shuts her door, but not before I catch a flicker of emotion cross her face, something melancholy, something cold and ancient.

4

ANGEL: 2020-100

Buried in the muddle of sky above the ice is the cloud house, cobbled together from all sorts of clouds—cirrus, nimbus, cumulonimbus, you name it. I fly there straight after leaving Yesi in the hallway. The air feels chilled and damp, and the moon hangs beside me, fat and sleepy. As soon as I pass the threshold, I see Charon, dozing on a chair built from cushy altocumulus clouds, like goose down. He must sense me, even though I'm not much to look at, and he shakes awake, pawing at crusts of drool on his chin.

"Delaying the inevitable, are we, young Padawan?" He means my mandatory nightly return to the Other Place.

"I don't want to go back there." I fight a shiver, just thinking about that shapeless hell. It's the existential equivalent of setting your world on fire and being left with one surviving furniture-clearance outlet intact to wander through, its lights turned off and corridors empty. I know I arrived there because of a moment of violence by my own hand, but I couldn't have known I'd be trapped *there*, just as I couldn't have known I'd get a chance to escape *here*, slipping through the sole exit door on the day it wobbled into view. Still, I'm only allotted a day pass here. Each night I must slink back to the Other Place: It's a gothic Cinderella-Persephone mash-up for the ages.

"First of all, too fucking bad, and second of all, that's not what I meant, kiddo." Amusement plays in his keen rat eyes. "You've got to suck one of the meat bags bone-dry before you jet out of here for the night. You've got to shuck its pretty little skull like a corncob."

I nearly choke on crystal spit. "Excuse me?"

He rises and shuffles toward the cloud fridge, its contours painted in impressionistic cirrus dashes, wrenching at an impossible handle to find a congealed cheesesteak sandwich waiting inside. "Are you feeling as *rosy-cheeked*, pray tell, as you did when you got here this morning?"

I'm not feeling great, truth be told. Spreading myself through walls and other surfaces is an exhausting business. I can't help but think of someone tugging through knotty hair with a fine-toothed comb. Walking through walls is like that except I'm the gunked-up hair. It's better to behave like a good little living person, flitting through open doors.

A fun fact hits me: When little kids shut doors on ghosts and shake under their covers, they're only keeping the tired, agreeable ghosts out; the angry, energetic ones will still be all too eager to barge through and raise hell. I wish I could tell Rob—he always giggled when I got spooked by the dark and pulled the sheets up to my chin, as if flimsy cotton would protect me.

Rob.

The rush of pain attached to his name knocks the air out of me a good three seconds later than usual.

Rob was Mama's miracle baby, born on a crisp fall day when I was nine years old.

But he was my baby, too, my baby brother. I was called Angel, but we all knew who the real angel to Liese's devil was.

He was so goddamn cool for a fourish-foot-tall, little, Bambi-eyed creature that it hurt. He's the only kid I know who loved the dark. He even closed his eyes whenever he enjoyed himself a lot, as if the absence of light, of sight, could help him relish it more—

But I can't think about him—I'm gagging already, my guts clenched up in anticipation of pain. Some days I can't think of him at all without choking. Other days a bright little memory nudges its way through before the pain can block it out. Is there anything safe to miss about him right now?

I think of him, eyes closed, tucked into a cocoon of warm, clean sheets every night. Eyes closed, feeling the random, grazing tickle of a salty wind when I took him to the pier. Eyes closed, sighing and flopping onto the grass after a game of tag, his every eight-year-old muscle oxygenated and warm. I just hope he's still—

I stop myself cold.

"I'm just tired, okay?" I snap at Charon. "Get off my case." My polite charade is donezo, as far as Charon goes. It's also easier to be an asshole when you're invisible-ish.

He snorts. "Tired! That's rich. You're not tired. You need to feed."

"Feed?"

He tsks me before setting his sandwich inside a cloud microwave and slamming it shut. "You're greener than I thought," he says, fiddling with grayed buttons on the blurred dash. "Others feed on humans' dreams," he communicates, as if speaking to a toddler, "like little piglets at a metaphysical teat."

"But I'm not made of anything." An escape should be an all-inclusive kind of deal. "Why can't I nap and gorge on cheesesteaks like you? Be a vegetarian?"

"Do you get how vegetarianism works?" The microwave beeps. "Relax, kid. Chugging their human sauce doesn't hurt them. Imagine they're semitrucks on an uphill slope through life," he says, scooting a flat hand forward and up. "You're lightening their burden." A second, concluding beep.

He opens the microwave, plucking out the steaming cheesesteak and playing hot potato with it as it burns his dirty fingers.

I scan the empty cloud shelving. "Don't you have a plate for that?"

He shoots me a withering look as he holds the disintegrating organlike sandwich by its dripping edges. "No."

I feel nauseated.

"What happens if I take a hard pass? If I conscientiously object?"

With an elbow, he slams the microwave shut. "Then you'll be shunted back to the Other Place, Gandhi. I can conscientiously promise you that. You're an Other now. Revel in it."

Revel in it.

And the truth is, even though reveling sounds over-the-top, in a spring-breaker kind of way, I don't want to be forced out and miss my mother's Argentina. Not yet. Not before I've had a chance to figure out why I'm here. I rationalize feeding in my head:

Is feeding a grosser, cruder version of being a narcissist like Liese, who needs constant external validation to *survive*?

Okay, just kidding. "How good does my fake tan look?" is as gross and crude as it gets. But maybe Charon's right and we can gain

56

energy without someone or something else losing its own. Maybe cosmic balance isn't mandatory.

Yeah. Nice try, Angel.

I must be silent too long, because Charon barks at me. "Don't overthink this. Now beat it, okay? Time to get a move on." He motions at the cloud door with his designated sandwich hand, dotting his belly with grease.

When I don't move, he brings the cheesesteak to his slimy lips and hesitates. "Try the ghostfucker if you have any trouble."

"The ghostfucker?"

"She's a little thing," he says, holding his free hand out to waist height, "about yay high. Silver ringlets, sort of a consumptive albino Orphan Annie look. Always has her nose in a book."

He's talking about Yesi. Yesi, who sensed me. Yesi, whose trembling hands explored the darkness, seeking me.

All is quiet at four in the morning in Yesi's baby-blue bedroom; the moon, through the bathroom skylight, casts a cool glow onto Yesi's face. It's as if the universe itself is acting as an air traffic controller, showing my sticky fingers where to land to feed. But I can't do it. I can't feed from the ghostfucker.

I shouldn't call her that. I shouldn't. She's Yesi. I know she's Yesi by now—she introduced herself to me. But I know it would be easier to feed if I branded her as one single thing and disconnected—choosing simplicity of thought over curiosity in the complexity of human nature. The less aware I am of her nooks and curves—the more I view her as a paper cutout of a human being—the easier it is to flatten her into nothing, all for my agenda. *Flick*—there goes the paper doll, smoothed to nothing at all. I've been the paper cutout before. I guess now I'm the flicker.

Yesi is sprawled in bed, arms stretched overhead like she's on a rack. Comfortable, though, by her peaceful expression.

I'll have to look into her face as I feed. I'll have to touch her, in the fake way I can. I shudder and look away.

That's when I see a stain above her head.

It ripples with the blue scarf she's pinned up, this stain—it judders into view. I approach and see that it's a crystalline ripple. Two ripples. They look like luminescent soot and vibrate in the air. Sort of what I must look like.

Others.

Others with their steaming hands on her skull, drawing in energy. I fall back in disbelief at what I'm seeing. Her thoughts, dreams, whatever they are—they look like liquid crystal threads, blooming a pretty blue beneath their shadowed fingers.

They don't acknowledge me. They don't react when I crawl toward them; they even shuffle aside as I approach. They must be weak, like me.

"Who are you?" I ask, even though I'm wary of them. Afraid.

They don't answer.

I look into Yesi's face one last time: She's oblivious as to what's going on. At peace with it all, in her painful ignorance.

The crowd gives me courage. I'm like the worst of us.

Trembling, I place a hand by her forehead, then another. I can feel her heartbeat through the veins at her temples. There's something so intimate about the exchange that I draw back at first. But I return my hands to her head and wait. I feel that *drawing in*, that singular tingling sensation where my fingertips should be—

She's dreaming. I can feel the brightly colored threads moving through her consciousness, like yarn on Circe's loom; her skin is warm to the touch, feverish. She's a deep sleeper. She's running along a field, running, running, running. It's summer. Like Florida in the pictures I've seen—thick air, I can taste the eucalyptus and citrus rind.

I take the thread of memory from her. Pull the gluey thread out of her, her breath calm and even. The dream gushes into my fingertips, my palms, my wrists. It gives me shape, its images flooding me. Sunlight illuminating baby hairs into a halo; a crimped red mark of elastic on skin; birdsong laughter. They seep into the hollow in my chest.

I feel good, too good. Like Hercules—no longer weak, in fact, never weak. Satisfied. *High* with it all. If sane consciousness is the skeleton that gives structure to a life, this must be the unpolluted marrow of those bones. Like my memories of Mama, of Rob.

Am I stealing the rooting of her happier dreams?

What will she be left with when the night is done? What does she get from me, from us, in return? My guilt, my pain—hopelessness, worthlessness?

An Other moves away, and two more rush in, like those piglets at a teat.

"Every Other for itself, I see," I say, guilt surging up into me. Guess it's not passed off to Yesi completely. No one around me says a word; we're all consumed by our using and abusing. I hesitate, still close to Yesi's scalp.

A shadow, almost human, flits toward me and latches on beside me. Latches *onto* me. Through me. An Other.

"You're supposed to ask for permission to come aboard," I say to it. Nothing in reply, of course.

That's when I feel leaking from the edge of my form: The bastard is trickling newly acquired energy from me. I shimmy away, and it follows greedily, silently.

"Stop it!"

No answer. Whatever my moon flesh is made of quivers as I weaken.

"Leave me alone," I say, shoving it away again. "Don't you have anything better to do? Like haunt some little girls?"

It's a bad joke because it's not much of a joke at all. I taste a sourness in my mouth. It doesn't reply, and the pressure doesn't relent. I have to flee if I want to preserve my energy; I have no choice. I run off, back to the refuge of the nut-brown girl's room.

"I'm not a good person tonight," I warn the room, as if anyone's listening. And yet: It's difficult to ignore that in my badness, post-feeding, I feel more substantial, more alive. *Real.* As if badness is my default setting, and I know I will feed as long as I have to. That must make me a true Other.

The nut-brown girl is alone, sleeping calmly. I can't know why no one's feeding from her—it's a mystery for another night. She's smiling. She looks *hopeful*, as if her dreams are transporting her someplace nice. She has no idea what's coming.

Seeing that, I can't stop from heaving onto the floor beside her bed.

Of course nothing comes up. Nothing can come. But I know deep in my crystal ribbing that I've done something ruthless to further myself.

I tuck myself into her closet, dreading my return to the Other Place. Souls aren't like steam, I realize. They're like viruses, spreading to the surrounding organisms, infecting them with their unfulfilled dreams and inescapable worries.

5

MAVI: ARGENTINA, MARCH 1978

In the morning, I wash up in the empty bathroom and dress in my best church clothes. Yesi must have gotten up earlier, because her wet toothbrush and towel are drying on the sink, and I find a note on the edge reading, *Meet at breakfast? Starving. Follow croissant smell & stampeding teachers.* I unlock my bedroom door and sniff divine butter in the hall, which has seen a cheery transformation. The skylights above, unnoticed before, work wonders, giving the polished wooden doors and burgundy carpeting a beautiful richness. Either that, or a good night's sleep erased my trepidations. Yesi must have been right—Vaccaro School feels off only at night. Just as some succumb to strange moods when the moon is high, so does this house.

I follow a determined—or deaf—woman hurrying down the stairs, to the right, into the stone hallway, and into the first door on the right to the staff dining room—that cavernous room of stone with one long table, now bearing a lavish spread of pound cake and pears and cereals and steaming trays of scrambled eggs and sugared ham and more. My mouth salivates. And only then do I see the *people*: At least two dozen people of all shapes and sizes mull about the display. People! I compose myself, even though I want to kiss their cheeks, shake their hands, cling to their shoulders. *Great to see you. Great to meet you. Great. Just great.* Alone, I questioned everything I saw, but around other calm bodies, I can become another routine-driven shell in a crowd. Stuffing my face. I hurry to the buffet and load a plate with crepes and apple slices and sausages and scrambled eggs and everything I can fit, no matter how the juicy contents spill and splatter onto one another. The woman I followed, wearing cat-eye glasses, tucks into a lumpy bowl of oatmeal with the same resolve I witnessed earlier, and I see *her*—that *her*—Carmela De Vaccaro herself, who cuts an impressive yet slender figure in a white pantsuit, standing tall by the artfully spilled basket of whole apples. Seeing her in the flesh is to see a glamorous actress in the grocery store. That she deigns to eat breakfast with teeth and a tongue like mere mortals . . . ! She's beautiful, surreal, every millimeter handcrafted by some god to form the Perfect Woman, lacking, of course, the sort of imperfection that makes some of us interesting. Her skin is poreless, wrinkle-free; her hair a glossy platinum bob that rejects the idea of split ends and flyaways existing. She is the mythical one who *has it all*. She speaks with a white-haired man, who holds an oversize mug of coffee, hands palpitating as he surreptitiously watches Carmela with bowed-head awe.

I bite into the croissant and stifle a moan at the taste of butter. Happy cows, I can tell. I haven't eaten pastries this delicious in months, and it reminds me of my early-morning runs for facturas with my mother. Yesi sidles up to me at the fruit station and, with tongs, drops individual blueberries into a bowl. Of course.

"Sleep well? No ghosts, right?"

"None at all," I say. "But then again they didn't have a fighting chance at haunting me. I crashed hard after the chocolate."

She grins. "Get your coffee and meet me outside?"

Agreeing, I obediently serve myself coffee, dripping a bit on the hand-embroidered tablecloth in my eagerness, only to feel someone waiting behind me. The hairs on the back of my neck prick to attention.

It's the young man from the window, his blue-white eyes truer than the ice.

"Have you served yourself enough?" he asks, nodding at my overfilled plate. "There's no weigh-in later."

My face immediately burns, and I know it has betrayed me. "I missed dinner because of you."

He's carrying an apple in one hand and a half-full cup of coffee in the other, watching, surely, my cheeks turn a shade of red little known beyond baboon's backsides. I know he enjoys stirring discomfort in people, and that makes it all the worse.

"You missed dinner because you decided to take a nap out front. I woke you."

"By spitting on me."

He raises a brow. "What a repulsive suggestion." He sets down his apple and extends a napkin toward me. "For your cheek," he says. I raise my hand there: croissant flakes. A pastry basket's worth. "Some of us are better than our base instincts," he adds.

I swallow and take the napkin, brushing his hand with my thumb and forefinger. His skin is icier than his eyes; he recoils, disgust curling his lip. I can't help but wonder if my hand is sweaty or if he caught a whiff of morning breath or if he's seen into the pinkish gum of my insides only to glimpse the black rotting bits—

"I see you've met my son, Domenico." Carmela smiles at me—it

63

must be a smile, as her lips turn up, but there's no effortlessness in the muscle movement—and I nearly choke. I wish I could hide the damned plate. The son. Of course he's the son.

"Miss Quercia has a great appetite for teaching," he says.

"Miss Quercia." She sounds out the syllables, as if the name is unfamiliar. How, I do not know, because she hired me. She does not acknowledge her son's double meaning, and whether that is merciful or cold, I'm not certain. "How nice."

With every second that passes, her distaste toward me solidifies. So I must speak up.

"Madame De Vaccaro," I say, hovering the plate low, "I never connected with your secretary, but I would love to review my sample curriculum with you when you have a moment—"

"It's not our moment now, I'm afraid." Her smile seems like less an expression of mirth than an accessory she was gifted by a relative and is forced to occasionally wear. "But it *has* been a pleasure to meet you. A true pleasure. We need fresh blood here."

The smile melts away. She watches me for a moment, evaluating, and I swear I can hear the gears whirring behind her eyes. It's the look someone at a meat-processing plant might give a cow about to be killed. As if I'm less than human, but also pitiable for it. I'm afraid she'll mention that she knows about my mother, about my sad predicament. I'm afraid she'll expose me and run me out before class has even begun. I can feel my desperate mind scrabbling for simple explanations, for denials, for control. Domenico sips at his coffee, watching the silent exchange with cold amusement.

But she nods to release me from the awkwardness. He half winks at me—fast enough to deny it later. And together, they float off, feet practically no longer touching the ground, as only those with aristocratic ancestors can.

I'm frantically reorganizing my plate with my eyes, wishing to disappear into the thick, custardy scrambled eggs on my plate, when Yesi reappears, still carrying her bowl of blueberries. Blessed Yesi.

"Where'd you go?" she asks.

"Nowhere. Just making conversation." I drop the croissant on top of the eggs. To hell with it. I will eat it all.

"Come, now, let's eat on the balcony, overlooking the ice. It's my spot." She pops the last blueberry into her mouth. It's unclear what she eats to sustain her body, but that's a mystery better solved another day, when I'm not about to sweat through my shirt. "I see you've met Domenico," she adds. "Resident dilettante and half-formed Lothario."

"So he doesn't teach anything?" Why am I not surprised?

She chuckles as she guides me toward the oversize and windowed double doors to the patio. "The girls don't need any instruction in that kind of thing."

I look around the room, locking eyes with Morency, who stands watching us stock-still by a swinging door in a floor-length black canvas sack. My face falls. Perhaps she's keeping tabs on the kitchen staff humming in and out as they replenish supplies. Perhaps she's putting a hex on us. I hustle out the door with Yesi.

The cold outside rushes us, bracing but welcome. And the ice field! The ice stretches out before us like scenery from another world entirely—uninhabitable and severe. Why would anyone choose to live beside this sort of view? To me, it's a reminder of unwelcome solitude, of how very small and insignificant we are, of the sheer *luck* that places like Buenos Aires were made habitable and developable by nature. I suppose if I had been the one to construct this mansion on a rock, I would have felt mightier.

"Isn't this sublime?" Yesi says, settling onto a chair.

I nod and munch on my croissant, glad to be paces away from a heated mansion.

"This might be one of the last days we can do this," she adds. "The weather turns so quickly up here."

I've a chance to scope out the other teachers as we sit. A handful of them, all older, all shuffling along with peaceable, flat grins. I feel a bit as if we've entered an old-age home. At least Domenico and Carmela have, gratefully, disappeared.

I meet Mrs. Hawk—Yesi's *Hawk*, teaching literature—an old woman with a beak of a nose who nods amenably and melts into a nearby chair in silence. And Mr. Dello Russo—Yesi's *Arma-dello*, the history teacher—who looks truly armored, his neck as thick as a tree trunk, who grunts and continues reading his oversize tome. I think I might have passed him on the stairs yesterday, but he makes no mention of it. And Dr. Molina—*Mole*, in Yesi's book—the science teacher–cum–nurse of the cat-eye glasses and oatmeal, whose face unlocks upon spotting Yesi; she sits by us and announces that two of the kitchen staff are fooling around. "But we don't know which," she says with the same intensity as her stride. "They always look at everything and everyone with such disdain. I haven't squeezed a word out of them."

I smile and load my mouth with more dulce de leche crepes hiding at the soggy bottom of my plate.

She brings her face close to mine, eyes enormous behind the lenses. "When is your birthday, dear?"

I swallow and tell her.

She scratches the numbers onto the pad beside her bowl, mumbling to herself, before peering at me. "You're a seven. Yes, a seven. That makes complete sense." She sets down her pad with a conclusive tap.

"Sorry?" I look at Yesi.

Yesi smiles gently. "Mole is a numerologist," she explains.

"Amateur," Mole adds.

"Undoubtedly amateur," Yesi notes, folding her arms. "What does seven mean, then? Conventional and domestic? Or was that just me?"

Mole looks back at me. "Yesi is upset that she's a six, you see. The caretaker." She takes a bite of oatmeal and swallows it whole. "Sevens are contemplative and spiritual. Aloof and distant at their worst."

"Aloof and distant?" Yesi laughs. "That's not Swamp Thing at all."

"I'm glad the name has stuck," I say. I like that Yesi feels she knows me enough to form an opinion of me, but I can't say she's right. It's a moment that slides the narrowest of wedges between her and me; I don't like to feel incorrectly solved, and I wonder what purpose this supposedly friendly and open personality of mine will serve in the context of Yesi's world. At least this incorrect label will help me keep my private affairs private, all with a cheery smile on my face.

"Seeker of knowledge, number seven," says Mole, reexamining her notes.

The older man with friendly, open features and curly white hair—positively lamblike—sidles up to us. "Dr. Molina, Miss Yesi, and dear Miss Yesi's friend," he says conspiratorially, "did you hear the sad news about the parallel lines?" His face is serious, earnest.

Mole snorts without lifting her eyes from her pad.

"No . . . ?" I look around to see what he means. "Parallel lines?"

Yesi bites her lip next to me.

"They have so much in common," he says, dropping to a whisper. "It's a shame they'll never meet." He pauses, grinning wide and slow. "But I'm *so* pleased that we get to!"

Yesi claps her hands. "Bravo, Lamb," she says, and I try my best to smile. Yesi is far quicker than I am. He chuckles, bowing stiffly, and runs a hand over his scalp.

"As the youngest teachers here, I expect you both to keep my sense of humor in . . . *line*."

"Punny," I say, shifting the fork I have in hand. He's a fool but an endearing one, I suppose.

"I'm Edwin Lamm," he says, extending a chilly hand to me that does not match his warm smile. "That's *L-A-M-M*, lest you jump to any unfair conclusions based on my unfortunate God-given mane." I choke on an apple slice. This nearly sets me off. He can't possibly be named Lamm. "Mathematics."

I elbow Yesi hard, and she elbows me back as I introduce myself. I can't tell what came first: Yesi's names for them, their own given names, or their unfortunate resemblances . . .

"Why did you come to Vaccaro School?" I ask. "Sorry if that's too blunt."

"Not at all, not at all, my dear. Your directness is refreshing. I was about to be forced into early retirement when Carmela found me," he admits, scratching his lamby pate.

"Early retirement?" He doesn't look too old to teach. He looks about as old as my Tío Adolfo.

"I'm afraid so." He lifts a hand. "I have the shakes, you see."

I can't tell whether he means Parkinson's or another disease. His hand, though dotted with age spots, doesn't appear to move. It sounds like a cover story. "I'm sorry to hear that."

"My gran has the shakes," adds Yesi. "Awful business."

After breakfast, Morency distributes handwritten schedules and directions to our teaching cottages, and Carmela waves us all off. She—or her anonymous pod of assistants—scheduled my class relatively early in the day, so I weave down the same winding path I climbed up yesterday to find my cottage, nearly a quarter of the way back down the hill.

This school looks like one of those charming villages snipped from a brochure, but the cobblestones are devoid of tourists—devoid of the neon splash of signs. No, CAFÉ HERE! No, PUBLIC RESTROOM, its walls of tiles begging to be defiled by an angsty teen. No empanada stands touting peso meat pockets. No gift shops full of miniaturized, seizure-inducing junk. I peek through the shuttered window of an unused cottage and find the interior dark, its contents impossible to see. But the glass itself is spotless. This mountain seems to exist inside some sort of time-exempt vacuum, in which dirt and dust and droppings and dew cannot accrue.

The English as a Second Language classroom, a petite cottage with no grand view, contains a large round table with eleven chairs and a blackboard. Morning light filters in through the ivy-cloaked windows. I smell freshly sharpened pencils. Someone's been in to stock the cottage with supplies for me. It's humble, yet perfect—the setting could've been plucked straight out of one of my dreams, if not the hypermodern brochure. *Perhaps I am meant to be here*, I tell myself. *Perhaps everything will be all right*. But I cannot shake the feeling, returning from yesterday, that something is wrong. I step around the room self-consciously, carefully distributing sheets of paper and pencils.

I hear a knock on my door in the moments before my class begins. I struggle to open it, an alarmingly heavy thing that has swollen in place, but when I manage, Carmela De Vaccaro smiles down at me, all white-blond hair and corporate teeth. You'd think she was fashioned in a lab somewhere: Her eyelashes are individually coated in a jet-black gloss, and a perfect red lacquers her respectably full lips. Even her eyeliner appears to have been applied by machine.

"Miss Quercia." She pushes past me into the room, a burst of frigid air trailing her.

"Is this our moment?" I ask. I want to clear the awkwardness; I want her to like me, so that she might protect me if it comes to that. The words of Tío Adolfo resound in my head.

But the joke falls flat to the stone floor.

She offers a sad little smile most closely related to a wince and perches herself on the edge of the round table. "I see you've managed to settle in." Head curiously still, she shoots looks at the stack of papers I've spread across the table as if they might crimp and crawl across the wood and infect her with more of that bland whiteness from which she already suffers.

"I—"

"We have a highly unusual setup here. But it's one I'm proud of," she says, swiveling a massive ring on her finger a couple of crucial millimeters. "And I'm so pleased you're willing to join this adventure with us. My family built this village over a century ago."

Or their serfs did. I smile.

"I feel privileged to be building on their legacy. And I'm glad we took a chance on you."

Just as you take a chance on us.

She speaks as if she can't deviate from the script of the promotional brochure. I'm glad to hear the words, as empty as they might be, because now, more than ever, would be the moment to express her private hesitation about me. Glassy-eyed, she waits for me to say my part.

"Madame De Vaccaro," I say. "Thank you for taking me in. I'm not sure how much you know about me, but it—"

She stops me. "Your past hardly matters here. You have a degree, don't you?"

A faked degree.

"You should be equipped to handle our girls. There will be only ten, after all." Ten. She lets that number sit for a moment, eyes drifting, but quickly collects herself. "You'll manage, if you keep their attention, that is. The success of your lesson plan will soon be determined." She checks her golden watch quite obviously. "They are late.

You should not allow such behavior going forward. They won't be inclined to treat a young teacher with respect—especially not one with such a different upbringing. You shall have to earn it from them."

My hands curl into fists at my sides as she appraises me.

"Now, the rules of Vaccaro School. No smoking, no drinking, no foul language. No wandering alone, especially at night. The house is old, and delicate, and you put yourself at risk by going where you shouldn't. And of course, no fraternizing with my son."

My cheeks flush, seeing as I've almost broken them all—these rules I swore I'd uphold.

"If you break these rules, you will be promptly removed from the premises, all pay withheld. It goes without saying that I will not provide a positive reference in that case, either. I have no tolerance for rule breakers." She folds her hands before her. "Now. Anything else?"

She's more cutting than Morency. Or perhaps more efficient in her takedowns.

I shake my head, speechless, and she rises.

"Do let Ms. Morency know if you have any problems. I expect you won't. At least, not from this moment forward, correct?"

Her smile is as beautiful and flat as before, but there's a tinge of maliciousness there, a hint of a threat, as if I could still become a bother worth crushing. She extends a hand to shake, and the flesh is cold and dead in my grip. She brushes off her pantsuit—or perhaps any trace of me from her hand—and leaves me to clutch my materials, praying I'll do well here and continue to be safe.

My class begins at 11:30 A.M. sharp; the clock reads 11:35. After straightening handouts set at each of the other ten places, I sit in a chair and wait for the girls to arrive, crossing and uncrossing my legs.

And I wait.

Rearranging the paper into neat fan shapes.

And I wait.

I hover by the window and peek out the clearest pane: no one.

By 11:50, I believe Carmela's embittered rant about the girls' lack of respect—to be fair, I would have blown off a young teacher myself as a thirteen-year-old, had my school not been run by two head nuns who patrolled the halls like rabid wolves eager for a sweet-fleshed meal of girl rump.

This gives me some inspiration.

I storm outside, making it about five paces with clawed hands before two girls dart around the corner and bump into me, falling back with wide eyes.

"Who are you two?" I ask.

There's Sara, quiet and pale, a bit conniving-looking, her hands neatly folded.

And blushing ferociously beside her, there's Michelle.

"We're so sorry, Miss Quercia," she whispers with no other explanation.

I smell charred flesh and singed metal, sharp in my nose.

I shuffle back a step as the sight of her sinks in.

Michelle. She is the spitting image of someone I knew as a child. Someone whose face will never leave me: a classmate, the daughter of a government worker named Falcone. *An empty-headed bureaucrat ignorant of the evil he spreads with every scratch of his pencil*, my mother had said. Her first name was . . . well, it doesn't matter now.

But Michelle: She has the same pale green eyes fringed by thin lashes, the same natural stripe of blond through her mousy-brown hair, the same round face, mysteriously free of cheeks to pinch. Michelle, who has gem stickers on her earlobes and avoids my eyes. I want to ask where she's from, what kind of trick this is, why she looks like her. But I can't, and I don't. I'll seem mad.

"Well, Sara and Michelle, you're late," I say, leading the two of them into the cottage.

I watch Michelle unpack her notebook and wonder how this could happen.

Perhaps she survived, somehow.

Perhaps . . .

It's Vaccaro School, come to frazzle me.

I zip those compartments in my mind shut.

"Where are the others?" I ask, once they're seated.

Michelle bites her lip and bores two holes in her handout. Sara stares back at me mutely.

I'm going to sweat through my shirt again.

Blessedly, as I'm about to explain their first assignment, the door swings open. Seven more girls stream inside: chatty and hungry after a morning of study, eager for lunch, behaving as if they've arrived on time—no, behaving as if they've arrived *early* for a salon appointment.

They do not even give me a glance. The popular girls lead, if they exist in a school of ten pupils: There is Mariella, a cherubic girl with pink cheeks and the blackest hair I've ever seen, braided into two thick ropes. Another girl links arms with her—the lankier Gisella, an intimidatingly gorgeous girl, if such a compliment can be made about a thirteen-year-old. Her own hair in a dark blond braid, Gisella purses her lips at me when she enters and whispers into Mariella's ear, both of them laughing. They choose their seats while the others wait, evaluating the room.

"Take your seats, ladies," I say in the nunniest voice I can muster. "You are late." If only I had a ruler to menacingly tap.

I notice the Vaccaro School uniform. A white button-down shirt with a Peter Pan collar, so sheer you can glimpse their undershirts, and plaid skirts rolled up far above the knee, unsanctioned by Morency. Knee-high socks. Loafers, some with coins slipped between the lips. They've been pulled from a teen movie—all at or around what I would call their Lolita phase; coquettish, not yet fully blossomed but coltish and aware. Still clutching or feigning to possess a waning innocence.

Rich girls, too, of course.

Silver bracelets, diamond earrings, pearly pink lip gloss from shiny tubes, oversize sunglasses perched on one head even though it's now overcast.

As they introduce themselves, I look around. Most of the girls whisper in groups or pairs as the others speak.

Diana, with greasy skin and an explosive mane of brown hair, spreading her many multicolored notebooks out. Christina, snorting when she laughs and slamming the table with her hands, nails bitten to nubs and speckled red.

Silvina, a malnourished-looking girl who looks from face to face, swiveling the charm bracelet on her wrist.

Luciana, freckled, her jaw permanently fixed. Homesick, perhaps. She refuses to look up from her handout, which is not that riveting, I assure you. And there's Isabella, with drooping eyes and a runny nose, who squeezes Luciana's hand beneath the table.

One space at the table remains conspicuously empty.

"Where's the tenth student, ladies?" I ask.

They glance at one another.

"I was told to expect ten students." As I say the words, I slow, taking in the shrugs, the scratching of temples.

"Don't be cross with the tenth girl, Miss," says Mariella gravely. "She isn't very sharp, so Ms. Morency insisted she massage her feet instead of tackling English. The future of those giant bunions takes priority."

The other girls look at one another, smiles erupting across their lips.

"You're wrong, Mariella. I heard the tenth girl's in Domenico's closet, sniffing his dirty laundry and imagining their first kiss," adds Gisella, batting her lashes and cupping her hands together. "Prince Domenico. Kiss me, Prince. Kiss me!"

My mouth opens and closes. I wonder for the briefest of moments if they've seen me act a fool in front of him. They couldn't have. Plus, *he's* the troubled one.

"I heard the tenth girl is rehearsing," ventures Silvina. "She's a child prodigy acting in a new show called *Vaccaro School of Pain*. Elements of sadism."

Scattered laughter—only a few know what sadism is, and Silvina shrinks back.

"I heard the tenth girl dropped out of school last-minute to live at a cattle ranch," says Christina. "Little did she know, the ranchers had confused her with a cow because she's gotten so . . ." She blimps up her cheeks with air.

Giggling fits; Christina's palms are rosy from hitting the table, which shakes beneath my forearms.

"Pirates took her and tied her to a boat headed to South Africa," adds Diana, whipping her hair back.

"She'll be the slave to a tribal overlord by next week," adds Mariella, resting her chin on her hands. "The poor thing."

Even Luciana and Isabella, the sad little couple, rock with laughter. "They're going to cook her into a soup," says Isabella, nudging Luciana in the ribs. "With coconut milk and green chilies and oxtails."

Michelle, little Michelle, whom I can hardly look at on account of the chilling resemblance, blushes and looks at her hands as if the most important message in the world is written into her knuckles.

Mariella holds out her hands to stop the chattering group.

"We're all wrong, of course," says Mariella, looking me in the eye. "We're all joking with you." The girls quiet down and look at Mariella with red faces.

I bite the inside of my cheek with what I hope is a reproachful look on my face and lift my notes—basic introductions. Glad that they've simmered down.

"She's in the trunk of my stepfather's car," says Mariella, cheeks rising in a minxish grin. "I do hope she's not getting hungry."

They hoot with laughter. Clap hands across their mouths.

So they're a spirited bunch. "That's enough, ladies," I interrupt. "Enough. Handouts."

They quiet, pick up their papers—some eye-rolling and whispering.

An odd little voice pipes up. "The tenth girl isn't a real girl."

Sara, who has been silent since she spoke the two syllables of her name.

Before I can say a word, Mariella slaps a hand on the table. "Oh, shut up. Way to ruin everything, freak."

Sara blinks at her with two dull brown eyes, unfazed.

"Enough!" It was all innocent enough, albeit macabre, this talk of little girls branded and kidnapped and packed into cars. I will talk to Carmela or Yesi or anyone else about the tenth as soon as possible. Perhaps I misunderstood or misheard. But the lone extra seat bothers me.

"We haven't seen a tenth girl," says Mariella.

My eyes flick over to her, trying to judge whether she's pulling my leg. "Let's move on, shall we?"

Gisella and Mariella smirk at each other.

"Can you introduce yourself in *English?*" I ask. "Gisella?"

She folds her hands on the table with exaggerated primness. "Dearest Miss Quercia," she says, in unaccented English, "you should know that we've all been learning English since we began to walk. Your handout is . . . inadequate."

The girls around her chuckle, as if they aren't still children. Michelle blushes an angry pink, mirroring how I feel—though, of course, I'll never show them. Carmela's office told me they were beginners. Novices. I can't decide if Carmela is disorganized, uninterested, or if there's something else afoot, but I sense Carmela has never been unprepared in her life.

"Wonderful," I reply, fetching a stack of lined paper to distribute. "Then you can each write a short composition describing yourselves and your homes in the next half hour. We can spend the rest of class getting to know one another better. Together."

Gisella's smile fades as she snatches the paper from me. Soon, the nine of them begin scribbling away, some with more vigor than others. My gaze falls to Michelle again, who hurries to fill the page before her with a loopy scrawl. I cross the room, trying to make sense of her resemblance. I think of what Yesi said, about how living in a haunted house helps you to explore all the dark nooks in yourself. To me, that still sounds more like a horror than a boon.

The half hour passes this way, and as I'm collecting their papers, Mariella and Gisella stand, gathering their bags.

"We have another fifteen minutes, ladies."

Mariella looks at me with pity. "Early lunch, Miss Quercia. I suppose your schedule must have gotten lost with the imaginary tenth girl."

Gisella bursts into giggles as they stroll from the room arm in arm. I know that losing my temper will lead nowhere. Most of the other girls trickle behind them. Michelle lingers, stacking and restacking her materials.

"You may go, Michelle."

She nods and tries for a smile as she exits. I collect the assignments scattered across the table and drop back into my seat to read. My mouth goes dry: Their written English almost matches mine in skill level, and my mother taught me English daily growing up, convinced I would need it to be independent and escape—or help—our country one day. As cool as the teaching cottage is, I sweat bullets, wondering how I'll rework my lesson plan to suit their higher level. I scold myself for not being prepared, for not loving the girls immediately, for letting them get to me with nothing more than sharp tongues. Before I lock up, I check my desk for dead frogs, my blouse for inky tears. No. Of course not. These aren't city girls—they're Vaccaro School girls. Lucky and confident beyond measure, rooted in themselves and vibrant memories of rich childhoods. Their mischief will be much more insidious.

The trek back up to the main house is arduous. It's oddly quiet because the girls are long gone. Halfway up, I stop, catching my breath, and watch the rock face for a sign of movement, for a sign of life. As if on command, a starship of a butterfly, its wings copies of autumn leaves, launches off a tree trunk beside me, floating off and fading to match the ghostly pallor of the steps. Blending in perfectly. I squint at the maze of stones, wondering if other camouflaged creatures observe in silence as they do. Biding their time and playing by the rules, until they can follow through with the plan some god or devil wrote for them, too.

6

ANGEL: 2020-200

The first day of classes. I burst back into the closet ready for action, and a bit queasy-quivery, too, like a kid who's inhaled a family-size pack of M&M's in his mom's van on the way to Disneyland only to realize sugar crashes are death. I press into room 7, look down, and see that I'm bisected by a chair—standing in it, not on it. Since I left, the nut-brown girl has wedged a chair in front of the closet door, below the knob, as if to lock someone in. *Me?* Has she seen us? Felt us?

I tsk her softly, thinking of what Rob would say about her amateur-hour ghost-prevention techniques, if that's what that bit of redecoration was.

But when I see her and Yesi at breakfast with the rest of them, they're no worse for wear. I circle Yesi, examining her guiltily as she cheerfully eats one blueberry at a time like some kind of baby deer. "Mavi!" she says, seizing the nut-brown girl's arm like they're the best friends in the world. Little does she know that she has about a few dozen other invisible best friends who can't get enough of her.

The room is chock-full of teachers and students, many of them a bit shell-shocked over the ridiculous spread (crepes!), but empty of Others, as far as I can tell. Maybe most Others have better shit to do this early. Maybe mealtime is too boring since we can't eat a damn thing. I feel a wobble of nostalgia for ramen noodles and chicken tikka masala and, oh my god, cheeseburgers. They're all as edible and tasty to me now as crumbling plaster moldings.

I hover around the coffeepots, eavesdropping and learning names, because, you know, it's my first day of school, too. The specter otherwise known as Morency (I think her first name is afraid of her) leans into Carmela De Vaccaro while I watch. "After her tardiness—missing dinner, Madame!—and wild roaming last night, she is proving to be a terrible disappointment," says Morency under her breath, smoothing her black skirts. As if missing dinner is like taking a hatchet to your neighbor. In that sense, there's only one person in this room worthy of capital punishment, of course—Mavi. "You should ask her to leave," Morency adds. "You should ask all the young women to leave—"

"Ms. Morency, if we all made decisions based on transient, substanceless gut feelings, then we wouldn't make much progress at all, would we?" Carmela banishes a speck of dust from her sleeve with a tapered fingernail. "Do leave the decision-making to me. The little girls are here now, prepared to learn and better themselves. Prepared to be a part of a greater cause."

Morency's jaw sets before she speaks. "A greater cause, Madame? I trust that—I trust that this has nothing to do with your . . ." She clears her throat. Waits a good three seconds—an eternity in Carmela's bone-chilling presence. "Tenth girl."

She speaks the words as if she's crossing herself, and a quiver runs through me, jelly-thick as an electric eel. Who is the tenth girl?

I watch Carmela smooth her jacket with a cold smile. In silence, as if she's teasing me and Morency by not answering. The edges of her lips look strained and vaguely wet, like she also just ripped the delicious head off a small and fluffy creature with her teeth and holds it back by the damp root of her tongue.

"The students should be at home with their families," Morency ventures to say, breaking the silence, "where—"

Carmela extends a perfectly manicured hand. "I won't tolerate a tantrum at this point in the game. We are committed." She looks Morency up and down. "And why must you wear black all the time? Black is a color for the depressed, for those in mourning. I never wear black. Because I keep hope alive," she says, chin high. "It is the most precious gift we have."

So what is Cruella de Vil hoping for, exactly? And what does it have to do with a tenth girl? I circle around to face Morency and see that her authority and nerve have melted away after Carmela's shutdown; she looks like a kid who's learned bloodthirsty monsters really do squat among the dust bunnies under her bed, and yes, they're interested in chewing off that foot you tuck out of the covers when you sleep. Carmela struts away from her, approaching Mavi and Whitewalker, and I get the wind knocked out of my crystal when Carmela refers to him as her *son*, Domenico.

Makes sense. Terrible, god-awful genes, or phenomenal ones, depending on how shallow you are. Whitewalker terrorizes Mavi, who's red-faced ten seconds into the conversation—she struggles to balance her overloaded breakfast plate after being deprived of dinner last night. I find Yesi and tap her shoulder until, mosquito-style, I draw her attention to Mavi. I guess feeding did help me gain some substance, and she and Mavi might as well benefit from it. Ghost charity. Yesi rescues Mavi, and they scamper outside with their breakfasts, two little garden rabbits who will survive Carmela's arctic wrath for one more day.

The teachers chatter about vacations, lesson plans, and other subjects about as interesting as bowel movements; the novelty of eavesdropping on conversations fades, and with it, the power of my invisibility.

I comb the cottages outside for the first time, getting the lay of the land.

It's quiet, until mousy (moley?) Dr. Molina passes me on the steps, carrying a three-foot-tall stack of papers in her bony hands, slipping and sliding on the mossy stones. She's seriously going to break a hip, and I'm going to be the only one to hear her wailing.

"Ooh!" she says cheerfully every time she skids on one and miraculously catches herself. It's like watching a train wreck as she approaches another set of steps, each step more treacherous-looking than the last, culminating in a missing step that she clearly can't see over her damn papers.

"You've got to be kidding me," I say, rushing forward to nudge her upward, so she doesn't plunge into the hole and roll all the way down the hill, shattering every single one of her fragile, rodent-thin bones.

She steadies herself with my help and notices the gaping hole while I groan with the expended effort. "Thank goodness," she says to herself, laughing and restacking the packets in her arms. "Lucky, lucky girl, Doctor."

"Luck has nothing to do with it, woman!" I snap at her. "Check yourself."

She wanders off, oblivious. And I wonder if maybe we're not entirely to blame for all the good and bad in life. If maybe luck is just another word for intervention by the unknown—someone or something we can't quite understand helping all of us along, shaping the rules of our reality.

High-pitched chattering reverberates down an alleyway around the corner from the cottage. I slink across the roof tiles and find the girls sharing a cigarette (to be fair, only three of the seven present venture to smoke it, and they cough, tomato-red, like they've chugged pureed habaneros). Two more of the girls stand off to the side—one looks dead-eyed and pretty damn evil, in a bland way, and the other is quiet and shy, with a twinkle of deeper intelligence. She toes the ground and glances toward the cottage. So that's nine girls. Only nine students. Who is Carmela's tenth girl?

"Honestly, Luciana, stop crying. Everyone's parents split up," a lithe, dark-blond girl tells the crier, crossing her baby-colt legs and taking a mouthy drag like Katharine Hepburn. "It's not a big deal. They'll leave you alone more."

Savage. She's wrong, too. Sometimes single parents get more obsessed with you. Sometimes one parent kills the other parent, skipping the separation process entirely and adopting the telenovela Hail Mary.

Luciana bursts into another long, honking sob like a braying donkey.

"Gisella," admonishes a gentle brunette, while another pats Luciana's hand.

"Parents suck. But you know what else sucks? This stupid school," says one black-haired girl authoritatively. The ringleader.

"This *haunted* school, Mariella," whispers the girl patting the crying girl's hand.

I snort.

Mariella shoots her a dirty look (*Peasants*) and continues: "And *life*. Life in general sucks." I nod along, feeling her nihilistic vibe. It's kind of wholesome and nice, to be honest, that they're smoking cigarettes angstily, trashing modern existence in person, as opposed to the contemporary alternative of face-tuning social media posts alone in their rooms. I never thought I'd say that, but it's true.

Mariella seizes back the cigarette. "I say we blow off the rookie teacher. That would cheer you up, wouldn't it, Lu?" The others glance at one another nervously, and it's abundantly clear that cutting would cheer up only Mariella, but I applaud her noble effort.

"How long should we pretend we don't know any English?" asks another, giggling.

"I'm sure she's peeing her pants. It's her first day *ever*, I heard. She's barely older than we are."

"God forbid I ever end up like her." A shudder. "Teaching."

"She looks like one of my old nannies," says a fifth. "I wonder how she became a teacher so *young*. Shouldn't that be illegal?"

"She won't be our teacher for long." Mariella takes another puff. "She'll learn her place is back in the gutter soon enough."

Learn her place.

"If not, I'm sure Domenico will show her," says Gisella, belting out a gorgeous movie-star laugh.

"You guys are such clichés," I grumble from over in the peanut gallery. Even without technology to help them along in finding vapid role models, they're still on the fast track to becoming assholes. They're like the landed version of Liese, who's biologically compelled to shit on me and Rob. Granted, that's because of how much she hates our communal asswipe of a dad for impregnating our (as in, Rob's and my) mother, but join the club. Point is, these girls are one bad latte away from being the sort of person who marks all her food in the refrigerator with a sticky note reading *Liese! DO NOT TOUCH!*

Even if it's a disgusting lemon yogurt that's going to expire while she's away on her cosmetology retreat (Liese, circa last year).

One of my most vivid memories was when Rob went off on his own and set up this whole old-school lemonade stand on the corner of our street so that he could raise money for an animal charity, on account of his dream of being a vet. I was the one who suggested the idea: He was pretty obsessed with his tablet at that point, with feeding and caring for a horrible, octopus-like electronic pet called a scoogi (who names these abominations?), and I would have done just about anything short of using child harnesses to get him out into the real world. He took to the idea of the stand. The problem was that Rob took this disgusting, expensive container of pink swirly lemonade in the fridge that Liese had bought herself—she was dieting, and it contained mystery Fit Lemon-Aid!™ herbs meant to make her waste away—and he poured it out, drop by drop, into little polka-dotted paper cups to sell. He got one, maybe two hits from pitying neighbors, and when I escaped my part-time summer job and came to buy my own cup, he proudly displayed his meager and fragrant Halloween candy bucket of cash (one dude had emptied out a pocket full of ones and cigarette butts into the bin, if that gives you any indication of our kind of neighbors—alternately generous and gross). "At least, if I'm not a vet, we can be on-tah-pah-noors, Angel," Rob said, and when I was about to laugh and ruffle his hair (God-given right of older siblings), we saw Liese marching toward us, gnarled blond hair flying behind her like Medusa's snakes.

"How dare you steal this from me," she said. She had a real uppity streak, something to do with being a real Aryan looker built in a lab while the rest of us looked like overdyed mistakes; she was swinging around the fancy monogrammed bag she bought like it was a weapon of poor taste.

I wanted to laugh, I did, until I saw Rob's eyes look all wounded. He's the kind of kid who felt bad stepping on *grass* for a summer because he didn't want to hurt a single blade. Her eyes scanned his handmade sign reading DONASHONS FOR ANIMALS!!!! (Spelling not necessarily a strength of future veterinarians or entrepreneurs.)

"When will you realize that you'll never be a vet, Robert? Do you know how many years of school that takes? Don't you understand no one has the money for it?"

"Scholarships," I said, crossing my arms in Rob's defense.

"You're delusional," she said, desperately trying to hold herself still. I saw that Rob was suppressing tears; he hated when people raised their voices (probably because of the loud fights that erupted over my dad, or, rather, the empty space that should have contained my dad), and all Liese did was raise her voice for stupid-ass reasons. "Your mother was a bit of an idiot, wasn't she? Living in fantasyland for years—look where that got her. Stuffing all these ideas into your head and going ahead and—well, I shudder to think what will become of you now with this idiot caring for you."

The second idiot being me, of course. Rob was crying softly, and I was clenching my fists. I took the jug of lemonade and held it out to her. "It's lemonade, Liese. Lemons and water. I'll buy you some more. Take it."

"It's cold-pressed and organic." Her mouth ejected the words automatically, and she flushed. "But that's not the point," she snapped, ripping the jug from my hands.

That's when her husband sauntered up, with—no joke—a pastel bag of supplements and protein powder in tow. He-who-must-not-be-named.

"What's going on here?" he asked. He was a faceless creature the size of a centaur, with thick veins threading through the skin of his arms; they popped up when he was hot or turned on (don't ask, please don't ask) or pissed off. They looked like writhing snakes—like something lurid. He set down his shopping bag and put his hands on Liese's shoulders as if she were a doll he could massage or crush, depending on his mood (she was). He smelled like beer, or yeast, and stale sweat mixed with bad cologne (*Macho Icy Mountain Fre$h!*).

"Angel took something without asking again." Liese turned red, looking chastened yet still superior.

His flat eyes flicked from the lemonade container to Rob to me.

"You need to learn your place, kid," he said. *Learn your place.* And his casual tone made it sound like a workout regimen suggestion, like *You need to do a dozen crunches*, and that's why his put-downs were so insidious. "You're living in our house, on our dime. You aren't some special dandelion." *Snowflake*, I thought. "And you shouldn't be indulging the kid." He nodded at Rob, who had gone silent. "That's the best advice I'll ever give you."

"You're right about that," I whispered to myself.

His eyes, which had gone unfocused, landed back on me as Liese averted her gaze.

You shouldn't be indulging the kid.

I would kill for *the kid*. Indulging him—encouraging his dreams, few and paltry and Skittlesy as they were—was a given. And could it even be considered indulging him when he'd gone through so much, so young?

He stepped closer, his fingers the size and color of singed mini-sausages tightening around Liese's collarbones. "What'd you say to me?" he asked, veiny-armed and amused. It was a challenge, not a question. A challenge he knew I could never take him up on, because I could never win.

I was silent.

"Speak up."

"Babe—" Liese started speaking, but he tightened his grip. There was even a smile playing on his lips, and I would've done anything in that moment to take a tire iron to his stupid skull and gouge a dozen gaping holes. A workout regimen I could get behind.

"Shut up, Liese," he said as casually as some people say *I'm fine, thanks*.

She tensed under his grasp, and I knew she was going to defuse the situation with some ditzy remark, like *Babe, leave it, I bought the T-bone steaks you like for dinner but you always know how to grill them up so nice so we better get cracking on the marinade*, because Liese, a bully herself, recognized that her husband was a bigger one. Takes one to know one, and all that.

His nostrils flared. "Speak up. Say whatever it is you have to say."

"Babe——" Liese said again, and it was more of a baby-animal squeak-groan. *Babe!* That fucking word! People have killed over less, and my hands were in fists, and I said, "Oh my god, be quiet, Liese," under my breath, and her face iced up (God was a touchy subject, He-who-must-not-be-named was a Big Fan), and he dropped his shoulders and in one fluid motion hit me with a brick of a hand, casually again, but so hard that I felt it in my deep-down face bones and sported a welt on my cheek for a week.

It was the kind of pain that was a delicious reminder of my hate—of his boring, ham-handed cruelty. I would have killed myself hundreds of times, just for him to have to mop up my subhuman steroid-free blood, just for it to stain his veined arms up to the elbows, really soaking down into his pores.

Rob stayed curled up next to me in my bed all night. I sang him the old lullaby Mama always sang him—the only time she mentioned God. He gave me his banana-yellow blanket to press against my cheek because his blanket helped everything, as magical blankets typically do.

"Did Mama get sick because she gave us her ideas?" he asked, as if Mama lived on ideas as we lived on air, on food, on water, or something mystical and absurd and childlike and beautiful like that. I told him no, even though I thought Liese's gaffe had helped him mine some deep truth about people. He asked again when we would go home, real home, and much later, when he thought I was asleep, he tugged his blanket back toward him and let silent tears drip into its tropical stripes. After that, I let him play with his scoogi whenever he wanted. And I—I shut down around Liese and He-who-must-not-be-named, *learning my place*.

But not here.

That's when I'm overcome with an Others-approved urge to scare the living daylights out of these schoolgirls, before they check a mental box that says, *Yes! casual cruelty—the thoughtless kind—is totally funny and* okay.

But how to accomplish a little thing like that?

"BOO!" I shout, hovering over them like a banshee. "BOO BOO BOO BOO BOO!"

They don't even budge. Fine. Way too predictable to work. Kill the ghost dead for trying.

My foot punts at the blonde's hair (kicking her head feels a little too much like curb-stomping a kitten), and girlfriend doesn't even register the breeze.

I can't lift anything good to throw, either. I try a forgotten notebook—nope. I try a nearby lantern, for the ghostly symbolism of shattering its glass. I'm struggling to deadlift a pebble on the roof above them when out of nowhere, I hear a rumbling. A roaring.

Feel it, more aptly.

An entire plane of roof tiles above me becomes dislodged and slides down the roof—shuttling through me, like it's a subway car, but also dragging me, like I'm a deflated balloon on the tracks. Slamming into the ground next to the girls. Shattering with a thunderous crash like a hundred terra-cotta pots.

If I were the lucky owner of one grade-A body, I would've been elegantly decapitated in front of this group of five-foot-tall seventh graders. Not even these brats deserve that.

Commence the shrieking (me included), the cigarette-smoking blonde shrillest of all. A few of them have scratches on their ankles from flying shards. Like little dancing rodeo clowns, they leap up and dust off their clothes and stub out the cigarette and collect their book bags and curse with varying degrees of success ("Good Lord!" is heard more than once).

"Um, I'm going to head over to class," says the shy girl. The creepy girl drifts with her.

The group splinters as more and more girls hustle toward the class cottage. Only Mariella tidies her braids as she watches them retreat. "Losers."

I sit back and wait, shaking, wondering if I caused a roof to literally break in two or not. I examine the blank swath from my spot on the ground. It must have been me, fiddling with the lower tiles, disrupting the balance, and causing the whole avalanche. *Do I not even know my own strength?* Damn, Hercules.

When the entire group—Mariella included—heads to class, I pat myself on the back for a pretty good-natured haunting. Whether or not poor roof maintenance was involved.

As I'm heading off, a cloud passes overhead: puffy, cotton-white, enormous. Your stereotypical dream cloud, the sort of thing baby angels pop out of, cooing and shooting arrows. I want to bury my face in it, suffocate in it, kind of like that girl who's famous for rubbing her face in fresh bakery bread (I always feared crust on her behalf). The sky beyond, a deep-lake blue, is richer and realer than any sky I knew. It vibrates, as if it's swirling with invisible, gelatinous fish. My eye catches on the ridge of the main building and travels along the seams of every cottage running down the hill.

That's when I see them, perched on the crest of the cottage I was messing around on, invisible to me until now. Sitting and watching.

At least a couple of dozen frizzing shadows—if you can call static shudders as much—of men above me. Hulking, bulky masses, twice my size. Not one or two—but two *dozen*. Concrete in a way I've never known.

Bile laces up the threads of my non-throat, knowing these Other reptiles were above me.

Knowing they did this.

Revel in it, I hear Charon say in my head. *Hercules*. One raises an arm to wave, a semitransparent, glassy arm as thick as my torso, and I hear laughter, the faintest baritone laughter, carried on the wind.

Every crystal light in me shorts out and goes dark.

7

MAVI: ARGENTINA, MARCH 1978

Mole joins me and Yesi for a lively—and private—lunch on the patio over the ice, which has softened in the midday light. I've come to learn that only dinner is eaten at one table together—as if night truly requires more community security on our part. During the day, it seems, we are safe. We settle in front of chicken milanesas, fried to a golden crisp and topped with chopped fresh tomatoes and basil, and Mole proceeds to spill her guts about everyone at the school, including Morency herself. It helps, after the embarrassment of my first class, to gossip. I wish I was better than it, but Marguerite's God knows I need it.

"I heard from the kitchen staff that Morency had an affair with an Indigenous man years ago, conducted entirely under the cover of darkness," Mole says. "When her parents found out, they insisted she marry the man. But when he saw her in the light before the ceremony, he ran off in quite the hurry."

"Oh, please," I say, looking at Yesi. "It's too good to be true."

"I found a photograph of her in her ghastly wedding gown," Molina replies, dropping to an elated whisper. "I'll bring it to you."

I do feel a bit of pity for Morency. But only a bit.

"To be quite frank she looks utterly different. Sad-eyed and small and charming," adds Mole.

"Small?"

"Yes, small. I swear it. A bit bloated already, perhaps. But it's as if the energy of that early disappointment funneled itself into overgrowth of the bones, joints, hair." She brushes a tendril of a vine dangling from the patio wall off her shoulder. "Like Vaccaro School itself. She's a derailed number one, through and through."

Yesi and I catch each other's eyes. For a scientist, Mole can be quite whimsical.

"So is that why she's at Vaccaro School?" I ask, setting down my knife and fork. "She's an old maid with nothing better to do than be a matron of a house?"

Yesi looks to Mole, whose nose twitches. "She must have known Carmela before. She's certainly loyal to her. I can't imagine why else she'd be here. When she found Mariella and Gisella smoking cigarettes with Domenico on the first night—"

My skin tingles. "What?"

"Well, yes. They were being silly. But Morency erupted into this rather magnificent rant about how no one should take one's safety for granted—not in *this house*. If she thinks it's so dangerous, you would think she wouldn't be here, no?"

I bite my lip.

"What's your theory, Mole?" Yesi asks. "Your theory as to why the school exists." She looks at me. "It's Mavi's favorite game. She has no idea why it should exist. She doesn't buy Carmela's reasoning."

I inaugurated the game at breakfast to beat the nerves. We invent more and more outlandish reasons: because it's a tax haven for Carmela (though we don't exactly know how—operating on the grounds of a national park, perhaps, and reaping government subsidies); because Carmela's using it as a front to slyly harvest a special goat's fur to make pashminas; because they've run out of money, and as destitute pseudo-aristocrats, they've managed to persuade the ignorant wealthy to send their girls here—they need the tuition as much as we need the final lump sum. I ignore the idea developing in my brain that this is a haunted house hungry for lost souls; no teacher or student has given me any explicit reason to think they are in a situation similar to mine. But after digesting my unpleasant classroom encounter with Carmela, I am certain there is more to this school than meets the eye—she hides darkness with her polished veneer, as no such person hides an educator's heart of gold.

Molina's nose wrinkles. "Carmela has been taking the airs," she says.

My breath catches. "What?"

"Carmela isn't well," she says, pushing up her glasses. "Mentally, I should say. Emotionally. She's up here to recuperate and feel useful. That's why the school is entirely off the grid. Unreachable by phone, satellite, you name it. Devoid of new technology. It's like a sanatorium. She needs the peace, you see." She drops to a whisper again. "You know she ran the second-largest cement company in Argentina for a dozen years, ever since her husband passed? Typical eight. Money and power-focused. Then her daughter fell ill."

Yesi and I look at each other.

"She has a daughter?"

"Well, yes. Had. Her princess. Domenico's younger sister. They held a quiet funeral, family only, a month before they approached me. Before they reinstated the school."

"No!" Despite the salaciousness of it, I feel an ache in my throat for Carmela. As cold and unfeeling as she seems, there must be a kernel of humanity there. Whether it's been lacquered with too much foundation and lipstick and dye to ever see the light of day remains to be seen.

"And how did they find you?" I ask.

"Pure, wild luck. I was an assistant biology professor in Bragado," she says. "My husband had just passed away—"

Yesi's face crinkles up. "Oh, I didn't know. I'm sorry."

"Yes, yes, thank you, dear. He was a terrible bore, however, and we hadn't said more than *Pass the salt* to each other in thirty years. In any case, we lived near the center where her daughter was seeking treatment, terribly elite place, thousands of pesos a day, out in the country. And she asked the head of the school if he knew of any teachers without families willing to relocate—"

"Ah."

"Yes, ah. So here I am."

We sit chewing on bites of chicken breast for several moments.

"So some of us are lost sheep," I say. "Looking for a new path."

Molina considers this. "It makes perfect sense to me that Carmela would seek teachers who could be entirely devoted to the school."

"At least for the term."

"That's right."

"Or be incentivized monetarily to be devoted."

Molina laughs. "Ah. Well, yes. I won't mind retiring in a few years. That's my plan, you know. Watch the girls graduate and leave. I've a cousin who lives in Miami whom I always forget about until I'm absolutely sick and tired of my present circumstances."

"You in Miami, Mole?" Yesi laughs. "Even the brash, thonged Floridians would shrivel up and die at your antics."

"If only there were more men here, my dear," she replies, fluffing her limp strands. "Only that divine creature Domenico. But he's far too young for me. Too much juice in him, and not enough fiber, if you know what I mean. I would suck him dry in a week."

We fall into hysterics; I spit out a chunk of tomato. "Molina, no!" Wiping my lip, I whip around to make sure he's not turning the corner.

"One of you should engage in a torrid affair with him," she says. "Or is one of you doing so already? Oh, please do tell me if you are. It would so brighten up this dreary mountain life of mine."

I look at Yesi and find her staring at me, smirking.

"I've been here less than twenty-four hours, for God's sake," I say.

"She wouldn't dare," says Yesi in a drawl.

"I'm certain he's an absolute savage in bed, though," adds Mole.

"Mole!" I whisper-shout as Yesi laughs at me.

"Mavi could get thrown out, Moley. Hush hush."

Mole sniffs the air. "Carmela wouldn't be all too concerned."

"*Not concerned* about her prince mingling with the commoners?" I say. "I received the warning, you know. Steer clear of him or suffer death by firing squad."

"No, no. There's only room for one such beloved in a family. I have it on good authority from a maid that he spends his days smoking hashish in his room. He's gone through several dozen grams. At least, that's the running estimate based on ash collected by the staff."

"No!"

We burst out laughing.

She wipes the tip of her nose with a grave expression. "It's troubling for a perfectionist like Carmela."

"What happened to her husband?" I ask. "I haven't heard much of him, only that he died."

"Oh," says Molina, waving a hand. "He was a five. Speedboat accident in the Côte d'Azur. A rudder cut his head right off—apparently, the coroner said he only felt a tickle on the back of his neck."

I swallow a lump of tomato caught in my throat.

After lunch, I read the girls' essays, gleaning strange little tidbits about their lives:

My name is Diana. and I grew up in Uruguay. then London. which makes for an exciting existence I should be most happy about. or so my father says. My father is an ambassador. and my mother was an actress. but not a very good one. or so my father also says...

I'm Silvina. My family is German, and they moved here in the 1900s, long before World War I and even World War II, in case you are thinking that we were Nazis. But we aren't Jews, either, God forbid. We live in Recoleta, in the large stone house at the end of the square facing the...

My parents named me Gisella after the opera about the woman who dies of a broken heart and is summoned back to kill...

Mariella Garibaldi is twelve years old and wishes she were still on the yacht off of Sardinia, where her family has a country home, instead of this heinous place...

Michelle was also my mom's name, and her mom's name, and her mom's. My father was French, and even though the Beatles are British, he liked to sing to me, "Michelle, ma belle..." Now they are both gone, and I live with my aunt, who takes her meals alone. She asks her maid to deposit a fresh can in my room each night for dinner. We eat only canned foods because she thinks fresh foods are tainted by the guerrillas or the military. I'm not sure which—it depends on the day. I'm happy to be here. So happy that sometimes I hear my soul sing when I'm brushing my teeth... It wants to spread itself out of my head like warm light.

And so it is settled: Michelle is no relation of the Falcone girl. Their resemblance falls to chance, and Michelle is simply a lost soul like me, which is why I've taken an interest in her. I breathe easier when my brain boxes this up and stores it away.

When I've finished reading, I draft lesson plans—more specifically, I rack my brain for a single shred of wisdom to impart as I wait for Carmela or Morency or some hybridized monster composed of them both to find me in my cottage and chastise me for being unprofessional and unprepared. I rustle up an old copy of *The Catcher in the Rye* and decide to plunge into it with the girls. It's creative, but I'm creative. Or so Mole said number sevens are.

No one comes to the cottage all afternoon but for Lamb, who comes bearing a scone and a thermos of tea, like a blessed angel. Dusk falls, and with it comes a prickling feeling along my scalp. Scratching at the panes of the cottage is only the scratching of overgrown vines; footsteps here and there are only Lamb and—in all likelihood—mice. But I buy into it already: the danger of dusk here. So be it. I will abide by the rules. I hurry back to the house to wash up for dinner and follow Yesi to the dining room, where someone has set the grand table for a lavish sit-down dinner.

Lit candles line the sides of the room, flames bobbing. Every bit of finery glimmers on the table: crystal goblets, silver candlesticks, and gilded plates that look one hundred years old. Fingers of steam curl from the overflowing platters of mouthwatering sliced meats drizzled in jus and grilled vegetables with char marks.

I tidy my hair and my skirt before draping a lace-edged napkin across my lap. "Has every dinner been like this?" I ask Yesi in a whisper.

She nods. "Eventually it will have to end. If they keep this up, Vaccaro School will be bankrupt in its first semester." She raises her chalice of grape juice to mine—per Carmela, *no drinking among the staff*, even though everyone surreptitiously tipples, or so says Lamb. "Cheers to draining the Vaccaro coffers with elaborate feasting."

"And cheers to adventure." I look around the table as I sip.

Carmela sits at the head, draped in ivory silk, with Domenico to her right and black-sacked Morency scowling to her left. The few of us teachers dot the sides, and the girls sit at the end, chattering among themselves, looking old-fashioned and darling in deceptively sweet, matching white button-down dresses with pearl buttons. Mariella holds eye contact with me and winks before I look away. Gladly, I've Yesi on one side, Lamb on the other. I clink my glass with his.

He grins. "Ah, yes, chin-chin, my dear! *¡Salud!* What a glorious house. What a magical evening. May they all be like this."

I ogle the plate of juicy steaks before me, wondering when I can serve myself, but Carmela rises and the table hushes. I catch Domenico staring at me, and he looks away, heavy-lidded eyes bored. I think of that bit in *Pride and Prejudice*—Lizzy overhearing Darcy say that she is tolerable but not handsome enough to tempt him.

"Welcome, all," Carmela says, spreading her arms wide. She, or a hidden makeup artist, has applied a symmetrical cat-eye to her lids. "I am so pleased to have all my staff and students here together for our first meal *en famille*."

Yesi coughs away a laugh at her French pretension, and Morency glares at us both.

"Vaccaro School is unique to all the world—many rich traditions are kept alive here. The first De Vaccaros made their life here after emigrating from northern Italy. Indeed, it was on this hill that they built a fort of unparalleled quality to protect themselves from the Zapuche Indians in the area, a fiercely territorial group who would, per my grandmother Domenica, peel the soles off the feet of foreign women they kidnapped so that they would not be able to run."

Yesi elbows me, and Mole, across the table, clears her throat. I glance at the girls, who do not seem to have registered Carmela's controversial statement. Gisella hurls a ball of rolled-up bread at Michelle.

"You sit inside that fort," Carmela adds with a wide smile, showing her animal-sharp incisors. "But it is so much more than that. It became a place of spiritual rediscovery for my family—imbued with hill magic, populated by wise presences from the world over that the Zapuche believed to be fundamental to their existence."

I frown. How did outsiders like Carmela and her family transform from despised colonial menaces to fundamental parts of the Zapuche's existence?

"It became a place where generations of my family learned how to adapt to the new world—how to reconnect with each other," she says, taking Domenico's hand, which sits on the table beside her. He blinks at her, as if realizing he is not alone. "There's an infinite, magnetic wisdom to this immortal rock—it is ultimately a place of inspiration, of healing. Our nine-month term here could bear the sort of fruit one might associate with a century-long golden age. Rest assured: You made the right choice in coming here. The school will bestow great gifts on us all. We must simply give it all that we can first."

I swallow and look around the table at the crooked half smiles and lifted chins and fiddling fingers. I expected more from Carmela's speech than oblique reassurance—more to rally us, more specificity to inspire us and give us a sense of her mission. I sense that most of us did.

"Can we eat?" I hear Diana whisper to Mariella from under her unruly fringe of hair.

Sara whispers to Mole across the table. Carmela notices and snaps.

"What is it, Dr. Molina?"

Mole hesitates. "It's nothing."

"Do speak up, Doctor," says Morency, her horseface sour.

"Sara asked me what happened to the family and the school that used to be here." She clears her throat. "Your family and their school."

Carmela's smile does not melt from her face as I might have expected. The table is silent, all of those seated riveted, despite the food cooling before us, untouched.

"You may have heard rumors of what happened to my family here," she says, dabbing at her right cat-eye with a crooked finger. "I will tell you the truth now, so to stop them. A virus affected the family and household staff some sixty years ago, sending them away."

"Did the students die?" asks Sara, eyes shining for the first time. Silvina elbows her, hard, and Sara ignores her.

"The school was closed until the property was deemed safe again," says Carmela without a waver. "I am pleased to share that we have passed every inspection with flying colors. The Vaccaro School will be named a site of historical significance by the government this year." The mention of the government sends the slightest collective ripple through the diners. Carmela raises a glass, her fixed jaw straining against taut skin.

Morency mutters under her breath, and Carmela snaps. "What is it now?"

Morency folds her hands in her lap with a martyr's wounded eyes.

"Ah," says Carmela, as if this is a signal. "I am also pleased to have Morency here as de facto head of household staff. She will handle any further questions you might have. As far as I'm concerned, I trust her with my life. She has been my right hand for many years, ever since her mother served as my nurse, and her mother's mother served as my own mother's nurse."

Morency blanches, nearly impossible to detect on her pasty skin. I suppose it wasn't the introduction she wanted.

"That's a lot of nursing," whispers Yesi.

"Hearty woman," I whisper back.

"She has Zapuche blood in her," continues Carmela.

"I did have the refreshing sensation when we met that her love would not be the kind I could run from," whispers Yesi, in an imitation of Carmela's imperious drawl.

I clap a hand over my mouth.

"Yes, Luciana?" says Carmela. I look over and see that Luciana has raised her hand.

"Michelle wants to say something," she says.

"Then *Michelle* should raise her hand and speak."

Michelle blushes. "I just wanted to say—"

"Do speak up," says Carmela.

She comes to her feet with a screech of the chair's legs. "I wanted to say that I'm proud to be a pioneer," she says. "I think we all are."

And the hardened edges of my heart melt.

"Suck-up," says Mariella with a cough, to chuckles.

"That's enough," interrupts Morency, standing. "Yes, the Vaccaro School was known around the world as a place of great learning of all types—a place where young women would emerge to be strong social players in a society that did not value them as it should have. Today, *we* will be our generation's pioneers. *We* will tap into the"— she glances at Carmela—"spiritual significance of this place and help build strong, brilliant girls to lead our country out of this murkiness. It is our mandate, and it is our will. Men have torn apart this country with their shadowy violence. We women will take back our futures and press on into the light."

Domenico scoffs and crosses his arms as Mr. Lamm claps.

"Brava!" he shouts.

And soon, the others clap, too. The girls giggle behind their hands. I have to say, I might warm to Morency yet—though my stomach turns at the mention of our country's present violence.

I raise my hand tentatively, eager to change the subject and emboldened by the lift in the table's spirits, to ask about the missing tenth student. Carmela nods at me.

"Should we be expecting a tenth student, Madame De Vaccaro?" I ask. "I was under the impression there were ten girls."

Morency looks into her hands, and Carmela's lips peel themselves back into a frightening smile. "She's been taken ill," Carmela says. "She will be here soon, God willing."

I glance around at the girls and teachers, surprised to find their interest isn't piqued. I can't let the subject go.

"Can you tell us more about her?" I ask. "When can we expect her?"

Morency slams a hand against the wood of the table—everyone startles but Carmela, lost in thought.

"That is enough," she says, eyes darting around. "The food is now cold because of these endless interruptions." My trickle of newly formed compassion toward her evaporates. Fine. I'll have to wait for this sickly girl to arrive to learn more about her. I catch Domenico's eye, and he raises his brow at me in the half a second before I look away. I distract myself by inhaling several lamb chops and a hunk of rare beef, unsure of when I will eat this well again in my life.

Oh, right. Tomorrow. God bless this school.

The teachers linger after dinner to enjoy a bit of sobremesa. A vacant-eyed Carmela rises to lead the girls back to their rooms in the westernmost branch of the house. She rubs at a spot on her chest with the heel of her hand as she waits for the girls to line up behind her. Her off-key speech endures in my mind, as does Molina's earlier story about her daughter's death. It must be torturous for her, for Domenico, to be surrounded by so many little girls of her daughter's age. Unless she inhabits a realm of enlightened reflection that's so above and beyond me that I can't recognize it.

While Morency gives instructions to the kitchen staff, Domenico rises—presumably to go smoke—and I impulsively excuse myself to go to the restroom, with a sidelong look from Yesi. Of course, I end up following his fading form down the hall, away from the staff stairs, unsure of my motivation—perhaps I follow because I've been prohibited from doing so. Or I follow because some clue in his behavior might illuminate the underlying mystery of the house. Or I'm fulfilling a sad cliché and want to needle him because he's melancholy and a bit frightening and ridiculously attractive in a way that seems impossible outside of fairy tales. I know he's not stupid—he must smoke to deaden some part of himself. To pass the hours while stranded here. I'll admit it—I'm not immune to the lure of the "complex" man, despite knowing I'd be better off with someone simpler, kinder. But . . . broad-shouldered and sure-footed as ever, he ambles down a route I've never explored, through the ballroom and down a hallway off the closet door I hid from Morency in with Yesi. I don't yet know why a man in his prime from an elite family chooses this rock as his place of solace, besides its being the path of least resistance. My world of opportunity is a grain of sand in his.

He turns right down another corridor, yet to notice me. I'm watchful, sneaking backward glances. By some stroke of luck, no one else has followed. He climbs a short flight of creaking stairs I don't dare to climb and stops in front of a doorway. He pushes open the door with a hand and pauses, as if he's aware I'm behind him, snooping. As if he's affording me this glimpse of his gorgeous royal-blue room with views of the ice—a startling white in the dark. There is a king-size canopy bed and a full sitting room. He lifts the half-zipped sweater over his head, offering a glimpse of a toned body beneath before his shirt falls into place. Flinging the fine wool like a rag onto a brocade sofa, he breathes in and out luxuriantly, the muscles of his back shifting beneath the paper-thin shirt and his skin.

"Don't follow me. Don't touch me."

I splutter for words as he remains still.

He doesn't turn to face me, and blessedly, I can't be sure he's speaking to me. He cracks his fingers, one by one, and my cheeks feel like hot coals.

"I know what you are, and you disgust me," he says. "You're hollow at the core. But having me won't help you. I'm nothing but a bad memory given shape by a disgruntled God."

And he shuts the door.

I sink to my heels around the bend. My hands tremble. Does he know, then? Does he know what I am? The cowardly daughter of a hardened leftist, on the run? *Having me won't help you.* As if I hoped to lure him in like a siren and use his family's influence to protect myself. What a fool I am to flout the rules of this place on my second night here.

I slink back to the teachers' residence hall, swearing not to follow him again. Promising to settle in quietly. But his final sentence lingers in my memory because I cannot make sense of it—those petulant, spooky words laid his loneliness and insecurity so bare. I hustle up the back stairs to my room, overwhelmed by the sense that the house's mysteries live well inside that murky, unhealthy place that steals bits of your soul should you linger there too long.

I try to sleep after my strange encounter, but I'm restless. Falling straight asleep would be too simple, too prescribed. I knock on Yesi's door beyond the pass-through, and after a few tries, she answers with a pen in hand, a smear of ink across her face.

"Go to sleep, Swampy dear. I'm working." She shuts the door with a wink, and my sad little effort to waste some nighttime hours together is aborted.

I peek out into the staff hallway and find it quiet but for the purr of a radiator. Hand frozen on the knob, I consider wandering out again. But after a good minute of contemplation, I close my door. I huddle on the bed under the yellowing blanket and my coat. The room still freezes my fingers and toes into numbness. A space heater would be nice, nicer than those imagined chocolates on pillows. Without the light of day streaming through the bathroom skylight—without any moonlight, as the sky must be covered in clouds—the room becomes as solemn as a mausoleum.

What would my mother have said about tonight, with its crystal pitchers, its lace fineries, and Carmela herself, her words as false and decorative as the rest? She would've despised the De Vaccaros, I know that much—she would've railed at their brushing aside old crimes. She would've told me to dig up the whole truth and expose it to light, not long after reprimanding me for wanting to fit in and hide the tender pieces of myself.

I try to call up happier memories with her, anything that might give me a feeling of warmth in the tomb of my room, but all I can recall in the darkness, at first, is the cyanide tooth and Manuel's teary-eyed face. And then Michelle's little round face drifts into view, coupled with the stench of scorched concrete and sweet gunpowder. A flash of the blackened crater where my classmate's apartment had been.

During that period of visiting cousins, some time after my mother encouraged me to think of Manuel's suicide with pride, she hosted a rowdy group she would not let me see. This was unusual: Toward the end of our time together, I was encouraged to participate, to bask in that particular glow of her righteousness. If her exclusion of me was an indication of hesitation or of fear on her part, I cannot now know.

Locked in my room, I listened as their voices waned and waxed, whispers to shouts. I overheard grainy talk of the horrific kidnappings, rapes, and torture committed by the military junta, of far-left guerrillas as young as sixteen—my age. I knew about all these graphic crimes, or much about them, at least, and I pressed my ear closer to the door, puzzled as to why I was excluded. And then my mother's voice, clear as a bell, sounded out: She said the name *Falcone.*

I recoiled, my stomach a bundle of live wires. Falcone: *an empty-headed bureaucrat ignorant of the evil he spreads with every scratch of his pencil.* My classmate's father. Feeling unclean and unwell, I tucked myself into bed and waited for my breathing to slow.

Her visitors were gone before I woke.

The following week, I was working on homework in our apartment when a powerful blast unlike anything I've ever heard shook the earth around me.

I dropped to the floor, then crawled toward the window. Nothing was visible outside except a distant cloud of smoke. Soon after, I heard the sirens and smelled that choking odor.

My mother was teaching that day, and I waited inside, chewing my nails to shreds, for her to arrive with news of what had occurred. But she arrived so late that night, smelling of wine, that I pretended to be asleep when she entered my bedroom and kissed my cheek.

I learned about it in school the next day. The Falcone apartment had been bombed by guerrillas. An amateurish operation, said one snippy nun to another, for the intended target—Mr. Falcone, the government worker—had been speaking with the building superintendent at the time. My classmate, whom I imagined had been working on the same assignment I had been working on several blocks away, had been the only one to die.

When I told my mother this, as she read the last of that morning's newspaper after dinner, she did not react. I prodded her, and she stood ever straighter, avoiding my eyes as she told me how tragic it was when the innocent died.

I knew, in the marrow of my bones, that she was in some capacity involved in this act. I knew which three syllables I had heard her say, at this very table, only a week prior. *Fal-co-ne.* And, without passing moral judgment—for I was ill-equipped to do so—I wondered how she believed she could keep this dark truth from me. How could she believe I would blindly follow her bright ideals, ignoring the existence of their darker shadows?

I sat there, chewing at the insides of my cheeks, remembering my Tío Adolfo sitting at this same table and denouncing terrorism on both sides, warning it would pitch us into civil war long before it did so. He had been right. Folding my shaking hands atop my napkin, I asked my mother to tell me what I could do to help our people without fomenting bloodshed, like Tío Adolfo.

I'll never forget how she looked at me, then, her eyes falcon-sharp, injured by my clueless criticism. She snapped at me to not be so naive. Once so much blood had fallen, the time for talk of peaceful protest was over. Those who had committed so many atrocities de-served everything that was to come.

My trembling worsened as I tucked myself into bed alone that night. If only we had all listened to people like Tío Adolfo before our country was locked into this cycle of hostility and brutality, I thought to myself. *If only it were that easy*, I heard my mother's voice reply, inside my head.

The Falcone girl's face was burned into my memory after that. I don't know what I might have done to help her—nothing, I suppose. I felt as powerless, then, as I had hearing about so many young left-wing victims. But I swore I would never forget that the world wasn't as black-and-white as my mother claimed—that within the shades of gray lived delicate truths important to Tío Adolfo's peace, if not my mother's brute strength. This was a knowledge I was desperate to protect and expand upon: Inside the gray was an answer, an answer needed in the future, but I would not find it unless I stayed alive to learn it. I have never felt so strong an instinct as that one.

And yet: I fear the gray now, delving into those dark nooks Yesi spoke of. I find myself burying the past, just as the De Vaccaros do, and desperate to uphold their incomprehensible rules, as if they will protect me in the future.

In my tiny bedroom, I fashion a pocket of air inside the blanket and breathe, fogging up the space. Hundreds of kilometers away, young people as courageous and principled as my mother fight and die every day, while I hide myself here, pondering the mysteries of an old house. Why has my classmate returned to haunt me here, in the form of a student? What could her resemblance mean?

It means the past will not remain hidden, no matter what you do.

Waiting in silence to feel tired, I hear a rhythmic creaking and dis-tract myself with thoughts of the girls' first assignments. A rumbling follows, as if a train passes underfoot. At night, the house breathes and groans audibly.

That same damned draft's ice-tipped tendrils weave in through the closet door and circle me as I squeeze my eyes as tightly shut as I can manage. At one point, when my toes are twitching back and forth to frantically combat the cold, I hear soft laughter from beyond my room.

"Yesi?" I call into the pass-through.

Hard at work defining the ghostly house noises, or so I imagine, she does not answer.

8

ANGEL: 2020-300

Once I'm fed, I cook up an elaborate plan: a way to explore Vaccaro School in full, while hiding in plain sight. It's a grand plan I'd like to say I conceived of ages ago but forgot to follow through on—one that requires the help of one of my personal Vaccaro School all-stars. A hateful, pasty prince among pasty men (not to be confused with *pastry* women, like sweet-smelling Mavi).

The whitewalker.

After the teachers head off to their second day of achingly tedious classes, I find him, alone and dazed. He's in his same royal-blue upstairs room, rolling a "special" big-boy cigarette—there are four butts in the ashtray already, but better there than in an unsuspecting teacher's hair. He's watching the ice melt through the window (spoiler: it's not).

"Do less, Domenico." He could be waterskiing on the lake. Enjoying a bottle of chilled chardonnay on the terrace. Seducing the paltry ranks of women and men in the house (you know what they say about men with necks the width of fire hoses)!

I grab him by the shoulders, as I did the other day, and mush him around. Can I squeeze myself into his arms? Into his head?

He jitters forward at my touch and picks up the manila file before him. His day job at the house? Doubtful. The folder reads: PRIVATE—CARMELA DE VACCARO.

"Okay, props," I say as he flips through the pages. I can't help but read over his shoulder: It lists staff details, collected for Carmela by a private detective by the name of Alack Sinner. To my deep and enduring sadness, the majority of the files are boring and predictable. But some salacious details do catch my eye.

Dr. Molina's page reads, *Lack of discretion. Evidence of severe obsessive-compulsive disorder.*

"Psycho," Domenico says.

"OCD is a serious mental illness," I snap back. "And have you even watched enough true-crime documentaries to know what psychopaths are?"

He flips on. Yesi's page reads, *IQ = 153.*

I cross my arms, waiting to see how he can insult a girl genius.

Below it reads: *Prone to delusions and lapses in memory.*

"Freak," he says.

I shake my head.

Mrs. Hawk's page reads, *Delicate constitution, migraines, and narcolepsy.*

"Peasant."

"You're not giving me a lot to work with," I reply.

Mr. Lamm's page reads, *Hypochondria. Possible evidence of inappropriate relationships with students in past teaching positions.* My jelly eyes squinch up, trying to make sense of it, based on what I've seen of the man.

"Pedo," Domenico says, his creativity at its peak. I throw my hands in the air and give up.

Then Mavi's page. Mavi's father left her family at a young age, and the government arrested her mother last year on suspicion of guerrilla activities and took her to a state facility for the worst enemies of the state. A hellhole described, chillingly, as one that *no one ever returns from alive.*

I swallow hard. Mavi's mother is as good as dead. And worse—her last place of residence is listed as *none*. Did Mavi outwit the detective? Or was she living on the street?

I've always had a soft spot for the underdogs. It's not so unlikely that Mavi and I would have been friends.

Tendency to form inappropriate and intense attachments.

"Guerrilla slut," Domenico says to himself.

I frown at him. "Seriously, Domenico, wash your mouth out with soap."

Toward the back, I recognize the face staring up at me as . . . *Domenico De Vaccaro. Evidence of severe depression and self-destructive behavior.* I let out a low whistle as Dom's fingers close around the page, crumpling the edge. I catch, in minuscule print: *Deeply manipulative narcissist. History of sadistic behaviors. Episodes of animal killing and sororal abuse.*

I shiver. He doesn't have anything to say about his page, unsurprisingly. He flicks on his lighter and holds it up to the sheet until a flame licks at the lettering. I don't know whether to feel sorry for him or hate him. I guess a bit of both.

He takes another hit from his joint. He lifts the photo of Mavi attached to her evaluation and strokes it. "We'll teach the little slut, won't we?"

Half of me gags—Who says that to himself? Out loud?—and half of me feels a judder of genuine fear. "No, we won't, asshole," I say, pushing his shoulder. I'm denser today, more crystal-concrete, thanks to Yesi, and my hands slow as they knead his flesh. But he doesn't answer. Doesn't even wince. Maybe he's too stoned.

He picks up a red pen, draws an *x* over her left eye. He repeats the process on her right one.

Deeply manipulative narcissist.

He draws cuts on her like some amateur graphic novelist, deep gashes dripping fake inky blood. He details every drop.

History of sadistic behaviors.

I remember the way he watched her from his window, like she was a fast-food meal he would devour and forget.

He colors over her arms, leaving stumps. He draws in hash marks of rot. An exposed bone.

Episodes of animal killing and sororal abuse.

I remember his dropping a lit cigarette on her.

I knew cruel cowards like him all my life. I dart fingers into his flesh to no avail, blazing with more and more rage that comes from a place I couldn't even identify inside myself.

People who take their strength, their power for granted. People without the emotional strength to be kind.

I take hold of Domenico's shoulders, and he shrugs to himself. But I am persistent. I hold on.

He cracks his neck with a series of disconcerting pops, as if re-adjusting himself internally. I continue to press on. My fingers press in through the spongy parts of his body—the skin, the muscle—like glutinous syrup through a fine mesh sieve.

I hear the first clicks, like teeny-tiny Legos attaching themselves to joints and bones, and my crystal material merges with every inch of Domenico's muscle; it's like pulling a coat around an unruly dog and strapping it up tight, tight, tighter, until the poor thing suffocates. It's uncomfortable for both of us—at least, I imagine it must be uncomfortable for him—in its snugness, but I feel his matter accommodate mine, filmy as it is.

He shudders, seizes. He murmurs, so animal and plaintive, but the sound dies in the back of his throat.

I blink open my eyes and look out onto the ice, ripple-edged and gray in the morning haze. I think—

I am him.

Dom.

Holy fuck.

9

MAVI: ARGENTINA, MARCH–MAY 1978

How to describe the passing of time at Vaccaro School . . . ? At first, I thought that time in a new place is a wild creature you can't quite get your hands on, much less tame. You can only aspire to trick your brain into feeling comfortable with time's quirks—into feeling it's contained, or better yet, the experience of it, shared.

But here, at Vaccaro School, time kicks the side of my head at random. I'm left out cold, wondering if I'm eight or eighteen or forty-eight; mothered, motherless, or mothering; dead, alive, or something in between. Then the feeling fades, and I go about counting seconds and minutes, logically, with only a growing dread in the base of my stomach. Waiting for the next kick.

Here are the only consistencies: Nights stretch on endlessly. They are cold and empty corridors to be walked alone. Nightmares rise through the floorboards, ooze through forgotten cracks in the walls: Usually I hear echoes of my mother's voice, fervently discussing government policy as a young, soft teacher with Tío Adolfo years ago or proselytizing young, soft students as a hardened professor. Or she herself appears, disappointment thick in her eyes, from a slick-walled well of a prison; or Michelle materializes, that unlikely double of my lost classmate. Ragged holes and sores spread through their flesh, as if my unconscious mind can't even be bothered to sculpt them in full, creating gruesome impressionistic mannequins instead. Tears dry on my cheeks as I wake (do I?) to the sound of the closet doorknob shaking. I don't know who's trying to get in, but I fear it, because I do know that seeing its face will change me beyond recognition. I cocoon myself in my coat and four (yes, four) new blankets, dumped in my room by a grim member of the cleaning staff. The air around my bed is always frigid: a pocket of misery in the damp confines of the house.

What's worse: I also feel watched. Sweat pours down my neck as I fail to shake the feeling that I'm not alone in the privacy of my bedroom. It's as if the invisible demon inside my closet can see me through the walls and enjoys watching me squirm as it rattles my door.

In a fit of rationality (or not . . .), I become convinced a child has been visiting my room and causing the disturbances; I hear girlish whispers at night from underneath my blanket and in between the webbing of my dreams; I smell the headiness of dairy—spoiled milk, as if the girl sips on a repulsive refreshment while she observes me. But which girl could it be? Who would do such a thing?

None of them, beastly as some seem. It can only be stress. Altitude. A panic attack. *Homesickness*, Yesi says in the light of day, because I haven't mentioned that I lacked the main prerequisite for that feeling—a home.

Days, blessedly—perhaps expectedly—are as short and sweet as nights are long. Once the evening gloom evaporates, I wake to Yesi humming in the bathroom, and we breakfast with her beloved bowl of blueberries. It reminds me of my old morning routine with my mother: eating medialunas together, flakes dotting the kitchen table. Her hands holding up the newspaper. The scratch of the pencil tip. Circling. Underlining. *¿Que pensas de esto, Mavi?* she would ask in the Argentine *voseo*, pointing to a bit of news and waiting for my every unformed opinion. Endlessly patient in helping me hammer it out. When I saw the special logic in her view, she smiled at me like the sun. I can hear the birds that gathered near our windows in the mornings when summer turns muggy, preening and cooing calmly. There are few animals here, and no newspapers at all—only the ice outside the window and the occasional work of fiction. But the ritual of it grounds me. It allows me to affix a smile on my face and pretend I am nothing more than a good teacher, oblivious to the world beyond this rock.

Breakfast is followed by a rush of class, and lunch with Yesi and Mole of ham-and-cheese sandwiches or simple salads and more chicken milanesas on the patio. And Mole—immune to Morency's suspicion—persuades her to let us enjoy a Yesi-style nightcap of chamomile tea (we're still afraid of breaking Carmela's no-drinking rule) after dinner so that I can slip off to bed sleepy and toasted warm. We take over one of the sitting rooms we've discovered, off the winding brocade maze, full of first-edition books. It's a treasure trove, to say the least, and we delight in flipping through them, in marveling at what may very well be precious leftovers from the previous incarnation of the school. Mr. Lamm joins us on a couple of occasions, with his secret snifter of brandy, regaling us with stupid jokes that have, to my chagrin, begun to make me laugh.

Lamb is a gem. During our second week, on what will end up being the final beautiful day of the fall, he finds us all at breakfast to invite us and the girls to a special outing for lunch, precleared with the powers that be. We ask what we can bring, but he tells us, with a mischievous grin, to bring only ourselves and meet him by the front steps of the admissions entrance. When Yesi and I arrive, we find the girls whispering around Lamb, who beams, extending his hand to us like a boy asking the most beautiful girl he's ever seen for a waltz. He escorts us down in the rickety funicular—my first time seeing the contraption that I should have taken the day I arrived, covered as it is in vines—and we see that he has already spread a checkered picnic blanket and propped open baskets filled with finger sandwiches of cucumber and smoked salmon and chive. The ice field looms before us, an earthly sky with constellations of fissures. We toast to the parallel lines with the iced mint tea in our glasses and while away the afternoon. Even the girls break out into grins, fall back onto their elbows, and chatter among themselves about lipsticks and half-remembered boys and the chameleonlike butterflies landing on our shoulders, their wings churlishly stealing the color from our shirts for themselves.

Lamb toasts us a third time in his excitement. "And none of this would be possible without Domenico," he adds.

"Sorry?" I say, choking on my tea. "You can't be serious." We haven't spoken since that unsettling moment in the family-quarters hall.

"Why of course I'm serious, my dear. Who do you think carried down the picnic baskets? These old bones? I thought he was fishing for an invitation."

Yesi looks at me. "It's a good thing you refused him one, Lamb."

Lamb nods, a far-off look in his eyes. "Oh well. I didn't think it would be appropriate with the girls around. He still smells of . . ." He stops himself, eyes widening at the girls, whose ears prick up. "He still carries on a friendship with Mary, err, Jane."

Mariella sneers. "You can say he was smoking dope. We're not idiots."

"We're old souls," adds Gisella.

The first time Domenico speaks to me alone, I flinch, expecting a cutting insult to come from his marble-sculpted lips. He finds me in a musty sitting room, alone, warming myself by the fire—the weather has already taken an even brisker turn—and reading while Yesi works, undisturbed, on her manuscript in our library. I call this sitting room *the deer room* because a large stag head stares down on those seated inside. Its only other defining feature is a hideous wooden armoire as tall as Morency, covered in colonial imitations of tribal carvings.

"Can I come in?" he asks, giving me a passing glance before scanning the bookshelves for God knows what. "I need to check the room for something."

He never struck me as the kind of person who cared whether he was intruding.

"You're looking for *something*," I say automatically, unable to shut my mouth for a single moment.

"Yes." He steps forward, and there's a jerkiness to his movements, like he's a dog shaking off invisible fleas. I attribute it to withdrawal from the unknown substance, and I wonder if he's concealed an old stash of smoking supplies here. I wait, watching him as he moves through the room, muscles rippling beneath his fine white linen shirt. My heartbeat could break my ribs, and I only pray it isn't audible to him.

Unsatisfied with his search, he turns and catches me staring. "Mind if I sit?"

It feels like a ruse. An abstruse one. But who am I to deny a master of the house? "Be my guest."

He sits—lowers himself—into the tufted chair beside me, and I

120

notice with surprise that his eyes look clear and full. "What do you think of Vaccaro School?"

I choke on air. Small talk? Well, he's certainly warmed to me since the first days of commenting on my diet. Since he did—or didn't—warn me against pursuing him in that hallway. I didn't know he was genetically capable of polite small talk.

"Are you serious?" Not that I am capable of it, either.

He chuckles, sapphire-blue eyes shining. Their warmth and vibrancy concern me. "I'm serious. Be honest."

Because now is such a prime opportunity for candor.

"Come on." He folds his arms across his chest and leans back. "The grittier the better."

"I like the girls," I say tentatively. "The students."

"Okay." His eyes drift, and it's a terrible drifting that some stupid adolescent piece of me wants to stop at all costs.

"But sometimes I struggle to comprehend the bigger picture."

And he blinks to attention. I tell myself it is harmless to address the history of the house. To address why it is back in existence. That it's not a dangerous excuse to keep him here, because just thinking those words *keep him here* makes me feel queasy and pathetic.

He leans into me, shoulders straining beneath his shirt. "The bigger picture?"

"Yes. Why your mother—why Madame De Vaccaro—is trying to bring this school back now."

He looks into the crackling fireplace, silent. I rub the chair's upholstered buttons beneath my fingers, dreading his reply. How brilliant of me to criticize his mother's actions. And to ask why *now*. When now is a time so soon after his own sister has died. When now is a time fraught with danger, even if we don't feel it on this isolated rock.

"Have you felt something dark here?" he asks. "Something sinister?"

A shiver chases wicked thoughts down my spine. I remember my many nightmares, my sinking dread every time I must tuck myself into bed for another night's unrest. Could someone like Domenico De Vaccaro have felt that same inexplicable fear? I think of what he said that night by his doorway, and I'm suddenly overcome by a powerful urge to stop him from falling back down into that melancholy pit. I'm afraid of what he might say—I'm afraid he might become the man he was before this strange and new conversation of ours.

"That's not what I meant," I say carefully. "It's just that it's so isolated, and the group of girls is so small. It can't make much economic sense. It's not to say I'm not impressed that your mother wants to preserve your family heritage."

He sighs, sits back in his chair. "Well, there's also sort of this Walden Pond component to it all. You know, isolating these special kids from the world at large, which is oversaturated, overwhelming, and bringing them somewhere quiet and peaceful to learn, plain and simple. There's something nice about that. Especially since these kids aren't really their parents' top priority. I don't know—it's a wholesome learning experience I wish I'd had. It wasn't this way where I grew up."

I widen my eyes at his sudden loquaciousness. "Paris?"

He looks away. "I guess what I mean is, when you have a fractured family as a kid, it's nice to pretend you could develop a second family at a school like this."

His sudden vulnerability sends a shiver of a different kind down my arms; it blooms into something hot in the pit of my stomach. "I'm sorry about your family," I say, unsure of how else to reply. I think of his lost sister, his lost father. "I lost my own mother recently."

"Yeah. Well. Losing a parent when you're young sort of feels like losing a leg and then learning to live with the limp," he says, shrugging. "You're never quite like the others, and they know it. You can

122

definitely be happy. But in a sense it's always there. The space where a leg should've been." A wry smile. "You get it."

I do. "I didn't take you to be such a philosopher king."

He chuckles. "I'm definitely not. I guess you brought it out of me." He glances at me quickly, then looks away again. "Everyone craves an experience at a place like this, removed from the world, where it almost seems as if no bad can happen, at least once in their lives," he adds. "No opportunity for loss. No distractions. I don't know. Maybe I'm wrong."

"Plenty of distractions," I say before he catches my eye and my mouth slides shut.

"What?"

Argh. I look at the stuffed deer head with untoward interest.

"It's nice to talk to someone," he says.

"I thought it wasn't allowed."

His brow furrows.

"Um, your mother? Madame De Vaccaro. She said it wasn't allowed. *Fraternizing*." I sound like an idiot. "Not that I care one way or the other," I add, tugging on my hair.

"Fraternizing sounds awful anyway," he says nonchalantly, coming to his feet and winking at me. "I'm sure we can come up with better things to do."

I bite back a smile.

I return to the deer room the next day, wondering if he'll be lured there by the same curiosity I feel. Sneaking through the corridors, I burst into the room. I find it empty. My shoulders sag as the deer head stares down at me judgmentally. I settle into the leather armchair Dom occupied last night, and that's when I notice freshly chopped wood piled beside the fireplace. Someone's been in since we were here.

The doorknob rattles, and the door creaks open. I see a foot encased in a pebbled leather navy loafer first.

Dom follows, fighting a grin when he sees me.

"I was about to lay a fire," he says as I blush rose red. "Join me?"

Like clockwork, he meets me in the deer room every day to talk about an unpredictable range of topics, with a genuine curiosity and teasing humor I warm to immediately, as well as an accent I can't quite place but decide is an upper-class quirk. This newly sober Domenico loves listening to songs I've never heard (he teaches me one called "Space Oddity"), eating exotic dishes I've never tasted (he promises to try to cook a chicken dish from India for me), and using technology I can't begin to comprehend (what is an "eye pod"? I dare not ask again). We move our chairs closer and closer as the days pass. One day, I lock the door behind us with a delicate *click*. Another, I kneel alongside him to light the fire, the sides of our bodies mere centimeters apart. *He smells like soap and fresh-cut grass*, I think, just as he says: "You smell like facturas."

My mouth twitches as I wonder whether it's a bizarre compliment or a veiled insult: It serves me right for smelling him. I should glimpse into his eyes to check, but I know looking into them will lead me to liking him a bit too much, so I refocus on the firewood. "I don't smell it. But I suppose thanks are in order," I say drily. "Fresh facturas are the number one Argentine comfort smell, aren't they?"

I can feel his cheeks rise in a smile—that's how close we are. "Is there a ranking for comfort smells?"

My heart flutters, a butterfly I wish I could forcibly pin down. "Why shouldn't there be? You're not a real person if you've never had one. My comfort smell is wet pavement."

He lights the match. "Hmm. I thought most people pick gasoline or ink if they go the inedible industrial-supplies route. Why wet pavement?"

I settle back onto my heels. "During the summer, my mother used to wake me up at six in the morning so we could walk the streets to get the first steaming batch of—well—facturas from the bakery. We used to pass all the *porteros* washing down the sidewalks, and there would be this smell wafting up from the wet pavement. I can't explain it. It's chemical and dirtlike and sweet with this secret layer of old garbage. That was my comfort smell." I grin as the fire catches. "Everything delicious has to be slightly corrupted to qualify as delicious."

We watch as the fire crackles to life, the edges of our fingers almost touching.

He turns toward me, fixing his blue eyes on me. "What do I smell like?"

"Fresh grass," I whisper before I can stop myself.

We meet eyes, and lightning strikes the top of my head, trickling warm down my shoulders, arms, hands, fingers.

But then he bursts out in a laugh, the heartfelt kind of laugh you'd want to hear every day of your whole life if you could, and he stands. "Because of the weed? Thanks."

"No!" My face pales, but I quickly recover and start laughing, too. Relief rushes over me like I've plunged into a refreshing lake during a hot summer: The tension is broken.

I settle back into my chair, tingling, and it's in that moment of silence that I hear footsteps outside. Dom and I lock eyes, mine wide. Have we been too loud? How could I expect this to continue with me unnoticed?

The doorknob rattles, and a dreaded voice calls, "Who has locked this door?"

The relief turns to icy panic: Morency. Dom silently points at the large armoire in the corner of the room, and we both rise to our feet.

"It's just me. Domenico," he shouts back.

"Open this door immediately."

He opens the armoire door with the slightest creak and helps me climb inside its cramped quarters. *Sorry*, he mouths, before shutting me in. He turns the key in the lock.

I huddle there, in the pitch-darkness, my heart slamming against my ribs, as he unlocks the door and Morency rushes inside. I could shrivel up and die as I silently inhale the ancient wood smell—coffin-like.

"Why have you locked this door? What kinds of iniquitous dealings have you brought into this house?"

Despite the terror coursing through my body hot as bubbling oil, I bite my lip to stop from grinning at the absurdity of her accusation.

"Iniquitous dealings?" he repeats. "I'm reading alone, Ms. Morency." I hear fingers tapping a book. "I just didn't want any meddling kids barging in here."

"I don't believe you." She stalks around the room, and I hold my breath, rivulets of sweat snaking down my neck. She sniffs the air, so close to the armoire. I pray to God I don't smell like facturas right now.

"Have you been . . . smoking cannabis in here?" she spits.

"No, Ms. Morency." I hear the soft crinkling of leather. "I swear."

"If you are lying to me," she says, "I will ensure your weekly shipments on the supply boat stop at once."

I take a slow breath in.

"I'm not lying, Ms. Morency," he says.

Silence. I fear my chest will burst, my blood pumps so hard.

"Master Domenico," she says, her voice closer to me than ever. "Your armoire is breathing."

I press myself farther back and shut my eyes, as if that will help me disappear, when I know that I will be discovered if she opens the armoire door.

"That's ridiculous—" Dom says as the doors of the armoire shake, locked, and my entire body clenches.

The shaking intensifies.

"You really shouldn't break that, you know," Dom says. "That's the only piece of furniture my ancestors brought from the old country. It's real Corinthian oak. My mother doesn't want it opened, and she'll be very upset if you damage the paneling."

The shaking stops.

I hear nothing, but I imagine Morency's lips setting in an angry line. Then a girl's voice shouts in another part of the house, audible even inside the confines of the armoire.

"I have my eye on you," Morency hisses before I hear the rustling of her skirts as she leaves to chastise another member of the house.

I exhale, rubbing at my eyes. A minute later, I hear the room door closing and Domenico fiddling with the key to the armoire. At first, the door won't budge, so I press my weight onto it to help push it open. At last, it bursts open, and I fall into him, collapsing against his warm chest. He holds me up, and I can feel his heart beating, almost as fast as mine. I don't want to move, until I remember myself.

"Real Corinthian oak?" I croak.

And he stifles a laugh, which I also instinctively muffle with my hands, until that same pleasurable shock rolls through me as my hands touch his lips. I flinch away, my blush penetrating even my toes, now, I'm sure of it.

"What?" he whispers, smiling.

Who are you, Domenico? Why are you good now? I want to ask. *Why do you act like an entirely new person?* But it is a mystery I shall have to investigate in secret.

By the next afternoon, we switch to a new sitting room, hidden in a remote corner of the house and untouched in years by anyone but us two.

As for the girls and myself: Their advanced intermediate English level means that they can almost appreciate Holden Caulfield—or suffice it to say that his exploits hardly even scandalize them. They are brilliant—unnervingly so. I understand Yesi's early description of *special*. In that monstrous cliché of young teachers, I'm ashamed to admit that I learn almost as much from them as they do me.

But it is not easy to feel a rapport with them. I cannot stop myself from thinking, class after class, that they are entitled brats—lucky little girls receiving a (purportedly) world-class education over the ice, with no idea of the expense nor the amount we all must cater to them. And to make matters worse, they lie—yes, lie—like their lives depend on it, weaving together the most inane stories to derail any and every lesson.

One morning, Silvina drapes her charm-bedecked wrists atop the table and tells the class she cannot focus because she went to sleep with her hair *loose* and woke up with a *fishtail braid*.

"I felt tiny hands on me," she says as the attention of the class falls on her blushing roommate. You'd think the gorgeous fishtail braid was the black plague from her tone. *Is your braid disrupting the flow of blood to your brain?* I want to ask.

Another day, a sullen Luciana, who has remained mute for days despite my gentle encouragement, informs the class that God is punishing her by leaving red finger marks on her forehead as she sleeps. I examine her forehead for any sign of irritation. "Could they not be pimples?" I ask her, at which point she grimaces and replies, with utter disdain, that "an impoverished backcountry orphan like you, Miss Quercia, cannot understand someone of different stock like me, but that is not your fault—God made us all different for a reason."

Well. I had to stop myself from laughing aloud. Whatever gave her the impression I was a poor orphan, I can't know (good on her, though), but that was enough to goad me into replying, "And God and skin-care products help those who help themselves, Luciana," in a tone that might have been altogether too cutting for the average weekday morning.

On another day, Morency bulrushes me outside and hands me an envelope. Just as I believe she's serving me with the terms of my resignation for God-knows-what-offense, she tells me, "To include in your evening reading." But, of course, I don't wait until the evening, and I tear the envelope open before lunch, neck prickling.

Ten files—nine full and one blank. The girls' files, describing their backgrounds, their family situations—packed full of salacious details. Why would Morency give these to me now? If it is because I asked about the tenth student at our first dinner, why would she furnish me with an empty tenth file?

I piece together their stories as best as I can. They are special, these girls, albeit not in the ways I believed. Some of the details are unreadable, appalling, disgusting, and I nearly allow my eyes to race past the worst. I'm not easily disturbed, but even so, I feel my heart slamming around my chest like a trapped and frantic bird as I slow down to absorb the lurid details.

Gisella: *Born to a serial philanderer of the Argentine intelligentsia and his third wife, who had an affair with his editor, resulting in a high-profile separation, her nervous breakdown, and her relocation to Switzerland. Gisella has not celebrated a birthday or holiday with her family since she was five years old, and after the arrest of her father, she will not ever again.*

Diana: *The daughter of a general who recently faced scandal for embezzlement and the public abuse of his wife, a former actress with bipolar disorder. The mother took to the streets with Diana, living in a roach-infested hostel for several weeks, before being found and committed. Diana weighed a skeletal twenty-two kilos when found, versus the average forty. Her mother has not been seen since, and her father placed her in our care before possibly fleeing to Uruguay.*

It is too grotesque to fathom.

Silvina: *Her prominent German-Argentine family housed escaping Nazis in the forties before discovering the matriarch was from half-Jewish stock. She starved herself to death, dying from heart failure in their family home in Recoleta when Silvina was six. More recently, her father, an infamous lawyer, has been accused by the military government of pursuing the release of criminals of the state.*

Michelle: *After the disappearance of her parents, two members of the wealthy bohemian socialist set, Michelle was orphaned and began living with her aunt, who eagerly awaits each child-support check but provides little care for her. A lawyer noticed Michelle was living in a poorly ventilated and unheated attic and arranged for her to be sent to the school.*

Mariella, she of the yacht in Sardinia: *Subjected to systematic physical abuse by her stepfather and shuttled from school to school by her mother as a form of escape. Her mother refuses to acknowledge the abuse outright and leave her husband, an arms dealer with ties to the current military government.*

They are all special girls. Special in that they have been damaged by the same world that seemed to grant them tremendous luck at birth. They were all sent here, to the boondocks across the ice, to hide. To hide and be safe, like me.

It makes me pity the girls, and to my dismay, the pity begins to caramelize into something like bittersweet affection.

Luciana: *Beloved and outspoken author mother sick with ovarian cancer—her estranged military-supporting father and much-older brothers sent Luciana off, unwilling to keep her around while the mother (primary caretaker) goes through treatment abroad.*

I remember how Luciana's skin has looked splotchy, her shoulders drooped; a weight grows inside me. An all-too-familiar weight—guilt. I overlooked the girls trying to make Luciana laugh in class—never considered she might soon be motherless, too. It is a strange type of solitude, when your family anchor rusts and breaks apart, setting you adrift.

I'm heading over to lunch after collecting my papers the next day when I find the group of girls huddled by the front door of the main building, where I fell asleep before my warm welcome. I hear soft crying and cooing and hurry toward them to see what's happened. They're all present but Sara, who is ill with some form of cold.

"What's wrong?" I ask. I know it is the mother's illness I read about; I can see from the corner of my eye that Luciana is crying with Isabella's head on her shoulder. Michelle wipes at Luciana's cheeks.

"It's nothing, Miss," says Mariella, crossing her arms in front of her chest with a flare of the eyes. Her feistiness, the result of fending off an evil stepfather.

Michelle whispers to Luciana. There is wordless conferring among the group—exchanged glances, indistinct shrugs.

"It's that Luciana's mother is sick," Michelle says, tugging at the corners of her Peter Pan collar. "They're very close." The girls watch me from the corners of their eyes, lowering their heads. Jaws hard. Picking at cuticles.

"May I speak with Luciana?" I ask, parting the group. Mariella raises a brow. The others settle back. Luciana regards me with tear-filled eyes.

"I'm so sorry this happened," I say, sitting next to her on the steps. Mariella snorts, brushing a ball of lint from her skirt hem.

"*Really?* You're not going to tell me it's all going to be fine?" Luciana asks, choking back tears. "You're not going to tell me to keep my chin up? You're not going to tell me that this happens to everyone eventually?"

I hesitate. Because ever since I lost my mother, I have never wanted to hear that life would get better, even though I know it likely will. I never wanted to hear that I should have faith or use the power of prayer to help myself and not wallow in self-pity. I wanted some-one to echo what I was feeling—or, at the very least, to truly *hear* it—so that I would feel less isolated in my devastation.

So I shake my head. "No. I won't." I hold her eyes, unflinching, until she buries her head in my shoulder. I choke down the shock and rush of sympathy.

"We're here. Understand?" I wrap my arms around her. We speak for some time, in a group. I don't have a solution, a quick fix—I couldn't. I've never even been able to grieve my mother properly, because some part of me maintains hope she survives. But for once, I feel like time's effect can be predicted.

Mariella sidles up to me as we stroll to lunch. "You did good for once," she says, nudging me in the side before hurrying on to catch up with Gisella.

I walk on with Luciana, who holds my hand tight and whispers, "I'm sorry I called you an impoverished backcountry orphan, Miss Quercia," before blushing and looking ahead at the other girls. I squeeze her hand and smile. If it weren't for her earnestness, I might have burst out in a laugh.

But not every day runs as smoothly. One day at dusk, I go down to my cottage to find a misplaced assignment, and I hear a series of bone-crunching thuds in the alleyway behind the structure, as if thugs are pummeling someone. I run out to find Michelle, her doll body limp in a corner behind a trash bin, her mouth and knees bloodied, as if she fell from a great height. I lift her up into my arms—either she's featherlight or I'm stronger than I think—and run her to Mole.

In the makeshift nurse's office, Mole uses smelling salts to bring her back and checks her eyes for a concussion.

"You were lucky Miss Quercia found you, Michelle," Mole says.

She looks at me and readjusts her glasses on her bridge. "She might have been out there unconscious for hours."

As Mole bandages up Michelle's superficial wounds, we ask Michelle why she was running around before dinner.

"I wanted to ask Miss Quercia a question," she says. "And something pushed me, and—"

Mole stops her. "Pushed you? Who pushed you, dear?"

"I don't know," she replies, face turning crimson. "I didn't see anyone."

I feel like Michelle is lying—lying to protect someone or to protect herself from scorn. But Mole clucks with her tongue, scrambling my thoughts. "Well, get some rest."

I sidle up to Michelle when Mole turns her back to rummage through a dusty cabinet for a painkiller. "Are you sleeping well?" I ask her. My nights at Vaccaro School are a singular misery no other adult in the house claims to share.

"No," she says. "But I never have. I have strange dreams about my parents sometimes." They've died, the two of them—I know that from the file. She studies me with her cherubically round face and her familiar eyes, ringed in deep blue. She lifts her chin to the side, inspecting me further.

"What is it?" I ask, skimming my cheek, as if there are crumbs there. I feel a shiver pass through me. I'm meant to care about this girl; why else would God have made her look this way?

"You saved her life," Mole says as Michelle shuts her eyes. "You're a regular guardian angel."

If only she knew why Michelle's face perturbs me so. "Oh, please."

We leave her to rest in the cot, and Mole accompanies me to the door.

"Her aunt's a vile woman, I've heard," she mutters, confirming what I read. "Were it not for the inheritance in a sealed trust, she would've been dumped somewhere already."

"Don't say that." I glance back at Michelle, whose chest rises and falls beneath the graying lilac blanket.

Mole rests a swan-white wrinkled hand on my forearm. "You mustn't get too attached," she whispers. "They're so different from us."

I don't think to ask her what she means—though I gather she's referring to our class difference. My first reaction is nothing but simmering frustration. I've begun to feel entitled to care for these little girls. Heaven knows how it happened, but I feel it is my duty to protect them, perhaps Michelle most of all.

I invite Michelle to share tea with me and Yesi that evening after dinner, as Mole decides to read magazines in her room alone. We figure we can still get away with it—Morency assuming Mole is involved. We all dress in our pajamas—mine a blue pair liberated from Yesi, which belonged to her grandmother, two sizes larger than her own—and drop into the plush chairs by the sitting room fire. Yesi reads me and Michelle excerpts from a travelogue in exaggerated voices until tears stream down our faces.

The door to the sitting room creaks open around nine. The cold returns—a chilly draft that sinks into exposed strips of our skin.

Yesi looks at me. "Close the door, would you, Swamp?"

I press the door closed, only to be pushed back into the room by it. I see skirts, flaring black, before—

"Where is Dr. Molina?" asks Morency, a tower of black, as she crosses her arms.

Yesi stands to attention on instinct, while Michelle falls back into her chair, as if to melt into the soft leather.

"This is wholly inappropriate." In two strides, Morency reaches Michelle. "You have abused your privileges. You should be ashamed, keeping a student out this late, what with girls getting lost at night. Must I truly patrol the house, ensuring everyone is safely in bed?"

My eyes flick upward to catch a shadow of concern pass over Morency's face. "Girls have been getting lost?" I think of Michelle falling behind the garbage.

She frowns and plucks Michelle's hand from her side, ripping her from her seat. "And *in pajamas*. To bed. All of you. Now." She jerks Michelle toward the door. "Michelle. Now."

Michelle's knees wobble. "Can't Mavi and Yesi escort me to bed?"

"How dare you refer to them with such informality." Morency's free hand curls into a fist. "They are your teachers, and you are their student. Never forget this."

She tugs on Michelle, who looks back at us with watering eyes before vanishing into the dark hall. Yesi and I silently replace the books on the shelves and wipe down the rings of tea made by the mugs on the wooden side table. How can Morency behave with such harshness toward us for trying to bond? Wasn't that the intention of her giving me an envelope of the girls' secrets—to better connect me with them? We hurry toward the staff hall, and Yesi links her arm through mine.

"I hate her," she says aloud.

I understand: I, too, feel like a pest to be swept away by the broom of Morency's skirts.

"She treats us like children."

"Worse." I squeeze her arm. "But it can't be easy single-handedly protecting us from the evil of the house, and all that."

Yesi laughs, her blue eyes flat as coins.

"I wonder who was lost," I add. "What could that even mean?"

"It means some of the girls have gone hunting for the dark prince again in a desperate effort for entertainment. Don't you remember being that age? Wandering around, baiting dangerously complex older boys, hoping they'll even look your way?"

I blow the air from my mouth. "Not really."

She bursts out with another laugh, this one authentic. "Me neither, Swamp."

Smiling, I look ahead. Were it not for Morency, it would have been a perfect evening, the kind to make you believe in the potential for sweet dreams. We weave our way to the staff hallway as I think about what I'll choose from the breakfast buffet tomorrow. *The scrambled eggs have been a touch overcooked lately*, and the absurdity of the thought makes me laugh. The crepes continue to hold their own.

Yesi grips my arm. "Who is that?"

I look down the hall and see only darkness. "Who?"

"Lamb?" She tightens her hold.

But I've noticed now: It is a man's figure. He stands a head taller than me, his slow approach menacing.

"He doesn't look familiar," I whisper to her. His gait is both hesitant and malignant in its disjointed looseness.

"Oh, hush," she whispers back, tugging me closer still. "Must be kitchen staff."

I can't make out a single feature. The hallway narrows, and I graze a miniature chair, tripping to the ground and pulling Yesi with me. The shadow rushes forward.

"Fuck," it says, hoarse. Breathless.

I take the outstretched hand: Dom. His hand singes mine where they meet.

"Jesus, Domenico, you scared Mavi," says Yesi, brushing herself off. I shoot her a look. "And curse a little more loudly, I think Buenos Aires didn't hear you."

"I scared you?" There's no sarcasm in his voice, only surprise tinged with concern. As if I'm some kind of superwoman. Yet he's still holding my hand. Cautiously, carefully, not so much as something wounded, but as something that might disappear. His hands are warm to the touch, too warm. They send a strange and invigorating charge through me—I cannot help but think, over and over, how different he feels now from the first time we touched, at the very first breakfast. His fingers were made of ice then.

He stares at me, and I feel naked. He lets go of my hand to right the chair, glancing at me with a suppressed cheekiness as if to say, *The chair is the only victim of a fright here*. "Are you hurt?"

"No. Of course not. But what are you doing so far from your room?" I say before I realize it sounds like I'm nagging an owner of the house. "Not that it matters," I add, fussing with my hair.

"I've noticed something," he says, fighting a grin. "Every time you tug on your hair, you're lying."

My hand freezes. I can feel two sets of blue eyes on me: amused in different capacities.

"But to answer your question, I'm only exploring," he tells me.

"That's just lovely," says Yesi, pulling me forward with her. "Speaking of exploration, we're off to our beds like two good little teachers, to explore the riveting world of the subconscious. Right, Swamp? Right."

"Sleep well, Swamp Thing," replies Domenico, walking away from us.

"You are so incomprehensibly screwed," whispers Yesi, ferrying me onward. I turn back to see one of his hands raised in farewell.

This house, with its shrinking rooms and meandering halls, with its wild fog—none of it feels quite real most of the time. It's as if the house constructs an elaborate fairy tale for each of us—a gothic mystery for Yesi, a bildungsroman for the girls, a strange sort of romance for me . . . warping our perceptions to better suit its private fantasies.

I'm ashamed to admit it, but only during my time with Dom do I feel clearheaded. Awake. We have a rhythm, now, in the house, and only he rips me from its lulling embrace.

What will come of it?

I'm suddenly conscious of the winding, circuitous path my blood takes through my veins and arteries. I look down at my hands, and my nails are still bitten down to the nubs, plus a touch swollen and dirty around the beds—the humanity of that reassures me. If they looked perfectly clean and polished, too, I might think I'm in the throes of a hallucinogenic drug.

IO

ANGEL: 2020-1000

Sometimes inside him I shake like I've been dipped naked in icy waters.

Not because I'm scared of what I've done, nor because I fear losing control of this Greek god of a flesh machine.

It's because I'm so *powerful*, and strength is a singular type of beauty I always felt too removed from to understand.

I feel the energy coursing through his veins, blood powering ropy muscles I never once acknowledged in the old world. I couldn't even tell you if my old body was *ever* in possession of these muscles, this cartilage, these ligaments—there's a length to this body that's impossible to render familiar but instinctively embraced, if that even makes sense. I've absorbed an extension of myself, effortlessly. Like a concert pianist nailing a ridiculous chord during one practice, as if by magic. I've broadened my handspan on the cosmic keys, my footprint on the sand of the new world, in more ways than I can understand.

I can do more than see as he sees. I can smell as he smells—skunkiness, musk—and taste as he tastes. His heart beats faster, and it's my heart, beating for me.

I explore myself.

The stretches of flesh I thought would scandalize me like a little kid finding a dad's *Playboy* . . . don't. It could be the nerve endings, tingling and bright, all for me. I take hold of a forearm, an ankle, anything handle-like, and it blushes red or chills blue-white under fingertips of pressure. *Mine.*

Everyone should have the privilege to experience this before they die. Or after, as it happens.

When I try to speak at first, even to clap my hands, I feel a bit slow—I'm the accident survivor, coaxing every inch into understanding the PT specialist's instructions. I'm the baby dumped in the pool for the first time, flailing and agape. The actions follow the commands in inconsistent waves.

But pretty soon, I come to my feet easily enough, a crescendo of muscular dominoes.

I explore the house.

I need to see every corner of the house now, in my new body; I need to talk to everyone, in my new body; it's like Christmas Day for good Christian kids, and yes, I'm not oblivious to the legitimately absurd creepiness of treating a body like a gift from merry old Santa Claus.

I imbue Dom with my intentions—take this hall, wrench open this door. I'm not sure if that's how it works, if mindfulness plays a part in this. At first, I wander the halls, jerking around like an idiot playing a zombie in a haunted house. I find a cabinet full of sliced bread and eat a slice mindlessly, mouth barely closing around the doughy hunk—jaws misaligning so that I worry I'm going to bite my tongue off.

I stumble past Dr. Molina, who blushes and hurries along the burgundy hall, even though I don't acknowledge her. I ogle my hands and remember for the thousandth time that I'm reincarnated as a six-foot-tall husky crossbred with a Milanese male model. I wonder how much he takes advantage of his effect on others. I don't have access to his interior thoughts, I don't think. I would be afraid to access them, if I'm being blunt. What if I came across terror, resistance, fear? What if I came across leftover sadism, and it flooded my synapses with something explosively bright and sweet I've never known?

I learn after trying to inhabit Dom sober that it's easier to enter someone who's under the influence of drugs or alcohol (oh, how infinitely pleased every sex ed teacher I've ever had would be to hear a dead seventeen-year-old confirm this). Happily, Dom goes to *town* on his stash every morning. Pros and cons: My silky-soft hair reeks of weed, but in general, my body relaxes, chill as can be.

Sometimes it's too loosened up. One day, heading down a short flight of stairs near the student hall, I bump an unattractive painting of a ship off the wall with my shoulder—the brief burn of pain comes. You'd think that since I'm not the permanent owner of this body, it'd be like dinging a car rental I'm not on the hook for. But it's not—I feel a lightning bolt of entitlement, closely followed by a *thundering* fear of my own fragility. As for the heinous, vomit-worthy masterpiece, I consider whether to rehang it or dash off when Carmela—*yes, the brood mare mama to Dom's baby colt, Carmela*—approaches me from down the stairs, clacking up the flight in her skin-colored heels, as I'm still clutching the frame guiltily.

I shape my mouth into a smile and try to formulate, in my head, a gracious but short remark obsequious enough to appease a tiger mom, when—

"What are you doing, you degenerate?" she hisses. Her eyes narrow to hatefulness; her tone cuts like I'm an underperforming peon at her cement company. "Make yourself useful and pray for your sister in your room. We shall have a serious problem if I find you in the girls' corridor again."

In the girls' corridor again? What the hell was Dom doing there before? Remembering the mentions in his file, I want to retch.

The body—okay, me, but the body when it fails—drops the painting on the stairs with a thud and simultaneously misses a step with my foot, drop-kicking the frame in some incredible gymnastic display.

It gives the distinct impression that I've blown off Carmela's request (demand?) and attempted to boot a hole in her precious artwork.

And I'm still strutting forward. Mic drop.

"Damn you, Domenico," she says to my back. "Don't you dare cross my path again when you're in one of these moods."

Ha! Muahaha! And I can't help but smile (internally) at the fact that she didn't notice the *change*, even though (or because) I behaved like an actual nutcase. I still vehemently believe that any change in mental state should be visible through the eyes, or through the posture, just as evil thirteen-year-olds can select, from a crowd, the most vulnerable of their peers through the widened eyes and hunched shoulders—that cry for invisibility. My eyes must read as glazed as ever for Carmela not to notice a difference in her precious son. Either that or Carmela's outright ignoring the unsettling changes in her house. And my possession of Dom is only the tip of the iceberg.

I leave Dom each day in pain, feeling weaker than ever—unbelievably sore, but lacking the ability to build muscle, really an athlete's hell. So each night, to sustain myself, I feed from Yesi right before the sun's meant to come up, which feels like the most banal evil routine now. As I flit away from her room, I try to ignore the extremely physical red flags that crop up as the ice grows. With the passing of time, the house is becoming a hive of weird, hostile energy.

Before, I would only hear the tail end of a sneer here, catch a glimpse of the shadow of a bear-man there. But now groans and bitter laughter reverberate through the house as soon as the sun sets.

On a sick, self-punishing impulse, I edge past the girls' rooms after I leave Yesi. I've never been at night.

I'm in their hall when I feel a moistness in my fingertips.

I hear stifled gasps.

Slurping.

I squeeze through a gap by a door, and that's when I see them. Feel them, mostly.

The frizzing shadows from my nightmares; those constellations of sooty jizz.

The Others swarm the girls' rooms. Too many to fit. Feeding in slobbering packs. Too many to stop, too many to discourage.

I can't bring myself to look at the girls. Easy prey.

I've mostly ignored the girls during the day because they just giggle and flee when they cross my path. So it was easy to brush aside the bags under their eyes ripening to the color of a fresh bruise, their reactions slowing. The weird one—Sara—must be affected most of all. The one who has a cold.

It makes sense that the girls would be targeted this way: The more vulnerable the subject, the easier she is to feed from. As if it's any consolation, the Others don't notice me in the middle of their slippery debauchery. But I can't help but wonder what else they're doing that I've been oblivious to while in Dom. Are they also possessing people in the house, as I am? Would I even notice a change in anyone's behavior?

∞ ∞ ∞

In the daytime, in total disregard of Carmela's warning, I snoop around the unlocked rooms in the family's quarters, the cottages, and the common areas in Dom. (Man hands! Convenient for opening jars, drawers, and so much more!) I eavesdrop in Dom. I also train daily to acquire new skills to unlock house secrets: I painstakingly practice picking locks, and I read in Dom. I never read much at all before, but you'd think I'm a regular bookworm because I devour every dusty, forgotten book in the house, landing on some compelling info about the Zapuche tribe, but mostly getting lost in footnotes more times daily than there are washboard rungs on Dom's dumb abs.

Per a book published in 1908 by an especially sensitive and passionate tribal historian, I learn that a Zapuche shaman did curse this spot in roughly 1708. She did it in hopes of protecting the tribal territory from pre–De Vaccaro European colonizers—by shredding the cosmic wall between the living and the dead with this curse, she thought she could enlist the aid of Zapuche spirits in their ongoing territorial fight. Surely the fiercest Zapuche warriors throughout time would not let their holy land be lost.

Unfortunately, the tribal historian and the interviewed Zapuche elders agreed this curse backfired, to put it lightly. Hostile spirits of all kinds and from all ages flooded the land, from the moment that the curse was laid through the unforeseeable future.

All just as Charon said.

But then . . . there's more.

A sacrifice of a young girl—once per generation—was the only identified method of protecting the tribe (and every other inhabitant) from the unholy *Otros*, or Others. Each sacrificed girl would safeguard that generation until the next. This sacrificial ritual was continued until so few Zapuche remained in the area that those still here . . . stopped. The tribal historian claimed that according to the elders, Zapuche numbers in the region fell to near nothing by the second half of the 1800s, when Domenica De Vaccaro instituted her school.

It's the one fascinating tidbit I extract, and it sends adrenaline-laced shivers through me. Not just because learning about it provides a brutal context for my existence here, but because it aligns with those Zapuche bedtime stories Mama told me as a child—stories I thought sprung from her imagination alone.

Every story began the same way.

Have you heard the Zapuche legend of the girls? I hear Mama say, in layers of memories from years ago. I would shake my head every time, even though I'd heard the legend at least a hundred different nights. These were carefully woven stories from her own childhood, set in the Argentina she rarely revealed, and every glimpse was precious. *In every generation,* she would say, *a young girl was sacrificed to the Zapuche gods, in a great ceremony on a cliff beside the ice, to ensure the safety and peace of the tribe. She knew being sacrificed was a weighty honor, one she could only hope to live up to someday. Because, Angel, when the girl was sacrificed, she did not die—no, she lived on in a new form, removed from the tribe but gaining great powers. Becoming like a god herself. She could move clouds and ice. She could connect lost relatives. And most important, Angel, she could tell you the color of your soul. What follows is one of her adventures in Patagonia . . .* And that's how every story would start. They were bedtime stories rooted in truth, that truth being their common preface, pulled straight from legend.

The girl possessed unfaltering, luminous kindness. She was ancient yet aware of every generation's travails. She faced unimaginable loss and became only stronger—all of this after being thrown from these very cliffs.

Could she actually exist?

Maybe I'm here to find her.

∞ ∞ ∞

One day, while I'm cruising the house for more books describing these girls, I barge into a sitting room with a deer head, finding Mavi by a fire. I rattle off a sad excuse for hello and hesitate as I scan the room, wondering if I should engage with her. And if I do, should I impersonate Dom? I'm so tempted to slip into that clichéd detached-asshole personality and see if it just clicks into place when I'm in this body. I prepare the words in my head: words that will cut and titillate in one stroke. I heard enough of them back in the day to know what could work, but I never felt the kind of unwavering, testosterone-fueled hubris you need to speak them.

I sit, ready to go, when I notice the way her eyes catch on mine and stick, before moving slow as caramel over the rest of me. She bites her lip. *So this is what it's like*, I think, feeling that burst of self-confidence that's sharp and bright enough to distract me from its artificiality.

She returns the next day, and the one after that, so I must do something right. But I have an IQ higher than a grapefruit on my good days, so I obviously wonder: *Is she returning to the deer room because I'm a sparkling conversationalist or because of Dom's scorching hotness (exhibit infinity: his twenty-four-pack, loosely skimming all his artfully cut shirts)?* Does it matter? It's hard to say. But I crave every afternoon with her: It's addictive, being seen and heard this way. Like she's fortunate to breathe the same air as I. It's a drug so intoxicating that sometimes I lose track of who I'm meant to be.

It's after a couple of weeks together and a near-capture by Morency that Mavi and I make plans to meet after dark.

"It's a full moon tonight," I mention offhand. "The view of the stars above the cascading ice will be mind-blowing."

"I suppose it's not in the cards for me to witness that." She hesitates. "My room doesn't have much of a view."

And then I remember. Of course: Her room, room 7, is windowless.

"We could meet later," I offer, heat creeping into Dom's cheeks. "In the dining room." Neutral territory, in between us both.

She raises a brow. "Are we not acquainted with the same Ms. Morency? There won't be an armoire for me to hide in in every room we visit."

And I know it's not fair of me, but I want more than this existence of sneaking around to dead, enclosed sitting room after sitting room with her. Of craving an accidental touch.

"We can come up with a cover story if we're caught," I offer. "You can blame me."

"Oh, I'll definitely blame you," she replies, but with a quick nod of the head and flash of the eyes, she agrees.

I head down to the dining room early, watching the stars twinkle through the glass of the French doors. Never in my life did I see a sky like this: precious gems on unrolled velvet.

I hear footsteps behind me, and then the whisper, *Dom*.

She's there, behind me, grinning like a fool, cheeks flushed and brown eyes bright in the dark. She's so close I could bridge the gap between us in less than a second. I can feel her breath.

I take her hand and pull her out onto the patio, where it's bracingly cold, but the entire sky spreads before us, the dreamy indigo blue of the galaxy in old movies. And the ice, it glows as if lit from within.

"It's magic," she whispers. She shivers next to me, and I can't tell if it's from cold or awe.

I search for the constellations I know, but I can't find them. Maybe it's a Southern Hemisphere thing. Still, there are explosively bright stars shimmering everywhere, enough to create our own.

"Do you see the giant sleepy eyes?" she whispers, pointing just above the ice. "And the lit candle? And there, next to it, the house with the smokestack."

I nod, even though I can't keep up. "I see a rose," I say, tracing it with my finger.

"Where?" she asks, leaning closer. She's shivering harder, now, her teeth chattering.

"Here," I say, moving to take off my jacket and give it to her. I drape it over her shoulders, and my fingers graze her collarbones. She trembles and sets her hands over mine as if to adjust the jacket, but really keeping my hands there. I can feel her heartbeat through the place where our skin touches. I realize I'm holding my breath, and I pull her a half inch closer, settling my arms around her, her back to me as we stare up at the sky.

"I see it," she whispers. "The rose."

We're silent for a long time as she melts deeper into me, and for the first time, with my bear arms around her, I feel as if I'm helping someone feel safe and secure—as if I'm capable of protecting her from all harm. I've never managed to feel that before. Even when I comforted Rob or Mama, I never felt confident I could protect them forever. After all, how can anyone feel confident about something that falls to chance more than effort or will? But something about this moment with Mavi—the hormones, my muscles, that addiction she feeds in me, whatever—gives me the mistaken impression that I could. And I never want to move.

"Do you think they're watching us?" she whispers.

"Who?"

She tucks her hair behind her ears. "The family we've lost."

I rub my hands together. My mouth becomes dry all of a sudden. This has taken a turn. "What made you think of that?"

She shrugs. "It's so vast out here. I can't believe souls just . . . vanish once the bodies are gone."

I swallow hard and hope she doesn't feel the uptick in my pulse. "So . . . where do you think the dead go? I mean their souls." It spills out against my will, hot as bile.

She inhales deep, scans the sky with her eyes. "I should probably say I think they become angels, watching us from their clouds in heaven. But that sounds . . . too easy."

I shiver, hearing my name from her mouth. "I read about Hindu reincarnation once. The soul is eternal, and it returns to a new physical body after each body's death. In every cycle it learns something new."

"I like the sound of that. I think I'll change my answer."

We're silent for a while. "So you don't believe in ghosts, then?" It comes out as a whisper. She as good as told me she didn't believe in them in our very first conversation, so long ago now, but since then, she's mentioned the "inexorable feeling of being watched" at night, which almost made my eyes bug out of my skull.

"No. I don't believe in ghosts."

I swallow the knot of heat in my throat. "Wouldn't you want to see your mother again?" All she's said about her mother, the professor, is that she's dead. Not disappeared—just dead.

She stiffens, and I worry I've upset her. "Whether I would want to see her has no bearing on the existence of ghosts. I don't believe her consciousness could make an appearance here expressly for me. That's all." She clears her throat. "A ghost—a ghost would not be the person we love." And the reality of the situation dunks me in cold water again: I'm seeking connection in a place where it's impossible.

We're silent for a long while, and she slowly relaxes again in my arms. "We're both here right now. I think—I think that's what matters, Dom."

And I stop to consider that maybe, just maybe, she's right.

It's minutes before morning when I leave Dom to sleep—I've overstayed, and I'm sure he'll sleep like the dead for the whole day, because possession wipes him out as much as it wipes me out. I miss him immediately. My second-rate crystal tissue feels flimsy, dispersible by a few gusts of wind.

I'm slipping into a new self. A self that finds expression only through Dom's form. Old human habits die hard: Sometimes I *need* his body now because it empowers me in a way my shapelessness in the Other Place never does.

I fall up through a skylight and watch the ice, which expands greedily as the cold worsens. Before, I could have watched for hours, but a new claustrophobia poisons the beauty of the view for me now. I hate the ice and the inert yet smug inevitability of its growth, which seems at odds with everything I know about the natural world. This world is changing for the worse, day by day, when I want it to stay inert.

As I flit back into the house and toward room 7, Others gush from the other girls' rooms, spilling into the halls in their bacchanal. Their feasting is blind in its intensity—vapors shudder past like greedy alcoholic younger brothers hovering around a wedding's open bar. They are too busy to notice me. I elbow my way past, and no one gives the slightest resistance.

I squeeze inside Silvina's room and find a gruesome scene: Others dripping from the headboards, tentacles made of shadow and light draped across the prone, shrimpy lumps in the beds. Silent, slippery torture. I hear either the suction of the feeding or the whimper of a girl or my own imagination turned perverted composer, and I can't look or listen anymore without heaving.

I've never seen so many Others in one place—have never had the courage to mull around them, I should say. But I force myself to look and listen. To be aware. To stop imagining. It's only then that I notice: There are no bodies in the beds at all. The shrimpy lumps are made of sheets.

Silvina, Christina, Diana, Mariella, and Luciana are sitting on the floor behind Silvina's bed, clapping their hands together. They're playing a twisted version of patty-cake, or something slap-centric like that. Silvina's cheeks look chapped and red.

Mariella stands, cross-eyed, and does a rickety cartwheel, her black hair flapping into her mouth. She gives a strange, desperate peal of a laugh and stands on her hands, then her fingertips themselves, teetering with an athleticism I haven't seen outside of Olympic gymnastics.

Christina gnashes and sucks at chocolate-covered fingers as if they are cobs of corn.

Diana brushes at her hair as if pulling weeds from roots and flings the clumps of unruly strands across the carpet like confetti. Her face is peaceful. Her face is dead, even though her limbs vibrate with tense energy.

And Luciana. Luciana crawls on her hands and knees with agonizing slowness toward the window overlooking the ice, raking the carpet with her fingernails, eyes rolled back into her head. Half-moon fragments of her nails wedge into the rug along her path—as if she's so desperate to move forward and to hold herself back at the same time.

These are not normal girls.

These are Others acting out, no longer content with feeding and haunting alone.

Is this who I am, too? A fool playing in a meat shell, shunting off another soul?

I float away, meandering past the other teachers' rooms. Only to find more Others still.

Most of the teachers sleep on as the creatures explore the threads of their subconscious, testing each for valuable energy. But there's one anomaly: The hawk-nosed teacher lies in bed, eyes wide open and unblinking, mouth open in terror as an Other picks its way through her skull like an old white guy picking through a quail carcass with his teeny-tiny mother-of-pearl-handle silverware.

She is aware of what's happening. Like an unanesthetized patient. Paralyzed. Conscious throughout a surgery. I try to push him off, and I'm met with powerful resistance. *You won't be joining this country club.* When I feel other threads clinging to me, probing for energy, I push away.

I heave onto the ground, expelling nothing for the thousandth time. I tell myself she cannot feel a thing, even with her eyes open. Some people sleep like that. Narcoleptics. But I know it's not true.

Charon's been lying to me with his claims that feeding doesn't hurt. *I've* been lying to me. Weaving together lies as tight as my crystal strings are now bound around Dom's flesh.

What's more frightening still is that outside of Dom, on nights like this, I question what I am. My senses and sense of self fail me, pitching me into complete darkness. I can't wait to be back inside of him again tomorrow, my crystals wrapping him like tangled nanoscale Christmas lights that only I can see and celebrate. The world around us dark and encircled by broken teeth of ice.

11

MAVI: ARGENTINA, MAY 1978

We receive word at breakfast one morning that Mrs. Hawk has left the house for good. Carmela announces in between sips of coffee that Mrs. Hawk wished to pursue another opportunity—corporatespeak for *no proper explanation shall be given*. Mole tells me behind a hand that Mrs. Hawk had problems with her heart and hurried away on the first supply boat out; Lamb swears no boat arrived or left, as he spent dawn by the ice, enjoying the cool air before the fog rendered such a pleasure impossible. Despite the inconsistencies in the rumors, the whispers subside as soon as a brisk prayer for her health is said and buttery platters of softly scrambled eggs emerge from the kitchen. I eye my fellow teachers and Carmela as they chatter for the rest of the breakfast hour, privately wondering how we can carry on with our days like nothing at all has passed.

I tell myself my shock isn't warranted. Mrs. Hawk might have been planning her leave privately with Carmela for some time. But when I peek into her room after breakfast, some of her possessions remain, and a member of the cleaning staff roams, vigorously disinfecting every surface with a foul-smelling liquid. A simmering anxiety fills me.

"She was fine only last week, wasn't she?" I whisper to Yesi as we venture down to class. "Could it be—?"

"Swamp, as someone obsessed with developing fantasies, I have to say, what's the use in inventing one in this case, when it's obvious she'd had her fill of this place?" she asks me, shaking her silver head. She links her arm in mine. "She was old, Swamp. Not everyone is up for the adventure," she adds, pinching my wrist affectionately. "Her loss."

I suspect Yesi's quickness in processing the news has to do with her assuming the woman's literature duties. But I cannot sweep Mrs. Hawk out of my head so easily. The chemical stink of her vacant room pervades every corner of my memory. I wonder, for the briefest of moments, if the old virus afflicting the house has returned and Mrs. Hawk and Sara were the first to be affected. If this were the case, perhaps Carmela would hustle Mrs. Hawk out of the house under cover of darkness to shield the rest of us from that knowledge. But Sara remains here, and I am told she is recovering.

So I cannot allow myself to dwell on these morbid fantasies.

Later that day, I race to make dinner with the group—sliced beef and onions, plus potato croquettes—sliding into my chair as everyone's about to begin, and I nearly fall back off when I see a goblet filled with real, blood-colored wine inside next to my table setting. Wine! I'd thought the evening would be a somber one, on account of Mrs. Hawk. I dip a finger inside to watch the crimson liquid drop. There must be a mistake. But Yesi looks at me wide-eyed, her own lips purple, clutching her goblet like it's a talisman. Carmela, too, catches my eye and nods at me, a veritable smile playing on her stained lips. She turns back to speak with Armadello, the dullest man there ever was, looking like a kindly deity in her flesh-colored sweater coat.

"What's the occasion?" I whisper to Yesi. "Shouldn't we be more . . . subdued?"

"Shut. Up. She didn't die. She left," she whispers back. "Now drink it before I drink yours."

"Join us for a cup, Mavi," Carmela calls over the table without a mention of my tardiness. "In gratitude to Mrs. Hawk."

A few of the others clink glasses. Morency, I notice, is conspicuously absent, and her space is empty, so I feel no disapproval emanating from her corner. Dom's is empty, too. I cradle my cup. The groups around me chat about previous jobs; the girls giggle when Lamb mentions he worked as a butcher's assistant until he couldn't stomach the carcass smell any longer. He cannot, to this day, look at blood without fainting dead away. I press away the rare slice of beef on my plate with a tight smile and down my glass of wine in one long gulp, eager for it to rush to my head. Not another word is spoken about Mrs. Hawk, and, oddly, the feeling in the house is one of general merriment. I try to embrace it. After all, I hardly knew the woman, I tell myself.

"Can you tell us more about the cement company you owned, Carmela?" I ask aloud when there's a lull in the upbeat conversation. Yesi kicks me under the table. But I may as well take advantage of her good humor.

A smile erupts across Carmela's face, her sharp teeth a blinding white. For once, she's not judging us, tight-lipped. She's not icing over the atmosphere in the room. I have complimented her in a way she finds appropriate, and as such, we have all been blessed. "Well," she says, folding and creasing her napkin once, twice, "it was fascinating work, operating at the highest levels of international industry. I was responsible for brokering more than a dozen massive deals before the governmental troubles arose." I look into my glass of wine as Yesi refills it surreptitiously. Diana whispers, *What troubles?* Carmela's smile wrinkles. "But, of course, it didn't offer the potential for personal satisfaction that Vaccaro School does," she adds in a tone brittle enough to give me pause, to give everyone pause.

Mole sniffs audibly. "You should give the girls a business seminar, Madame De Vaccaro."

The girls smile and waggle their heads like otters, implicitly understanding when to suck up and to whom. "Yes, Madame De Vaccaro!" says Gisella. "You absolutely must!"

"We might have a mini Carmela De Vaccaro in this very room," adds Lamb, clapping together his hands guilelessly. "Empresses of business! Imagine! Now that would be a fearsome sight, a pack of ruthless girls raiding the corporate world! You should teach them, Madame De Vaccaro. What it would be like to have your own child follow you into your business . . . ! Well, not your child, per se, but a child, a child you've educated"—his eyes freeze with a vaguely pained look, as Mole's widen in warning—"that's a dream I've always had, myself, there being a child I might have a hold over—that is to say, with whom I might share my passions . . . Wouldn't that be . . . just . . ." A gurgling sound like that of an animal in anguish dies in his throat.

Yesi drops her eyes to her plate as I choke on a sip of wine. The unsubtle mention of Carmela's dead daughter could never go unnoticed, not with the way gossip travels here. After several seconds of silence, a quiet moan escapes Lamb's mouth, and he bows his head.

Carmela smears the neatly folded napkin across her lips, the resultant bloody lipstick stain visible from my seat. "I am an administrator, Mr. Lamm. Not a teacher."

The rest of the meal is a solemn affair, even though Carmela bestows one or two more bright and false smiles upon us all. She permits us to shepherd ourselves back to our rooms since Morency is otherwise engaged.

It's a short enough walk, but I can't see straight from the wine. I take a series of wrong turns with Yesi, both of us stumbling and laughing so hard my sides ache.

"That poor, poor dear," says Yesi, swinging me around by the hand, spinning me as we tango. "He would make a magnificent villain were his intentions at all baaaaaaaaaaaaaahd."

I punch her in the shoulder, hiccupping in tears. "After his butcher story I wasn't sure I could stomach seeing a Lamb go to the slaughter." I fall onto a miniature chair with my knees in the hall, its legs or my legs creaking ominously as I sway.

Yesi, red-faced and nest-haired, takes my cheeks with her thumbs and forefingers. "Oh, my little Holden, my fiercely independent and naive and cynical and affectionate and darling little Holden. If I could keep you from ever living any deaths or abandonments or disappointments, I would."

I take her hands and swing her around, laughing. "You've lost it, Yesi."

We slow, and hand in hand, I sing the lullaby my mother used to sing me growing up: "*Que linda manito que tengo yo, que linda y bonita que Dios me dio . . .*"

"It's *blanquita*, not *bonita*, isn't it?" Yesi asks, stopping me.

"My mother changed it," I explain, the walls spinning around us. "*Todas son bonitas, aunque no sean blanquitas.*"

The rest of the stroll blurs; we read the winding walls like braille to return. Seven, seven, thank goodness I've found seven, placed the seven in the seven, seven times seven. I drop onto the bed and fall asleep with my filthy Mary Janes still strapped, humming the lullaby to myself, as if it can allay all my latent fears.

It is the dead of night when I wake from a dream of draining the bathtub, full of frothy, rancid water, with my mouth. *There's a motherless one here*, whispers a girlish voice from the closet as I splutter. I am covered in sweat, disoriented, and shivering. I curl my feet up only to feel the soles of my shoes rasp against the sheets. *There's a motherless one here.* Because of the skylight in the shared bathroom, the moonlight bathes my room in a faint, otherworldly glow. My room door has been opened, a draft blowing through, and the closet door has been, too, exposing the gaping maw of the closet.

I see a sliver of white, slipping out of the darkness within. Her. A little girl, her long and greasy hair draped in front of her face and hanging over her shoulders like a yoke.

The intruder, I think. How did she get in? I swear I locked my room door. I swear it.

I squint my eyes at her in the dark. She's pale and impossibly reedy; she wears a disintegrating and stained lace nightgown that exposes her skeletal arms and her knobby ankles.

She is unfamiliar—not one of the little girls I know here.

She shuts the closet door with a single finger, all while adjusting her neck with the other hand. The sound of each vertebra cracking sends a tremor through me. No, she's not like the girls I teach. That's when I stop breathing, hoping I won't catch her attention. Hoping I can melt into my bed and become invisible. Hoping I can fall into a safer realm of sleep and forget this encounter.

Yet I continue to watch her, pinching my eyes into slits. Riveted and terrified.

She moves about my room with the self-possession of someone who does not feel the eyes of others on her, splaying the pages of my books, rifling through a pile of clean and folded clothes. I smell a rank waft, ripe and aged, like the meaty interior of a used plaster cast.

Could she be a ghost, or the ghost of someone lost to the curse sixty years ago?

She drops a crumpled shirt of mine and moves toward the chest, placing both hands on its fine wood with delicacy. Her feet are bare, lacy blue with cold or a strange form of rot, and none of her steps make a single sound on the floorboards.

In fact, as she moves, her feet do not brush the ground at all.

She lifts a book I've left on the chest and lets it slam onto the chest hard, her black eyes darting over to me with cold mischief.

She sees me startle. It was intentional—a trap. I shut my eyes tight and feel a surge of intense, bone-singing fear. There is only silence in the darkness, except for my heartbeat, which I wish I could stop. Will she touch me? Will she go? *Have courage, Mavi.* She can't be older than twelve. She can't intimidate me.

I open one eye, still praying she's gone—only to muffle a shriek and shrink back into my sheets. She's much closer, so close I can taste her foul breath, and she's leaning over me like an otherworldly animal. She blinks her two dark eyes at me. There is a twisted hopelessness about her, a flattened affect to her that only exists in children who have cut themselves off from the world after terrible harm.

Is this creature the tenth girl? The tenth student?

She may be unfamiliar, but she does resemble someone I know. It's in the curve of the jaw, in the hairline. But who? She stands, bones still cracking in her spine, amusement playing on her dry lips.

"English teacher," she whispers in a charmless singsong. "You're awake."

My throat closes at the label.

"Won't you answer me, English teacher?"

I freeze, only my heart galloping at what feels like hundreds of beats a minute in a useless body. She moves even closer, bringing her stench of putrefaction with her, and kneeling onto the edge of my bed, her black eyes wide. Their corners are red and encrusted, as if she's ill. My mind, my body warn me not to engage her. I silently beg her not to come closer. I need her farther from me.

"Or don't answer," she says. "I've only come to tell you that the Others are coming."

Who is coming now? My eyes flash to the open hall door, on instinct.

"Aren't you going to ask who the Others are?" she asks in a rough rasp. She simulates patting my head, and I withdraw, swallowing the painful knot of dryness in my throat.

My reply is barely audible. "The Zapuche?"

She smacks her dry lips. "No." She wilts back onto her pin-thin ankles at an unnatural angle that should snap them. "*The Others,*" she says with emphasis, taking her own long and filthy hair in her fingers. "The Zapuche opened a path for them with their curse. They come from all corners of the globe. It's already starting. I know you've felt them." She plays with her ropes of inky hair, twirling them roughly. "They're always watching, always waiting. But they visit most at night. Passing drafts and whispers—that's them. You understand?" A few long strands come loose in her hand. "They're taking over this house again. And now that they've made one little girl sick, the rest will follow," she says, letting the hairs drop onto my bed. "No one should have ever come back here."

They've made one little girl sick. Sara. A common cold, Mole said. Coughing, fatigue, nothing more. I pinch my leg to see if I'm awake—it stings precisely as it should.

"I don't understand," I mumble.

160

"Speak up," she replies.

"Sara has a cold."

She takes the ends of her gnarled hair in hand and picks through them. "It looks like a cold, like a virus, but it isn't. The virus is a lie crafted by the De Vaccaro family. Do you understand me yet? The Others like to cause trouble."

The virus is a lie? "What are the Others?"

"They're not like you." She breaks off a knot of hair. "But they want to be like you. They want to live, to breathe, to laugh, to eat. But they cannot so easily. They need energy, and they cannot get it as you do. They borrow it from you instead. A little at a time, a little more, a little more, until you can't lift yourself from bed." She tilts her chin toward me. "Get it?"

I shake my head.

Her lip twitches, and her hands drop her hair. "Well, in any case, you'll see soon enough."

She settles her bony hands on her knees and takes a breath, as if fortifying herself. "I am going to encourage you to leave, now," she says, enunciating carefully. "I'm going to encourage you to leave and take everyone else with you. I know you're not likely to listen until it's too late, but I am telling you that leaving is the courageous and intelligent choice in this scenario, no matter what you may think."

I process her suggestion. To *leave*? To leave now, when we've only just arrived? When each of us has given pieces of ourselves to this place? We've come here and done our damnedest to settle down. We must make the best of what we've been granted.

A jumble of outrage and fear unlocks a new courage in me, and I sit up in bed and try to turn on my lamp. To face this odd creature in the light. I keep eye contact with her as I fumble for the switch, failing to find it in its normal spot. She stares at me, rubbing her hands together, as if keeping warm, and I realize it: Her face resembles a face I've gazed at for many afternoons. She looks like Dom.

Could this be Carmela's lost daughter? I stop searching for the switch, shivering in the dark.

"Who are you exactly?" I whisper.

She slips off the bed, uneasy, as if noticing the recognition in my tone. "I don't matter. I'm a memory. This warning is all I'm good for."

"Then—then how do you know all of this?"

"I know the residents of this rock better than you," she says, turning from me and gathering the hem of her nightgown in one swooping motion. Stepping toward my open door.

"Wait!" I call. "Where can I find you?"

"You can't," she says before rushing toward the hall and disappearing through the doorway.

I push to my feet and follow her, peering into the empty hall, and even drifting down its unlit length.

"What happened to Mrs. Hawk?" I call out into the dark.

No one answers.

As my mind sharpens, I notice that my arms and legs shake so badly I cannot keep myself upright. This was all a waking nightmare, I tell myself. A nightmare brought about by drunkenness.

But she looked so *real*. The tenth girl, if that's what I should call her. I want to trust in what she told me, and that terrifies me more than her visit itself. Her message stirred intense feelings of horror and relief in me, as if my body and mind know their appalling intuitions about this house have been confirmed.

I'm a few steps into the pitch-blackness—the moon, so temperamental, has disappeared again—when I feel a presence close.

"Is that you?" I ask, pushing my hands into the darkness.

"Miss Quercia," comes a deep voice. I jump—I can barely discern the speaker's shape, but it's massive, rangy.

When I see a loose bun, unraveled into a long braid, my blood runs colder than ever.

"What are you doing out of your room at this hour?" Morency asks. The whites of her eyes luminesce. "It isn't right. It isn't right for you to be out like this. And to be shouting about Mrs. Hawk, after—" Silence swallows her words.

I cross my arms to stop their tremors. "There was a girl, Ms. Morency. A little girl. She didn't seem well. She came to my room and—"

"Enough. No little girls roam this hall. Enough of your stories." She wraps the black cloth around her shoulders; the bones stick out like handles. "Stay in your room at night."

I fall back toward my room, shaking still, and she waits, a motionless giant in the dark, until my fingers connect with my doorknob.

I close the door behind me, triple-checking the lock, and nestle back into bed, but it's difficult to fall asleep, even buried under the layered blankets and breathing into the safe pocket of stale air. Too much adrenaline floods my veins.

I will admit it: Despite my stated lack of belief in the paranormal, I prayed for a midnight message of guidance after my mother was taken—after she died, if I'm to believe what my godmother told me. I remember what Dom asked me once: *Wouldn't you want to see your mother again?* In truth, I did keep a boxed-up hope in the back closet of my mind that my mother might visit me in some form, strong in spirit as she was. Surely she could figure out a way to speak to me one last time. To tell me she was in peace, or to tell me to perform some duty for her. To urge me forward, following in her footsteps. But, of course, she never came. No one did.

Yet here, at Vaccaro School, two mysterious presences have crossed my path already, unbidden:

Michelle, who resembles the dead for reasons I cannot comprehend.

And this strange girl, this supernatural intruder. *They're always watching, always waiting. But they visit most at night.*

Are her intentions entirely good? Or could she be one of these devious creatures she warned me about?

Surely there could be no nefarious reason to warn someone about danger.

On impulse, I rise and open the closet door in the corner, as if to expose her hiding place. But the closet is still empty, even if it feels as quietly carnivorous as before.

Vaccaro School has tightened its hold on me, and now it tests my pressure points. Tests my perceptions, my strength, my belief in the impossible. I've been asked to give pieces of myself, and now I've been asked to leave. What horrors are to follow her warning? This question perks up the hair on my arms like each one is a ghostly stinger left behind by an old pricking.

I play my pitifully limited reel of memories in my head to calm down: my mother at the piano before she left, playing old songs Papa must have loved with a dreamy look on her face. Smiling sadly when she notices me. Eating medialunas each morning together, flakes dotting the kitchen table. Her hands holding up the newspaper. The scratch of the pencil tip. Circling. Underlining. *Mavi?* Those birds that merrily gathered near our windows in the mornings when summer turns muggy, preening and cooing. It is mental exercise, to try to recall them with such clarity, with such detail. These good memories I take for granted are threads that bind me together. Snip one and I might unravel.

After spending a while gathering them, tending to them, bright colors flood my brain, and I drop off into a shallow, troubled sleep.

After washing up the next morning, I groggily find a loose clump of dark hair at the foot of my bed, and I stare at it for a good minute before tucking it into my coat pocket with an unsteady hand. *The girl was real—her warning real, too.* As far-fetched as it might seem.

I hurry down to breakfast, pouring myself two mugs of coffee, holding the milk, glugging the coffee down, and refilling them both. Ignoring the odd looks, I struggle to open the patio door without free hands—an awkward endeavor involving elbows and ring fingers—before Mole takes pity on me and outstretches her hands to take my coffee mugs with a knowing look. It's too wintry for the others on the patio, at six biting degrees Celsius, more or less, and it's decidedly gray and ominous. But I still draw the door back with a creak, and frigid air blasts in. Restorative, in my mind, but Mole recoils, handing both cups back as I step out onto the frosted stone. "If you have to vomit," she says quietly, tugging the doors closed behind me, "do so over the balcony." Behind the window, she winks and mimes my knocking on the door when I wish to be let back inside with the rest of the sane people.

I wish Yesi was around so that I might explain what happened—I associate her with rationality, but I haven't lost my impression of her interest in the macabre and otherworldly. If anyone can reconcile me with last night's nightmare, it will be her. She isn't at breakfast, though, and this morning, both entry points to her room were locked. It took all my composure not to break into full-handed smacks of the bathroom door to wake her hungover self up. *What if she was also visited?*

I take in the brisk air as deeply as I do the caffeinated mud-water, with a mind to those old-fashioned mountain health retreats, and I will myself to find reassurance in the thick, protective clouds and the ice. But it's impossible: The glacial field approaches the house with the gall of a silent rogue army, as if it might accost us up here someday.

We are all trapped on this rock; the house itself is an ancient gilded cage. Who exactly watches us from the sky, from the ice, as we putter about, as we go along our trivial lives cluelessly inside? My visitor was only the first to show herself, and the Others won't share her benevolent intentions, if I am to believe her. I drain the second coffee cup—the dregs now room temperature after a minute outside—and Dom appears in the corner of my eye by the patio window, speaking to someone out of sight inside the breakfast room. His smile makes him look boyish when it's genuine. I frown without thinking, reminded of the girl's resemblance to him. And for some reason, I never expected him to have friendly relations with other people in the house, either. I thought his friendship was private and reserved for me alone, as absurd as that sounds. He notices me watching him and raises a hand. I fall back from the window and look off into the ice in what must seem like embarrassed shock. I ignore the flutter in my chest as my thoughts return to the girl from last night—my mind parses through every available image in hopes of deciphering whether she was fantasy or reality. Alternating icy breaths and scalding coffee should have ushered me back into reality, but all it does is punish my throat for my being unreasonable.

I bump into Yesi at last in the snaking ground-floor hallway on the way to class. She's carrying an open box of chocolates in her hand.

"Thank God," I say, seizing her shoulders. "You slept in?"

She shakes her head. "God has nothing to do with it," she says, grinning, and extends the box toward me. "Want? I spent some time on the book in the sitting room. I'd been neglecting it." I ignore the chocolates, and her face darkens as she shuts the box. "Swamp?"

I take her free wrist—thin as a twig—and drag her in the direction of the front door.

"Jesus, Swampy," she says, falling behind me. "Slow down."

"Something happened to me last night." I drop her hand as we climb down the front steps, through a fog so thick we cannot see more than a meter before us. We pass a swinging arm, which ends up being attached to Mole herself, who waves at us, the odd couple, before we dart past into the fog once more. "I've been wanting to tell you about it all morning."

"Something happened? Vague. Terribly vague." She tucks the chocolate box under her arm with a wary glance at the cobblestones, but she keeps up with my pace as we pass what must be the science cottage, engulfed in murk. "Can't you tell me inside, where it's warm? I don't have my coat, and I wasn't built for single-digit temperatures—"

"Either I've vivid dreams," I say, slowing to a stop before the English cottage, its telltale awning riding atop the mist, and pushing inside with a grating rasp, "or I was visited by a ghost."

She narrows her eyes, opens the chocolate box, pops a square into her mouth, and chews the bite thoroughly, thinking. "Mmm. Caramel."

"That's all you have to say?" I ask, my breaths turning shallow. The classroom is still frosty, its windows entirely whited out, and I need to click on the space heater and find a coat, but my mind's running too quickly to prioritize. "A little girl came to me in my room. A little girl who looked so much like Dom. Look—" I rustle inside my pocket and pull out the clump of hair, showing it to Yesi. She wrinkles her nose in disgust, and I let the hair drop. In the light of day, it looks a lot like my own. "She warned me that creatures are coming for the girls," I tell her. "*The Others*, she called them. Will afflict them with something that looks like a virus but isn't. The supposed virus Sara has right now."

"Awfully specific for a ghost," she says, biting into another neat square.

"She knew the De Vaccaros. She could be Carmela's dead daughter. Don't you think?"

She swallows. "Well, Swampy," she says, closing the box once more with studied nonchalance, "maybe she was the ghost of Carmela's girl. Though I'm sure she wouldn't survive any visits outside their palatial family wing." She smirks. "*Survive* was a naughty choice of word."

"I'm being serious, Yesi," I say, frowning. I'm surprised, to be honest, by her blasé reaction, even if I am being ridiculous. You'd think a writer could manufacture a more imaginative and encouraging reply. "I am telling you this little girl was a real ghost, whether or not she's a De Vaccaro. And she was instructing us to leave."

"A *real* ghost. Well. I'm glad she was a real one." She turns from me to switch on the space heater. "With real shedding problems, apparently."

I ignore her. "Do you think the Zapuche curse is real?" I ask her in a whisper, unable to drop the subject. "And if it is, do you think we could find one of them, nearby, and have them . . . reverse it? Then we wouldn't have to leave."

Yesi turns to look at me with a startling mix of pity and surprise in her clear blue eyes. "Just to be safe," I add uselessly, the words leaving a metallic tang in my mouth.

"There are no more Zapuche here," she says carefully. "By the midfifties, the entire local tribe was run out of the area by government-backed loggers. You must know that. For all we know, they've been exterminated."

I feel as if a heavy stone has landed upon my chest. "Exterminated?" I say in that same whisper, because it is all I can manage.

"Now, listen, Swamp. You said you might have experienced an

especially stimulating dream. The house is spooky. I'll give your little ghost girl that. But I don't think there's any more to it than that. After all, aren't all old places a bit scary? The idea of the history here alone." An abominable history. I drop into the nearest wooden chair. She places two hands on my shoulders and squeezes. "The booze did you no favors, Swamp darling. And Mrs. Hawk's departure clearly rattled you. I don't blame you or the little ghost girl in that wonderful head of yours."

She's condescending to me. I bat her fingers away and drop my head into my hands so she won't see the disappointment there. I've never before questioned my sanity in a serious fashion, and last night's shared bottle of wine couldn't have muddled my mind as much as Yesi suggests. I take a deep, cleansing breath.

Suppose Yesi is right. The altitude doesn't help, nor does the isolation . . . My old paranoia might have manifested itself in this nightmare of a girl.

"Fine. I need to relax." I will relax, I think to myself, as my heart only beats harder.

She smiles with closed lips.

"So how's the book?" I ask as my mind swirls with all the unknown evil of this world, lurking out of sight. "Speaking of ghosts. Real or unreal."

Her eyes are already distant. "Like a living, breathing thing. Like a greedy, suckling child."

I spot her box of chocolates, sitting on a desk and encased in shiny, fancy gold wrapping paper that I only just noticed. "At least you don't have to feed it."

She laughs, warming her hands before the space heater. "Oh, Swampy. It's twice as hungry as the average infant. If I don't feed it pieces of myself daily, it turns into an absolute monster of a thing."

∞ ∞ ∞

In class, I ask the girls to read their compositions aloud to the others, which sounds like a sly way of convincing them I'm an attentive teacher when in truth I'm unable to focus whatsoever. I appraise them all from my seat at the table, as if I might see traces of a disguise one of them used to prank me last night. Michelle catches me watching her and stumbles over a few words, but the others manage their presentations quite well. I hold her back after class and consciously try to prevent my hands from convulsing, my eyes from twitching on account of my unwise caffeine consumption earlier.

"How are you doing?" I ask, smothering my hands in my pockets. "Sleeping well?"

"I'm a bit tired," she says, blushing. "But I'm fine. Why? What is it?"

"So you and the other girls are doing well?" I look away as casually as possible. "Even with Mrs. Hawk gone?"

And she hesitates, slipping her book bag onto her shoulder. "I guess so. We didn't know her well. She suffered from bad migraines and missed class a lot."

"And Sara? Have you seen her today?" Carmela has limited her visitors, claiming that it's too much activity for her. To her credit, Carmela has been tending to Sara herself—the one sign of motherly devotion and care I've seen in her.

"Oh. Well, Madame De Vaccaro did let me see her this morning," says Michelle, smoothing down the limp hair beside her part. "She's doing so much better—bursting with energy. You wouldn't believe it."

Yesi leaves me for the book after our classes, again, with an apologetic and pitying pat, and Mr. Lamm has taken over the sitting room as his private pipe-smoking den, making it impossible to penetrate without hacking up a lung, so I wander the house for a while until I'm due to meet Dom.

I comb the serpentine hall for a doorway I haven't seen, a nook I haven't explored, but despite my best efforts, the house loops me around and back around to the same set of tired rooms. So I peek into those musty but familiar sitting rooms, searching for fresh evidence that something is amiss.

I encounter no one but Gisella, curled up with a book and very much alone. She registers my intrusion a second late and, with none of her characteristic nonchalant grace, struggles to conceal the cover with splayed hands.

"What are you reading?" I ask, unable to resist and expecting something forbidden.

She bites her lip and shows me: *The Haunting of Hill House* by Shirley Jackson, in English, nonetheless.

"Don't tell the others," she says as I'm about to compliment her taste. "They keep asking me to paint their nails because I'm the best at it." She frowns haughtily. "But I don't run a stupid salon."

And the Gisella I know is back. I suppress a smile. "Do you like it?" I ask, pointing at the book.

She nods, silent. Her fingers crawl across the cover, as if itching to reopen it.

"I'll look for more for you," I tell her, smiling and shutting the door on her private escape.

Every other sitting room remains untouched—most are woefully ignored by the current occupants of the house. The last people to enjoy them are surely long dead; the air has never felt as stale, choked full of dust composed of shed skin cells.

What am I searching for?

The girl, holed up somewhere, filling a familiar space with that strange stench of hers?

Mrs. Hawk, whose disappearance maddens me still? A part of me doesn't believe the woman could have left of her own volition.

Or do I hope to find someone who will either accept what I saw last night as truth or blast its veracity away entirely in blunt, serious terms? Not brush me off as a hungover wreck, as Yesi did?

Perhaps I should look for Morency. She respects the darkness in this house as much as I now feel I should. And she's the only one to truly do so; every other occupant is cavalier about the rules, barring dearest Carmela. Morency was also missing at last night's dinner, yet present in the hallway of my nightmares last night. It cannot be a coincidence.

I knock on her door for several agonizing minutes with no result—a good thirty seconds between attempts. I head back downstairs in the general direction of the family's quarters, accessible through that stone hallway. If I know one thing, it's that Morency will smell my trespassing presence. I follow the route that Dom took the night I pursued him. Before he was my friend. I slow by his room, and the corridor is pin-drop silent.

"Morency?" I call. "Yoooohoooo."

Nothing. I press on. The hallways in the family's quarters boast vaulted ceilings; the decor is richer; the overall feeling is airier, as if they've afforded themselves alone the privilege of easy breathing. I wonder where Carmela works during the day—if she keeps any photographs of her daughter, the would-be empress of business, in her room. If I might recognize her daughter in those photographs.

I wonder, also, if she worries for herself or for Dom being here, the spot her family was pushed from sixty years ago—if she worries that the De Vaccaro family is doomed to a type of tragedy that runs much deeper than a virus. I shiver in place. Morbid, unruly thoughts. Perhaps Yesi's right, and as a narrative builder, I should be put out to pasture.

I leave the family's quarters and fetch some calming tea in the deserted kitchen, eager to put my mind to rest during my daily conversation with Dom. Surely he'll tell me if my imagination runs too wild and dark.

The fireplace crackles as I cross the threshold of the latest sitting room and spot the top of Dom's head. Relief crashes over me all at once, and I settle beside him, careful not to spill my tea. He looks up from his book, *Tropic of Cancer*. I've never read it myself, but I know it was considered obscene for years and years. Of course he's reading it.

"You looked like you were going to leap off the balcony this morning," he says, turning to face me, and his resemblance to the girl last night—in the dark, slashing eyebrows and the pointed chin, too—silences me.

I fake a smile and bring the tea to my lips as he watches me.

"Mavi?"

I swallow and clear my throat. "Only testing out my wings before the weather gets too bad. Missed you at dinner," I say, trying for a relaxed tone.

"Will you think I'm a degenerate if I tell you I slept through it?" he asks, flipping the page.

"Not especially. I already think you're a degenerate," I say, recapturing my shaky sense of self. "But I'll be infinitely jealous."

"How was it? Especially awful?"

"More or less."

We sit in silence, my pulse heavy in my throat, my hands, my heart. He evaluates me, brow raised. "You look weird. What's wrong? Which one is it—more or less awful?" His eyes are a baby's blue, a robin's-egg blue, that blue of all things supposedly pure.

I exhale and smell the lingering fermented remains of last night's excess. I'll tell him. I must tell him. "Supremely awful. I can't believe you missed it. No one brought up Mrs. Hawk's departure at all. Your mother served us all wine, and people unraveled. Lamb made the mistake of mentioning your sister—"

"Mrs. Hawk's departure?" he asks, shutting his book. "Which one is she again?"

"—and I fell asleep half-drunk with my shoes on and had the strangest nightmare. A little girl in an old, ratty nightgown warned me that trouble was coming to the house in the form of ghosts. *Others*, she called them." I expect him, for a moment, to laugh it off, and there's an expectant smile on my face. I refrain from including the salient detail of his resemblance to this girl: Perhaps even now I'm afraid a mention of his sister will upset him. It's one of the odd triggers I notice; every time I mention her, he breaks eye contact.

But now he leans toward me.

"Only a nightmare," I add, light as air. "I must have been thinking about the virus your mother mentioned at dinner the first night. You know how these things are," I say, even though I don't have a clue what I'm talking about. He watches me intently, and I expect him to tell me I'm full of nonsense. My mouth goes dry, and I point at the book. "What's it about?" A pathetic save.

"Oh. Honestly, I don't know. I've only just started."

"What's your favorite bit so far?" I lift the tea to my lips.

He folds open the book to the first page and shows the line to me: *The cancer of time is eating us away.*

"So the first page."

He laughs, but it's short and not heartfelt. He sets a hand out on the table between us, double the size of mine. "I want to hear about your nightmare. Come on. Tell me."

I'm trembling now. I hide it with a manic smile—my exhaustion setting in. "Oh, please. It doesn't matter."

"You wouldn't have said anything if it didn't matter, Mav," he says. "I sort of like to think I know how you work by now. At least some of the time."

So I exhale, and my overworked brain urges me to trust him.

I tell him everything, and though the nerves do not lessen, a weight melts, bit by bit, from my shoulders. He asks me to repeat every detail twice—to swear I am recounting every word exactly as it reached my ears.

As I finish, the curiosity in his eyes is undeniable. "Are you afraid?"

I can't help but remember his earlier mention of something sinister in the house. Of ghosts.

"Sort of," I admit. I run my fingers through my hair. "Well, I don't know. Should I be? It didn't feel like a nightmare. But the literary seer of domestic ghosts says I'm being ridiculous." I bite my tongue before mentioning the tragic, lost Zapuche and their infamous curses. "You mentioned ghosts here before. What truly happened to the inhabitants of this school sixty years ago?" I ask him in a whisper.

He rubs his hands together for a good moment, watching the flames dance before us. "It wasn't a virus," he says at last. "And you didn't have a nightmare."

Though he speaks gently, his certainty chills me more than the memory of the girl's visit itself.

The dinner bell rings, jerking us out of our seats in our hideaway, as if someone was, indeed, watching us. I lose the opportunity to discuss the matter further—though perhaps that's a blessing, because I don't possess the courage to dive into that dark realm just yet.

12

ANGEL: 2020-1200

A ghostly creature with a delicate humanity. Visible to Mavi as more than rippling air or a fraying, otherworldly swatch of threads. This girl who snuck up on Mavi in her sleep sounds lifted from Mama's tales, with her wise warnings and her pragmatism. A dead-perfect match for the sacrificed girl in the house history books: protector of humans, with powers beyond comprehension and knowledge of the godforsaken pack of Others.

My mind's aflame with thoughts of this mystical tenth girl and all the questions I want to ask her. Need to ask her. But how to call her out to speak with me?

I never thought I'd say this, but I'll find an answer in the books. The issue at hand being that I've scoped all the good ones—only Carmela's personal collection remains to be liberated.

Sweeping through the family's quarters in Dom, I jiggle every door handle. Locked. But I can peek through keyholes, and crouching, with one eye open, I find Carmela's office empty.

After checking around the corner, I hold my breath, then slide the two unfurled paper clips into the lock. Dom's heart jackhammers as I jimmy it. When it clicks, I exhale and open the door, venturing inside the one place I haven't gone before while visible: Carmela's private rooms. Time to put the man hands to good use.

On the solitary bookshelf, I spot a couple of repeat Zapuche tribe history books and an Argentine social register. I nose my way toward her desk, detecting different details while in Dom: She keeps no personal items here at all except for a framed photo of a child's footprint, inscribed with the identifying letter *M*. Not Dom—his sister, maybe. I drag my thumb over it, wishing I could access Dom's memories. I pull open the heavy drawers, expecting stacks of paperwork, but Carmela keeps offensively, irresponsibly little material in her desk for an administrator. Specifically: no material at all. No curriculum plans, no official-looking documents, no dossiers on the students and staff. (Dom must have squirreled away the only one.)

I size up Carmela's bulging armoire next and scour the room for its key. There aren't many places to look since everything is so damn empty. I spot the key wedged under the leather writing mat on her desk, the most obvious hiding place ever. *Do less.*

Despite their new lock-picking skill, it somehow takes the hands a solid ten seconds to jangle the old-fashioned key around in the lock and swing open the chest. Inside, I find a single Zapuche tribe history book, published in 1925 (!), my most contemporary find yet. At first glance, it reiterates information about the shaman curse, *los Otros*, and the girl sacrifices, but I tear the relevant pages from the book with a silent apology (you won't be used to roll joints! I kind of sort of promise!), shoving them into my pants to devour later.

The rest of the armoire contains nothing but dust.

You are the worst principal I've ever met.

And yet: As I think the words, I realize her shittiness must be intentional on her part. After all, it's abundantly clear she was born to execute. A female cement company CEO in a time when that's unheard of, pivoting to single-handedly found an isolated historical school after losing half her family.

A master of public image: polished to shine on the surface. Unmovable below. I remember her false smiles, her hollow speeches.

A born executor, plainly going through the motions. Biding her time. Keeping hope alive, as she said to Morency on the first day of classes.

But what does she hope for? What does she wait for?

I try to knot together the disparate loose threads in my mind: the tenth girl, her warnings, the Zapuche legends, De Vaccaro family history . . . But I can't tie them, turbulent as it is in my crystal head.

The only noticeable changes here come in the form of the growing ice, and the presences of the Others, strengthening by the second.

Could it be the Others she's waiting for? I wonder, since all she keeps are Zapuche history books. A family member who knows the legends could be aware of us—of the danger we pose.

My hand shakes on the chest handle, rattling the metal. I push it forward and slam the chest shut with a louder-than-expected clang.

"What do you think you're doing here?" says a shrill voice from the doorway. My other hand drops the key like it's made of molten iron.

Carmela bursts in, crossing her arms with fury from hell in her eyes as if she has to physically straitjacket herself to keep from strangling me (acceptable) and dinging her manicure (unacceptable).

WWDD? Quickquickquickquick.

"So?" she asks, tapping a heel. Slate gray today.

Dom wouldn't watch her like a deer in the headlights. He would act. He would pounce. He would be the bobcat in the woods.

But I'm not Dom.

"Uh, nothing," I say, smooth as silk ties from the mouth of an overworked clown.

"Is that so." Her indignation feels forced to me; a glitter in her eyes tells me that this exchange delights her, or at least satisfies some twisted expectation she had. There's a shade of Liese in her, for sure. But I don't have time to play another bully's game. I've experienced far too much emotional growth.

Okay, maybe not, but I'm six feet tall, for Pete's sake, and built like a ram, if not a bobcat. At least some parts of me are. The words surge up out of my throat, unstoppable. "What do you know about a tenth girl?"

The shimmer in her dies; she runs the slip of her tongue neatly along her top lip, a half-seductive, wholly reptilian motion. "What did you say?"

"There's a tenth girl here," I say, crossing my meat arms. "A girl who comes out at night. When were you going to tell me about her?" *Bitch.*

She won't meet Dom's eyes, calm as she remains. "You don't know what you're talking about." The eyes flick a foot farther from me like they've spotted a roach on the ground.

"Were you planning on hiding her from me?" I rub my hands together, a new charge building. "From all of us?"

She surprises me by sitting in the chair before me, spine erect. She briefly scans the room, as if the words she needs are on paperwork strewn about, but—whoops!—there are no papers anywhere because she's a fraud principal.

But she shakes her head mutely, as if I'm the mad one.

"She warned us about this place," I add, leaning closer, wondering if more information is helping my case or torpedoing it; by my luck, this last sentence must rattle her battleship, because her eyes widen, exposing a sliver more sallow-white. "Well?"

She presses her lips together before speaking. "You have seen her." I can't tell if it's a question or a statement of fact, but I sense the tremble of emotion there.

My breath catches, and a palpable energy surges afresh through my veins. "Yes," I lie. "She was wearing a white nightgown, and her hair was long and dark."

She interweaves her fingers and waits for more; I only have what Mavi told me, and with every passing second of silence, my *lack* is showing like an ugly pair of flowery underpants under a perfectly decent skirt on a windy day.

"Liar." She spits out the word, doesn't so much speak it. "You don't understand what you're talking about."

As I gape, her fingers straighten. One rises to the corner of her mouth to adjust an invisible, straying speck of lipstick.

"Um, why would I mention her, then?" I ask. Well done, Dr. Smooth.

She looks away: reframes something ugly in her mind, rehangs it. To no avail: It's still ugly, judging from her mien of contempt. "What is it that you want, Domenico?" she asks with more than a sprinkling of condescension.

I want answers. *What do you know about this girl? Is she the one my own mama told me about nightly? What do you want her to do for you? What do you think she can do for me, Angel?*

But strength responds to strength.

If only I could be a superior damn detective—access her son's years of experience with her and squeeze out more information without giving her a drop in return.

"You wished to inform me that you know of her," she continues, latching onto the pregnant silence on my part like a greedy, little, bump-obsessed vampire. "You hoped to convince someone that you are more than the valueless simulacrum of a living, breathing man. Is that it?"

I'm silent, a bit dumbfounded—thoroughly convinced I've never heard a more elegant put-down of My Fair Dom. Her hands curl into fists, turning a purplish pink. She exhales through her mouth like a SEAL practicing box breaths. When she catches my eyes again, she looks oddly overcomposed, and a dart of terror rips up my spine.

"You fail to think matters through, Domenico. Each and every time. Your every purposeless action, your every half-formed thought reflect only the worst characteristics of your parents. The parts I have spent my life trying to cull from myself, and the parts that murdered your silly, narcissistic father." She smiles grotesquely, lips pinching into a thin, pink-edged line. "Tell me: Is this what you desired? An admission of my hidden, shameful feelings toward the son I should love?"

As she speaks, I wither. I know her fury is directed at Dom, of course. But nothing so eloquently severe should ever be said by a parent to a child. Even Liese's and He-who-must-not-be-named's blunt rage was often blind and lacking teeth.

Can she hate Dom so much? Can she hate herself so much? Can she relish these moments of cruelty for their own sake, or does she enjoy punishing herself?

Watching me blink at her like a lost calf, she mashes one temple with her fingers, smearing some kind of flesh-colored makeup. "Get out," she snarls. "By the grace of God, *get out*."

I launch myself toward the door, chastened and hypermobile at last. "Um, okay, sorry about this," I say, vaguely horrified and shocked yet still blandly corporate, like a fast-food manager fielding a complaint about a thumb in a fried-fish sandwich.

"You're *sorry?*" she snaps. I swivel back: Her eyes swirl with a complex hatred I've rarely seen, one that requires shared biology. One that reveals unmistakable horror, the shame she herself mentioned, and there, underneath it all, the love she tried to hide.

"Never mention the girl to me again," she says. "And *go.*"

I do as she says.

But as I rush into the hall, I feel it flooding me, sickly sweet on the heels of my humiliation: a desperate urge to find this tenth girl. The enigmatic creature whose name, when mentioned, could force someone as formidable as Carmela the Great to splinter and crack.

After dropping off Dom, I race over to the cloud house to grill Charon and find him seated, cirrocumulus book in hand. He groans. "What is it now?"

"Reading anything good?"

He shuts his book, and it dissipates. "This isn't book club, butt wipe."

"The tenth girl. Who is she? The little ghost girl who warns the humans about Others."

He settles back in his chair. "In their infinite wisdom, the Zapuche believed a special girl could protect the rock," he says with utter uninterest, as if reading an airline safety card for the hundredth time on a flight because he forgot to pack his own entertainment. "Not quite an Other and not quite a human. They thought she could grant wishes if found." He pauses. "As if she's Betty Crocker and wishes are miniature fucking cupcakes."

"So she's one of the girls from Zapuche legend? The girls who were sacrificed to protect them from Others?"

He scoffs. "Protect. Yeah, sure." He narrows his eyes. "Been reading house history books in your free time, huh?" He purses his slicked lips, appraising me. "I just don't get you, kid."

"What's the girl's deal? The one who's in the house now?"

"What's her deal? How am I supposed to know, you inarticulate moron? I'm not her keeper. I've never even seen her. But if the little mongrel's still scrounging out an existence, I bet she hates our guts. She strikes me as the uppity type. With morals. You know what I'm talking about."

He snaps his fingers, conjuring a book from the thick air, and resumes reading. I squint at him, trying to gauge whether he's being an honest or dishonest asshole, but he doesn't even acknowledge me. Further attempts at asking him for information only lead to his politely requesting I bugger off to a moist and foul-smelling five-foot-long place I'd rather not mention (my own colon).

But now I know she exists, and purpose is a set of wings, strapped to the unexceptional so they can fly.

I'll find her, Mama.

13

MAVI: ARGENTINA, MAY 1978

Despite my newfound belief in Vaccaro School ghosts, a couple of nights pass in relative calm, without a single abnormal sighting—I sleep in healthy patches, tossing around my blankets, awakening in the oddest dreams. Every one features me and Dom together on an unnamed beach, a dark city street, or a leafy suburban park—surrounded by throngs of strangers, our skin glistening from an unusual humidity. I cannot hear our conversation, because I am distracted by the overwhelming feeling of being watched by hundreds of curious, shaded eyes. When I peer more closely at the strangers around us, their features blur until they vanish. The vaguest promise of doom hangs in the air, but nothing ever comes of it.

I never experience dreams set in what could be a hypothetical future, and these fill me with a lingering apprehension. How am I meant to interpret them? Should I bother at all with a pursuit as silly as dream interpretation?

I am unnerved by a change at school, however, and it's nothing I could have foreseen in my dreams: One morning, the gray redoubles with a vengeance, so thick that it eats away the toe of our every footstep. Each teacher is made to pick up the girls at her previous class and escort them through the nasty brume to her own. After mine, the last before lunch, Morency herself comes. But Michelle must peel off, because she approaches me while I'm grading a few essays.

"Miss Quercia?" she whispers, squeezing the paunch of her teddy bear–like book bag. I expect her to apologize for her recent class-time naps. Only yesterday, I turned my back to the girls for a moment and found that they had propped little folded paper animals all over Michelle's sleeping form, as if they'd taken to living on their heedless host. When I tapped Michelle on the shoulder, she startled and smiled up at me dreamily, the animals remaining in place.

"I wanted to . . ." She stops and grinds her nails into the bag's leather, shaking her head. Her lower lids tremble, and in that moment, I notice the distinctly blue tinge to the delicately veined skin beneath them. "You asked how I was the other day. Why?"

I hesitate and set down my pen.

"Do you sleep well here?" she adds, propping the bag on my desk.

"I suppose that depends."

"Have you noticed anything at night?" She flattens her palms on the wood grain of the desk. Her nail beds turn white. "Have you felt anything at night?"

I will my facial muscles to remain immobile. "I'm not sure I know what you mean. Homesickness?" I remember her awful aunt, who locked her away and served her canned foods. "Altitude sickness?" To hold on to my sanity here is to grasp at straws.

Rubbing at her pale moon face until her cheeks turn pink, she sighs and looks at the floor. "I sometimes think someone is in my room at night, is all."

"What?" My breath feels trapped inside my rib cage. "Someone who isn't your roommate?"

Her chin drops to her chest in ashamed assent, and a phantom fist clenches around my guts.

"Who?" I want to take her by the shoulders. "Who is it?"

"I don't know." She scrubs at her cheeks again as if warming them. "I thought, at first, it was another girl. But she didn't laugh; she didn't make noise. She only watched. So now I think it's someone else. Someone just watching."

"Watching you?" I ask, thinking of my own visitor. "Has Diana said anything?"

Diana, her roommate, should know if anything out of the ordinary was happening, but Diana has not been the most forthcoming student with me, spending most of her time coloring in her rainbow of notebooks and ignoring questions, speaking, instead, only out of turn. But Michelle shakes her head. "I wanted to know if you felt the same thing, and that's why you asked."

"Michelle, don't you think we should discuss this with someone else . . . like Madame De Vaccaro?" The thought is a terrible one, of course. I can't imagine Carmela De Vaccaro quelling anyone's fears or anxieties, though she did manage Sara's sickness well, if Sara is truly recovering. "Perhaps you caught what Sara has? We should talk to Madame De Vaccaro."

Her hands squirrel into her blazer pockets and ball into hard lumps as a violent color stains her abused cheeks. "That's exactly what I didn't want to happen," she says in an unfamiliar, strangled pitch. "That's why I came to you."

"All right, then," I say, plucking one hand from her pocket and smoothing it out. "We won't for now, okay?" She tenses up as I say *for now*. It must be hypocritical of me to refuse to trust Carmela for a moment yet refer Michelle to her for her own troubles. "You can trust me."

"But you don't believe me."

That isn't true—I'm not prepared to admit to a child what I believe. "Of course I believe you. But I'm sure there's a rational explanation for your feeling uncomfortable and not getting any sleep," I lie. "Perhaps you're having nightmares? Nightmares you forget when you wake?"

Her hand feels gelid and limp in my grip. "When you have nightmares," she says, slowing her words down, as if patiently explaining a phenomenon to a younger child, "they feel real, and they take you to another place, but when you wake, you are brought back to where you are, and you know the nightmare was not real."

"Yes," I say, wary of where she's headed. "I think that's true."

She stares at me, unblinking. "This isn't like that. This is nothing like that," she says with the dark authority and clarity of a doctor providing a patient with his unfortunate clinical diagnosis.

Chills run up my arms. "But you're *sure* someone's there?"

"Yes. But I can't see them."

Suffice it to say my blood runs cold. This is surely no dreamlike visit from an amicable ghost. These are the wily ghosts I've been told to fear. I don't know what to say, what to do, and a sour taste blooms from the root of my tongue.

"I will look into this myself," I promise. "And in the meantime, we'll find you some chamomile tea so you can get some proper rest tonight."

From her flat smile, I can't tell whether she's satisfied or horribly disappointed. I escort her back up to the house to wash up—our pace three times as slow as usual, for we must count each of the hundred and fifty steps now.

As I lunch alone, I single out the fears in my mind: What if spirits are, indeed, hurting the girls? Spirits I can't control, much less understand? What if I can do nothing at all to help, once I do learn more about them?

I do my best to box up these fears, seal them shut, push them to the edge of my thoughts. Because despite these stacks of worry crowding my brain, I still know the right thing to do. I will listen to Michelle. I won't write off her behavior as evidence of insanity or hysteria or homesickness because it's convenient or the logical thing.

Because I believe her.

I look for Yesi after lunch, finding Diana, instead, sprawled on her stomach in a sea of colored pencils in the deserted ballroom, a pad of paper in hand. Peering over her shoulder, I see she's sketching the bizarre mural of the demon and the farm girl in extreme, gory detail.

"Good work," I whisper, and she flips over with a focused look on her face.

"I'm redoing it," she says. "So that it's more realistic."

"Oh?"

"The girl wouldn't just sit there like an idiot." She points to the glaring peasant girl on her page, wielding something sharp in hand. "She would notice the demon, even if he's invisible, and she would stab him in the neck."

"I see." I fold my hands, not knowing whether to admire or fear this pastime of hers. I clear my throat. "Diana, I take it you—you haven't seen anything like the demon in your room at night?" Lord, the euphemisms I must use.

Her cheeks turn bloodred, matching my own embarrassment, and she shakes her mop of hair before flipping back onto her stomach and burrowing into her sheet.

"Well, carry on," I encourage briskly before leaving her to what

I have decided is important work: revamping the most tasteless parts of this dated house.

I find Yesi at last, toiling away on her book in a grungy sitting room, and I decide to present her with my latest flimsy scraps of evidence, in the form of what Dom and Michelle have told me. She as good as laughs at me, and when I rise to leave, faint footsteps trail after me into the hall. "Oh, Swampy," Yesi says, precious book tucked under one arm, as she grapples for my wrist with her free hand. "Nothing to worry about. Don't worry. Truly." When I stop, she neatens my hair, like a girl's, and I wave her aside.

I march on, passing a painting of a shadowy and unwelcoming landscape that rests askew on the wall. "I don't understand. You're fascinated by the macabre history of the house, drawn in by all the gloom, but you brush off what I told you as *silly*? What about what Michelle's going through? That doesn't alarm you in the slightest?"

"Oh, Swamp Thing . . . !" She cuts off a laugh, bounding after me. "She's a *child*. You shouldn't become one, too. If it's anything more than a story, it's sleep paralysis. I've heard of children having frightening episodes—you know, finding themselves unable to speak or move for a couple of moments before and after sleep. Feeling inexplicable doom and all that. Frightful thing."

I'm unconvinced, but I slow. Yesi's behaved strangely ever since I told her about my visitor. She's ignored me, patronized me. But why? I glance back at her, clutching her precious book, and an explanation hits me like a frozen shard up the spine. "Ah," I say. "I see it now. You resent that a wild and mystical creature visited me and not you, patron goddess of all things ghostly."

Yesi's look is razor-edged. "I am not jealous of your nightmares. I don't play the role of the vulnerable, susceptible young maiden, myself. Though it's quite clear that there are those in this house who adore it on you. Mavi, the fragile lady plagued by haunting messages from the other side. Just the thing to inflame a twenty-five-year-old male's overactive libido, especially one who reads *Tropic of Cancer*, which would have been brushed off as a breezy sex memoir had it been written by a woman."

I feel rooted to the ground, feet tingling. "Excuse me?"

She crosses her arms over her book. "Don't patronize me, now."

"Dom's not like that," I say, crossing my arms back at her. "He understands that I don't confuse fantasy and reality. He treats me like an adult."

She snorts with laughter. "*He's not like that*. How can you keep spouting that drivel? Listen to yourself." She points a tiny finger at me. "Don't get yourself into trouble with that addict. He will take advantage of you. And, Swampy dear, if he's put ideas into your head, I'll murder him myself." Her eyes are glassy, reflecting the antique-yellow light from the tarnished hall sconces. "There's no such thing as ghosts," she adds, voice wavering. "Not even in a house with a bloody past."

I watch her, stunned into silence. Only one coherent question comes to mind. "Then why are you writing a ghost story?"

A part of me, the vindictive part, hopes to stump her. I hope to force her to sputter out a transparent lie or immediately confess some odd vulnerability. But instead, she places one hand on her hip, still clutching the book firmly with the other arm, her expression hardening. "I write my ghost story to exorcise myself of a fear of the unknown," she says, as if it is obvious, before turning around, powering toward the staff stairs, and climbing them two at a time.

"What?" I rush after her. "The unknown?"

"The great unknown," she says over her shoulder. "Why are we born the way we are, at this time, in this place? It overwhelms me, this feeling of randomness."

"And how do ghosts remedy that?"

"Ghosts are an invention of people looking to reconcile themselves with the peculiarity of memory, with the randomness—and permanence—of loss, with unfathomable inner selves," she says. "Ghosts are one of the first and best metaphors!" I can't tell if she's pivoting or exposing some tender inner truth in grandiose terms. I'm learning there is a hardened core beneath the layers of whimsical dreaminess, of game nonchalance. She slows until I've caught up to her. One step above me, she rests a hand on my shoulder. "Change has been hard on all of us, Swampy. Chin up. I believe you saw a little girl—consciously or subconsciously—who warned you about this place. I'm not saying you are silly. The house is a mystery to everyone—it brings out so much in each of us." Her hand drops from my shoulder, and she scoops up mine. "I care about you, Swamp. I worry about you. Don't become unwound, be it over a man-child or a bad night. I don't want you to waste any more afternoons falling prey to any kind of evil spell. Will you promise me that?"

My cheeks burn: She's chiding me for my afternoon encounters with Dom—the ones I thought I had kept so secret. I nod to appease her. If it will take time away from him to restore my friendship with Yesi, so be it. "And to think that, at first, I thought you were one of those wilting Victorian flowers who scribble in diaries all day and believe in the paranormal more than the normal," I say.

An unconvincing smile stretches across her face. "Well, you've just described an unfortunate stereotype of female writers, Swampy. Good on you." She leaves me, continuing down the hall.

If only she believed I was more than the unfortunate stereotype of lovesick maiden.

I wend my way back to the empty kitchen for an apple and a cup of mint tea. The leaves tinge the water a grassy green, a relaxing enough sight, though my hands tremble as I hold the cup.

A gray-cheeked cleaning woman enters. She ignores my greeting and scrubs a dish with a frown by the solitary window facing the ice.

Mole told me the staff sleep in a different building; they limit their time inside this house as much as possible. They sense the sinister inside its walls.

She sets the dish to dry on a rack as I look over her shoulder: Blackened water runs from a colossal new crack that has shot through the ice since morning. How is it that we can even glimpse it? A rare window opens in the fog, enabling us to witness this ominous change. I am overcome by a crawling sense of dread.

"Devil's floodgate," she mutters as she leaves the sink and drifts toward the door.

"Sorry?" I call after her. "What do you mean?"

But she is gone.

That night, I dream that Dom and I are trapped in an unfamiliar sitting room in the house, windowless and decrepit. He speaks to me with palpable desperation, but I cannot understand him. As I read his lips, a tiny hand, small as a tarantula, wriggles onto my shoulder, then another. More and more of them crawl onto me—shrunken, sticky, strong versions of Yesi's—and I am tugged away from him, back into the damp dark.

14

ANGEL: 2020-1400

The next time I nudge a history book out of Dom's shelves, it feels like waterlogged roadkill and smells even worse. It serves me right for thinking I'm some kind of Zapuche academic. I drop it onto the floor and rinse Dom's hands, wondering if it's the weed or reality. But when I pull more books off the shelves, all of them are blackening and decaying, as if their pages are made of flayed human skin. The contents of so many erased by moldy speckles. I wonder if the devouring fog has bibliocidal tendencies. Or maybe Book Black Death exists. I flatten out the pages I ripped from the 1925 Zapuche history book in Carmela's office, already flimsy and wet in Dom's hand.

"'In 1918,'" I read aloud, out of creepy habit, "'Zapuche staff members assisting the De Vaccaro family at the Vaccaro School wrote letters to their displaced families sharing news about a "sickness" afflicting residents of the house. It was posited that a girl had not been sacrificed in some time to *los Otros*, and the spirits would naturally become hostile once more. After many of the residents of the house perished—and failed at various attempts to flee—it is said that a couple of remaining Zapuche on the staff were persuaded to sacrifice their own daughters for the "greater good." The outcome of this grisly endeavor is unclear: It is said that the procedure could not have been entirely effective, since they lacked full tribal knowledge of the ritual. However, a limited number of residents did escape the land and survive.

"'No further information is known about the final girl sacrificed.'"

As if I couldn't dislike the De Vaccaros more, I now know who deserves credit for their survival. Who was sacrificed? Could she be the little girl who warned Mavi to leave this place?

"If you can hear me," I say aloud to the empty, swirling air, "then I'm sorry."

Dom's heart feels heavy as lead in my chest, knowing I'll only discover answers to these questions inside the demented heads of some of the current residents.

Namely, Carmela. But after our loving exchange, Carmela must have privately declared World War III (definitely a cold war) against Dom because she won't speak to him, much less acknowledge his existence—an inconvenient turn of events, in that she's my number one resource to grill about the girl, and a convenient turn of events, in that I'm scared shitless of her.

Silver lining: Dom himself hasn't been in the mood to escalate the animosity on his off time, either, much less participate in the world at all. He exclusively smokes and sleeps during the short gaps I'm away from him. *He needs me too now*, I think, with a flutter of one-winged joy. *But that's only because I made him need me.*

I wander out of Dom, returning to Carmela's quarters and newly intent upon spying. After all, I can't do as much as a vitreous web of spirit, but at least I'm invisible and free to track Carmela. Research reveals that she spends a lot of time in her bathroom primping and in the sickroom, whispering to Sara and patting her hand.

Sara, who was meant to be "doing better," looks as pale and limp as a threadbare dishrag—to be honest, she looks this way most of the time, anyway—and doesn't answer Carmela, much less lift her desiccated little head. There's a cheerful, false desperation to Carmela's voice that freaks me out—it's the kind of tone the money-grubbing relative uses with the dying, loaded patriarch in old movies—but I guess she is where she should be for once: with the sick student.

As Others drift in and out, never lingering long, I remain, convinced my spying will reveal a useful nugget. Believing the tenth girl will visit the sickest girl in this house if she deigns to visit anyone at all. I wait as boredom sets in. As I begin to feel feverish. Nothing out of the ordinary happens until just before dinner, when Morency walks in on Carmela Nightingale "caring."

"That's quite enough for today," Morency says gently to Carmela, moving as if to place a hand on her shoulder, but never breaching a foot-wide radius. She carries a folder in her right hand, and she extends it, as if it's the only safe appendage with which to prod her boss. "You should leave the girl now, Madame. That's quite enough. You mustn't tire yourself out."

"I will remind you, for the dozenth time, that this is not your school," Carmela says, swallowing Sara's hand in her own, like a child hoarding a special shell. "These girls are not your responsibility. They are mine."

Morency pauses, with a glance at Sara. "If you were so concerned about them, Madame, you would send them home," she replies, smacking the papers down on Sara's nightstand.

Carmela rises, swelling up like an affronted Napoleon. "How dare you speak to me that way." She checks the wrist her watch should be on, but the skin is bare. "It's time for dinner. Watch the girl, and don't make a fuss. I shall return shortly." She storms out of the room.

This. House. Restless and overwarm, I feel a sudden urge to shake Morency's shoulders. Jolt her into recognition, into action. *You think everyone should leave? Don't just tell your good-for-nothing boss. Shout it from the rooftops.* But I don't.

Everyone here is so helpless.

I float-pace the room, struggling as a new wave of unfamiliar heat passes through my crystal. Morency settles beside Sara, who is on the verge of sleep now, and dips her head close.

"I've brought you more assignments," she says, aligning the stack of papers with her bedside table. "As you asked. You completed the others so quickly."

Sara does not reply. Morency sits beside her for several long minutes, watching her with a furrowed brow, until my eyes glaze over. I've wasted the day, puttering around these fools. I should've stayed in Dom.

With this thought, the blistering heat I've been feeling in my torso crescendos; it doubles me over, and a sudden, painful weight streams from the lengths where my arms and legs would be. It's like I have gangly phantom limbs, having spent so much time in Dom, and a cramping agony overwhelms me, flooding in from nerve receptors I don't have.

"FUCK THIS," I shout, reeling from this pain that shouldn't be. New pain, at once shimmering and incinerating, like gastric reflux from hell. I know what it is: It's my returning craving for concreteness, and it's unbearable.

Sara gasps awake, as if I've screamed in her ear, gulping in huge breaths as if it's her first time breathing.

"Oh my god," I say as Morency mutters, "Goodness."

Sara looks straight at me, eyes burning bright as fireflies. "When are you going to bloody leave?" she asks. I point a crystal finger at my own chest area. Dumbly.

"Language, Sara. Language. And I shan't leave you until you fall asleep," says Morency, leaning forward, as if to block her view. "I know it can be lonely to be ill when all your friends are in class without you."

"You must be dreadfully bored," says Sara with an unusual crispness, looking through Morency as if her imposing form is crafted from glass. As if I'm the one draining all the heat and light from the room. I know for sure, in that moment, that she's speaking to me.

"You can see me?" I ask her shakily. Her pupils dilate. "Do you know the girl?" I ask her. "The tenth girl?"

She scoffs, and those raw little eyes cling to me, like some ancient troll's, defending its mountain pass. "Be gone. I'm telling you right now that I will not sleep." She blows air from her mouth, and a thin strand of reddish saliva drips from the corner of her lip. "I will not sleep, damn you."

I stagger back. She says it as if I'm waiting to feed from her (I'm not). As if she *knows* I feed (can she?). I choke a little, her pupils tunneling into me and digging out my guts.

She can't just see me.

It's as if she can see beyond me: into the hellish gulch in my soul that holds all the cruelty and evil and misery I'm capable of. Every wrong I've ever committed. All the desperate needs and desires I try to conceal, too. Powerful, motivating shit I can't even identify or understand myself. She smells the guilt—a fear of inadequacy. Feels the pain of loss that radiates from every cell of my being.

"I understand," says Morency, carefully, clinically patting

Sara's still hand. "But good little girls always do fall asleep. They always do."

A noise of disgust blasts from Sara's throat. I drift back into the wall, with her eyes still hot on me. Contemptuous. "You can't have me," she rasps. "You can't have me."

The wall engulfs me as I back farther away from her, and my crystal aches as I understand her meaning. I don't want her. Jesus, I don't want her.

Sara and Morency sit in silence for a time, the lights dimmed, until Sara closes her eyes and appears to sleep, her frail chest moving rhythmically, her birdlike limbs weighed down by a thick blanket. Morency releases a sigh and rises with a series of cracks.

"Sleep well," she wishes Sara's sleeping form. "You'll need your energy."

I drift out of the staff hall and back up to the desolate family's quarters. I sluice up through Dom's bedroom, where I left him to rest before dinner.

He's still asleep, his hair all mussed exactly the way Rob's used to look, with this big cowlick at the right temple—the furred patch Rob would twirl and twirl and twirl when he was nervous and his blanket wasn't within arm's reach.

It hurts to look at.

Squinting, I can imagine Rob grown. I can imagine him closing his eyes on pain I can't unsee, if only by virtue of being older than he was when the losses tore through us—with less of that youthful resilience. I can imagine him meeting a girl or guy as intriguing as Mavi. I can imagine him loving so much more than I've ever been able to love, and it's a love that builds on itself, filling any old lunar craters left inside.

I would've given him my life in a second. But what good does carrying that promise do me? It's not proof of anything—not proof that I'm good.

After all, I think of Sara—of all these girls whom Mavi cares so much about. I don't torture them as the Others do, but I'm still not moved to help them, no matter how much they appear to suffer. A good person might try to help them, but to me, they don't feel real enough. Not like Rob.

Not like Mavi, I think, and the thought sends a jag of fear through me. My time with her fills those same craters in me now, artificially or not.

I turn to Dom: I want to cover him with the marled blanket on his bed, as I did Rob, were I able to with my crystal hands. But since I can't, I let him sleep on.

As I'm flitting out, a sliver of light lines the leftmost threshold of Dom's door for a moment.

Someone's watching him. Us.

A thin strip of white.

I fly around the bend, squinting at the light. It's running away.

A waif.

I fly faster, as fast as I can go.

Shit. She's running. A little girl I've never seen in classes, in an ivory gown that skims her ankles.

Unkempt blue-black hair in a fringe brushing the hollow below her narrow shoulders. A little girl with features as fleeting and ghostly as mine must be, to those who could see my ungodly flesh. She flips her head back at an impossible angle as she runs, and for a hot second her eyes look right at me. Not through me. Serious eyes, black and full of judgment.

Immediately, I know she has to be the tenth girl Mavi saw.

They're not like you, the girl had said, according to Mavi. *But they want to be like you. They want to live, to breathe, to laugh, to eat. But they cannot so easily. They need energy, and they cannot get it as you do. They borrow it from you instead. A little at a time, a little more, a little more, until you can't lift yourself from bed.*

The girl's right, of course; she's nailed us on the crystal head. I can guess what she thinks the color of my soul is: black as a goddamn pig roast forgotten on the barbecue after an apocalypse.

But I still bolt after her.

I race after the wisp of white linen.

She runs on two feet the length of my palms, as a little girl does, until I stop looking so close. And then she glides.

Glides an inch above the air. She darts, dances, flies toward the window overlooking the ice.

I only race.

She climbs onto the windowsill, gripping the frame with her hands but bicycling her slender feet through the glass like it's air.

"*Wait!*" I lunge for her, falling several feet short. "You're the tenth girl!"

And thank baby Jesus on toast, she stops, swinging her feet around so she's seated, facing me, chin pressed to her chest. Her blackened hair hangs in her face, shrouding her features. It's so long it looks as if it's never once been cut. She's got a stain down the front of her dress, a greasy splotch that wavers in the low light. Trembling, she drops the frame and holds her belly as if the sight of me makes her sick.

"I'm Angel," I say.

She doesn't answer—only turns to gaze upon the ice like it's calling her.

"I know you," I say, breathless and senseless as I can be. "My mother told me about you, I think. About how you were sacrificed, and how you gained powers. How you can connect lost family members and tell people the color—"

She releases her stomach and holds out a solitary finger.

I stop.

"I don't speak to your kind," she whispers before crossing her arms over her chest like a corpse and falling back off the sill, through the glass, and into the ice. Her inky hair flies back and up, revealing and concealing a final look of calm on her face, as if she's done this countless times before.

I race forward and peer down into the abyss of snaking fog, looking for a plummeting body.

"Wait!" I yell into the void. "Please!"

I need to know how she can see me. How she can act like me but look like them. I need to know who she is and how she became it.

But she has disappeared. Peering into the abyss, I don't see even a wink of a white gown. She dove into the ice as if it's a cool pond.

Why was she wandering a house packed full of my kind with her impenetrable calm? Why did she peek in on Dom when she did? She must have heard me when I spoke about her in him. If only I'd stayed inside him a few minutes longer—I might have hid who I am.

I don't speak to your kind. I fall back into the suffocating confines of the house, as shapeless and empty as I feel inside. *It's not my fault I'm this way*, I want to shout after her. There's this power inside each of us that could flame up at any time, torching the world or igniting a revolution. There's this power inside each of us that could extinguish itself and leave our insides an iced-over wasteland of suppressed passions and blunted points, freakish and half-grown, strewn with craters, by forty or sixty or eighty.

Don't you feel it?

It's not just me. It's every single one of us that can feel love and loss. That's our burden, in exchange for life.

Without Rob here, without Mama here, it's so much harder to protect my own flame, so much harder to give it enough kindling to manage itself, contain itself. I'm here alone, in the near darkness, waiting for some lost and hidden desire to surge out and take me by the throat. Like the one that brought me here.

Who is the tenth girl?

She might be a fiery Zapuche legend.

She might be a mild-mannered mystic.

She might just be a lost little girl.

She is a pack of mysteries fit into one ivory tendril. But the only mystery I've solved is that she doesn't want to speak to me, which is exactly what I need her to do.

15

MAVI: ARGENTINA, JUNE 1978

The days after my strange quarrel with Yesi are especially gloomy; besides the ravenous fog, consuming everything around us, an angry drizzle spatters the skylight. I wake wondering how Michelle and Sara slept, since the former has napped through our latest classes, and the latter has yet to reappear in class at all.

In the morning, I layer my heaviest corn husk–colored blanket over my coat, channeling an elegant woman wearing a shawl to the opera and succeeding at looking more like a wet newborn horse, complete with the greasy mane and quivering legs. Yesi must be furiously working in her room, because she doesn't answer my knocks.

As I head down to breakfast, a step cracks under my foot, and I lurch forward, clinging to the wall in shock and recovering my balance. An entire stair plank has rotted through—its stench thickens the air. I could have tumbled all the way down. I push the thought from my mind and hurry along to the breakfast room, only to find the patio doors locked shut, with kitchen staff posted by them, sullen guards who won't answer my questions as to why. I cannot see the ice mass for the screen of grayish white outside the window; if I squint, I swear the ice has approached, but then again, these heavy clouds play tricks on us.

I am seated, munching on an underdone piece of toast, when Mole enters the room, frazzled, strands of hair poking out of her head in every which way.

"It's Mr. Lamm," she whispers to me, eyes swollen behind scratched lenses. "Oh God, Mavi, it's Mr. Lamm. This damned place is going to kill us all. I don't know how much more I can do on my own, I don't. I'm telling you."

I want to settle and console her, but my thighs feel glued to my seat. "What is it, Mole?"

"He suffered a heart attack last night."

I drop the toast and interlace my quivering hands together beneath the blanket. "Where is he?" I ask. "How is he?"

Mole exhales. "He's in his room, resting. He won't be teaching for at least a week, I assure you, though the poor dear was mumbling about someone filling in his lesson plan. I gave him aspirin and nitroglycerin, and he stabilized. I think he'll be fine—it was a minor one, if anything, but enough to give us all a fright. It was a reminder that we need a proper medical team up here for this school to be fully functional one day. I'm unsuitable to handle all the house's needs. Oh, Jesus . . . And imagine if no one had found him in time? I shudder to think. Morency—of all people—found him, you know. It is a miracle. He was alone on the hill," she says. "By the funicular dock, shaking and soaking wet. He could have caught his death. It's the strangest turn of events. I can't quite wrap my head around it. He was half-clothed, and there were uprooted vines partially strangling the poor thing. Morency outright asked me if I thought he was suicidal, and I said no. What on earth could she be thinking? But I searched every corner of my mind for an explanation and found nothing—what exactly was the silly old dear attempting?" She nudges her drooping glasses up her nose.

She doesn't have a chance to continue, because Morency appears from nowhere in a flash of black. "Dr. Molina?" she says, scowling at the two of us. "I require your assistance upstairs at once."

With a heaving sigh, Mole shakily dabs at her temple and follows Morency out.

When class time arrives, the clouds have lifted the slightest bit, and I am surprised to find the girls huddled around the table, whispering like left-wing conspirators. They're coloring in elaborate get-well cards for Lamb, it looks like—using Diana's colored pencils and pens. It brings a smile to my face, until I notice the anomalies.

Sara has returned—she alone sits back in her chair, arms crossed, her face so translucently pale that it looks bruised. I should be glad to have her back, but my stomach churns, feeling her deep-set eyes bore into my back. Lord help me.

And there are only eight. There is no Michelle.

"Welcome back, Sara," I say as cheerily as I can muster, slotting my folder into the crook above my hip. "That's kind of you girls to write cards for Mr. Lamm. I know he'll appreciate them. But where is Michelle?"

"She's going to flip out," whispers Luciana, drawing a blue pencil across her card in broad strokes.

Silvina viciously zips her pencil case shut. "Favorite," she coughs as I secure my blanket-shawl around me. It's still freezing inside, and my stomach is a bundle of live wires.

205

"Miss," says Mariella, of course, standing up out of her seat with an impatient glance at the others, "Michelle isn't well."

"She's being a baby," hisses Silvina.

"She feels tired," adds Diana, folding her card in half. "And I don't think she's being a baby."

I set down my papers, noticing that the space heater has been turned off. "And where is she?"

"She's with Madame De Vaccaro and Ms. Morency and Dr. Molina in the sickroom." Mariella looks at Gisella, who sits gray-faced beside her. Michelle must have been the reason Morency called Mole upstairs. And the sickroom—the sickroom is new, it seems. I turn on the space heater with a faint click.

"How odd," I say evenly, passing out the exercises I've written up with trembling hands. "But class must go on. Seats, please."

Mariella settles, tugging on her braids, and Sara sighs and blows a raspberry.

"It's not odd. It's logical. It was only a matter of time before the rest of the girls got sick," Sara says, fixing me with a contemptuous look that spits, *You dumb bunny*. I keep my jaw from setting. It's as if she can read my worst thoughts. I've taught myself not to indulge my distaste toward her, but sometimes it's difficult to ignore the feeling that some children should not exist. I'm not sure what scares me about Sara. Every sentence she speaks seems menacing, every action rooted in some hidden, incomprehensible cruelty. "Illnesses travel in close quarters, and all that."

"Shut up," whispers Gisella under her breath, her hands bunching up. I watch her for a moment, grateful for her interruption, and find myself hoping the color will return to her unusually pasty face.

"Shut up?" Sara smiles without an ounce of warmth. "Oh, pretty Gisella, beautiful Gisella, *divine* Gisella," says Sara in a mocking sing-song, running her own stiff hands up her arms and her chest and her neck like a woman who has lost control of her body to a lascivious man. "I can't bear to keep quiet until you braid my hair like yours, in those luscious rows. All I want to feel is you touching my long, thick strands. I might just die if you don't satisfy me."

Silvina chokes out a laugh, but everyone else is stock-still, watching her. Gisella's mouth falls open. Some of Sara's words sound lustful; others, cold as ice.

"Oh," she continues, arching her back. "To feel your pretty little fingers separating them, stroking them, thumbing my naked scalp." I fight the impulse to retch as she trembles with overacted delight, lunging across Mariella's desk to snatch Gisella's arm with white fingers.

Gisella chokes and shudders away.

"Don't you want to? Touch and be touched? Oh, dear Gisella, won't you be my very, very, very special friend?"

"That's enough," I shout, snapping my fingers at Sara as Mariella shoves Sara's arm away from Gisella. "No more performances. There is no place for that kind of behavior here, Sara. Stop now. You may go to Madame De Vaccaro's office if you cannot comply."

She whispers unsavory words under her breath.

"Excuse me?" I say loudly, hoping that I'm not shaking. A horrific transformation has come over her. A girl who seemed only quietly off before seems entirely possessed.

She grins with uneven teeth so small they cannot be adult.

"Morency thinks it might have been a bad batch of fish that's leaving a few of us a bit tired and queasy," interrupts Mariella, covering Gisella's hand. "That's all it is. Enough nonsense."

"A bad *catch* of fish," says Diana, and Mariella throws her hands up.

We begin the lesson, but try as I might to engage them, they seem more preoccupied with their nonexistent manicures than the passage in the book. Sara can't even be bothered to open her copy, despite insistence on my part. "No redeeming qualities," she offers as her sole explanation. She crosses her arms at me, and I at her: She is resolute in her uncouthness and better off ignored, at least for today—at least until I regain my patience with her and lose that niggling fear.

When the time comes for Gisella to read a portion of a homework essay, she sways on her feet. "'Phoebe says she does not want to ride the carousel, at first, because she is too old. Holden knows she wants to ride it, so he . . .'" She licks her chapped lips with a thin, lethargic tongue. "'He buys her a ticket. The carousel runs even though it is winter, and . . .'" She drops the paper, and as it floats to the floor, she stares up at me abjectly. "I can't continue, Miss Quercia. I'm sorry."

Could she have been so adversely affected by Sara's pathetic show? "And what's wrong, Gisella?"

Mariella shoots to her feet defensively. "You can see she's not well, Miss Quercia. Can't I read in her place?"

I ignore her. "Gisella?"

"Sick to my stomach," she says, sitting down and laying her golden head on the desk. I watch her carefully, wary of falling for some kind of prank. I am not ignorant of the vulnerable fair-maiden act, after all. But the poor thing looks fairly ill, unless she's pulled the chalk-on-the-cheeks trick.

"Mariella, you will take Gisella to Dr. Molina after class," I say calmly.

Mariella fetches Gisella's paper from the ground. Mariella whispers into her ear, and for once, she looks quite somber. "No more little fishes for you," she says aloud.

Gisella looks as if she might groan. She manages the class, though, with her satiny head down, her reedy arms draped across the desk.

"I'll take these to Mr. Lamm, too," says Mariella, toting the stack of cards as she helps Gisella out at the end of the class. She's loyal, that one. Blooming into someone else in the time I've been here—

someone responsible and keen. If only all the girls had taken to their relative independence in the house this way.

Sara exits the classroom last, despite showing the most limited interest in my teachings. She slows by my back, coming so close I can't bear it. I can even smell her, this woodsy, musky scent, like the sweat of a full-grown man. She's whistling a tune that evokes the American Old West. She tugs the door shut, relishing every creak the unoiled hinges make. I glance in the door's direction as soon as it catches the frame, only to find her peering at me through the window, stone-faced. She salutes, and the same wicked smile stretches her pale lips.

After a solitary lunch of soggy lettuce tucked inside slips of ham and old bread, I visit Michelle in the sickroom, a free room in the family's quarters that has been converted to a cheerless, airless space with two cots, a crumpled burgundy rug, a lumpy taupe sofa, and a lone lamp. The air smells of sickness, of damp. Morency lets me squeeze by with an enormous frown, and Carmela rises from her seat beside Michelle and folds her slender arms with a similar glumness. Her nails haven't been freshly painted, and even her face is more bare than usual. She whispers with Morency so I take the opportunity to slip in next to Michelle. She lies in one of the cots with a wet charcoal rag on her forehead. "How are you feeling?" I ask, kneeling beside her and dabbing her with the filthy thing before casting it aside.

She burrows into her stained pillow. "I could sleep a hundred years," she says, curling onto her side so only a few centimeters remain between our faces. She looks half the size she was, a kidney bean, as if she's withering before me. "Have you figured out what's happening?"

"I'm still trying," I reply as softly as I can. "Can you tell me anything more?"

"When I'm awake, I feel this ice in my bones. It's easier to sleep, but I don't get any rest when I do. I—I go to this . . . place." She swallows, the slightest flush spreading across her cheeks, before locking eyes with me. "It shines like scales, and there are other people there. She's okay, Mavi," she whispers, a weak grin spreading across her face.

Cold fingers trace down my spine. "Who is okay?" I ask her.

But she doesn't answer, her eyes hazing over.

"We'll call your aunt to come get you," I say, covering her cool hand with mine. The thought of Michelle suffocating in an attic beside stacks of old canned legumes makes me sick. Still, she must be sent away, if the house is causing this. If Others are whatever Others might be.

Her eyes refocus. "I can't leave the school. You don't understand." She clenches her hand around mine, pricking my skin with her unclipped nails. "All I want to do is sleep. Please let me sleep."

She's a shell of a girl. I promise her that I will come every day to sit with her while I investigate what's happening. As I leave, I smooth her hair down at the part, the way she likes. But she's too exhausted to react.

I speak with Morency as I'm leaving, and Carmela returns to her spot beside Michelle's bed, plopping the rag on Michelle's forehead. "Ms. Morency," I whisper, "I was hoping I might stay with Michelle overnight and make sure she is comfortable." It's less a proposal than an entreaty.

The slit of her mouth pinches together before she speaks. Her eyes dart to Michelle and back to me. "That is wholly unnecessary. Madame De Vaccaro will remain with Michelle until she falls asleep. This is a common flu, Miss Quercia, not the bubonic plague."

My brow wrinkles.

"Sara recovered, as will Michelle," she says, folding her hands one way and then the other. "I will not furnish you with an opportunity to make mischief in the evenings."

"Mischief? What——?"

Her long nose scrunches. "The madame must not overhear a syllable of your prattle. I thought you might have learned to hold your tongue in her presence. Looseness of one's tongue leads to looseness of one's morals, Miss Quercia. Regardless—you mustn't leave your room after dark."

What is she worried about? The mischief I'll cause or the danger I'll face? These damned rules make no sense. "And why shouldn't we leave our rooms?" I ask, the pressure in my chest building. What does she know that she won't tell us? Has the girl warned her, too? Has she seen the dangerous ghostly Others in this house? Or does she have more malicious intentions? "Did something happen to Mrs. Hawk?"

Morency's eyes flash to Carmela as she crushes my wrist in hand. "Hush."

I rip my arm away. "Have you spoken to Michelle about what she believes is afflicting her?" Any secrets she knows will not remain undisclosed for long. Any and all information about the darkness of this house must be shared among its occupants. I think of Yesi; how I could use her self-assuredness now, how I could also use Dom's mollifying presence. Looking at Michelle, who lies wan and lost—far worse than Sara ever did—I wonder what more we can do. The girl suggested we flee; what can be done when that is not a simple course of action?

Morency cocks her head at me. "Out. Before——" Her mouth closes as Carmela glances at us.

I remain still, my gaze back on Michelle. "It's just that Madame——"

Carmela's head snaps back to us at the sound of her title, and Morency interrupts.

"How many times must I repeat myself? What exactly do you expect will happen to her at night, in the heavenly calm and quiet of the sickroom?" she asks me, her voice a growl as she physically maneuvers me out. When I turn back to object, she slams the wooden door a centimeter from my chapped nose.

As I storm away, I hear screams of laughter in the hall. I loop around to find the source and encounter Luciana around a bend, her own nose a centimeter from the bare wall, her fragile shoulders rocking hard.

"Luciana?" I ask, rushing to her.

Her grotesque mask of a face turns to me, tears spilling from her glossy eyes, and she shrieks with laughter, an all-consuming laughter that shakes her body with a violence that looks painful. She raises a shaking hand, pointer finger hyperextended at the joints, and gestures at the blank wall before her.

I lean in, and I see nothing at all. Perhaps a speck of mold.

"Are you all right?" I take her by the shoulders, and she wrests herself away, still hysterical as a hyena.

She wipes at her eyes roughly, ripping out eyelashes yet laughing still, and races down the hall. I gape at her disappearing form, wondering what on earth has gotten into the girl and why it chills me so.

A break. I need a break after the madness I've witnessed inside and outside the sickroom.

I miss my meeting with Dom, remembering my promise to Yesi, and find her on the patio for teatime. The kitchen staff sentries have gone, and despite the frigidness of the day, she thinks it's pleasant enough to take the air for a short while. She hums to herself with a cup of tea and a draft of her novel in hand.

"How goes it?" I ask, motioning at her manuscript. I've never glimpsed it, I'm sorry to admit. When I asked to read it, Yesi told me that it would hurt her feelings too much if I started it and didn't finish it, so she'd rather not share it, which I found to be an altogether disappointing reason.

She shrugs, setting it down and stroking the cover with dreamy eyes as I approach with my plate.

"Awful, what happened to Lamb," I say.

"Odd," she admits. "But Moley says he'll recover."

I nod once. "I'm more worried about the girls, to be honest. Michelle's taken such a turn," I whisper before lifting a piece of pistachio pound cake with my gloved hand and taking a bite.

She stares into the swirling tea leaves in her cup. "Michelle, Michelle, Michelle. I have to say that you didn't show nearly as much concern when Sara was ill. You're letting your unusual attachment to Michelle get the best of you. And my, how *boring* that girl and her common cold both are."

I stare at her, mouth full of crumbs. "Thank you for the psychoanalysis, doctor, but—"

Our table rattles, and Yesi snaps to look up; it's only Mole coming through the patio door. I beckon her over, as this is the first chance I've had to speak with her since the morning, but she ignores my summons. She sits at a table away from us and nods wearily at me before cracking open a book and nibbling on some pound cake. For once, she looks uneager to gossip, hunched into her coat. I don't blame her.

"Mavi," says Yesi in a low and measured tone, so that Mole cannot overhear over the wind, "I'm worried about you. You're plainly looking for someone to lap up every half-baked theory you spout— someone who will take up a pitchfork with you at a moment's notice. Well, I won't provide the same warm little comforts as Domenico. I'm sure he held you close as he mirrored your every opinion, but—"

"Oh, shush. I didn't even see him to—"

"He couldn't possibly have one bad intention, could he? With an

213

angel's face like *that*?" she says, her voice rising. "Tell me, just how many fingers does he have stuck up inside of you at any given time? And I do mean that in the puppeteering sense, though I'm very fond of the lurid alternative." She takes a prim sip of tea, eyes piercing me.

I feel punched in the gut hearing this after staying true to my word. "Moley?" I call out, rapidly swiveling away from Yesi in my chair, its legs grinding against the stone floor. "How is Lamb doing? When can we visit him?"

Mole sighs, lifts herself out of her seat, and edges over to sit at our table with her plate. "Well, Mavi dear, I'm so impressed by his progress. You can go see him whenever you'd like—I think your company would cheer him up quite a bit. He has no memory of last night, I'm afraid, but he's in good spirits. To be frank, I'm more concerned by certain complaints made by the girls."

"What?" I feel the pleasant burn of affirmation, especially welcome in front of Yesi. "What do you mean?"

Mole's pupils dart behind her glasses. "I saw Gisella privately, in her room, after you sent her to me," she says carefully, cutting into the dried-out crumb with a measured look at us. "Because of her aches and light fever, I was immediately convinced that she was in the early stages of the same strain of influenza Michelle suffers from. It's highly treatable on-site." I feel Yesi's gaze of superiority settle on me as Mole continues. "I was going to have her sleep in the sickroom tomorrow if her condition worsened. But then she pulled me close." She deposits her fork on the plate without taking a bite. "She told me that men . . . that men come to her in the night and . . . touch her. That they give her the illness."

I clutch my stomach, and Yesi pales. Men sounds so much worse than *them*; it humanizes these evildoers, lends a perverse and pedophilic dimension to it all. "Men come to her? She didn't say whom?"

Molina shakes her head and breaks apart a clump of cake with her fingers, which are blue with cold. "She said she couldn't tell. But before you get yourselves into a tizzy, here's the rub. She said they weren't real men—they were ghost men, ghost men the size of three men combined, like the demon in the ballroom mural, come to punish her for thinking unclean thoughts." She brushes off her fingers, pauses. "And Michelle, well, as you both know, Michelle complained yesterday of a lack of restful sleep. And she made a mention of visitors today, too, before Gisella did. It intrigues me that one girl should be afflicted by these delusions, only for a second girl to share them and expand upon them the following day, all the while living in the same dormitory. Now, I'm no psychologist, but it seems as if we're now facing a bout of hysteria brought on by the influenza." Mole picks up her fork once more. "And when considered in tandem with Mr. Lamm's strange heart attack . . . well . . ."

I pause. "Mole . . . are you suggesting Lamb was involved in the girls' . . . claim?"

The color drains from her face. "Oh, no, Mavi. Not at all. No, no—as a five, Mr. Lamm is careless at times, even irresponsible, but I wouldn't think him capable of hurting a child in a thousand years, and I do not believe the girls are victims of abuse in general. You misunderstood me. Every man here has been vetted by Carmela herself. In all likelihood, the girls were rattled by Mrs. Hawk's departure and Mr. Lamm's attack, and perhaps they've invented this story to cope with their stress."

I set down the cup I've been cradling—the tea inside has long lost its heat. "But there's no reason for little girls their age to lie about this."

"Oh, my dear," says Molina. "That is beside the point, though of course there is. These little girls are practically ignored at home. The school is, in a sense, their stage."

"You can't possibly believe they would invent a story this

outrageous for the sake of gaining attention," I say, picking up my cool cup again with tremulous hands.

Mole sips some tea without answering, and I stare out at the blank slate of ice, ominous and sickly green at this moment. I swear it looms higher than usual, and it feels like some gigantic god has turned its pallid cheek to us here on this rock. "I don't know," replies Mole.

I lean on my elbows. "Shouldn't the sick girls be sent home before whatever is happening gets worse?"

"Well, now that you—" Mole's eyes bulge, and she dips toward her plate, her hands rushing to her throat as if she's choking. She wheezes; she can't take in any air—it's plain as day. But she hasn't taken a bite of cake. Is it the wind? Or the cold, closing her throat and bringing on a form of asthma? Her eyeballs swell, as if they could pop.

Yesi and I rush to help, and my hands encircle her brittle torso when she self-corrects and straightens. Cracking her neck, bone by bone. My hands snap away from her shoulders, which feel so warm beneath my fingertips now. And she turns, inspecting me with chilly disdain—an unfamiliar, confident expression I've never seen on her at all.

"No need to blow this out of proportion," she says in a monotone so unlike her normal register. "The girls will move past their delusions if they are handled carefully, and their flu symptoms will pass with time, as Sara's did." She sets a hand on my wrist like a manacle, her skin searingly hot. "God forbid Carmela has to send home students during the first triumphant semester back at this place—that would ruin the school for the rest of time. She'll bring in a city doctor now. A psychiatrist, too, to address the girls' fears. And I'm sure she's called their parents. Framing the situation more lightly, of course, but . . ." She shrugs with a smug and distant look on her face and releases my hand. I'm left with a welt the size of a fat roach. "The stupid little bitch," she mutters to herself, pushing back her chair with a discordant scrape, abandoning her plate on the table, and strutting inside.

I stare openmouthed at her back, but Yesi looks only a touch dazed and bewildered.

"Mole's right," she says to me, crossing her arms haughtily. "The girls will survive. Now stop blathering on before you upset them even more."

I stamp back through the stone hallway, furious that showing concern for the girls has earned me only contempt from high priestess Yesi. I feel it: Even though I've tried to follow the house's absurd rules, it is rotting around me, poisoning the bonds within and making me feel rootless once more. The tenth girl's advice floods my mind, sweet and acid-edged: I can still leave this place behind. The city might not be safe, but I can reinvent myself elsewhere.

I toy with the tempting idea of escape as I simmer alone throughout dinner, swallowing soggy string beans and bland humps of beef that seem a lifetime away from the delectable feasts we once enjoyed. It should come as no surprise that Yesi and I don't speak once, but I do listen idly as the girls chatter.

Gisella joins the table for dessert, still pale, yet relishing her plate of flan with a new book in her lap. She's wrapped in a large coat, her hair released from its braids in gorgeous curls. I'm so unexpectedly relieved by her return that I can't help but smile at her, and she waves at me, brightening—and dare I say, with that gesture, my instinct to flee begins to settle into a manageable impulse. The adult in me is willing to admit that not every relationship I have in this house is withering.

As we wrap up the meal, Dom grins at me from the end of the table—all warmth and earnestness. I look away—concerned Yesi will spot me eyeing the dark prince as she sparkles over her pot of custard next to me. But then I remember words she once said to me: *If you can survive living in a haunted house . . . you can come to know all the oddest little nooks in yourself.*

Perhaps I was wrong to promise the high priestess I would stay away from Dom. She of all people knows there are many hidden nooks in a person, most of them obscured from view. She doesn't know him, so she cannot know that he does not mirror my every thought, as she claimed. No—his hidden kindness has simply unlocked forgotten doors inside me, surprising the both of us with what lies behind them. When I have shown him those dark corners of myself, he views me not with Yesi's derision but with an inexplicable wonder, like I'm a creature too complex to understand but too special for him not to accept any bit of me offered forth, with gratitude.

No, not all my bonds in this place have been poisoned.

I catch Dom's eyes and smile back at him.

One thing is clear: I cannot leave this godless rock just yet.

16

ANGEL: 2020-1600

Before the house dinner, I find Charon in his cloud cottage, thumbing glumly through a blank cloud book.

"It's you," he says, hardly glancing up. "My fair-weather friend. Do you only talk to me when you want to pump me for info? Or do you need help bending your morals today? Or perhaps you'd like me to massage your conscience like a good little geisha?"

"I know you saw her," I say, ignoring him. "You must have seen her. The tenth little girl. Just now. She dove out of the window." Bored, he continues paging through the book. "She's about the same age as the others, but she's wearing this white gown. She's got black hair, and—"

"Are you cracked, kid?" he asks. "You couldn't have seen a tenth little girl. You're losing it."

"I saw her, and she exists. As much as you or I exist. You yourself told me she hid here! And Mavi's seen her—"

"Oh, so that's what you need help justifying today—screwing someone in the house with your Ken doll dick."

Like a hot Japanese blade through pig fat.

"Screw you, Charon."

He tsks me. "Everyone has their motivations, fears, and desires, but Jesus, yours are a trip. You're wasting your goddamned time messing with that little English teacher."

"I'm not messing with her. We're friends."

"*Friends.* Stop it, kid. Don't be a goddamned fool. You know how this works. Don't make me lay it out for you. She's supposed to fall in love with the son. Get her heart broken. Funnel it into her teaching and become a bitter-ass bitch. She's just that kind of girl. You know girls like her. We all know girls like her. You're not special. She's not connecting with you because you're different. She thinks you're someone you're not. She'll never meet the real you. She'll never know the real you. Got it?"

"That's not true." I fight the tremors overwhelming me. She did miss our last meeting. "You're lying to me. Again. Just like you lied about feeding not hurting them." He scoffs, frowns, wags his open book in the air—the curmudgeonly old man scattering pigeons. "Just like you lie about not knowing anything else about the tenth girl," I continue. "Just like you lie about who knows what else."

"You presumptuous little fuck," he says, snapping the book shut so that it evaporates. "I'm not lying now, for your goddamn record, but that doesn't mean I have any responsibility to tell you the truth. Just like you don't have any responsibility to tell *her* the truth." He smirks. "Friends forever, right?"

I don't reply.

"Let me guess: You keep her around because you want her to one day absolve you of what you've done, over a heartfelt little conversation with two cups of tea in front of a crackling fire." He wiggles his fingers, imitating the flames and sending an involuntary chill through me, as I wonder how much he's seen and how much he knows. "But no one in the house will absolve you. No one in the world can absolve you, alive or dead. We carry what we've done forever. And any darkness inside you stemming from those choices is yours and yours alone, until the end of time. Don't foist it on anyone else. Learn to live with it. Ride the tides of darkness."

He's wrong—he has to be wrong. I'm not trying to rope some poor sucker into sharing the burden of darkness inside me. How could I be if I haven't even told Mavi who I am? If I haven't told her about Mama, about Rob? If I haven't told her about what I've done?

"Piss off, Charon," I say, but I'm the one who storms out of the cloud house as he sits snugly in his seat.

When I drift back to the house in time to pick up Dom for dinner, I'm the one who's gutted—I'm the one who's pulled under by the swell of black below the floating crust of cloud.

Mavi stares into her plate at dinner, twirling strands of hair between her fingers. I hate myself for it, but there's no stopping the flood of relief and reassurance I feel in seeing her again. I periodically half wave to catch her eye, but try as I might, I can't transmit any kind of message across her wall of chestnut hair, not from my chair of honor next to Carmela (who fingers her steak knife as if she's going to wedge it between my knuckles if I so much as breathe too loud). I finally catch her smiling at me as Dr. Molina rises to lead everyone to their rooms.

Mavi strays at the back of the group. I follow her, waiting for a lively uptick in the staff discussion about butchering methods, and I pull her into a sitting room at random. She falls into me.

"This wasn't your brightest idea," she says, face flushed, craning her neck in the direction of the fading chatter.

"Desperate times," I say as I shut the wooden door behind us. "Where have you been?"

She presses herself against the splotchy silk wall. "With the girls. People have been dropping right and left."

I stare back at her blankly, and she looks at me as if I've had a lobotomy. "Mrs. Hawk, of course "—speaking of lobotomies—"and Lamb's heart attack, Michelle and Gisella . . ."

We hear some muted whispering behind the door, and her eyes tear away from me, fearful.

"Don't worry," I say, gripping the knob. "They can't hear us."

She tucks her long hair behind her ears. "You've witnessed Morency's Olympic hearing. Second only to her wrath. And did you forget that mixed-gender discussions lead to artificial insemination and death in this house?" she says, and though I know she means it as a joke, there isn't a hint of humor left in her voice.

"Listen," I say. "I saw her. The tenth little girl. The girl from your waking nightmare. She came to my room when she thought I was napping earlier."

Her posture stiffens. "You're kidding."

"Long black hair, wearing a stained gown?"

Her fingers fly to her throat. "What did she say to you?"

I rub my hands together, shaping my thoughts into words—why hadn't I considered exactly what to say earlier? It's an opportunity to help her, to be useful by injecting any little tidbit I can, but I'm tongue-tied. "She told me to look out for the girls," I say. "She told me they are visited at night by spirits."

Mavi takes my forearm with her hand and grips it hard. Dom's skin blazes under her touch, a sensation so intense that I am convinced it's my own skin. "What else?"

"Nothing else," I say awkwardly. I can't exactly reveal the girl's sole pronouncement—*she ran off because I'm an evil remnant, Mav.*

"I can't believe she came to you, too," she whispers back. "They're here, then. The *Others*. Michelle told me that she feels as if she's being watched. Harassed while she sleeps."

Michelle must have it worst of all now. I remember that she's Mavi's pet: the round-faced, shy one, with kind and calm green eyes. My brow wrinkles.

"And now Gisella's on about the same—*men* touching her, Dom. It's sick. Obviously, at first, I thought about abuse, but I can't picture anyone here committing such an atrocity." Her jaw sets. "I'm done hypothesizing. I'm going to sneak over to the girls' rooms tonight—I have it on good authority from Mole that your mother and Morency will be gone by midnight. They've been gone by then every evening with Sara." She looks up at me, eyes raw and red. "We need to solve this, Dom. Not only for the sake of the girls, but—" She stops, nibbles hard on her wine-colored lip. "You should know something. I can't just leave this place."

I clear my throat. "What?"

"I can't go back to Buenos Aires."

I stare at her in silence.

"My mother was arrested by the military government," she whispers, biting a fingernail.

I know this, of course, but I let sympathy wash over my eyes. I pull her deeper into the sitting room, and I reply evenly and without judgment. "What happened?"

And to my surprise, she tells me, in hushed tones.

They arrived before dinner: three men in suits and a woman who smiled at me with teeth as rectangular and perfect as Carmela's when I answered the apartment door. I had been reading Austen—forced upon me by my mother until I learned to love her—on the worn sofa in our living room. I was meant to be in the kitchen, helping my mother cook dinner. Being a good daughter, as far as I knew what that is.

"Is your mother in?" the woman asked, pressing on the door with a scrape of her nails. Her hair was too shiny to be real, as were her teeth. I could hear my mother's criticism in my head: Why would people buy fake versions of these body parts unless they wanted to hide themselves to a terrifying degree?

I hesitated to answer her. It wasn't that strangers rarely came by the apartment—they did—but they rarely came by in polished, polite groups who deigned to inquire if Mother was home. I felt a painful burst deep in my gut. "No," I said, standing taller. She still towered over me.

"We know she's here, Margarita Victoria, and we'll come inside either way," the woman said with a smile that cut. Unendurable pressure built inside my head as I heard faint frying noises from the kitchen. "It's time. Why don't you let her know?"

My ears popped. It wasn't time. It wasn't time. It was never time. I trudged inside, not feeling my legs, only their eyes on my back. In the kitchen, my mother was coating chicken cutlets in bread crumbs to fry while humming to herself. This I could have told you even without seeing her. Milanesas, my favorite meal as a child. I could smell the oil heating in the pan.

"Who is it, mi amor?"

"Three men and a woman," I whispered. "In suits."

I will never forget how the blood drained from her face. I might have been the last person to witness her in the full bloom of health before that moment. For all her shows of strength and defiance, for all the times she'd hosted those she called "cousins" mere paces from my bed, she still feared the military setting foot in the space she shared with me.

"Did you speak to them?" she asked.

In my silence, she had her answer. She wrapped her fingers around my shoulders.

"Mavi, what did they say to you?"

"They know you're here," I said, panic working its nailed grip to my throat. "They know." My eyes filled with tears, acidic and hot.

"They were civilized," she said, as if that were some consolation. "Go now. Go to your abuela*'s cupboard closet." It had a false back, this cupboard closet, which led to an enormous hidden room in an adjacent apartment my mother had acquired in secret. The cousins' room. My* abuela *was a hoarder, my mother said, and she kept piles of mildewed clothing and newspapers there until my* abuelo *noticed and snuck the piles out at midnight, blaming hungry rats the next morning.*

"The cupboard?" I asked my mother in confirmation. "They'll find me."

She took me by the hand—or, that tender notch between palm and wrist—and held it firm. When I was on the cusp of adolescence, we'd rehearsed a routine many nights having to do with this cupboard, the same cupboard the guerrillas hid inside. She told me that if she ever instructed me to hide there, I was to stay inside the closet for three hours after hearing no one. I was to proceed to my godmother's apartment, taking the bus and speaking to no one. I had giggled at this at the time because she treated it half as motherly law and half as a zany game she had invented.

But in that moment, I was angry and terrified that this had come to pass.

"I am yours," Mother whispered to me in that kitchen, holding me against her and reading my scalp with her fingers as if to memorize the feel of my head. As if that would be a consolation to us both. "You are mine. The color cannot be stripped out of us." She kissed me firmly on the forehead, so firmly I felt her chapped lips might be imprinted there forever. I ran to the cupboard and locked myself inside, pushing aside a forgotten

bundle of newspapers. Confused, terrified. Counting seconds in my head at a breakneck pace. I didn't hear anything happen. I thought she must have evaporated. I don't think they hurt her, at least not there. Not inside our building, where the neighbors might have heard or seen.

Some part of me knew those were the last words she would ever speak to me. I was not a fool, even if I hoped and prayed every day that I might be wrong. I couldn't make sense of her words for a long time; any other parent facing this situation might have said, I love you or Be strong, or some pale and desperate version of the two, poeticism—or should I say creativity alone—failing them in a time of unspeakable horror, which isn't to say the standard powerful words fall flat in such a moment. What I mean to suggest is that she'd had the time or the foresight to rehearse final words. That was more difficult to forget.

How furious I was. At her, for the thoughtless risks she took, thinking them noble and high-minded. At them, for their brutality and lack of humanity and understanding for their people. At myself, for shutting myself away when she spoke to those cousins. For failing to act, but more so, for failing to educate myself, so that I could better understand what kinds of action deserved to be taken.

I am yours. You are mine. The color cannot be stripped out of us.

How enraged I was, too, that she spoke of color being stripped from us by them, when she had allowed the color to be stripped from herself and her countrymen long ago, deciding what was black and what was white. All in an effort to be strong.

I waited for a long time in the cupboard, shivering and crying some minutes, incandescent with rage others, as silently as I could bear. This required the repetitive slamming and mashing of my good-for-nothing face with my obedient, soldierly hands. She hadn't turned off the stove, oddly, and the oil bubbled and burned, adding to my panic. I could smell the scorching from the cupboard. It was a wonder it didn't burn the apart-

226

ment building down. When I was about to leave the cupboard—certain that hours had passed, my bladder full to bursting—I heard footsteps and tensed up.

"Margarita Victoria," called the woman. Crisp and unapologetic, unruffled and fully justified. "Margarita Victoria, you shouldn't be here," she said. "Come out. We're here to help you. We're here to protect you." I didn't say anything. I was raised to have faith in strangers but never the government. I can't know what they would've done to me. Hopefully, I will never know. "Your mother was not who she said she was. She was a spy against the state. A guerrilla agent."

At the time, I clamped my teeth down on my tongue, despite recognizing the truth in her words. My mother was no spy, but she did resist oppression in the ways a professor could. She stuck fast to her principles.

All I wanted was to step out of the cupboard and beg her to reconsider. I would have told her that my mother was a teacher. Too passionate, surely, and a single mother, which might have been a shameful stain on a Catholic society, but she managed the role of two parents well enough for me. I noticed that I didn't have a father far less than I should have. She was the best cook of milanesas and best inventor of bedtime stories, a distinction quite separate from reader. She smelled of backyard honeysuckle and milk and tried to treat others with kindness. She believed she could bring out the best in every soul, even if it wasn't that soul's impression of its best, and she would do so even for this woman's blackened and hardened one. But I bit my tongue, too sane to believe she was telling the truth, too afraid to disobey my mother, and waited until the woman left. I relieved myself in the corner, terrified the trickling sound would call them back out, and swallowed my own saliva until my mouth felt as dry as cotton. I crept out of the cupboard a good day later. I saw the charred pan on the stove, no longer burning. Even a monster had its limits, I wanted to believe, and that woman had spared me and my neighbors by shutting off the gas flame.

I gathered a few possessions. Too few, in retrospect. And then I climbed aboard the bus to my godmother's house.

When she finishes, her face is as pale as snow.

I'm speechless. I tell myself what I feel is sympathy. Pity. But it hits me all at once, in a brain-melting surge, that what I am is awestruck. By her confidence in her vulnerability. By her truthfulness and directness. By her kindness, even now, in a universe where kindness is too often a footnote in a forgotten book in an abandoned library. By her ancientness and her freshness, all at once. It doesn't make sense that I should find a person like this now. Here.

"I know it's a lot to take in. But I'm tired of following rules that don't make sense, and I couldn't conceal my past from you anymore," she says. "Do you—do you think hiding here makes me a coward?"

My palms are slick with sweat. How can I possibly answer that question? If she faced certain kidnapping and likely death by staying in the city, how could I tell her she had been wrong to flee, even if fleeing meant abandoning her mother's fight?

"No. You have so much courage. You made it here alone." My heart aches. "And you're so young. The young, the curious, we . . . we need to stay alive and learn everything we can. So when we're older, we can fight smarter, together."

I realize how much of a hypocrite this statement makes me: We need to stay alive? Really, Angel? But speaking the words to her makes me believe them. Fun fact: The heart can pump us full of mind-altering poisons forever. Even when we've done absolutely everything in our power to kill it.

She looks at me strangely, then, her eyes glowing with sadness.

"Thank you," she whispers.

"And I'll be by your side tonight," I say, because no other words will do.

She reaches for my hand, her fingers brushing the veins pulsing on top of the bones. "You're one of the good ones, Dom."

Sometimes I wonder if she felt she knew Dom at all before me. If she did, she must have noticed a difference. She must have noticed more than just snatches of my influence, more than the edges of my soul. She must wonder what happened to him. Because I'm not as good an actor as I'd like to believe.

But I don't ask her if she wonders any of this. I just smile, eyes wrinkling.

You're not special, I hear Charon say. *She's not connecting with you because you're different. She thinks you're someone you're not. She'll never meet the real you. She'll never know the real you.*

But even if that's true, I can't ignore this new desire in me, a desire rooted deep, deep down in my spongy rotten core. A desire I can't identify at first. It's a cousin of that searing curiosity—of that unquenchable thirst to learn more about her.

It's a desire never to betray this person, and recognizing it sends a tremor of acid-edged fear through me. Because I already have, time and time again.

17

MAVI: ARGENTINA, JUNE 1978

I confess: In the royal-purple room, I bare myself, weaving for Dom the gloomy tale that roots me. Somehow—*somehow*—I leave feeling as if I, the impoverished orphan Mavi Quercia, could carry and re-shape the entire broken world, when perhaps a wiser woman would feel vulnerable and more than a touch afraid. But the truth holds: Though I may wonder why Dom changed, I no longer question who he is now, not at all. This Dom is good, no matter what secrets the hidden nooks in him contain.

Even so: I can't reconcile the confidence I feel around Dom, his oversize hands warm gloves around mine, with the inexplicable help-lessness I feel when thinking about these unknowable spirits haunting the girls. How can I kill worry without also murdering that precious tenderness I feel? I think they stem from the same part of my overactive brain. I need a noble distraction until the late evening. So before I return to my room, I deviate from the prescribed and lawful path to check on poor old Lamb.

I knock on his door once, hearing a muffled noise from the inside. *Come in*, it might've been. I push inside and find him wearing a voluminous taupe sweater and pants, seated in a plush cloth chair. His forest-green room is blessed by two of these chairs, plus a narrow bookshelf, as well as a cocktail-size table crowned by a few glasses. He reads a mathematics journal by the look of the boring, numeral-filled cover, and he perks up when he sees me.

"Miss Mavi?" he asks, setting down the journal. All-white eyelashes fringe his eyes like snowflakes. "You've caught me up when I should be resting in bed. Dr. Molina will be none too pleased. Oh, but it is a pleasure to see you!"

I can't help but smile. He looks well—full-faced, only a shade greener than usual.

"How are you feeling, Lamby?" I ask.

He smiles warmly. "Much better, my dear. It's so kind of you to visit—and the girls, the girls, too. They brought me sweet alfajores with dulce de leche and warm tea!" He motions at an empty mug, eyes bright. "I had a bit of a scare, that's all. You know the elderly and their health—nothing to be done about it but keep a good attitude. And I am much improved." He gestures to the matching tufted chair opposite his. "Please make yourself comfortable, won't you? I must be a good host. Ah—wait. I've just the thing." He stands, his back cracking, and pulls a book from the shelf titled *The Blind Widow Weeps*. "I have a delicious treat for you."

I sit, settling into the cushioning. "A novel?"

"Not quite," he says, chuckling. With quivering fingers, he wiggles a yellow-labeled bottle of brandy out from behind the book: a secret stash. His eyes sparkle when he faces me. "Have a tipple for me? A bit of sobremesa. It will calm my own nerves to smell the stuff. But Dr. Molina's strictly prohibited me from drinking it, naturally."

"Oh, I don't know." It would take the edge off the evening, but I glance at the door, wary, and he notices, chuckling again.

"I know what you're thinking, Miss Mavi. But I've never been caught before, and we shan't be caught now. If anything were to happen, anyway, we would blame my influence."

He pours me an amber glass on the antique, dusted-over table in the corner, and I sip the brandy, out of curiosity more than anything else. It's punchier than I would've thought, tasting of dried apricot, lip-smacking plum, and cinnamon. Delicious indeed.

Sitting once more, he clears his throat and moves his long fingers along the journal edge. "Now. I must ask, while I have you here— how are Michelle and Gisella? Dr. Molina suggested there was a bug going around. I'm concerned they haven't had her full attention on account of me."

I run a fingertip along the glass's edge. My head feels heavier after my second sip—a pleasant weight. "Oh, Lamby. Don't even think of it. The girls will be fine. They have to be," I say, sounding hollow as ever—and possibly tipsy, which is near impossible. He watches me intently, urging me along in silence. And I speak, explaining the girls' conditions as I run my hands across the chair's seams. It doesn't make sense to unload on poor Lamb, but something spins inside my weighted head already—perhaps it's the root of my tongue, feeling light as air.

He closes his journal. "This is serious indeed. Do you have any theories as to what is causing the disturbance?"

I look toward the door and drop my voice to a whisper. "Spirits?" Could it be the first time I've spoken the word aloud as a serious possibility? A blush creeps across my cheeks.

"Oh dear. Ghosts," he whispers. "Victims of the virus, you mean?"

I want to take him by the shoulders and shake him. *It's not a virus*, I want to shout. "Not really, no."

He smiles. "Yes, I, too, believe that Madame De Vaccaro likes to whitewash history," he says unexpectedly. "She knows more about this school than you might think. I overheard her telling Sara odd details about the Vaccaro School's sordid history when the girl was ill, and I was surprised, to say the least." I look up, surprise of my own cutting through my tipsiness. But he doesn't catch my eye. "Should we make contact with these ghosts? Ask if they're incensed Zapuche or irate De Vaccaros?"

I fail to read his expression. "You're teasing me, Lamb."

"Oh, Mavi, dear, I am no godlike figure who understands why one being should exist and not another," he says, watching me carefully. I must shiver, because sympathy floods his eyes, and he moves to tap my hand. "Ghosts or not, you mustn't be afraid of what's to come, my dear. We mustn't try to kill fear in its bed. We must shake its hand, as it is a noble adversary, and inform it that we have a long list of tasks to accomplish, and it may try its best to stop us, but we plan on accomplishing them all."

I exhale, willing myself to take his words to heart and calm down. I swirl the brandy in the glass. It coats the edges and melts beautifully along the curved sides. "You're truly enlightened, Lamb. An underfed, overfurred Buddha."

He chuckles to himself and tops off my brandy, only to regale me with one story, then another, then another, culled from some strange part of his memory, interspersed with the occasional math-related joke, as no evening with Lamb would be complete without that oddity; my worries dissolve, and I myself melt into his chair, the glass of brandy nestled in my lap. He nudges me awake some time later, and all I remember is stumbling to my feet, but I arrive at my room without being detected, sleepy and warm, dipped into that misleading, milky limbo between reality and dreams, where nothing truly seems to matter to us, yet we are closest to the black abyss running parallel to our world.

When I wake, parched and gasping for water, it's after midnight. I'm late to meet Dom, still dressed in my day clothes. I tug on my coat and slip out the door, shivering. The hallway is so deathly silent, the sort of quiet that makes your pulse throb in your ears. Not a sliver of gray moonlight ekes past the autumn grime on the skylights, and dust chokes the air, so that my breaths come in ragged. My mouth feels lined in soot. I tiptoe down the hallway, past Morency's room, down the broken staff staircase, expertly navigating around the missing steps. I turn right into the stone corridor leading to the family's quarters, down a long stretch, hearing the discordant and melancholic grinding of an appliance somewhere, and I climb up to the door of Domenico's blue room, noiseless as a mouse. I knock once. I wait, breathless. My blood cools in my veins.

Footsteps patter against the floorboards in another area of the family branch—perhaps Carmela returning from seeing Michelle. I wait, hunching against the wall unconsciously to make myself smaller. The creaking of a door somewhere. Shallow breaths—my own? I rub at my arms as furiously as the silence allows, fighting a building chill. I knock a second time.

Are the spirits here right now, watching me? I find myself thinking about snippets from my conversation with Lamb: Who are these ghosts, exactly, and where do they come from? Does everyone pass through this forsaken place as they cross over? I think of the many who have disappeared in the past few years. I place one palm against the wall beside Dom's door—if the walls could only talk.

I'm about to try the doorknob when it rattles. I fall back on my heels, and the door opens, exposing a slender, looming shadow.

Thank the Lord. It's him. Dom. Smiling, his blue eyes sharp when hit by a patch of rare moonlight. Every time I am with him I am surprised by how concrete and alive he feels next to me—so much more than anyone else in this strange place.

"Ready?" he asks, his voice more of a tired croak. He holds a hand to his throat. The skin there is raw. "Let's go."

I fight the impulse to take him by the arm, as I do Yesi. He leads the way down the dark hallway, past his room, loose-limbed. I'm shivering, and even with him in front of me, the panic threatens to return, nestling itself into my throat. The hallway narrows, curves. I thought the sickroom was next door to his. I thought we were steps away, but I must have been mistaken. The carpet is wet here, squelching beneath my shoes, but soaked through by what? There are no windows, no skylights. The air asphyxiates with its noxious thickness.

But at last, we arrive in front of the sickroom, and I struggle for breath before pressing open the door. Everything is still. The room, lit by a bay window overlooking the ice, glows. When the clouds part, the ice takes on a phosphorescent quality at night. I spot one familiar lump in bed, rising and falling. It's ominous how rhythmic the movement is. I sweep back the sheet, arm unfeeling: Michelle's sleeping, sandwiched beneath the covers. She smiles in her sleep, cheeks the color of iced-over greenery in the moonlight.

"She looks fine," I whisper, shaking my head. "She looks absolutely fine." And if Gisella isn't here, it means she was well enough to sleep in her own room after her brief reappearance at dessert.

"You're right to worry, though," Dom whispers back, rubbing his hands together.

In the moonlight, Dom's face looks ghostly and melancholy, the skin nearly transparent. Squinting, I think I can see the veins carrying life through him. I'm struck by how strange bodies are as shells for souls. How peculiar it is that memory funnels your love for someone in the quirks of their body. I feel I love my mother in the wide and proud smile her flat face made, in her solid hands and delicate, over-long fingernails. But these features mean nothing at all at the end of days, besides being private totems of that love. I sit beside Michelle, who doesn't stir. I see the Falcone girl's face on her, recriminating me, and I wonder again what kind of manipulation this is on the part of the universe.

My hand hovers by her cheek, as if I can gather some clue about the quality of her sleep—is it healing? I'll feel terrible if I wake her during her first hours of good sleep in days, if not weeks. We wait, and we wait, but nothing changes in the room, nothing changes for her, her wide and catlike smile. I feel a bit dumb in the head, a bit disappointed, if that word can be used to describe missing something you fear seeing so much. I'd expected a confrontation. I'd expected evidence . . . I'd expected my own fear to surge up.

Dom comes up behind me. "Maybe they're leaving her alone to-night," he says, breaking off. We ignore the implication—that *they* have moved on to someone else.

We wait there longer than we should. Michelle doesn't stir once, her breathing soft and steady. I sit beside Dom on the floorboards by the door. His fingers brush mine, and they're warmer than average, febrile. Closing my eyes, it's as if I can see a warm and golden light emerge from the pores of Domenico's transparent skin. I shudder as it suffuses my fingers through Domenico's, seeking, hoping, healing.

After I adjust Michelle's blankets, we leave the room. Outside the door, I look down the shaded and damp hall. It's a long way to the girls' rooms.

"Should we check on the others?" I ask, struggling to swallow. "We better check on the others."

Dom looks at me, eyes dark and unreadable. I hear the creaking sound once more—emanating from somewhere in the walls. It's the sound of someone unwelcome opening a splintered screen door.

"Better not," Dom says, head following the noises. "Wait here." He turns a corner, and I'm left alone.

"Wait," I whisper, pulling down my sleeves to cover my bare hands. "Wait!"

His footsteps fade. I rub my hands together through the canvas-cotton, gray in the dark. I don't want to be left behind. The hall looks so different at night—hostile and shadowed. A draft ruffles the hairs at the base of my neck, and I startle.

I peek around the corner and don't see him. Don't see him, because there are more bends, more curves, as if this is an organic structure, the gut of a centipede. I run forward, stumbling on my feet. How is it that I am still feeling the brandy in my veins hours later? I'm so sluggish, yet so chilled.

"Wait," I whisper with more urgency. The hallway is too dark and narrow, compressing me. I hurl myself into a bend, but when I lose sight of my own hands in the dark, I slow. He left me alone. He can't have, but he did. I curse myself and flip the collar up on my coat. I step forward—

It's then that I feel them. A damp gust strikes and melts into my flesh; an electrical charge trickles closely behind. I shudder with revulsion, unable to control myself. Intrusive, overwhelming, knee-weakening. A wave of icy nausea guts me. I curl over and wait for the sensation to pass. But it doesn't. It intensifies, as does this feeling of weighty doom, humming through my upper jaw, hitting the lower like dripping acid. And strengthening behind me, exuded from the cracks in the old charcoal paint like a foul smell, are those old voices. Whispering at first, then guttural, they clash into a building screech of long, dirty nails on a chalkboard. I drop to my knees, unable to take in a breath, as my ribs won't unknit. Another electrical gust sweeps through me, its darted charge like hundreds of fishhooks. I've lost all sense of direction, all bearing. I could be floating in air were there not so much pressure on my ribs.

Something hooks beneath my shoulders and drags me onto my feet like a puppet. My brain, woozy from the brandy, can't be sure if it's me or another force guiding me. From that tidy cabinet in my mind emerges an overwhelming fear, a rangy, athletic fear. But in the same moment, an all-encompassing force corrals the fear behind a door, shutting the door, smoothing over the door: apathy. It maneuvers me, gathering its energy from the impossible tightness in my chest. A sign of impending death, perhaps, but I'm being walked and watched even as I deteriorate inside, succumbing to that tightness.

A pincer seizes me by the arm. A firm appendage with the feel of a cool rubber glove claps over my mouth. I can't take in breaths anymore. Any clear vision remaining narrows to an uneven, dime-size spot. I'm dragged out of the hall, down another passage. Helpless, hopeless, I screw my eyes up into the darkness.

And there, an oculus. Pale blue, full of hope. "What's wrong?" is whispered, the voice a distant rush. "Are you okay?" Familiar. I can't shake my head. I'm rooted in place. "Do you want to go back?" The blue eyes are Dom's. Dom's. He takes me in his arms, placing two soft hands on my face, and I feel another series of pops through my joints, another jolt. The tightness abates. I fall limp, loose in my bones again. Dom props me up and brushes the hair from my forehead. "What happened to you?"

The feeling of relief overwhelms—the return of control. I'm flooded by gratefulness and fear and sadness . . . And I don't know what I'm thinking, but with his face—angles eased—a few centimeters away, I fall into him, and in that moment, I'm so eager to prove he's real. A hot tide inside me swells up as I look into his pale eyes, and I move closer and closer still, until I can feel his breath on me, sweet as apple.

I press my mouth to his: That same delicious current startles me, but instead of flinching back, I melt into the softness of his lips, that sensual reminder that we're both present and human and sane and not alone.

He falls back, wine-red mouth agape.

"I'm sorry. I . . ." I trail off before he can say a word. He trembles before me, and I wish I could reach for him, but I feel an odd looseness inside my head now, as if something broke off and rattles around there.

"It's okay," he says, bringing me close. I can feel his heart, this strangely precious living gift between us. "You're drunk, Mav. I can't believe I didn't notice."

Drunk. It feels like an insult of that moment, and my relief drains away, leaving only humiliation and panic. I push to my feet, falling again because of the weakness in my legs. "I'm not *drunk*." But I am, and I want to cry, because my words are so thick with emotion, and that makes me feel even more like a fool. Instead, I walk from him, gathering myself.

When I glance back, his face is a mask of confusion, mirroring what I feel. I have only one certainty now: This was not the fault of the brandy.

I have met them at last.

Pain made them real.

The Others.

I hear footsteps again somewhere—soft and rasping, like those before. And though I now know I have no hope of hearing the Others move through the house, much less identifying them in the light, I slow, almost unconsciously, until I hear Dom's own footsteps behind me.

18

ANGEL: 2020-1800

It's inhuman. Gruesome.

In front of my eyes, Mavi tenses, becoming as rigid as a frozen steak, one of those cardboardy brown bricks hand-carried to your door in a branded cooler by a dowdy, sweating salesman. And after she gasps back to life, she crackles like that same piece of tough meat dropped onto an overheated grill. Watching her endure the life cycle of an Argentine's favorite food is enough to make me vomit.

Is *that* possession, the process I submit Dom to daily?

It looks belligerent. Barbaric.

Unlike Dom, Mavi frees herself from the state with relative ease. But I can't forget the dead look in her eyes before her release. I can't forget her abnormal surge of gratefulness afterward, as if I've done her a great service by existing beside her.

And I can't forget the kiss, an automatic motion that seemed to swell out of the spot between her collarbones, toward me. As if she couldn't help herself.

She's supposed to fall in love with the son, I hear Charon say. *Get her heart broken . . . She's just that kind of girl. You know girls like her. We all know girls like her.*

Is she doing what she's always been meant to do? Trip and tumble into a stale love story with a beautiful fleshy meatbag heir, the only potential impediment being his dislike of her? The personality inside of him otherwise not mattering at all?

I don't believe it. But her hot and wounded eyes—so desperate to justify very real emotion, after I tell her she's drunk—they also linger in my memory.

"I'm not drunk," Mama said that afternoon, which meant she was. And she was almost never drunk. I followed her as she stomped into the bathroom, reeking of white wine, and upended a plastic container under the sink, dumping all her cosmetics onto the ground. "Come hang, Angel."

I looked at the assortment of mini-lipsticks and eyeliners strewn on the tile like they might rear up and bite me. "Aren't you supposed to be saving the world today?"

She'd volunteered for a laundry list of human rights organizations in her spare time, and she'd been encouraging me to join her for ages.

"Moved to tomorrow."

Which was never good, coming from the woman who almost tattooed *tempus fugit, carpe diem* to the bottom of her foot.

"You're going to have to organize all this shit," I said.

"Exactly what I'm doing," she said, patting the rug. "Come on. Sit."

I sat cross-legged in front of her: She looked especially thin and girlish on the floor before me. The weight had been melting off her slender frame recently, because of work, I thought. I could've easily encircled her wrist with my hand.

An eye shadow slipped through her fingers, and I looked up, catching her eyes just glowing at me.

"My precious Angel. I love you *so much*," she said, cupping my acne-flecked cheeks in both hands.

"Mama, stop," I groaned, throwing her from me. That was Mama. She could always find beauty when it wasn't there.

"Fine," she said. "Be that way." She sifted through the lipsticks. She wiggled one, a light apricot. "Oooh. Blushing apricot. 253, 213, 177. Nice. Reminds me of your favorite blanket back in the day. The one with the stars." She sighed, with a dreamy grin on her face, and uncapped the lipstick. "Do you still have that beat-up little scrap of it somewhere, like you used to?" It was true: I'd carried a gray shred of that beloved baby blanket in my jeans pocket until it disintegrated in the wash a year earlier.

"Mama!" I laughed. "Cone of silence. And that color was and always will be nasty. It looks like an eighties hospital sofa."

"And eighties hospital sofa suits olive skin." She tapped her freckled lips, and her eyes widened. "Shoot, is Rob going to do that same thing with his yellow blanket? I should've gotten him one made of Teflon." She painted her lips blind, hand quivering once, without smearing one speck. Then she pouted, smiled, and stuck her tongue out. "So?"

She was right: The color did suit her. Her lips didn't look as scary as expected. I opened my mouth to say *Could be worse*, but when my eyes reached hers, I saw they were wet and too heavy on me.

"So precious," she said, grinning at me, and her voice cracked on the last syllable.

Man, she was drunk.

"Are you going to tell me why you're drunk now?"

Her eyes went sharp, and she started jamming mini–eye shadows into a plastic container that clearly wouldn't house them all. "It's just work. Today was bad, Angel. A guy—" She stopped, breaking off again. I held a hand to hers, calming it and preventing continued angry-organization. She looked up at me. "A monster strangled this little girl."

"What?" My heart beat hard. She never shared details about work with me. I had glimpsed her on her computer on weekends here and there, but I never saw her in action.

I was endlessly curious. But I never disturbed her privacy. There were boundaries in our relationship, set a long time ago. We could be best friends. I could speak openly with her about almost anything, and I had. Just not her past, and not her work. You'd be surprised how full and loving a life you could lead without talking about those two cornerstones of a normal person's existence. But we weren't normal. Our connection was rooted in something that would be light-years long if unraveled. Something stronger than diamond but intangible on this plane. We sometimes called it cheesy things like mafia rules or kindred spirits, depending on how much bad TV we'd watched that day. But we recognized ourselves in each other, and that recognition cut deeper than the mother-child bond. Deeper than killing for each other, deeper than living for each other.

"He throttled this little girl. Or I guess a group of men did. It's hard to know. They're just . . . animals. It's nothing I haven't seen before at work. But this sicko I work with—my brain-dead partner turns to me after we look at the body and puts her hands around her own throat and goes—*bluuuuurgh*." She shook her own throat, popping her eyes out. "As if it's funny. I just can't do it anymore." She reached for my hands. "I'm sorry. I shouldn't be telling you this."

Visions of a limp-necked little girl Rob's age swarmed me. "It's okay, Mama. I'm always here for you. Don't say you don't know that."

She laughed shakily. "You shouldn't be saying that to me. I'm the mom." She released my hands, covered her face, and uncovered it just as swiftly. Her eyes were burning hot as coals. "Shit, Angel. Some people just don't get what this life is all about. We all go through our own personal hells at one point or another; we all inflict pain on others or ourselves intentionally or accidentally at one point or another; we all lose shit that we thought we couldn't live without, but there's still so much beauty and love and wonder to be found around every corner. How much pain do you have to be in to forget that and give in to the dark, you know?"

I shook my head—she got grandiose like this sometimes, ranted about life and what it meant. Sometimes I didn't know if she was oblivious or enlightened.

"Promise me, Angel—wonder, until the very end?"

"Wonder, until the very end," I promised, as I always did.

"Now let me clean up all this junk," she said, gripping my face. "Get out of here and do your homework." She kissed me hard on the cheeks, over and over and over.

"You're so *drunk*," I said, laughing.

I don't understand it, but I feel those threads of forever kinship—the kind that can be as soft as spider's silk and harder than steel—take root in me and reach for Mavi now. It's something more than garden-variety must-jump-your-bones lust. And she must feel it, too, or she never would have confided in me before.

But then Charon's words echo in my head for the millionth time. *You're not special. She's not connecting with you because you're different.*

She thinks you're someone you're not. She'll never meet the real you. She'll never know the real you.

If he's right, I need to know. Before I'm in too deep.

I know exactly what I need to do, as soon as I'm fed and rested and tucked back inside my fetching flesh costume. I need to tell Mavi who I am before this whole house goes to hell.

19

MAVI: ARGENTINA, JUNE 1978

I oversleep the morning after sneaking around with Dom, missing breakfast. Now that I know these creatures—ghosts, Others, spirits—so intimately, now that I know without a shadow of a doubt that they exist to harm us, it's difficult to summon the courage to crawl out from under my blankets. Not because I am afraid—what protection would my blankets offer, after all?—but because I am overwhelmed by the amount of information I must gather to help the girls. At least that's what I tell myself. I rack my brain to remember what the tenth little girl warned of: *They need energy, and they cannot get it as you do. They borrow it from you instead. A little at a time, a little more, a little more, until you can't lift yourself from bed.* But she said nothing about the pain I felt last night.

Why are only the little ones and Lamb falling ill—because they are the weakest? And how on earth can Michelle and Gisella see *men* near them at night, when I saw nothing at all?

In my rush to wash up and scavenge a bite to eat before class, I nearly don't notice the folded note slipped under my door. *Please see me in room 1 before breakfast*, it reads. *Ms. Morency.* My blood goes cold. I've long missed breakfast, and I can't know when she left this note. Could she have seen me last night, with Dom? And why do I still care whether she has?

I knock on her door, and blessedly, there is no answer. So I dash down to the empty breakfast room, snagging a piece of soggy toast and a cup of tea from the picked-over display. I take a sip of my tea and look out onto the ice beyond the windowpanes, muddy gray today to match the building clouds. In fact, I cannot distinguish between the two texturally. The ice will just build and build into a wall, fencing our rock and impervious to everything but spring's eventual thaw.

"How'd you sleep?" a deep and familiar voice asks behind me. I turn with a jolt. But it's Dom, standing by the door to the breakfast room. He shuts it, so we have privacy, and I ignore the bubbling shame and desire I feel.

"I've slept better," I say, trying for a smile. "Shouldn't have had that cup of brandy with Lamb."

He sits next to me. "Something possessed you," he says. Icy fingers run up my spine. "That's what it looked like, at least. Did you see anything?"

Of course, that's what I feared and hoped he would say, because once he has confirmed what happened, there can be no excisions from my memory. I can never again convince myself in the light of day that I am not so vulnerable, that our foe isn't so powerful. I cannot convince myself that what I experienced last night was a strange kind of love and fear intermingled—madness.

No—I'll have to remember the truth. A powerful and suffocating force washed over me, its evil and possessive effect as obvious to Dom as it was to me. I look out onto the ice, trying to formulate some reasonable and truthful reply that won't topple me.

"I didn't see anything, no. But you're right," I whisper. "They're here—whatever we want to call them. And now we need to work out what they want. There must be a way to satisfy the spirits and leave us unharmed. The question is, how do we satisfy the Others if we can't even communicate?"

Dom looks a bit flummoxed. He rubs his palms together again—he does this each time he's considering what to say. "We have one point of connection already."

"We do?"

The breakfast room door creaks open, and I leap from my seat. A group of silent kitchen staff floods the room, clearing the leftover breakfast display with a robotic swiftness. I flare my eyes at Dom and hurry off, leaving him seated alone.

In class, only six girls are present, fidgeting and doodling. The mood is somber. Six sets of eyes are trained on six sheets of paper, and even Sara contains herself, looking a bit beaten down. Michelle remains in the sickroom, and I suppose poor Gisella has returned there. But someone else is missing.

"Where is Luciana?" I ask.

The girls whisper as an uneasiness stirs in me. No one speaks up with an answer. Am I to understand that Luciana has fallen ill as well over the course of the night?

I have no choice but to work on *The Giver*—chosen only because it's another adolescent-friendly book I've found in English in the house; Lord knows what I'll do after this. I ask them to detail a memory of significance to them—positive memories only, in as vivid terms as they can manage. I hope the easy assignment will uplift.

"Perhaps it's baking a plum cake with a favorite grandmother," I say. "Perhaps it's playing long games of summer tennis with your father. These are memories that root us, that remind us of that for which we are grateful."

They play with their pens and pencils and erasers for the first fifteen minutes, building hills of eraser crumbs. Silvina whispers with Mariella until I fix them with a pointed look. They stare up at the ceiling as if the stucco provides answers in braille, if only their fingers could reach. Sara alone writes, slowly but dutifully, which is troubling. I persuade myself to look at her with pride.

"What's the problem, girls?"

Mariella snaps her gum. "This is a crummy assignment, Miss Quercia." She drops her pencil, glances at Silvina, who gnaws on the dry fringe of her lip.

"Thank you for your gratuitous assessment, Mariella. But it only asks that you think creatively. Surely you have a good memory on hand? Like the yacht you mentioned in your first composition, perhaps?"

"The yacht?" she replies, her voice wavering. She sucks in a gum bubble with a crack. I can see her mind whir as she tries to regain her footing.

"Miss Quercia," Silvina says, a mischievous smile blooming on her face, "have you even ever *been* on a yacht?" She nudges Mariella, as if to produce a chuckle, but both of them look at each other instead, unsettled.

They're rattled, the girls. Be it by Luciana's absence or something else entirely.

"Is there another assignment we can do?" Mariella asks in a plaintive tone I've never before heard. She chews fiercely at her gum, awaiting an answer.

"No. And chicle." I point at the garbage can.

Mariella rises, spits her wad of gum directly into the pail, and curtsies, as the rest of the class giggles.

All I can do is sigh. "To work, girls. Please."

Twenty minutes in, while the others have written barely a word, Sara slides her paper forward on the table. She smiles angelically, an off-putting enough sight for me to say *good work*.

"Miss Quercia, might I read an excerpt to give the other girls some inspiration?"

Am I to trust her transformation? She is all sweetness and politeness today. I look around at the other girls, who seem to mirror my nervousness, but I urge her on, eager to give her a chance at redemption.

She clears her throat and reads:

"'She's in a room, and there's a man above her. A man slender as the horizon line with fingers cold as ice. He touches her head, down to her chest, down to the space—'"

"Sara," I interrupt, masking an internal shudder. "Enough." I expect to hear giggles, but in their place is a terrible silence. Silvina's cheeks have gone a shade of green little seen outside a frosted-over vegetable garden.

"You don't love it?" A maniacal grin distorts her face. "It should feel intimately familiar to every girl here."

I am dumbstruck. Mariella balls her hands into fists. We sit there as the seconds tick by. None of them will look at Sara, that beast of a girl.

"It's about her pregnant mother at her ultrasound, obviously," snaps Mariella, shooting Sara a look of triumphant anger.

I am so grateful for her interruption I could kiss her cheeks.

"Right. An interesting perspective, but we were looking for something more current." I look around the table, desperate for someone else to speak up before Sara feels compelled to reply. "Have any of you chosen a memory?"

Mariella clears her throat. "Can we use class for inspiration?"

"If you must."

She looks around at the others, whose eyes drift to their pages as if they've received a telepathic message, and they scribble away. They leave their papers in a neat stack by my place at the end of the class—all except Mariella. The rest of them file out the door, one by one, and then Mariella steps forward, her assignment in hand. I hold out my hands expectantly.

"I did try to remember a story, Miss Quercia," she says to me, her pale face marred by deep undereye circles. "You have to believe me. I must just have a headache today because of everything going on."

My heart softens because I've never seen her this cagey. "That's just fine, Mariella."

"Thank you." She thrusts the paper into my hands, marked by her sweaty fingerprints. "I need to go check on Gisella and look for Luciana now," she adds as she hurries out.

There is a carousel, it reads. *I'm in my blue coat, and I'm reaching for the gold ring on my tiptoes . . .*

She's written about a passage we discussed while reading *The Catcher in the Rye*. And I don't believe it was an effort to serve me attitude—I remember the fear marking her face.

The lunchroom is empty but for a meager stack of ham-and-cheese sandwiches. I linger for a bit, wondering where everyone is—feeling paranoid and excluded all the while—before taking a sandwich to my room. On the way, I try Morency's door again, but she doesn't answer. I swear I'm going to break into hives awaiting this meeting with her. I consider leaving a note under her door but decide against it after kneeling by her door for a good five minutes, note in hand. *I'll try her later*, I tell myself. Tucked inside my room, I flip through the other sheets. The girls have stolen other passages and passed them off as their own memories. If it's a joke, I don't understand it.

I come to Sara's essay. I hadn't even glimpsed it, tempted as I was to chuck it into the trash. But I wonder if she elaborated on the page. I am surprised to find only a single line of text, written in uneven, intricate Old English lettering.

You are all fucked.

Gasping, I crumple up the awful paper in hand. Should I show it to Morency? What good would that do—proving I can't control my students? Proving Carmela right?

But Sara can't be allowed to terrorize the other girls.

I spend the rest of the afternoon before my meeting with Morency fretting—turning over ludicrous theories in my head about the nature of undead spirits, running my fingers over the spines of the prodigious book collection in the sitting rooms downstairs, hoping for a book to serve as my bible in this strange fight I am entering. I feel a stickiness on my fingertips, and when I pull away from the books, a pus-like mildew plasters my fingers. Upon closer inspection, it stains every spine—the darkness prevented me from noticing it at first. The books themselves are being eaten away.

Before dinner, I try Morency's room again. Room 1, at the head of the hall. The door is double the height of the others—fittingly. Intimidatingly. I knock and wait, smoothing my wrinkled shirt, my matted hair. I don't expect her to answer this time, either, and with a hint of relief, I turn to return to my room when the door clicks and creaks open. Morency, dressed in a haughty frown and all-black funereal garb that brushes the floor. She must repurpose extralarge, charred medieval witch rags for her outfits.

"You've kept me waiting long enough. At this rate breakfast will begin soon." With a nod of her slicked head, she urges me inside.

I could eat off the floor of her mahogany sitting room, sparely decorated but impeccably clean, with its own unused fireplace, crowned by a cast-iron mantelpiece. Her bedroom must be off one of the other shut doors, long and skinny as Morency herself. There is a bizarre fun house aspect to her quarters. She settles on a chair, posture straight as a rod, and fixes her hawkish eyes on me, without gesturing for me to sit on the uncomfortable-looking brocade sofa to my left—a blessing in disguise. We are nearly the same height when I am standing and she is seated, a baffling trick.

"Luciana has run away," she says, clasping her hands on her lap.

It takes me a moment to process her disclosure. I feel as if her bun has swallowed my own head and popped it open like a grape. "Luciana?" I step toward her, my blood flowing hot now. "But where could she have gone?"

"Nowhere," she says. "Not with this mist. We will find her eventually. Mr. Dello Russo has been leading a large group of house staff around the property in search of her. You may join in after we speak."

I am speechless: Have I been dallying all day while the others have been occupied with this? We sit in silence as she gives me the evil eye, and I struggle to grasp what's keeping her from excusing me— what's keeping us from leaping up and joining the search.

"I have heard it said," Morency says at last, "that certain staff members anticipate the reprise of the house's tragedy of some sixty years ago. I wish to relay to you that promulgating obscene rumors such as these will result in your immediate dismissal. Talk of the virus is unacceptable. It upsets the girls, and it upsets the staff."

The damned virus. I know in my bones that it's a smoke screen used by Carmela and Morency to conceal the Zapuche's true history here and their curse. But for a moment, I wish it was a virus. I wish these signs of spirits we've felt were . . . symptoms. Quite physical and entirely explicable. The thought makes me shudder; considering that I may be going mad because of some unknown, true illness. "I don't understand what this has to do with me." Unless she thinks I've been scaring the girls with rumors of the virus returning. She thinks I scared Luciana into running away.

She tut-tuts. "You mustn't hide your sins now, Miss Quercia. Madame De Vaccaro is aware of your propensity for indiscretion."

I pale, never expecting to be accused of a hypothetical crime I did not commit. "Ms. Morency, I only worried about Michelle to you in private. I never said a thing to anyone about a virus—"

She holds up a claw. "Do consider yourself lucky that I am handling this situation myself. It would be a shame to attract the attention of Madame De Vaccaro when she is preoccupied with more important matters. As punishment, you will go without your evening meal tonight. Stay inside your room after the search. Do not request food from the kitchen staff, and do not ask a soul to bring food to your room. I will know, and you will face a more severe punishment. Is that clear?"

My jaw hangs open in shock. She hasn't said a word to me about sneaking out of my room at night, nor befriending Dom, yet she zeroes in on the most absurd claim of all. I'm not sure whether to be relieved or incensed, but my face smolders with shame. *I'm not a child*, I want to tell her.

She grimaces, taking my silence for an imbecile's admission of guilt, surely. "I do not take pleasure in penalizing young people. I do believe that most intelligent beings learn from their mistakes," she says. "In time. You seem to be the exception to that rule, what with your proclivity to speak at will without a care to the consequences—as a beast might, were it granted the privilege of speech. Consider this punishment a warning, Miss Quercia."

254

I am numb: Morency's flawed conclusions stem from her personal logic, the logic of the ruined and hopeless world she inhabits. "How very kind of you."

I know it is a mistake as soon as I say it. Her mouth shrivels to raisin form at the hint of sarcasm. "Miss Quercia," she says, "I am not a kind person, but I am a fair person." The air hangs heavy around us as she fights a tidy, tiny grin of self-satisfaction and as I process the inherent madness of her statement. "Well then. Anything else?" she asks. "Speak up now, or we shall leave to join the search."

I stare back at her. She was the one to ask me here, the one to rip me apart, the one to . . . well. I compose myself, tugging together the muscles in my face like I'm wrapping an odd-size package with string. Realizing her smug attempt at dismissal affords me a rare opportunity. "There is no virus. So what do you know about the Others in the house with us?"

She inhales sharply. "Have you lost all ability to form coherent thought?"

"I felt them, you know," I add, ignoring her and gaining courage in my last-ditch effort. "Whatever they are. And I know you've felt them and fear them, too. That's why you make us stay in our rooms at night. You know what I'm talking about—"

"If Madame De Vaccaro were to hear a word of your ramblings, the consequences would be severe, especially for a young woman in your position," she says carefully. "I fear that you may have been overwhelmed by the requirements of your position, Miss Quercia— the need to behave as an adult, hearing you speak as such. Happily for you, I know that these past couple of days have been trying for you and the rest of the staff, due to Mr. Lamm's attack and Mrs. Hawk's sudden illness—"

My heart leaps into my throat, a choking mass. "So Mrs. Hawk was ill? She didn't leave for a better opportunity?" I feel like a fool speaking the words.

Morency pinches her lips together. "She was ill, and she left without advance notice. That is all there is to say. There are more pressing matters on hand, such as the welfare of our girls."

"When did Luciana disappear?" I ask, fists clenching. "How do you know she ran away? Couldn't she be somewhere inside the house?"

She fixes both black eyes on me, wills me to avert mine. But I do not. Luciana would not run away. She wouldn't. How could she survive on the hill alone, in the cold? Could she be staying with a staff member? Could she be—?

"Luciana left all her possessions in her room, and as such, I am certain she will return in due time. We are not discussing one unruly girl. We are discussing one unruly teacher. Now, I am willing to pretend I heard you say nothing. I do not agree to do this often. Do get some rest tonight, Miss Quercia, and never speak of this aloud again. You may take comfort in the fact that God has a plan for each of us, and he rewards the obedient. If one follows the rules, everything else becomes irrelevant." She flattens back her hairline and rises to her full height, an ebony tower.

"But I need to understand why the rules exist," I say softly, surprising even myself. How can anything as banal as house rules matter when girls and teachers alike are being tormented and disappearing?

She steps toward me, affording me a view of her chin, the refuge of one long stubby strand of black hair. "I must remind you that you are an employee, Miss Quercia. Could it possibly be a good use of your time to question the rules of this house and the philosophy behind them?"

For the briefest of moments, her question seems sincere. But I am reminded of her disdain for me most of the time, and every fiber of my being wants to pluck the hair from her chin in a petty little rage. She is maddening, a sphinx. I feel as if no combination of words I can conjure up will, when spoken, convince her of my good intentions, of my desire to help. And simultaneously, I remember my tenuous position here and her threat with regard to Carmela. Clearly, candor will get me nowhere with Ms. Morency. I feel myself fold like a paper figure. "You're right, Ms. Morency," I say. Her eyes narrow, convinced I'm making some pitiable play at humility. "I think we started off on the wrong foot," I add. "I'm eager to do a good job. To do well by the girls. To be liked by the other staff."

"To be *liked*," she says, long nose wrinkling. "To be *liked*. What a lofty goal for an educator. You have entirely missed the point." My mouth opens and closes as she shoos me outside with bony fingers. I swallow and move toward the exit, eager to escape the paradoxically claustrophobic confines of her giant-size room. It's windowless, too, the sooty fireplace the only point of access to the outside world.

"And, Miss Quercia?" she says. I turn back to find her pointing at a large, watery brown stain on my skirt, unnoticed drippings from my tea this morning. "This is a house of education. Do try to look tidy."

The fog outside is thick enough to taste; I feel a drizzle, too. Standing still, I cannot see my own feet; the cloud dissipates for mere seconds every time I take a step. I feel as if I am being smothered—it would be easier to swim. We conduct the search by forming a human chain, assisted only by a rope procured by Morency. The rope is our lifeline, especially as the cobblestones beneath us, once so even and immaculate, crumble. I am the link between Mole and Morency—Morency tugs me forward on the rutted ground, and Mole eases me up every time I stumble. There is no way Luciana could have made it far in this clouded hell. Every so often, Armadello calls out his own name, so that each of us may answer with ours in kind and ensure no one else gets lost. Carmela is not present: I suppose her excuse is that she is monitoring the girls, who cannot be permitted to join the search, either.

I sweat inside my coat. How are we meant to find Luciana when we cannot see one another? Lighting our lanterns only makes our trekking more difficult, lighting up our individual air pockets and blinding us further.

Mole and Armadello urge us to give up for the evening shortly afterward, and everyone else accepts this. *Silly girl*, I hear whispered.

I spend dinnertime in my room, imagining no one discussing Luciana's absence at all, the search long forgotten, just as no one discussed Mrs. Hawk's disappearance. When the clouds consume one of us, everyone else seems to forget them. *Sustained terror doesn't suit the house's private fantasy for us yet.* I imagine Yesi, sparkling and bubbling with gratuitous wit, enchanting those around her. I imagine Mole's conversations with Diana, in which she explains Gisella's and Michelle's conditions in über-anesthetized terms, translating their chilling description of a ghostly man into childspeak's *bad dreams*. I imagine Carmela, toasting us all for remaining in a house that is degenerating—a house she may very well know is tainted beyond hope.

There is so much falseness in this house.

I haven't any relevant history books in my room to piece together new theories about the house. So I try, briefly, to sculpt my future lessons into tools to distract the girls—to distract myself, too. Good literature temporarily pulls us out of a difficult moment; great literature suggests a permanent model for strength. So: *The Giver*. Only the Giver and his trainee are permitted to carry society's memories, and everyone else is stripped of their collective past to form part of a colorless, emotionless world.

As I simmer and scribble, the air in my claustrophobic square room grows thin, and when eleven in the evening arrives, piles of ripped-up-paper confetti cover my bed like first snowfall. *Enough*. I come to my feet and slip on my coat. *Fight* it is.

I move through the hall with no hesitation. Hesitation will kill me here at night. But I do think to myself: *Fool, fool, fool*. Traipsing around without Dom, without anyone. The *1* hanging on Morency's door glints at me, and the house itself remains suspiciously quiet, muting its own groans and cracks as if to goad me into exploring more deeply. I fold my arms across my chest and push on down the steps, skipping the missing planks. The ugly paintings on the hallway walls hang askew, as if someone's knocked them; either that, or I've developed vertigo. I ignore them and march on. Soon, I hear the hum of the refrigerators. The ticking of a phantom clock I've yet to spot in daylight. The faintest rustling, like a rope dragged along distant floorboards. I shut my eyes when I nose into the stone hallway, counting out the steps that remain. Sixty steps. I know it now, and by treating it like a game, I hope to trick my blooming fear. I imagine a sunlit garden path, scented by roses. My foot collides with the stairs—disintegrating, too—overestimating the distance by a step. I open my eyes, glimpsing a darting shadow at the top.

"Hello?"

There is no answer, and I climb on, taking the steps two at a time; you'd think I was eager to meet the trailing electric tentacles from last night. I shiver with revulsion just as I spot two shadows scampering around the first bend. Smallish, hunched. As I round the corner, sick to my stomach, a silken hand covers my mouth, and I whip around, my first impulse being to bite down—

But I see a familiar, pearly finger held to thin lips over my shoulder. It's Yesi, wearing her robe, widening her blue eyes, her silver ringlets tied into knots at the base of her skull.

"Jesus!"

"Swamp," she says, clamping down on my arm with that smooth vise of a hand. "You missed dinner."

"What are you doing here?"

She holds a finger to her lips again, and the second shadow slinks back around the corner. I squint in the dark: Mariella, with her two long black braids. She places her hands on her hips.

"I was escorting this one back to bed," Yesi whispers.

"I was looking for Luciana," Mariella says aloud. "She left clues, you know. Bitten nails in the carpet in her room. They lead toward the window—"

"Shh!" we both whisper back.

She glowers at us. "I'll find her."

"We will continue to search for her in the morning. And now you will return to bed," says Yesi, seizing her by the wrist. "It's dangerous to sneak about like this at night."

I nod along, even though my heart swells at the thought of Mariella searching so courageously for her friend.

After we leave Mariella frowning and tucked in bed, Yesi and I scurry back through the dark halls.

"Now will you tell me what you're doing here?" I ask. "I know you weren't patrolling for wandering girls."

She crosses her arms. "I spoke to Mole again. She recounted the girls' symptoms as described quite poetically by the both of them. And of course it sickened me. All that talk of men fondling them, far beyond where my imagination would've gone at their age. She's wrong to think it's hysteria." She lets me go and crosses her arms. "Luciana still hasn't been found, and I just know something awful happened to her. This would be the perfect place for someone to abuse the girls, you know. They've been told to trust everyone—that this castle on the hill is their salvation from parental carelessness, their righteous path to a special kind of womanhood. They've been told that Carmela double- and triple-checked everyone's background—which I doubt, by the by. And Mole's too exhausted to do right by these girls; between you and me, she should be retired. But in any case, I can't blindly trust Carmela and Morency to make the right choices anymore now that Luciana's run off, too. I needed to see for myself what happens to them at night. I just need to." She looks me up and down, pinching my coat between her fingers. "It looks like you've decided to do the same? I can't say I'm surprised. You've had your head on straight all along. Sort of."

"Oh, Yesi." I take her in my arms, and she softens in them. I know this is the closest thing to an apology that she'll offer at the moment, and I can accept that if it means I'm not alone tonight. Perhaps that makes me weak—or simply human.

"I'm relieved to have you here, too, you old Swamp Thing. Christ, it's spooky up here. And I thought we had it bad in the staff hall. Now come on," she says, pulling me by the hand. Breathless, we dash to the sickroom and push open the oak door. The room is silent and dark—clouds blanket the moon tonight, and the ice looks drab beneath them. Yesi and I draw back the flowered coverlets on the two sickbeds to find Michelle and Gisella, two warm bundles, snoring.

We sit on the sofa by their beds and wait. Wait for an incident. Wait for a visit from the malicious unknown. "We should go to the other girls' rooms instead. Surely we'll witness a disturbance there," I whisper to Yesi. "After all, Luciana wasn't in the sickroom last night. She was in her own room."

She squeezes my hand with her loving fingers of ice. "But the others seem fine. This is our best chance of discovering what ails these two." She releases me to drape a butter-colored blanket over our shoulders. "Patience."

I settle into the sofa, determined to patrol the night and do right by the girls. I will myself never to forget the warnings I've received, both friendly and hostile, about this house and its residents—be it from a petite ghost girl, fruit of my dreams, or that startling, electric blend of fear and apathy I felt last night in the halls beyond this room. My strength lies in those memories, I think, and my experiences will inform my actions now. But how it soothes me to have Yesi nestled beside me.

A clap awakens me. I can't believe I've fallen asleep; I look around, bleary-eyed, and though the room remains dark, I see the outlines of shapes in the room, furniture shapes, illuminated by the ice's supernatural glow outside the window. My hand shoots to Yesi's, cold and withered in her lap. I sense movement in the room and hear a creaking of floorboards.

A man's shadow appears. Leaning over Gisella, his arms outstretched. A groan of despair dies in my throat as I wish I could disappear into the wall. I dig my nails into Yesi's hand, hard enough to signal we're in trouble, and she awakens, too. "Did we fall asleep?" she asks, voice breaking.

The man's head swivels on its neck in a crescendo of rapid clicks. He does not shrink away, nor startle. He smiles, a glisten of wet teeth. I shoot to my feet, pulling Yesi up with me. "Who are you?" I hiss, immobile.

The man's freakishly slender fingers move toward the edges of Gisella's scalp. Her oval face looks solemn in the path of weak moonlight, lips parted in her dream-filled repose. Yesi rushes to the lamp on the far side of the room and tries the switch with a few shuddering clicks. The bulb has burned out. I can't make out the identity of the intruder from his position in the shadows, despite knowing every man in the house; he's shorter and more solid than Domenico. Rangier. And his posture resembles that of no one else in the house. It's animal in its energetic hunch—malformed.

Veins abuzz, I burst past Yesi and take up the base of the lamp in both hands. Without a second thought, I run toward the man and slam the frame against his skull with a welcome thud. He crumples against the headboard as I swing again and miss him, collapsing when the cord tangles with my ankles.

He straightens himself above me with ease, as if unable to feel pain, and I feel an excruciating stinging across my scalp—a clump of hairs torn at the roots. I grasp for his ankles, scratching at thin, hairy skin with my nails. Yesi shouts and charges toward him, and the pain on my scalp abates, but Yesi falls to the carpet beside me, panting, as the man scrambles to the door. Fleeing.

I struggle to catch my breath and pull myself up before helping Yesi to her feet. "Are you all right?" I whisper to her in the dark. She tugs me, wordlessly, toward the adjoining bathroom, where she turns on a functional light. A purplish-pink splotch spreads on Yesi's cheek, a hydrangea bloom printed on ivory.

"Are you hurt, Swamp?" Her voice is hoarse.

Blood-tinged flakes line my fingernails, and when I touch my scalp above my right ear, a ratty clump of hair falls. But the droning in my veins prevents me from registering pain.

"No," I tell her. "Are you?"

Her blue eyes water, and she proffers her fist. I squint to make sense of what she's holding, because, at first, it looks like a handful of snowflakes. But when I brush them, I feel a prickly bunch of white, short, and curly hair. Lamblike wool.

Above the sound of rushing blood in my head, I hear the softest sobbing: Gisella. I kneel by the edge of her bed. Her cheeks are damp, her nightgown mussed at the neck and riding up. "How could you let them in?" she whispers, drawing her knees into her chest. Her half-shuttered eyes don't catch on me; she could still be dreaming. "How could you?"

I gape at her. "I'm so sorry, Gisella." I adjust her nightgown, and she recoils, so I cover her snugly, as if that will help. "I'm so sorry. We came to watch you, and we fell asleep for only a moment—"

"They're disgusting." Her face is slick with silent tears. "Don't you see them?" I wipe the droplets from her face and must keep myself from drawing back at the dead feel of her skin.

Mole was correct to tread lightly in her conversations with the girls. I can't tell Gisella that I might have recognized the man, the solitary man who was leaning over her bed. That it might have been Lamb, her own teacher, he of the curly white fur. I can't process the thought yet myself. Lamb—whom I spent hours with only last night, who suffered from a heart attack the day before that? No. It's not possible. Yesi approaches us, face pink and wet. She swaddles herself as she observes Gisella.

"I can't take this." Gisella gasps, delirious. "They've taken Lu, and soon they'll take me." Bile rushes up my throat: This is Gisella, who has never been one to show weakness, if it can be helped. Yesi kneels beside her while I make my way over to Michelle, who has burrowed into her gray blankets. She eyes me from a pocket in her bedcovers—her expression jarringly dead and empty, devoid of trust. After a few seconds, she clamps her eyes shut.

Yesi feeds a babbling Gisella a handy glass of lavender syrup and water until she relaxes. I wet a washcloth with freezing water from the tap and press it to Yesi's cheek to curb swelling, too stunned to call for Morency or Carmela or even Mole. It is only when Gisella falls asleep again, and Michelle's breathing slows, that Yesi whispers urgently to me from our perches on the sofa. "It was him. To think it was him all along! There's nothing evil in this house but him. Christ. He's the pervert here to abuse vulnerable girls, Swamp. I can't believe I never saw it before. I can't believe I trusted him." She trembles, her nails crimping half-moons into the cloth armrest.

"You're saying that this whole time, it was Lamb?"

"I don't have a single doubt it was Lamb." She fishes around her pocket and juts out a fist of lamby fur. "He's been manipulating us all. He puts on this act of being an infirm, loopy, lonely old man so that we let down our defenses and treat him like the kindly grandfather we never had."

I think of how easy it would be to tell her he fed me brandy until I passed out, but I don't say a word.

"Haven't you noticed how he strokes their heads?"

I thought he patted their heads like a loving master pats his dogs', but perhaps I was wrong.

She shudders. "Oh, Christ. We need to tell Carmela tonight. We need to get him out of here." She stands, the towel dripping on her forehead. "I'll go right now."

I'm convinced there's more to the story—what with others in the house acting out of character, too. Take Sara, Luciana, and that outburst from Mole, and perhaps even Hawk . . . After my experience with the fishhook paralysis only last night, I formulate an idea. Perhaps the Others possess our friends. I'm afraid to say this to Yesi, though. Afraid because she's brushed off all my ideas about ghosts before.

"Yesi, you view yourself as the queen of logic and restraint, don't you? Then you must admit we didn't see him do anything to them. We must speak to him," I say. "The Lamb I know would never touch the girls. And he wouldn't have beaten you to the ground, either."

"It was self-defense on his part, once he'd been exposed as what he truly is and you walloped him with that lamp. He's a dangerous man. A sick man." Yesi's face contorts—the swelling admonishes me. "He snuck into the sickroom in the middle of the night and touched Gisella. God knows what he did before we woke. How can you protect him?" she asks. "You haven't even known him for more than a couple of months. Carmela must have plumbed the bowels of the earth during her recruitment. Imagine! A man retired for his wandering fingers." Her hands curl into fists. "How did it never occur to us that his shakes are an invention? That he faced retirement because of the vilest acts?"

I feel a sudden swell of nausea and hunch over my knees, bringing the heel of my hand to my mouth. Goddamn these Others.

Yesi pats me on the back before propping me up by my shoulders. "Enough of that. This isn't the time to be weak. We must tell Carmela right now."

A hot and rank froth surges up my throat. "I can't. I'm going to be sick." I run to the adjoining bathroom. I shut the door behind me and fold over the toilet, palms pressed against the tile floor, heaving into the bowl, nothing but bile in my stomach.

My attempt to learn, to help, to fight led to this most gruesome discovery. *We're so isolated here*, I think. *Trapped on this rock with the wretches around us, bleeding us dry and assuming control of us, one by one.* I curl beside the bowl to let the nausea pass. When I pull myself up and back into the girls' room, Yesi has disappeared. I shiver on the sofa until daybreak, watching the girls sleep as best as they can, scanning the room for more inexplicable evil. Only a patch of bloodred mold flourishes along a jagged crack in the ceiling.

Yesi and Mole find me as the sun rises beyond the ice. "Carmela wants to speak with both of us," Yesi announces as Mole rushes toward the sleeping girls. "She asked me to fetch you. Now."

266

20

ANGEL: 2020-2000

Sometime before dawn, I return to Dom's room, only to find that he isn't in bed. He's not slumped on his chaise under the royal-blue throw, staring at motes drifting through space. Not in his lavish marbled bathroom, collecting splayed onion-thin rolling papers. I feel the panic of a parent who ogled the electronics display in a Costco for *one minute*, only to turn and find his kid isn't at the chicken quesadilla sampler station, as promised: Dom's not in his room, period.

"Where are you, for Pete's sake?" I shout, as if he's a trained husky who will hustle back to me, tongue wagging, wondering who Pete is.

I circle wider: He isn't anywhere in the family's quarters. I search the house to find him, passing through the jigsaw puzzle of sitting rooms, of libraries, of staff quarters. The house is a haunted labyrinth—it would overwhelm if I couldn't break through walls. I poke my head through an upstairs wall and catch a glimpse of the breakfast patio below. The sun is about to rise, staining the flagstones a muted red.

That's when I see a figure, a solitary figure, slumped at the edge of the balcony rail, dangling feet in the void.

I drop beside him in the blink of an eye, recognizing his lankiness. "Dom?" I ask tentatively. The body turns to me, eyes glazed and dark.

It isn't the Dom I know, no—not fully.

It is his muscled skeleton, leaner than usual. His face looks gaunt and shrunken by sadness. *Have I not been feeding you enough food?* I think; and it's an incongruous enough thought in that moment that I feel a wave of anguish pass through me, salt-tinged and draining, as I avoid catching sight of his eyes again.

"I'm tired of this," he says, croaking like a corpse with dried-out pipes. He doesn't specify what he means, but I know.

"You can see me?"

He grimaces, kicks his leg.

I don't understand it—why he should have consciousness now, and choose this path, when he's been too drained of energy to try anything so drastic before. Has my hosting changed him irrevocably, too?

"I want you to live," I say, even though what I mean is, *I need you to live*.

How do I coax him off the edge, when I couldn't have pulled myself back, once upon a time? What unselfish reason can I possibly give him for living? He isn't conscious of his life anymore—he doesn't own that life.

I took it away from him.

268

He shifts more of his weight toward the edge, leaning into the wind. He wants to drop himself off the side like a soiled bundle.

I feel a sucking blackness inside, a swell of sympathy: I've been so quick to dismiss him as a loser unworthy of holding the reins of his own life when he's a human like Mavi, a human who deserves some shred of dignity. Who deserves some control over how his time is spent.

It's strange: Looking at Dom's own face now—the one spot I do try to avoid, when outside of him—and watching tears fall from his eyes, forming furious rivers on his cheeks that I didn't think him capable of producing, I almost feel as if my own cheeks are wet.

I pity him. But I crave more time here myself, even as the house and its inhabitants rattle onward to their assured destruction by Others. I care too much about Mavi, about Dom's strength, about the tenth girl herself and what she promises. And even though I fear my attachment, I can't deny its existence.

I try to flit inside him, to be the selfish hero and pull him back, and am met by a tremendous pressure. "Stop," he says, angling away from me, shoving at the air I inhabit, his bony thighs skidding on the railing.

But I have to persist and push inside him, knowing no other home. I can't say whether being host to a parasite like me is a fate worse than death. When I wanted to die more than anything else in the world, I wouldn't have allowed someone else to take over my body, to go through the motions while obliterating my own pained spirit. Even if it kept my loved ones satisfied.

No. Instead, I said, *Screw everything, my one right as a human being is to throw myself off the goddamned edge into oblivion whenever I damn well please.*

But I still can't let him do this.

It's tricky push-pull work, edging inside while pressing him away from the edge. Like slipping around icy, shifting scaffolding thousands of feet above the ground. And what's worse, I'm meeting too much resistance, too much more pressure than usual.

I'm still pushing when I feel a wobble inside Dom. I'm straining like a sumo wrestler locked in a rival's grip; manipulating all my crystal sinews in a way that takes overwhelming self-awareness. That's when I catch on a series of internal levers, one by one—and pressure releases.

A glimmer in the shape of a man exits him like a breeze.

Oh.

I understand all of a sudden: Someone else had usurped my place, but it wasn't Dom. It was an Other.

Relief blows through me: It wasn't him. It wasn't him seeking oblivion. It was a stranger, an impostor, a parasite.

How many Others have sat alone, overlooking the edge of the world, and dove onto the ice in a borrowed body? Is that what one of them did to Mrs. Hawk? To Luciana?

How selfish, I think to myself, shaking hard. *How irresponsible.*

But I have no right to call it selfish. I have no right to call it irresponsible, not with my past.

I look hard for the interplay of strange shadows and light around us. A constellation of silver speckles dances a dozen feet away—maybe. Or maybe not.

I enter Dom and corral his every muscle, leaning him back, nudging him onto the balcony like a toddler at the edge of a stair. I straighten my spine. I trudge inside, up the stairs, down the hall. I lay Dom down to rest in his own bed. He needs to sleep before tomorrow. He needs to sleep, to wipe the slate clean, to clear that look of total existential exhaustion still on his face.

I recognize it. I recognize that look from Mama's cadmium-yellow face in the hospital. *Cadmium-yellow*. Mama's skin was so yellowed and blotchy that day that Rob thought she had been painted up, that her thin and wan face was a mask painted to scare or, confusingly, amuse us, and I couldn't keep him from asking why her face was painted, and Mama asked, half joking, *What colors did the makeup artists choose today, Angel?* I consulted my phone and said 255, 246, 0, and she cackled for the first time in ages. Rob asked what the numbers meant, and she explained that it was a type of yellow. He asked Mama what that yellow was made of in the real world (if it was made of the captured sun, of daffodils, of peepee, of what), and since she knew the painterly names and RGB codes for the entire rainbow, she said cadmium, with a look in her eyes that told me she couldn't keep this up much longer, as much as she loved us. Cadmium is carcinogenic, which I found out later. Mama always did have a poet's sense of humor.

She died less than a week later, just after nine in the morning. Rob and I weren't there at the time, because Liese wanted us to keep up with school. No matter that first period was always useless, and I cut it anyway.

All I wanted in my old life was to accordion-open my time with those I loved, spreading the days so that every pastel hour felt like a single century, and then to accordion-close the time after those so painful I did everything I could to compress them into nothing.

This place has changed everything.

"Why did I let myself get in so deep?" I ask Dom as he drops off into an insensate sleep.

21

MAVI: ARGENTINA, JUNE 1978

"Enter," Carmela calls to me and Yesi.

In her office, a monumental wooden desk sits void of paperwork and personal effects—I see a calendar, a blank notepad, a modern and characterless lamp, and a glass of identical pens. She sits in her leather chair, arms folded, her face fully painted up and her platinum hair sculpted into its typical gleaming bob despite the early hour. She squares the notepad and takes hold of a silver pen. "Yesi was in a state earlier, so I requested that you and she both visit me when she was more composed, Miss Quercia. Are you prepared to explain exactly what happened now, Yesi?"

Yesi swallows, hands moving in and out of her pockets. "We were watching the girls last night, Madame De Vaccaro—"

272

"Which girls, Yesi?" she says, making not a single note. "Be precise, now."

"Michelle and Gisella."

"Was that sanctioned by Ms. Morency?"

Yesi bites her lip. "It was not."

"And it was not sanctioned by me. Why were you there, Yesi?" she asks, taunting us with her impassive expression.

"They're ill, possibly with a flu, and—"

"Yes, I know. Do answer my question."

"The girls shared concerns about nighttime disturbances, so I decided to witness the phenomena for myself, after Morency left them to sleep."

"Unsanctioned. As did Miss Quercia, it seems. Despite being told to remain in her room." I glance up to find her giving me a flat, chilly smile. "So the both of you were wandering the halls at night alone. Do go on."

"We were watching the girls, and around three in the morning, a man came into the room and leaned over Gisella. We rushed to fight him off, and he ran out. But I recognized the man." Hand faltering, Yesi pulls out the hair from her pocket and places the scraps on the table.

Carmela regards the bundle with the faintest hint of detached disgust and clears her throat. "And you can confirm you saw Mr. Lamm of our staff? The same Mr. Lamm who suffered a heart attack so recently?"

Yesi nods, chastened by the unlikeliness of it all.

"I will speak with Mr. Lamm this morning," Carmela continues. "I will also speak to the girls. But know that I cannot take such accusations lightly. I have no reason to mistrust you, Yesi, but if you have misrepresented the situation in any way, the consequences will be serious."

Even though I disagree with Yesi and am pleased by Carmela's reluctance to punish Lamb, the condescension in her tone grates on me. She's done nothing at all to help the situation. Luciana, as far as I know, remains unfound, yet Carmela sits here, imperious as ever. "In the meantime, your classes will be canceled while we evaluate the situation, and your future pay will be docked accordingly. Remain in your rooms, and speak of this situation to no one else." She picks up her silver pen. "You caused enough damage by informing Dr. Molina of your own accord."

"Dr. Molina is treating them," Yesi says.

"The situation has evolved," says Carmela crisply, setting down the pen. "This is outside of Dr. Molina's purview."

"You should send the girls home," I say, speaking up at last and accepting in that instant what the consequences are of wielding this opinion. "And the rest of us should look for Luciana."

"If the girls are sent home, then the school will be shut down. Is it in your best interest for the school to be shut down, Miss Quercia?" Carmela asks coolly. "What with your background?"

Yesi looks at me, confused, and the back of my throat aches. But I think of my mother and her cousins: I would sacrifice myself to spare the girls. I truly would. "It is best for them to be sent home. We all think so."

"And who exactly are 'we,' Miss Quercia? The two girls I see before me?"

"Some of us on the staff," I say. "Your son, too."

Immediately, I wish I had bitten my tongue. She scoffs—half incredulous laughter, half nonchalance. "I was warned by Ms. Morency that you were inclined to develop fantasies, Miss Quercia. Especially pertaining to my son."

My stomach drops, and I feel Yesi look at me with homicide in her eyes.

Carmela rises. "Ladies, I thank you for your input," she says in a tone that confirms our utter valuelessness, "and I assure you that I will—"

"Whatever you think about Mr. Lamm, or us, you have to acknowledge that the girls are suffering. And with Luciana gone," I interrupt, feeling the heat of tears coming to my eyes, "you must—"

Carmela stops me with a hand. "Do pull yourself together, Miss Quercia. Don't make me regret hiring a leftist troublemaker more than I already do." She turns her attention to the empty pad of paper before her. She hasn't taken a single note. "Is that all?"

I curl my hands into fists behind my back.

"Yes, Madame De Vaccaro," Yesi says for the both of us as my nails tear into my flesh.

Outside, Yesi marches away from me without a word. And I: Well, I could flay Carmela De Vaccaro myself with the frustration I feel toward her bureaucratic attachment to her pointless rules. I, for one, refuse to follow them any longer.

After I've eked out an hour or so of sleep in bed, Dom, of all people, knocks on my door. I'm surprised to see him, if glad, as always, even though my eyelids are still practically glued shut. I pull him inside, too exhausted and fed up to care a fig about decorum. Thigh to thigh on the bed, I tell him what I know about last night, about the man leaning over Gisella, about Yesi being sure of Lamb's guilt, about Carmela's brush-off, and I share everything that I don't know—why have the Others decided to take over our peers now? What comes next?

My words are a jumble. But as I speak, as I describe my confusion, a sentimentality mellows Dom's features, an open sentimentality tinged with sadness that I've never before witnessed.

It gives me pause.

I wouldn't call it a cousin of pity or concern—it reminded me of my mother's face the last time I saw her, the pained and adoring face of a person who loved me deeply despite keeping great secrets from me, the nature of which I could never fathom.

I look away shyly; it fills me with doom to face that expression a second time in a short life.

Before I can form the words to protest, he pulls me out of my room, down the stairs like broken teeth, through the chilly hall, into the breakfast room, and out to the empty patio, where the ice punctures the sky. The blustery weather wakes me like a cold-water bath. I extend a naked finger out into the wind; I know rain, proper rain, will pour from the steel-gray sky in mere moments, and we should be burrowing back inside the warm depths of the house. In consolation, I suppose, Dom fetches a woolly yellowed blanket and drapes the length over my shoulders with unsteady hands as I sit. He shakes as I've never seen him do, and cold doesn't seem to be the reason—his hands burn hot as ever as they brush my neck.

My stomach chooses that moment to groan like a dog in pain—when I ask to dart into the kitchen to scavenge a leftover piece of toast, a bruised apple, anything, he promises to cook me lunch himself after he says whatever he's trying to say. To *try* to say the words implies they're difficult to express. But Dom does and says everything with ease. The girlish part of me wonders for a split second if he's going to make some sort of romantic confession after our botched first kiss, but I don't think Lamb's story is one to put anyone in that mind-set, so I quietly worry, thumbing the blanket's edges as I wait for this secret to emerge.

"What's going on?" I ask with a gentle smile, trying not to shiver. "Couldn't resist the lovely weather?" I know I need to laugh off his zealousness. I need to put him at ease, because as I learned with Yesi, when those I care for become unwound, I risk becoming unwound myself.

No, a part of me—the weak part—wants to tell him. Not now. Please save your confession for another time. I can't bear it now. I can't, not after the evening and morning I've had.

His face freezes in an unfinished expression of fear, as if some crucial bit of machinery has failed inside. He watches the empty deck, hair windswept. Rain clouds the size and shape of tipped-over mountains race across the sky above us in double time, blown forward by severe winds.

"Listen, Mav, I owe it to you to explain myself," he says as if he's soothing a frantic animal. I fold my arms across my chest, feeling the first tickle of rain on my skin. "I know you've noticed a change in me since those first days in the house."

I contemplate him. Of course I've noticed a change. He cares about me. He's not embittered, not depressive, not cold, not jeering. But those days were so few that I can tell myself they were imagined. I curl my knees up onto the chair, wrap my arms around them. "What are you saying?"

"You deserve to know who you are. I mean . . . who I am," he says, rubbing his brow.

"Who I am?" A spatter of rain hits me on the cheek, and I wipe it aside reflexively. "Who you are?"

"This is getting all confused," he says, flustered. "Let me simplify this. You're Mavi. And I'm—I'm Angel."

"Angel." Two unfamiliar syllables my brain cannot process. *Angel.* Fat drops of rain fall onto my face, my arms, exploding into wet starbursts. I can't bring myself to laugh yet. I don't understand the joke. My cheeks flush. *Angel.* Is it a noun or a name? It must be a name. "What? But you're Domenico. Carmela's son. A De Vaccaro."

I'm humiliated speaking the words—feeling less purely rational than wholly unintelligent. I check his face for signs of madness: A jagged smirk, a winking sneer, but his face remains as smooth as an undisturbed lake. The effect is even more frightening: I'm sure he's expending great energy to keep it that way; either that, or the brain, overwhelmed, struggles to keep facial operations in play. My eyes flick to the patio edge, too few meters from us. How close the ice is now. A hulking mass.

"You've never once been wrong to think that presences gather here," he says, placing his hands flat on the table, sending another shudder through me. I can't keep my own arms still, and his hands, those hands, they're large and freckled and delicately veined and so real. "Presences do gather here. Spirits roam the halls invisibly, alongside the rest of us. They can even, at times, make themselves visible."

I swallow. "What? What are you saying?" My own hands are so fragile-looking and blue with cold; I tuck them into my armpits so they won't shake, but they don't stop, won't stop. And he won't look me in the eye; he's suppressing his own emotion. I wait for him to laugh or to cry; I wait for rage to swell inside me. I wait for a prescribed turn of events. I wait for a betrayal—the insecure part of me expects him to inform me I've been an idiot to believe in ghosts, that our friendship is as insubstantial and imaginary as they are. I wait for him—still—to reveal that hidden madness, an insanity he has learned to camouflage. A hundred conclusions flicker through my head as I watch him get speckled by the rain; for believing Domenico might have fallen for me as I did him, especially after those first days, the universe may now be giving me a colossal karmic middle finger. Whatever has gotten into Dom's head is either a grand joke or symptom of mental illness or evidence that I'm even more ignorant and minuscule in this universe than I thought possible, that all of us are, that . . .

Tears pool over in his wide blue eyes, and he scrabbles for my hands. To warm them, perhaps. I don't respond in kind. I can't.

But I'm taken back to the morning I met Domenico—when he teased me at breakfast and recoiled at my touch, as if everything about me disgusted him.

It would be irrational to think them the same person.

He's not Dom.

"You're one of them." Bile swells up my raw throat. "One of these *presences*."

"I arrived here like you did," he says, tears falling. It isn't an answer. He's not Dom, goddamnit. I want to kick him and punch him, but I'm so terrified that I feel as if I'm going to sob and vomit all at once.

"You're not a Zapuche. And you're not an old victim of their curse."

He shakes his head, wipes at his eyes. "Others come from all times, all places. It's this place—we're drawn to it. I told you. I tried to explain. I—I never wanted to cause any harm."

"I don't understand," I say, enunciating as clearly as I can. I think I'm crying, too; my cheeks feel hot and ice-cold all at once. He bites his lip. Domenico's lip. His face drips with tears and rain. "*Have* you caused any harm?" I think of Luciana, gone. Mrs. Hawk. The girls. I hear a sharp intake of breath, a gasp, a groan. From me.

"Of course not," he says. "You know me."

But I don't know him. This *Angel*, whoever this *Angel* is, whatever this *Angel* is, has watched us all from his stolen perch, played me for a fool, if what he says is truth. My Dom does not exist. "I don't know you. You lied to me." I rub at the moisture on my cheeks, unsure if these silly droplets betraying me are tears or rain.

"I'm the same person you've gotten to know," he says, voice catching. "Sort of." His meltwater-blue eyes droop so tenderly at me—it should wound my heart more deeply than the sharpest of his icy glances.

But he isn't Dom.

"Sort of," I echo.

"Please let me explain," he tells me, fumbling for my bare wrist again.

Its touch sends a crackling shudder through me, electrical and violent. It's not *his* hand—it's nothing but a tool used to manipulate me, hot as flame despite the frigid cold of the patio. Worst of all, despite my immediate fear and revulsion, some old part of my brain desperately wishes for the hand to remain there, because it brings a comfort to me that I cannot overstate. But craving an expired intimacy is worse than anything—a reminder of the permanent disconnect between mind and body. Where is Domenico, if Angel has taken his place? And is it inexcusable not to immediately wish him back?

It only started with the tremors, but I'm weeping, too, now; I hear it, and I taste it, salty thick, and I pull away, soaked to the bone, wondering how easily extinguished this flicker of consciousness inside me truly is, and how it has survived this long, a single wick alight in a gusty world. I push my chair back to stand, trip over a rain-soaked tile, and burst back through the patio's double doors.

"Please don't cry," he calls as I run. "Please! I don't—Please come back, Mav! Let me explain." And I hear him sob, too.

22

ANGEL: 2020-2200

I needed to take her where she could see the sky and the ice. Where we spent that first night together, under a blanket of stars. Where she could understand that the unknown isn't to be feared—it's to be carefully explored with awe, if she is willing.

I think of what we carved on Mama's gravestone: *Wonder, until the very end*.

Charon warned me not to consort with the other side: He told me it was time frittered away. But I've treasured every precious moment, and my only wish now is to strip away more of the artifice, to see those threads of kinship laid bare between us and to know if they'll hold.

So I took her outside, and I told her.

You're Mavi, I said, taking her hand. *I'm Angel*.

23

MAVI: ARGENTINA, JUNE 1978

I sprint from the breakfast room, down the stone hall, and up to the servants' quarters, dodging the broken steps in a breathless blur. *He's not Domenico. He's not Domenico at all.* The journey has never taken me less time, and I do not pass a single soul. Mind whirling, I burst into my room and rush into the bathroom, pounding on Yesi's door.

"Yesi!"

No one answers. She must still be sleeping. Sleeping or seething. Mistrusting us all. I know she resents me for failing to visit Carmela with her outright—for ruining her credibility by mentioning Dom in our meeting. Lord. Dom.

I don't know Domenico—I never did. Not beyond those early days of offhand cruelty, at least. Key still shaking in hand, I wrench my bag from underneath my bed, thrusting odd clumps of clothing inside, then packing every other pitiful item I brought (the hand cream and the toothbrush). It takes less than a minute to collect my Vaccaro School life. I toss my key onto the bed and skid out the door of room 7, flying down the mangled stairs, two at a time, nearly breaking my ankle on a missing step this go-around, zigzagging through the damask hall, its busy cloud pattern concealing patches of frilly dark mold. Damask, brocade, damn it all to hell. The house and its rules mean nothing.

I should have known. I should have known I wasn't befriending a reformed Domenico De Vaccaro. His incomprehensible vocabulary, strange accent, and utter lack of knowledge about Argentine politics were no upper-class quirk at all——more so a reflection of growing up elsewhere, in another time. That first shakiness in his bones could never be explained by withdrawal——the idea of taking over a body, mad as it is, fits so much better.

I should have known.

If such a spirit can exist and walk among us for weeks unnoticed, which of the rules governing our sad human existence still holds?

If I can fall for an impostor, can I trust myself again?

I plow into the locked front door, and as I fiddle with the series of locks above——since when have there been so many damned locks?——I feel the scratch of long nails against my sodden clothes. I flinch, falling into the thick wood of the door as a hand closes around my arm.

"Where, exactly, do you think you're going in this storm?"

Morency in the vestibule. Miserable, sullen Morency, whose beady eyes penetrate the walls with ease, as they do my own soul.

"I'm leaving." I hike the bag farther up my shoulder, aware, momentarily, of how violently I am trembling beneath her enormous palm. I tug away, but she keeps a firm grasp on me, her fingers as immovable as iron clamps.

"You left your room last night." She leans in so I can see the wetness of her rancid-smelling mouth. *Who cares?* I want to shout. I close my eyes and fight her grip, expecting her to hurl a string of insults at me, to spit on me, to—

"What happened?" she asks.

I stop, my fingers uncurling from the meat of my bag strap, and I open my eyes. She releases her hold, and the fact she isn't castigating me right now shocks me into brief clarity. "You were right," I croak.

"Go on."

But how to begin to explain just how unsafe this house is? How to prove that the dangers here are far greater than us, too powerful in their own right for us to understand alone? How can I convince this stubborn woman that we should all be leaving, every one of us? *This is a ruined place*, I want to shout. *There are unknowable strangers here who want to harm us. You must know this. You must sense them.* But my chest still heaves too intensely, my mind spins too wildly for me to say any of this.

"You were on the patio with Master Domenico," she says when I do not say a word. She crosses her arms, mouth puckered as if sucking a sour candy. "Can you assure me your exchange with him had nothing to do with your decision to leave?"

I swallow. Of course I can't. It has everything to do with my decision to leave. "He's—he's been possessed."

She glowers at me: The truth was the wrong answer. "Am I to take it that your deep concern for the girls of this house was all an elaborate lie to enable you to traipse around and debase yourself with Master Domenico? And now that your romance has died in its wicked bed, now that he has moved on from you, you decide that he has—what?—become possessed by an unfeeling . . . other?"

Weak light from the sconces flashes off the whites of her eyes.

"Excuse me?"

284

Morency, the one-track record, bound to repeat her exhausting, unoriginal, moralistic speech no matter what I say. And yet—I can't keep myself from trying, from screaming into the wind.

"There are ghosts here, Ms. Morency. And members of this house aren't in their right minds on account of the dark magic flooding this place. They're being possessed, taken over, whatever you want to call it. And I learned from—Well, it doesn't matter. I'm leaving. I won't meddle any longer. I won't risk losing my mind, too." I smear at the streaks beneath my eyes with my free hand, repulsed by the plastic feel of my skin.

I look up at her, her eyes black in the shadows once more, and I swear, for the briefest of moments, I glimpse a softness there—I cannot know if it is pity or fear.

"I cannot stop you," she says in no more than a hoarse whisper. "But the funicular is not running."

Of course it isn't. It's some punishment she's devised, I'm sure, for sneaking out last night, for fraternizing with the devil, for confirming her worst instincts about me. What a demon she is. I'm boiling mad; energy crawls down my arms and legs. "I'll walk."

"And the supply boat has been delayed."

"I'll wait for it on the dock anyway," I snap, turning from her and wrenching the door open at last. Outside, rain falls in sheets on the steps, and the fog is as thick as milk. I stagger back before pushing myself into the dense damp and dragging the door closed behind me.

"You'll be drowned like a rat in this rain," she calls as the door creaks shut and I begin the slow and perilous descent to the dock.

It could be half an hour later or an hour later: I've never been colder in my life, as the freezing humidity has nestled its way into a crawl space I didn't know existed between my bones and muscle. Each step takes twenty seconds to descend because I must first test my weight.

My thighs wobble, and I've rolled my weak ankles on loose stones a dozen times. My waterlogged bag weighs me down further, and as I shiver, I touch my fingers to my lips, feeling no warmth or texture of life on either end.

It could be said that I am in a state of panic, for I am no closer to the dock. I have not even passed all the cottages. My body feels like quivering lumps of mush trapped inside exhausted strips of muscle on the verge of shutting down. And my brain, my brain revisits the horror of Angel's revelation again and again. The loudest part calls me a fool, a fool, a fool, all while the quiet part asks: *But how was I to know that spirits could infiltrate the bodies of the residents of this rock for weeks on end?*

I rub my hands together to bring some warmth to them and immediately recoil as I remember Angel making the same gesture. I couldn't have known: That's the truth of it. Not when I only learned his kind existed long after meeting him. Not when he behaved so unlike the rest of them, handling me with care, day after day.

I slow by a cottage, trying to take brief refuge in one, then another, pressing my wet hands upon the glass, only to find them empty and their doors locked.

If Angel wanted to abuse us like the rest of his kind, surely he would not have treated me with such kindness, only to reveal the truth at last. Surely he would have another trick up his sleeve. I slump against the doorframe, teeth chattering and lips blue in the reflection of the glass. Mother: What would you say to me if you could hear me now? Would you call me naive for questioning this spirit's true nature, when his brethren are so evil? Would you call me weak for running from the house now, unworthy of that circle of fierce cousins you built around us?

I shrug off my bag. I always believed my mother's strength stemmed from her certainty. I thought her strength only grew when she doubled that certainty, instilling her black-and-white view in others.

I feel no such certainty now. More and more questions crop up in my head. My sole conviction is that conditions will not improve in this house of lost souls without intervention. To abandon my peers in this madhouse now, ignorant of this privileged and horrifying knowledge I have, would be cowardly and cruel. I might be the only person on this rock with access to someone who understands the darkness swallowing this house.

I think of proud Yesi, alone and vulnerable in her room. Of sweet Lamm, possessed and in poor health. Of Mole, bewildered yet desperate to help however she can. Of the girls, fighting against invisible torture, even as they fade.

I think it with a sinking stomach: I cannot leave them now.

Yet I cannot forget about Angel, too: this otherworldly creature who bridged an unbridgeable gap to tell me a most painful truth.

I need not be alone in this fight.

I rub at my eyes, clearing them of rain. Perhaps I was wrong about my mother's source of strength. Perhaps she knew strength comes from not feeling so alone, in spite of uncertainty, and she fostered that strength by drawing groups of cousins together around her.

You have so much courage. You made it here alone, Angel told me once. *And you're so young. The young, the curious, we . . . we need to stay alive and learn everything we can. So when we're older, we can fight smarter, together.*

It's time to let the old rules fall away and fight, now. I cannot run forever.

What to do when darkness overwhelms? That is one thing all of those I've loved would have agreed upon: We must gather up our strength and fight together toward the narrowing light. I hitch my bag back onto my shoulder. I know where I must go.

∞ ∞ ∞

Domenico—Angel—is still on the patio where I've left him, also drenched in rain, as if in penance. He must have been here hours, yet his swollen face looks hopeful when he sees me. I stand inside the patio door, towel in hand.

"Angel." I cross my arms around the towel to stop their convulsions. "An interesting name."

"I know," he says, wiping his face. "My mom named me Angel because she said I was born blessed, with a lucky star over my head."

I inspect him for some sign of a change, for some sign of possession, but I find none, only earnestness. He looks the same as always. Should I trust this curiosity and enduring affection toward this soul on my part, or am I still beholden to some flicker of dangerous intimacy felt toward what can only be a shell?

"So you had a mother," I whisper. "You were a living thing, once. A man."

What world, what womb does Angel come from, whatever *Angel* is?

He rises to meet me, as vulnerable as I've ever seen him. "I'm not like Dom. I'm different. But you can call me him, since I'm in him now." His lips tremble. "Do you care?"

Do I care that he is dead? A spirit?

An Other?

Of course I care. I hunger to know why he was granted this singular opportunity for life after death when so many others were not. What did he do in life to be deserving?

Or is his state a punishment, a limbo for souls with business left unresolved, as drilled into us by the ghost stories we hear as children?

But I bite my tongue, knowing full well that questioning this soul's existence will do us no good now.

"Why did you befriend me?" I ask instead.

"Because I've never met anyone like you," Angel says quietly.

If only it was that easy. And yet, this is the same Angel who was more assured than I was that every shade inside me would compose a glorious picture, even if its content remained unknown in full. The same Angel who offered up his love so readily—a tender, constant, boundless-seeming type of love I'd never seen. A type I never felt from the person I was closest to in the world—my own mother. And I'm not willing to throw that away until I understand why it was given.

"Will you be honest with me from this point forward? Will you tell me everything I need to help us?"

Two more questions I can only pray he answers truthfully because I cannot know for certain. And we know how flimsy prayers are on this gusty rock.

"Of course," he says, eyes blue and clear.

I can smell milanesa oil burning somewhere. This is a moment to test my strength—to trust my instincts and come together, or die. I steel myself. As I approach my own battle with such strange foes, I wonder how I will be. Will I become a hardened warrior like my mother? Or will a fundamental gentleness remain in me, like in Tío Adolfo?

"Then of course I don't care who or what you are," I say, throwing him the towel to dry off and breaking every rule I thought I knew about trust. "You are my friend, Angel. That's all that matters now." Both because I wish to believe him, this soul I have come to believe is good, and—and because I see no other path forward toward the light.

24

ANGEL: 2020-2400

After my grand reveal, no daisy chains were woven and exchanged. No one danced through the meadow across the ice, hand in hand.

Sure, I expected a blowout. But I thought that fight would be followed by blood bonds cemented; mafia rules. I can't say why, because in admitting the truth, I exposed a months-long betrayal. But at least Mavi still speaks to me, and that feels like enough. It feels like more than I deserve.

"We have a lot of work to do, Angel," she says, motioning for me to follow her through the empty halls and upstairs. "A lot of house rules to break."

I hesitate, tripping over my feet behind her. "Work? Rules? What?"

"You must tell me everything you know about the Others like you," she says. "That was your promise."

My face is still swollen from crying, and I pat it down, worried someone will see us or overhear us. "Of course. But you're not going to like it," I say as we pass room 6.

"I don't have to like it," she says, opening the door to her light apricot room and beckoning me inside. I sit beside her on the bed, with a glance at my closet. "Now," she says, "who are they?"

They being them, the bastard Others. *They* is generous, since she means *you all*.

"We're lost souls made of energy," I admit. Because that seems like a decent enough entry point. "To exist, to inhabit others, to do anything, we need to maintain that energy. To maintain that energy, we have to eat." I stop, consider my phrasing. Rub my hands together, as if that'll help me cook up a decent explanation. "It's not as appetizing a process as it is for you. When Others feed, it's on dreams." I think of every vibrant thread I've extracted from Yesi. "Others draw them out of their heads, like invisible fingertips sweeping through invisible cobwebs. If fingers were magnets, and cobwebs were metal fillings?" The tone of the statement rises at the end into a question, as if I'm a Valley girl, tripping inside her own phantasmagoria. Mavi sets her jaw, and I hesitate again. "I guess it can . . . dilute people's memories."

"You're feeding on the girls, and that's making them sick," she says, hands curling into fists. "And you possess them, too."

I blanch. "Not me. I would never do that to them."

"But you need to feed, too, don't you?" There's a sharp edge to her voice now.

I could say I feed from Dom. I've tried, after all. If only his dreams were nourishing. "There's someone here who doesn't appear to suffer when fed from." At least I don't think so.

She hides a frown, lips wrinkling. "That doesn't exactly make it more palatable to me. Who is it?"

I mumble *Yesi*, blood pumping hard.

"What?" she asks. "Oh, Lord, is it me?"

I shake my head. "Oh my god, no. It's not you. They don't feed from you. You're totally unpalatable, speaking of. Nasty, I think."

"I don't know whether to be relieved or offended," she confesses. "But that doesn't surprise me. I have nasty dreams like most nasty women. Who is it?"

I sneak a glance at the closed bathroom door. "Yesi," I whisper. "It's Yesi."

She bites her lip so hard it turns white before refilling with blood. "That's not possible," she says. "Yesi doesn't even believe there are real ghosts here. She thinks ghosts are symbols . . ." She trails off, her face turning gray. "Well, this would make her special. In a way she would detest. She—she wouldn't stand for it," she whispers to herself before clutching her stomach, and I think she's going to be sick, but her hands move to her thighs, gripping them hard, and she whispers, "Do you think she knows? She can't know."

"I don't think so," I reply.

"How can we stop them from feeding?" she asks, nails visibly crimping into the flesh of her palms. "I suppose I shouldn't ask you that. It's part of your survival instinct, I gather."

A ruby-red flush stains my cheeks. She looks like a little girl stranded on the dark streets of Buenos Aires, miles from home. Helpless. And it makes me feel queasy.

"There's some writing about sacrificing girls to fend off the spirits, but the Zapuche and their shamans were the last to know how to perform the ritual, and they're long gone," I offer, and she nods, drifts off in thought. I'm overcome by a desperate urge to give more, to help her, even if it will only hurt me. "But the tenth girl might know more. And I think she would help."

"The little girl who visited me? Is she one of you?"

I shake my head. "Something in between. A sacrificed girl. I think she's hiding here. Even—even Carmela is looking for her."

Her attention snaps back in full, as if Carmela's acknowledgment of the legend turns it into cut-and-dried history. "Truly? Carmela knows about her?"

I nod. "There's a Zapuche legend about girls like her."

Her eyes flicker with interest. And so I tell her the first story Mama ever told me.

In every generation, a young girl was sacrificed to the Zapuche gods, in a great ceremony on a cliff beside the ice, to ensure the safety and peace of the tribe. She knew being sacrificed was a weighty honor, one she could only hope to live up to someday. Because when the girl was sacrificed, she did not die—no, she lived on in a new form, removed from the tribe but gaining great powers. Becoming like a god herself. She could move clouds and ice. She could connect lost relatives. And most important, she could tell you the color of your soul. What follows is one of her adventures in Patagonia . . .

On this day, the girl happened upon a peaceful Zapuche village that had lived on guanaco—a type of wild llama in the region—for centuries. These guanaco were so gentle that they would graze within a hundred feet of the Zapuche, instinctually aware that the tribe only killed what they needed to survive.

But when foreign ranchers moved in, they killed the guanaco on sight, believing they competed with their sheep for foraging and pasture. They left them in the roads, rotting away and riddled with shot, so that they could not be used for food. Soon, the guanaco were decimated, and the Zapuche suffered in turn.

The girl recognized the problem, and she came up with a clever solution to help her people. Can you guess?

She would help the guanaco transform into butterflies around the foreigners—chameleonlike butterflies that could pick up the color of their lush Patagonian surroundings. That way, the guanaco could exist freely in their new form—but when captured by a Zapuche, they would reclaim their old one.

Mavi is lost in thought when I finish. "There are butterflies like that here," she tells me, eyes distant. "Ones that take on the colors of their surroundings. I've seen them myself." She settles her gaze on me, and it's much sharper than expected, even though her voice is soft. "But that's just a story, Angel. We can't simply fly away."

I clear my throat and blink away the humiliation. Of course: This is deadly real for her, in a way it could never be for me. "I think I can find more information about her," I say. "Real information. I promise." And I resolve to give this despicable source one final try.

When I leave her and Dom, I flit over to the cloud house. Charon's sitting on his cloud chair, pressing a cheesesteak between his dirty fingertips and studying the indentations. He grunts upon seeing me.

"Cute heart-to-heart with the English teacher. Feeling relieved and guilt-free now? Even though you sold yourself down the river with your little reveal?"

It chills me every time I remember just how much he witnesses in the house. I think of my tears on the patio, and I burn with shame.

"You know, I don't give her enough credit," he continues. "Telling her you can stay friends if you spill your guts about the Others? Brilliant manipulation."

"I'm not here to talk about that."

He sniffs at the soggy sandwich edge. "Aren't you a little miffed your girlfriend didn't inquire as to how your condition affects you?"

Charon asks, a smirk playing on his lips. "Aren't you wondering why she didn't ask you point-blank if you're dead?"

I blink at him. And even though I don't want to admit it, he's right.

Shouldn't it terrify her and exhilarate her, this idea of existing after death? Shouldn't it remind her of her mother and the other relatives she never knew? Shouldn't it give her hope of reconnecting with them—even if it's a misguided hope?

Shouldn't she wonder what happened to me?

But those conversations could fill a lifetime, and we've had no time at all.

"I came to ask about the tenth girl one last time," I say instead. "I need to talk to her. And I know you know her. You see everything in the house. Don't lie to me."

Belching, he shakes his head. "Jeez, sometimes I wish you were a Cabbage Patch Kid or a Furby or one of those mindless gurgling pieces of shit you can turn off. Logic just doesn't work with you." He considers me. "For Pete's sake, kid. You're supposed to be having fun. I've said it plenty, and I'll say it again: You're going to feel like all that time spent with the English teacher—all the time searching for this tenth girl—is a real waste someday. Nothing in there is real for you. Get it?"

"It feels real to me. Mavi's special."

He snorts. "Special is such an empty, piece-of-shit word. But to your point, she's as *special* as I'm *special*, kid, and my partner used to say I must've been hit in the head by an ass's hoof as a tit-suckling infant."

Partner. It's the first time I've heard Charon drop a nugget about his old life.

"You do realize this doesn't last forever?" he inquires before wolfing down a quarter of the steak filling.

I don't answer, feeling those same damn tears from the patio well up.

"You're in too deep," he says at last, mouth full. "You're a nice enough kid, but you care too much about shit that doesn't matter. The English teacher. *Any* human in that goddamn house—" He swallows, then blows the stinking air from his mouth. "Let's say your tenth girl exists," he continues carefully, setting down his sandwich. "What's she meant to do for you?"

My answer rushes to mind because I've known it in my bones so long, with or without admitting it to myself. It's impossible to speak it aloud without sounding completely unhinged, and I know it. But I say it all the same. "She can—she can reconnect me with my loved ones."

He groans. "There are no 'missed connections' here, kid. We're born alone, and we die alone. What happened to screw you up so much?" He lifts his sandwich. "Lose your mommy? Is that why you're desperate to pick up an emotional sugar mama in the house? Is that why you haven't diddled her?"

Am I so fucking obvious? Fury flames inside me, venomous words flaring up behind it. "You're a condescending piece of shit, Charon. You're so far up your own asshole you don't realize you're passive, hypocritical scum, spying on everyone else because you're trapped in a dark room all day, doomed to jacking yourself off and shoving cheesesteaks down your gullet. I don't need to put up with you, you pathetic old asshole. I don't need your shit."

"Bite me," he spits, hurling his sandwich onto the ground like a gauntlet. It bursts open, splashing the cloud with meat. "I can't be an asshole and be up my asshole, too. Kind of a have-your-cake-and-eat-it situation. But that doesn't matter—as always, you're missing the point. You've made your choice, looks like. Go suck at the teat of your little girlfriend-slash-surrogate-mommy a bit more while you still can." The bits of sandwich melt through the clouds. "The Others will bite off your crystal dick when they catch wind of you. And Others can die their own death, too, you know, and it's gnarly. But in the meantime, you're dead to me. Dead dead."

And he gives me cheese-flecked double middle fingers.

25

MAVI: ARGENTINA, JUNE 1978

I visit Yesi alone before what would have been her afternoon class time, slipping through the unlocked bathroom pass-through door. She sleeps in bed, as peaceful as an oil painting of an angel, tangled in her baby-blue sheets but undisturbed. I consider the monstrous details I learned from Angel—how the Others feed from dreams, and how quality of dreams differs—and wonder what richness there is to be mined from inside her skull right now. Angel says younger people seem to have richer dreams in term of quality of nourishment if not . . . flavor. It helps to be robotic in my thinking about it—to ascribe adjectives that make no sense, to be analytical and free of emotion, if word choices in your head can grant you such a freedom. Yesi is older than I am, but she looks as if she's only a girl. Can so shallow a factor affect the Others' perception of their feed quality? Or when

Yesi stopped growing, did biology preserve the purity and richness of some secret garden in her mind? I wonder when someone last fed from her dreams. Could they be feeding now, plucking glossy memories like plums? I don't feel any currents of energy in the air. Hear any rumblings. See any spiderwebs drawn from her temples. My human senses are woefully insufficient; I cannot imagine how this substance Angel believes is so integral to us human beings is stolen from her fragile body nightly. And worst of all: Her racked mind supplies the common feed for the monsters abusing us all.

I gently prod her shoulder, delicate and bird-boned. Her lids spread to show a sliver of periwinkle, and she half smiles at the bowl of blueberries I brought—the withered ones left from the last supply boat. "Did anything happen while I was sleeping?" she asks before looking up at the skylight in the bathroom, where a fierce rain now beats down upon the panes. "Christ, it's turned into an ugly day." Her peaceful expression hardens. "I suppose I shouldn't be surprised after the night we had."

She cleanses her face and settles back in bed to eat the blueberries one by one, as if in a trance. For the briefest moment, she comes out of herself to watch me carefully, recognizing that I've news. I gather the courage to tell her what Angel told me about himself. I spin the words together into a story she will accept as best as I can—she does me the courtesy of refraining from laughing outright, and the hairs on the back of my neck stand on end when I realize she's observing me with the faintest trace of fear. I wait until the end to mention the feeding.

"And who do they supposedly feed from?" she asks, crossing her arms. *"The girls?"*

"Anyone and everyone."

"Even us?" She waves dismissively, avoiding my eyes. "Oh, Swamp. Come on. Dom's pulling your leg. I can't be sure what his endgame is, though. Doesn't seem like the best way to charm someone into bed, by telling her you're a ghostly force bringing new life to an old body. Unless what he's trying to say is that his penis has mystical, life-bringing powers—"

"Yesi, I'm serious," I say as she trembles from cold. I unfold her arms and take her hands in my own to feed them some warmth. "They feed from our dreams, and with that energy, they can possess our bodies. Like they possessed Lamb. Like they possess Dom." I flinch when I speak his name.

She wrenches back her hands, and her knees flinch upward. The bowl topples off her lap, launching blueberries across the floor. "Have you lost your mind? Or have *you* been possessed by a lunatic? Is this some kind of elaborate ruse you've created to convince me that Lamb didn't harass Gisella? That he was possessed by some body snatcher? Because I won't believe it. I can tell you I've never been fed from. I'm not that kind of girl."

Now I'm the one who can't meet her eyes. I can't bring myself to taint this notion she has of her own self-sufficiency and power; it's as clear as day to me that Yesi is terribly strong and special, a creature of absurd brainpower, but the sense of violation is so keen in learning you've been fed from nightly that it overshadows any other vision of the self, at least temporarily. She becomes a unique victim without her own knowledge, a ghostly Lolita, a bag of unearthly flesh.

"He told me it doesn't affect us as much as it affects the girls. But the Others have fed from us at night," I say, treading carefully. "They take threads of dreams. It strengthens them, but it makes our sleep less restful. It can tinker with our memories." As I speak the words, I know perhaps I've said too much at once. If memory loss is a symptom of being fed from too much, Yesi will understand the level of abuse she's endured. And the girls—I think of the trouble they faced when working on that memory exercise days ago.

Her eyes lose focus. I take back her hands and squeeze them, still dreadfully cold. "Yesi?" Her face turns the pale shade of rotted cabbage. She runs to the bathroom and vomits blue spatter into the toilet. I rush after her to hold her hair back. When she settles back on the tile, I soak a towel and wring out the cool water to place it across her forehead.

"This is too elaborate a lie for you, Swamp," she says weakly. "I know you're telling the truth." I want to shove her and hug her at the same time.

"Why are they here?" she asks me. "And why now? I suppose it must have to do with the curse on this place." She regards me with bloodshot blue eyes. "Silly me. I thought it was the primitive Zapuche way of describing the virus."

"Do you feel them?" I kneel beside her. "Do you feel ill?"

"I've always suffered from a poor memory. Nothing more than that." She curls on the sodden bath mat. "My grandmother could tell me a story about an afternoon we shared a week or five years ago, and I wouldn't remember a single detail. I couldn't for the life of me do so now, either. I could remember plots of books just fine—just not the turns of my own life. She told me the ghosts were stripping me of my memories. I told *her* that her business about ghosts was madness. But she must have been right. My grandmother was right. I don't understand it. How could she be right? Spirits stealing memories. The premise itself is absurd." She fixes her eyes on me. "I don't feel ill like the girls. I don't, and I won't imagine that I do to force your pity and my own. But I don't know how to explain how I feel, lacking an impression of the shape of my past. I've tried and tried to explain it in writing. I suppose it's been happening so long I've been used to it—I'm not sure what my natural state truly is. Can any of us? But that's why I continue to write. Continue to draw the threads out of myself—to understand."

"Don't stress yourself, Yesi. We can leave. We'll shut down the school and move everyone away. Whatever is best."

"I'm not making myself understood." She takes my hands in her clammy ones. "Suppose it has nothing at all to do with this place?" she tells me softly. "I can't help but wonder if they follow me, Mavi. I think they might have found me again, along with a rich treasure trove of new victims."

I thought she might blame herself. I did the same, momentarily, when Angel told me he arrived when I did. Everyone considers oneself to be the foster parent to some terrible monster inside that courts disaster when given free rein.

"It all has to do with the Zapuche curse. I promise," I say. "Angel read about it in history books and showed me evidence."

"Evidence," Yesi says shakily.

"A shaman cursed the land, opening a path for spirits, with the intention of receiving their assistance in keeping European colonizers off their tribal land. But the spirits ran amok instead. So every generation, the Zapuche sacrificed a girl to keep the spirits at bay. When the sacrifice ritual was lost, so was the ability to fend them off."

"I suppose we can't just throw Angel out onto the ice as our sacrifice," she says coolly, crossing her arms. The humor returning.

"No," I say. "But Angel can help us figure out another way of saving ourselves. He knows so much about this. I promise." I think I mean the words. What does one call a liar who would die wanting to believe her lies?

She scrutinizes me with two shaded eyes. "Angel. You and your Angel. You seem so sure that Angel will help us save ourselves from his own kind. If you believe you can trust him, then why exactly is Angel who he is, Mavi? How can he be so trustworthy while still being one of these abominable creatures who sucks the life out of us?"

She drops her arms to her sides. "I think our lives will depend on untangling that paradox."

As evening comes, the rain builds on itself, minor storms coalescing into a force of nature of biblical proportions. Yesi and I spend all night huddled together in my bed, watching the thrashing against the lonely skylight pane. "I'd rather die than sleep again," she whispers to me as we wait for Angel to return, though both of us know eventually we won't have the option of melodramatically announcing our courage nor staying awake. I tell her Angel's legend of the tenth girl, with its mention of the chameleonic butterflies she, too, has seen, and the talk of sacrifices and fantastic powers brings a curious glint back to her eyes.

When Angel knocks, Yesi rises to open the door herself, and she inspects him for a long minute before opening the door wider. "I'm relieved to hear you aren't Domenico," she says, letting him by. "He was a real beast."

We can't help but grin at this odd olive branch she's offered.

"Now on to the serious business," she adds, dropping back onto the bed with a dark expression. "What next, Archangel Gabriel? Bestow upon us your message. Lead us from the darkness into God's light."

Angel's grin freezes. Once more, I am struck by the thought that he wasn't entirely aware of what he'd signed up for by revealing his truth to me.

"Why can't we escape with the girls on the next supply boat?" I ask, piping up.

As if on cue, the storm batters the bathroom skylight even harder.

"It's clearly impossible without God's and Carmela's help, Swamp," Yesi says, snapping at me. "Are you blind to the conditions outside? How would we distract Morency and Carmela, then bundle all the sick girls onto that tiny, flimsy boat? And in case you've forgotten, Our Lady Carmela manages the boat schedule."

"Yesi's right, Mav. Scratch the boat." Angel rubs at the skin between his eyes. "I still think we should focus on finding the tenth girl."

But I don't feel comfortable allowing this elusive, unidentified girl to be our only hope—our only focus. I remember the terror I felt when I encountered her in my room. "A little ghost girl who speaks in riddles and hides in the shadows, claiming she's good for only a warning. A little ghost girl Yesi thought I had hallucinated."

Yesi flaps her hand, dismissing me. "If she warned you about the Others, providing such specific information, I'm willing to admit that the being you saw was more than the physical embodiment of your psyche's warning that the unholy walk these halls. Again: Your imagination isn't that rich, Swamp." She turns her dictatorial gaze on Angel. "Still: Let's say this girl can give us knowledge of the sacrifice ritual that protects us against the Others—if such a ritual even exists. Why would you want to find her, Angel? Are you such a self-loathing Other? Or do you hope to fly under the radar and live on indefinitely in your charming little costume?" Yesi's words could decapitate a stone statue.

Angel crosses his arms. The tension in the air is palpable; our threesome can exist only so long. Are we forced allies, fighting a common enemy? Are we fools, or jealous friends? I resist the urge to pipe up and protect Angel from Yesi and vice versa. I pretend everything is normal, even though it can't be.

"Angel?" I ask in a tone as gentle as I can muster.

"If the tenth girl is one of these girls from legend, she can do more than force Others away. She can reconnect us with lost loved ones. She can—" He pauses, eyes clouding over. "Who knows what other miracles she can perform."

And somehow, even Yesi is silenced by this prospect. So I refrain from complicating matters by airing my long-simmering theory: that this ghost might simply be Carmela's dead daughter. How much easier it would be if she was a paranormal force of good who could help us fight off the hordes of Others.

"We can't sit around waiting for this girl to reappear. We should confront Carmela anyway," I suggest. "Whether it's to finally convince her of the danger we're in and launch an escape plan, or to mine her for information on this girl."

"Carmela almost murdered me with a letter opener when I pressed her on the tenth girl," Angel says. "She told me never to speak of it again."

"Then the two of us will pursue that anger in our exchanges with her. Crack her facade, and squeeze the truth out of her."

Yesi nods. "And if Carmela doesn't break open for us, we'll take advantage of the fact that you're her detested flesh and blood, Angel-as-Dom. The *Dom dominator*." She smirks, and Angel raises his hands in the air, as if accepting Yesi won this round.

And so our plan is set. Yesi and I will corner Carmela, that ironclad box of a woman, and break her open at last, with guile or force. Whether we'll find compassion or cruelty inside remains to be seen.

I cannot wait.

When Carmela misses breakfast, Morency offers no explanation. Instead, she announces that all classes will be moved to the dining room at breakfast, after Mole suffered a fall attempting to fetch papers from her cottage classroom in the storm. In the midmorning, a morning we cannot perceive but for the clock reading a certain way, while Gisella and Michelle recuperate in bed, the faintings begin.

First Isabella, in the stone corridor. Christina, in the breakfast hall. Diana, falling off her dining room chair. They faint dead away in their makeshift morning classes, young girls crumpling to the floor like old wilted flowers robbed of a vase. As Mole accuses them of succumbing to hysteria, of wanting to play hooky, we carry them to their rooms, limp and pale, where they inevitably complain of poor sleep. Of nausea. Of anxiety—a concept some of them don't even understand, yet can detail—*a rather unspecific but all-consuming fear*. They speak of being the victims of some inexplicable theft, a theft only Yesi can understand.

Mariella approaches me at lunch as I serve warmed-up soup and the last of the sliced fruit to the group. "Miss Quercia," she whispers to me before looking around the dining room, empty of all her friends except a glum Silvina. Sara refused to leave her bedroom. "What can I do?"

I inhale slowly. How can I feed her strength? How can I advise her to stay healthy when all her peers are fading? I cannot tell her to fight sleep, the only weapon I know, when it's clear she's buzzing from leftover adrenaline that is sure to dry up soon.

"You can eat well and nourish yourself," I tell her, sneaking her a whole apple and a double serving of mushroom soup, the best we have left.

She sets them down, eyes blazing. "I meant to help everyone else."

My hands wobble on the ladle: This girl before me has a strength I could have only dreamed of when I was her age. It might be my exhaustion, but I almost tear up, and my chest wobbles with pride.

I nod at her. "We'll do rounds to check on the girls after lunch."

"They'll get better, won't they?" she asks, brow setting into a strong line, as the electricity flickers in and out. "We'll work our hardest to cure them."

"Yes. We will do our best to help until doctors come." It is a gentle lie: I cannot know how a doctor would help us now, much less reach this rock. But I gather the food, placing it in her hands, then steer her by her delicate shoulders toward an empty seat by Silvina. "Now, eat."

By the time our sad lunch hour ends, Carmela has not resurfaced. Morency informs us that a doctor will arrive imminently for the girls. Yet shortly thereafter, the afternoon supply boat is canceled, and she orders the shutters to be shut, one by one, closing off Vaccaro School from the oppressive rain. Every able-bodied member of the house helps to lock us in further—six hands must tug each warped shutter closed, and three faces go dark anew when both sides are secured. Electricity is spotty, and more often than not, the house feels like a lightless tomb. Someone generously fumbles with damp matches, and new candles are lit for each of us to carry. Mostly tallow candles remain, and the smell of roasted animal fat thickens the air, reminding us of butchery and our rumbling stomachs in one go.

With our help, Morency converts an oversize and unusually warm carpeted sitting room on the second floor—once bearing a covered grand piano—into a larger sickroom. "It has the air of a refugee camp," she says to no one in particular as we inspect the fine lace of fungus growing along one wall. "Mess and misery included." We arrange nine cots in neat little rows of three, both hopeful that Luciana will be found and terrified all the girls will fall. Mariella and Silvina read to the sick girls, until Silvina drops to the floor herself, drained of the little energy she had left. An overworked Mole and I carry her onto another free cot. Only Mariella remains up, and though her face is gray from fatigue, she refuses to rest on the final bed, helping until Morency returns to relieve us.

Before dinner, Yesi, Angel, and I roam around the house, and the corridors are so quiet one could hear a pin drop. Carmela has all but vanished, and Sara has disappeared from her bedroom, too. We wander into the empty kitchen, only to find that many of its appliances no longer function, and a slippery grime coats its tiles.

"Where is the kitchen staff?" Yesi whispers, opening the cabinets to peruse the little palatable food left.

I can only shake my head: I haven't seen them in days, not since conditions worsened. Wary as they were of this place, they were adept at keeping its banal evils in check. It was a kind of magic we never appreciated. It might be twisted, but I pray they fled to safety.

We locate several cans of beans and tomato soup and go about heating them on the one gas burner that still works. At dinner, Angel, Yesi, and I share a table with Mariella, while Mole and Armadello make up another. Over our meager portions, we overhear Armadello lament the failed search for Luciana and Mole gossip about Mr. Lamm, as if Mariella isn't present.

"Sometimes they put on the sweetest facades," she says, her voice carrying from the other table. "No wonder he never married. And on top of it all, now we are short one more, caring for the sick and cleaning up while he lazes around in his room."

Mariella, sitting beside me, nudges me. "Is that true about Mr. Lamm?"

"Dr. Molina's weariness is getting the best of her," Yesi snaps, on her other side.

Mole drops her spoon with a metallic clang. Chastened, perhaps, she escorts Mariella back upstairs to tuck her in before resuming her sickroom shift.

Yesi fixes her critical gaze on a very pale Angel next as he tucks into his sorry bowl of beans. He stops eating midmouthful, and he excuses himself, explaining he must let Dom rest so they can recover their strength. I must watch him leave with a concerned wistfulness because Yesi flicks my arm.

"Stop that," she hisses. "Worry about our own kind."

He does feel like our kind to me. I almost remind her he is our only connection to the Others, but she does do more than her part by feeding him.

Before our sickroom shift, Yesi and I take Lamm some leftover beans and some crusts of stale bread with jam, but he can't even bring himself to the door to answer us. "Please go, my dears," he wheezes through the door. "Thank you for coming, but Madame De Vaccaro has asked that I stay here, out of sight."

But I push inside the forest-green haven, knowing better. Huddled over his miniature desk, he compulsively journals what he remembers and what he does not remember, as if to unlock some explanation in his memory. Yesi, hesitant, toes her way in after me and gasps: Fat clumps of hair identical to those she found in her grip are missing from his head and littered on the floor.

"I don't remember anything," he says, his teary eyes shellacked, as he raps his skull again and again with a roughness I've never witnessed in him. "I don't remember anything at all. But that, of course, sounds like what a monster would say if accused of such behavior. Does it not?"

"It isn't your fault," I offer softly.

"You were . . . you were possessed," Yesi adds, rendered inarticulate for once.

Convulsing, he shakes his bare head, convinced we're either devils come to ease out a confession or naive friends pandering to his delusions. We cannot persuade him of his innocence, no matter what I say. "There is a special place in hell for people like me," he repeats again and again. "I've fought my animal instincts all my life, only for my unconscious mind to betray me."

It sickens me to hear him speak this way.

"We should have kept trying to explain," Yesi tells me outside his room, her lip bloodied from nervous biting. But we worry about the pandemonium that would ensue if we revealed the hopelessness of our situation to our fractured group. "I'll recant what I said when we next see Carmela," she whispers to me. "Perhaps he'll listen to that soulless witch. It's the least I can do."

We spend another sleepless night, some of the hours mute, listening as the wind brings new sheets of rain crashing down. Cracks spread through our walls and ceilings like spiderwebs. Centimeter-long fissures grow to a meter or more in length, their edges jagged like rotted teeth, as if the house's walls are hungry.

We feed the six sick girls stories of our own invention (including the Zapuche legend of the girls, sanitized of sacrifice mentions) and the last fresh vegetables in soup in an effort to keep them awake—their conscious hours are maddeningly few and far between. Watching them yawn only makes my own eyelids heavier. While Mole tends to them, wiping their brows and administering syrup with a worsening resentment, Morency shuttles around uselessly, moving furniture, lighting candles only to blow them out, deciding an irresponsible number are lit, and staring at the walls colonized by mold. She also tries, repeatedly, to rattle open the shutters, and I cannot tell you what she looks for outside. But she needles us less. She hasn't mentioned Domenico or the rules since I stayed. Her shrill severity softens into a palpable internalized anxiety.

"Where is Sara?" I ask her as I spoon broth into Diana's mouth.

"With the madame," she replies crisply.

"And where *is* Madame De Vaccaro?"

"Occupied," she says as Silvina's body rattles with a gasping, choking cough one cot away, drawing our attention.

"Do you agree with her decision to keep the school open?" I whisper—total provocation, I admit, because how could a sane person agree?

She glares ferociously, setting down the bowl of clear soup she'd been feeding Gisella with a clatter, soaking the linens with oily drops. "The heavens rule us now."

And I suppress a scream of frustration.

Yesi and I search for Carmela ourselves as soon as we are excused from our duties. The knot in the pit of my stomach grows more gnarled as we wander the corridors—chilled to the bone, hearing nothing. Where in God's name has she been during these horrific hours? If she is with Sara, she must know the severity of the girls' symptoms, as well as just how much the situation has deteriorated in the past day. She was moved enough to call the doctor, so surely we can persuade her to send for a larger boat to take the girls home at last.

I feel ready to tear off Carmela's face. But Yesi advises me to tread carefully around her, since she conceals her knowledge of the house—of the tenth girl—for reasons we cannot understand. Yesi contrives an official purpose for our visit to her, to prevent her from shutting us out as she did last time: to formally recant what she said about Lamb. "Perhaps we must play by her set of rules to outfox her," she whispers as we pass Carmela's office door a third time. And I had sworn I would never follow her rules again. But perhaps this is different.

I stop Yesi, then, hearing lively chatter where there was once silence—enthused parroting. Carmela, all sparkle inside her office, engages in an animated, upbeat, one-sided conversation, like nothing I've ever heard. We press ourselves up against the crack to listen and wait, hand in sweating hand.

"Of course," Carmela effuses. "Anything. Anything." A block of silence, perhaps the faintest, gravelly whispering. "Anything at all."

"Who is she with?" I whisper to Yesi. She shrugs.

"Must you go?" Carmela asks, a note of anxiety tempering

her elation. "Must you? Don't leave the child. She's a shell without you—a shell!" My shoulders stiffen. But there is no audible reply. We allow another couple of minutes of silence to pass before knocking, hearing only sniffling and the shuffling of paper.

"Enter," she calls, her voice stiffened.

When I glimpse the scene inside, my knees buckle.

Carmela sits in her office chair, fanning herself with her pad of paper, her hair tied up into a loose twist. She has closed her own shutters, too, and the rain batters against them. Her candles are lit, and her hair looks bone-white in the low light, her skin waxy and thin. Perhaps it's the lack of eye makeup, but she looks simultaneously childlike and wizened.

And beside her is Sara.

Sara, slumped in a chair, blending into the darkness behind her, clothed in a dirtied smock dress, sunken eyes misted over. She's breathing, barely. Her ribs crumple inward.

My shaking hands curl into fists—was Carmela talking to her? This sick child, who should have been in a sickbed all day?

She's a shell without you.

Sara, who for so long defied me and shocked her peers with grotesque behavior, is, indeed, nothing but a shell before me.

My stomach plummets as I recall what happened with Lamb and with Angel. Hosts to energetic parasites.

Must you go?

The truth cracks me over the head: Sara has been possessed by an Other, who has since gone. But how long has the poor girl been possessed? When was the true Sara first lost to us? I glance at Yesi and find her eyes wide and fearful—gone is the determination we shared as we searched for Carmela. Gone is the certainty we could persuade her to listen to us.

"Well?" asks Carmela sharply. "Speak up."

So she knows. Carmela must know. About the Others, about possession. What else could this odd coupling mean? Sara has been possessed by an Other, and Carmela has used the child to convene with this Other. I think back to how attentive Carmela was to Sara when she first became ill, weeks ago. Was she possessed from the start and sequestered by Carmela in the first sickroom to be used as a mouthpiece? I lick my dry lips. "What is Sara doing here?"

Carmela smiles with arctic coldness, mouth sealed shut. We wait in silence for an answer that doesn't come, as her longer-than-life shadow flickers in the candlelight.

Yesi clears her throat. "Mr. Lamm is a victim," she says at last, breaking the silence. "He was possess—"

"We have spoken to the student in question," Carmela interrupts nonsensically, "and have decided that until the matter is resolved, Mr. Lamm will remain in his quarters. That is final. If we require your further assistance, you shall be made aware."

Her droning fills me with rage: I cannot listen to a moment more. I must crack this woman. I must show her we cannot be brushed aside.

"Madame De Vaccaro—"

The shutters crash against the windows, and I will myself steady.

"We know about the tenth girl."

My mention is meant to shock her—to provoke her. But all that results is a silence. An abatement in the rain, if only for a moment. Yesi's hand turns to ice around my forearm. I cannot bring myself to hold Carmela's gaze. But I watch as her hands fold on the desk.

"No, you don't," she states. "You know nothing at all. Once upon a time, I might have condescended to claim I admire your imagination. But to think that you, an ignorant child, could wrest any shred of control in this situation: Well . . . that is a failure of logic."

Desperation surges up in me, its hot claws racing up my throat. I will not be shut down. "We'll find her, and she will help us again," I say, regurgitating what Angel has said to me so many times, desperate for its pale venom to burn her. "She warned us, you know. Warned us about this place."

"That's quite enough, Miss Quercia. Any warning you believe you received was quite unintentionally given."

A shiver runs up my spine. Could she be correct?

"Th-that's not true," I stammer. I remember the girl's flat black eyes, her ropes of hair torn out by the roots. A tormented creature. "She told me herself no one should have returned here."

"Oh, do stop babbling, Miss Quercia. I am an imaginative person, too. Far more imaginative than you are, as it happens. And I am certain there is nothing you could ever invent that would rattle me." She raises one hand toward the door. "You may go."

But I push on. "She told me there are evil forces in the house causing people to act out of character, and I now know this to be true." I glance at Sara, whose jaw hangs loose on her cadaverous face. "As do you."

Sara doesn't register my words. But Carmela settles the pad of paper she's been thumbing back onto her desk. "Forces, you say?" She looks at me, her eyes twinkling malevolently. Intrigued at last. "How curious. And how can I be sure you two have not been possessed by these same ghouls and have come here now to harass me?"

I swallow hard, surprised by her taunt. "Because, Madame De Vaccaro," I start, the courage in my words strengthening, expanding, and beating faster inside me, "we have come to tell you we will fight them and escape, with or without your help."

I will admit: Glowing from my pronouncement, I expect her facade to dip. I hope she will reveal some scrap of knowledge. I pray she will explain herself.

But instead, peals of laughter burst from Carmela's throat. Cruel, melodic laughter that contorts her face into an ugly and inhuman mask, all sharp angles and shadows. She laughs for what feels like a minute as my blood turns to ice, and Sara sits motionless beside her, betraying nothing.

She wipes tears from her eyes. "The soles were skinned from the feet of the members of this house long ago," she says at last, an incredulous, condescending smile splitting her face. "How, exactly, would anyone fight, much less escape?"

In that moment, the room spins on its godless axis. The terror that engulfs me is as hot as scorched grease, and my face feels as if it has been burned off and hangs in mangled strips of half-melted flesh.

I remember the early days, when we playfully considered why Carmela started the school. Goat fur, we said. Subsidies. Oh, we were naive fools. Perhaps this has all been a sick experiment for Carmela to dabble in evil spirits. To conjure up a cohort, with us as the devil's feed. *Vaccaro* means "cattle herder," after all. Carmela has acted true to that name. She has herded us together like cattle, prepared us for an inevitable slaughter. But why? Why invite the inhuman power of the Others into this historic house? How can this be the legacy a powerful woman will accept? These are the words I wish to say, but I am bereft of speech in the moment, my mind a turbulent hive of stinging thoughts.

The candlelight flickers beneath Carmela's chin, giving her shaded slits for eyes and craggy cheeks. "Now please see yourselves out and shut the door at once. I need some private time to clear my head and listen to the rain. It has a most pleasing sound after the shrillness of the last few weeks."

As I gape at her, uncomprehending, Yesi drags me toward the door, and I stumble on my feet.

"Out," she says once more as I hesitate, giving a last glance at Sara, whose eyes fail to recognize me even then.

Trembling, my traitorous body listens to Carmela. I find myself following Yesi out; she shuts the door quietly on this wicked woman and the poor, withered child she uses as a puppet.

I once believed Carmela wielded an inexplicable power over us that moved beyond class divisions and the employee-employer relationship. I called it charisma—an admirable confidence, even. But perhaps she gained this power from her dealings with the Others themselves.

This woman of endless competence is doing the devil's work.

As if summoned by Carmela, the storm worsens; the wind cracks shutters, shoots metalwork off the roof, rips away tiles. Mariella, whom I never expected to see succumb to anything or anyone, drops off into sleep as she's dabbing Gisella's brow. Angel and I carry her onto a free cot: Not a single girl remains in good health.

"A doctor isn't coming," I whisper to Yesi and Angel, wringing a wet rag in my hands over a pail of murky water and draping it across snoring Mariella's forehead. "A rescue boat isn't coming. We need our own plan."

We pace the sickroom, wiping the girls' brows as suffocating terror builds and Morency knits an ugly gray scarf by the closed window.

"We must learn more about the sacrifice ritual," Yesi whispers back with a glance at Morency's looming, useless presence. She hands the two of us open cans of cold soup, then opens one for herself. "And to do that, we must find the tenth girl, once and for all." She looks drained of all life as she dips her spoon into the soup.

"Who exactly do you believe this tenth girl to be?" interrupts Morency from her rocking chair perch. We all lurch to attention, and I glance at Yesi, then Angel, wondering just how much she has overheard as she glares at us. "It should be clear to you by now that there are rooms in this house to which you shall never be granted access, and suffice it to say that the tenth girl rests there comfortably." And with that, she takes her knitting in hand and storms out of the sick-room. A cool draft follows her, blowing out a swath of lit candles, and we all shiver as we blink at one another in shock.

"Well," Yesi whispers, setting her half-eaten can in her lap. "If that's true, there's only one miserable zone we're prohibited from accessing."

"The family's quarters," we say in unison.

"The same quarters we've trawled time and time again," I add.

"But this time, we'll bring the house down, if we have to," says Angel.

Even in the candlelit dark, I can see his and Yesi's sunken eyes flash. Defiance allows hope to burn a little more brightly inside us, warming us as we wait to be relieved of our sickroom duties.

Mole arrives shortly thereafter, sniffing at us oddly, then word-lessly sitting in the corner, scratching notes into a book with increasing fury. She hasn't been quite the same ever since the sickroom opened. It reminds me that we cannot know when the remaining members of this house will fall. We cannot know who will be the next victim of possession. We only know it will happen. And the risk is so much greater during the perilous evening hours. Of course, without outside light, we have been pitched into endless night.

Mole watches us from afar, eyes hooded, as Yesi raises her empty can to ours, expression grim. "Cheers to tearing this decrepit house apart, one filthy stone at a time."

26

ANGEL: 2020-2600

It might only be a coincidence. But after my fight with Charon, after Carmela shutters the house, the Others notice me, like sharks drawn to more concentrated blood in the water. When I enter the house through Mavi's closet door, I barely have time to brace myself. The Others don't bite—they don't break. It's worse. They focus their limited attention on the little hidey-hole where I keep myself outside of Dom, and they come for me all at once, extracting every bit of strength I gained from Yesi in threads, just as I pulled those stringlets from Yesi.

Imagine a miserable flu: the kind where you forget you were ever healthy, you've puked bile and the residue from ice chips and saltines for the tenth time, and it hurts too much to sit in bed, much less watch TV. It's like that, except more active; little pieces of my being—

whatever makes *me* exist here in this membrane of nothingness—are sucked out by a phantasmagoric vacuum. I don't know what happens to those bits of my consciousness—I hope there aren't bits of my soul floating inside someone's crystal jambalaya body. I lie prone, too weak to fight back. And I think of the girls. If this is the agony they're going through, I don't blame them for gurgling in bed, flitting in and out of consciousness like terminal patients. To be punched and bitten and spat on would be better than this. I might still have the energy and state of mind to groan and cry and spit back and scream. For a regular human, injuries can be borne because you know—hope—your body will heal itself in time. Pain is brutal and disorienting, but not *always* a source of utter hopelessness. I think of Mama, who preserved the hope she might heal miraculously until she was so close to the end. Here in this universe, I don't know what the deal is for the girls, but I lack the ability to heal. Because Others fight for energy, gaining and losing based on feedings alone.

This could be a fatal mistake I've made, messing with Charon and straying from the pack of Others. I can't apologize to him, because every time I visit the cloud house, he's napping and can't be awakened—snoring so hard I suspect he's faking it to blow me off. And I don't know when the Others' attention will drift.

I once thought that the poignant, everlasting effect of death was the total extinction of the self as a presence in the universe. Now I am not sure. Death might be nature swallowing your matter—some part of you remains, digested as it is, to nourish and give life to another life-form. Even if the other life-form is something like an Other.

I guess there are pros and cons to this kind of life. When I waste away, there won't be any unseemly decay, no pus, no gore—no breaking down of the body. I won't have a mangled body to leave behind as evidence of a struggle or an existence. I will disappear, like a vision blinked away.

I refuse to tell Mavi or Yesi. It's no hero's noble proclamation to say my troubles pale beside theirs. And this might come off as pathetic, but I guess a part of me also fears that Mav wouldn't care much at all. Which is totally her prerogative, after the horror show I dragged her through.

Still, being with them is a bright pinhole shining in the darkness, the size of a flipped coin: a reminder I can't lose all of myself, I can't disappear in full, because then I can't find the girl and, yes, help Mav. This urge to help hasn't filled me since Mama and Rob died. It feels noble and shining to dedicate myself to helping her until I disappear—the King Arthur in Camelot.

When I experience a surge in energy—a minor respite from being sucked dry—a new solution occurs to my sluggish brain. If the Others know where I enter and exit the house, and target me there, I should figure out where they access it, too—maybe I can stop them from entering at all.

A simple realization follows: Every teacher's room has its own closet. Every. Single. One. The girls' rooms, too. I mean, okay, duh, but it could make sense as a unique—albeit obvious—entry point for every Other. I return to one of the closets in Morency's room. She's praying by the dying fireplace. I rest my crystalline hand on the flat wood of the closet door. Could it be that easy? I dart my head in, out. Only darkness.

But darkness is normal—darkness is a home for an eyeless soldier. I repeat the process I go through in Mavi's closet. I feel a buzzing, a humming, a building hope that this may work.

But nothing happens at all.

The Others do get tired of feeding on froth, eventually—at least for the day. They leave me, and I float in a trancelike state to Dom. He lies stock-still on his bed, staring up at the ceiling, as if making sense

320

of the constellations there. Constellations? I squint up: fruit flies. Drawn to the decay of the vegetable that is Dom.

Over the course of a few minutes, I press myself into him again. It's comfortable, even if I lack the full abilities I once had, swinging his arms limply, failing to smile evenly. I won't have much more time in him—this already feels borrowed. But I fix my eyes more closely on that bright spot, my pitiful nobility, the coin spiraling in space.

27

MAVI: ARGENTINA, JUNE 1978

We creep through the winding damask halls together, Yesi, Angel, and I, then tiptoe through the crumbling corridors of stone, lit candles in hand. Their flickering light lends everything an antique look—furniture shadows tremble on the spongy burgundy carpet, and our own contours grow malformed appendages and odd lumps while our backs are turned. There is no doubt: We are the bits of cud washing between the house's teeth. The floors shift beneath our feet, and not only because of the rotted planks—a hall that is claustrophobic and fetid in one moment becomes vaulted and drafty the next. While we hope to scrutinize every room in the family's quarters, every nook, we cannot keep track of which corridors we've passed through and which we haven't, because they all merge into one freakish house of mirrors. I tread through at least three versions of a sitting room in a row, the same shocked guanaco head mocking us over the unlit fireplace. I swear I hear the faintest throaty laughter, too, echoing around the chambers of my head. I run my finger along the dusty bar cart in the corner of the sitting room as I leave each time, only for the river of my finger's touch to disappear.

"But didn't we . . . ?" I ask Angel, taking the bar cart's brass handles in both hands before rubbing my eyes.

Yesi turns my shoulders back toward the door with her gentle child's hands. "You mustn't worry," she says, as if she understands. "The house knows we're tired, and it's trying to be funny."

Perhaps Morency was right: There are rooms I shall never be granted access to. Vaccaro School is an unholy maze with no exit and no relief. We pass an unreachable balcony and doors that open into a wall of bricks—bricks, in a house of stone! We rip open closet after closet, creating an informal inventory of each style of handle or knob, only to be met each time with an identical, random assortment of old woolen odds and ends. Hands heavy with blood, I tear the same mucus-green coat, the same vomit-yellow sweater off their hangers, scattering them on the closet floor in mulchy heaps until I must catch my breath. I drop to the ground and look at Yesi, who bites her lip. What's worse: The racks of clothing conceal nothing. Not a single closet contains a false back, not even a hole fit for a mouse. There isn't a forgotten coin, not a mothball, not a tangle of hair. I check the corners myself on my hands and knees, while the flames of the candles dance frantically and exhale desperate threads of smoke. Angel pulls me to my feet without a word. I am losing my mind: The house has been growing rooms as our backs are turned, I'm sure of it. It grows them like malignant tumors, these rooms, these physical bubbles of noxious memories from another era.

It is by an upstairs pantry that we succeed in finding an unsettling architectural quirk. Angel has passed the site every day on his way to every meal without noticing this: a tucked-away staircase, its entrance seamlessly integrated into the stone so as to become invisible. An optical illusion! I could leap out of my skin I'm so light-headed with joy. The staircase leads downward to a mezzanine level of the house we did not know existed. A giddiness fills the air at the prospect of a concrete discovery; Yesi's irises are wild above her solitary flame, in frightening contrast with the indigo-colored bags under her eyes. Could a girl be waiting here, somewhere beneath our feet?

Angel presses a finger to his lips and descends cautiously, as if heavy footfalls might scare her away. We follow, hearts in our throats. At the bottom of the stairs, we press on into the darkness and find ourselves before a wall of stone, thickly grouted and impenetrable. I feel for edges, for knobs, for latches. I kick at the slabs and massage them with equal enthusiasm.

"*Please*," I whisper, begging it to allow me forward. I put all my weight into the stone, and I swear I feel it yield for a moment.

But there is no exit here. We must spend an hour rubbing every seam, and this hopeless work puts me on the verge of tears. When I do groan, Yesi nips the skin on my wrist with her fingers in silent warning, and we tramp away.

Angel pulls me up a set of stairs—at its base, before it had rotted away, I hid from Domenico all those weeks ago and heard him tell the empty hallway he was hollow inside. Perhaps he knew of the Others. I squeeze Yesi's hand—I can hear her doll-size feet dragging beside me. She hesitates on the last step.

"We've done enough for tonight," she mutters, releasing my hand. "We'll be trapped here for who knows how many days in this storm. I might as well—I might as well sleep."

The hairs on the back of my neck prickle. It might be the image of the girls, snug in their beds, dead to the world for half days at a time. I still don't want to sleep, bleary-eyed as I am. I thought Yesi wouldn't want to, either. Sleep here is as close to insensate death as is possible in this world. I look at Angel, whose fast-blinking eyes reflect the desperation and alertness I still feel. There are these silent moments of communion with him that make me wonder if he truly is an angel, if I am ruined, or if we are both.

"Go on, then, Yesi," I say, for the both of us. Of course I don't want to leave her alone, this little fairy of a creature before me, all silver hair and heavy-lidded blue eyes. But she is the safest of us all, in her way. Even if she invites them in, she won't be any worse for wear. She gives me a limp hug and floats back off into the darkness.

Angel takes my hand, and we move on. The trouble is, we have nowhere left to go—well, almost nowhere. The only spot we keep returning to, unable to understand its access points in the dark, are two strange landings on a corner of the upper floor of the family's quarters. As we stand on one landing, we can see the other, separated from us by a balustrade and a steep drop to the ground floor. It's an architectural prank—a logical person's nightmare. Without a bridge, who could access the landing across from ours?

"Have you ever been over there?" I ask Angel. "In Dom or . . . ?" The landing is bare but for two doors. One leads God knows where *inside* the building. The other, a strangely knobless door, must lead outside the building itself. Two doors we cannot reach.

He shakes his head. "Too bad we can't jump across," he says. You'd have to be a deer to manage the leap. I have a vision of throwing the deer head over my shoulders and bounding across. Who's to say any rules of human life still apply at Vaccaro School? When one pillar of your existence is shattered, you're free to question the solidity of all the others, as you like. Surely the tenth girl would find the sight of my trying the jump amusing, after her dive onto the ice before Angel.

Being separated from the rest of the household in such a way would suit the girl—and it would match Morency's description of an

325

inaccessible corner. Angel peeks down into the wide abyss again—he can sense where my chain of thoughts leads. It is a fall to snap necks.

"Don't even think about it," he says, watching me peer over the edge again. "I can go there on my own, out of Dom."

I bite my lip. "But even if you do make it over there later, I won't be able to join you," I say. This fact feels inordinately important. I rub at my temples as if it will energize my failing brain. I look closer: It's difficult to tell in the near dark, but yes, the landing does have a door leading to the outside of the building, suggesting it opens onto a balcony of some kind. On our side, there is *no* door leading outside— only a shuttered and locked window. I crouch beside the window frame, juggling my lit candle, and feel the stone below, which is a lighter color than the stone around us, as if it has been recently placed and lacks weathering. It is abundantly clear to me in my mad state that this window was once a larger opening—a door, too?

"Look!" I shout to a baffled Angel. "Did you ever look out this window before they closed the shutters?" I ask him, feeling at the seams of stone with one hand, as if they will commune with me. "There must be a porch outside, connecting to the door on the far-side landing."

"There *might* have been a porch."

"I'll climb through the window to the door." I point at the landing. The hinges on the door open inward. "Easy." I blow out my candle and throw the stub across to the landing with the pack of matches.

He watches me for a long moment, candle flickering by his chin. "I'll go first."

I grimace at him.

"For obvious reasons," he says, motioning to his Dom body. "Not because I'm some macho piece of shit." He hands me a candle, and I toss it onto the landing as he moves toward the window. "Let's see if we can even open the shutters."

I follow him, and we work together to unlatch it. One lock jams, and Angel knocks it with his foot until it pops free. We wiggle the panel of glass up—the external shutters remain closed—and a burst of wet, bone-chilling air sprays us both, extinguishing the candle.

"Jesus." I clear the mist from my eyes. A vicious wind whistles through the open slivers between the shutters; it is only a matter of time before someone hears the whining and finds us here like a couple of drowned cats. We hurry to push the glass farther up, farther up, our sleeves and torsos soaked, and contrive a large-enough entry point to the patio I am sure waits outside. I spit the water from my mouth, clear it from my nose. I squeeze my eyes closed against the bursts of wind and rain, ignore the chill penetrating my slick skin. Angel presses at the external shutters to no avail, before kicking at them again; one of the two flies out and cracks against the stone facade before unhinging and flying toward the ice. I can't help but recoil. The sleet, strong enough to crack glass, soaks us and the surrounding carpeting with gray water, thick with ice crystals; my skin stings as I pinch off clinging bits of ice.

Angel the courageous pokes his head out of the window and darts back inside, red-cheeked and dripping. "There's no balcony," he says, wiping his eyes with his back to the opening. "Only a ledge about a hand's width wide."

Only a ledge. I swallow the lump in my throat and shiver from the wet cold.

"I can go," I say, pulling back my hair. "I've small feet. You can hold on to me."

He doesn't meet my eyes. Miniature crystals fringe his eyelashes. I frown: He looks sickly in the dim light, and I remember his complaints of weakness. "The invincible one always goes first," he says, smoothing a fleck of ice off his cheek. "Seriously, Mav, this isn't about my trying to be a knight in shining armor over here." He shuts his eyes, turns back to the window, and swings one leg over the frame.

I take his forearm in my hand. "What happens if you fall?"

"I don't know," he says, flashing me a look. "Does it matter?"

Of course it does, I want to say.

"Don't be an idiot," I say instead. And yet, I urge him on. I rub the soaked fabric on my arms and wait as he positions himself on the window frame. At least there appears to be some kind of ironwork anchored to the side of the building between this window and the door, supporting a useless, shattered lantern.

And the door: The door is an oddity itself. Its frame hangs there in the middle of the house's outside stone wall, leading nowhere. I'm swallowing my swollen heart as I watch him sidle over to it, shaken by wind and rain. He can barely see—neither can I. The faintest, eerie light emanates from nowhere at all—distant light reflecting off the ice, perhaps. He takes one pace, two. A whining of the ledge, audible over the rush of the storm. As he gropes for the handle, he sways on the ledge, dips a hair. The ledge is giving, giving before my eyes. I could choke. If Dom's body falls, if his skull cracks, where does Angel go? And Dom—is Domenico's spirit lost? It occurs to me then that Dom already is. But I don't care. I've only ever cared about Angel.

I'm desperate to help this person I can't ever know. I lean over the railing and reach for him, as if that will stabilize him; he takes hold of the knob at last and turns it to no avail; the door won't budge. He presses on the door with the handle turned, and there's a shift of some sort. He lifts a foot to use the stone wall beside it as leverage, and a massive groan rips through the metalwork of the ledge. He replaces his foot.

"It's jammed," he shouts into the wind, "I can push—" The shifting rain breaks off his words. The storm will tear him from the ledge and crack him on the ice below. I know it. As the thought courses through my frantic mind that I might lose him, a hundred belated questions bubble to my lips: *Where do you go when you aren't in Domenico? What are you like? Could we ever meet as ourselves?*

328

He takes the knob again and kicks against the door with a heavy foot once, twice, three times, the ledge weakening, but the door creaks, metal against metal, and he falls against it.

The blessed door opens inward.

I watch from inside the house as he collapses in a heap on the landing across from me. "Lord Almighty, Angel." I droop onto the railing with relief, waiting for my pulse to slow.

He sits up and props himself beside the open door, which threatens to suck him back out. "Don't come over, Mav," he says, wheezing. "That sucked so much."

"It's fine—if I scramble over right now, I can make it." I peer out onto the ledge he traversed. It hasn't collapsed. "I'm not letting you go on alone."

He aborts a sigh, too familiar with me now to know he would get away with such a proposition, and leans out the door, propping himself against the edge with his hands outstretched and ready to take mine. The wind abates for a moment, and I pull myself over the window ledge, the ridges digging into the skin of my palms, before tenderly dropping each foot onto the ledge, like a tightrope walker after ankle surgery. The sky, black shot through with swirling gray masses, shudders and breathes above us. Clouds form a giant maw, spreading wider, gnashing their teeth, hungry for fools. The ice mass beyond does not console; there is no softness to its facade. My skull would smash open upon it like rotten fruit. My fingers, gripping the grout of the window ledge, are blue.

"Come on, reach," Angel says, his words blurred by the furious wind. "I've got you."

An irregular flash of lightning highlights the angles of his face. The absurd truth is that I believe he does have me, this inhuman soul, a kindred spirit, a safe haven. I close my eyes to protect them from the sleet and reach for the ironwork above—

"Jesus, Mav, are you stupid? Don't close your eyes," he shouts. I wrench my lids open. He's only a meter and a half away. I wiggle myself down to the ironwork, and I clamp one hand around it, which sticks to the iron like a tongue to a frozen pole. I edge along farther, feet slipping against the pitiful ledge. When I lose feeling in my fingers, a sharp pain stabs my mouth—I've bitten a chunk of flesh from my inner cheek. But Angel's outstretched hand is only a couple of footsteps away now. I breathe through my mouth, tasting metal, and release one hand from the ironwork, lunging for him.

"Just a little bit farther," he says. "You've got this." His hand glows in the turbulent air. I only notice it as I sweep his fingertips with mine: It gives me the fleeting impression that he could disappear and reappear at any moment, like the lightning itself.

A creak beneath me precedes a stomach-dropping fall of a few centimeters; my tiptoes alone remain planted on the ledge—my hand still clutches the ironwork.

"Reach now!" Angel shouts. Without thinking, I swing myself over to him, shaking and shivering, weightless for a single moment, and he clutches my hand, wrenching me up so hard my arm might crunch out of its socket.

"Let go of the damn post," he shouts. But I can't. Intellectually, I know I must—my grip on it is weak—but physically, I cannot. He squeezes my hand and wrist until they ache, a pressure I feel despite numbness. "Come on. Trust me."

I let go, dropping onto the ledge with both feet; with a groan, it bends to nothing, supports flattening against the stone exterior. My legs pinwheel in the air, smashing against the stone, bruising my knees and providing no grounding; I'm sure I'm done, I'm falling, I'm dying, having managed nothing. But instead of the colossal drop, an excruciating pain roots up my shoulder, and I hang in the air. Angel pulls me up, limbs dragged over the rough stone, up, up, and over. I gasp and paw at the floor of the landing edge dumbly with my dead hand. With a groan of adrenaline, he reels me in beside him, and I clamber, like a drowning dog, onto the landing island, heart boring a hole in my chest.

I burst into tears—stupid, hot drops that blister my iced cheeks. Angel pulls me farther inside and kicks the door shut.

"Goddamned stupid," I splutter, curling into myself as he takes me in his arms. I look up at him, wet eyelashes shrouding his eyes. As far as my eyes, my ears, and my hands know, Angel does not exist beyond this temporary human shell that is indubitably not him. He cannot exist as his true self in any way that can be proved by my measly human senses. Yet he does exist, and he is here, holding me, risking himself on my intuition.

Yesi once said that ghost stories help us reconcile ourselves with the unfathomable and unknown. In spending time with Angel, my own life has become a ghost story, and I am glimpsing the wonder in the darkness. What if the beauty of our relationships on this earth is in their transience?

Lightning illuminates the landing through the lost far window, still sucking the room out into the abyss as Angel holds me tight.

"You're okay," he says, pulling me to my feet, and with his pronouncement, I feel I become so. *Okay.* There's a special faith in our relationship. And while I might not understand its nature in full, I know it is one of the most delicate and precious commodities in this world.

We collect ourselves, take stock of our candles and matches, talismans in the dark. Angel uses a match to light our two candles, bringing the landing back to life. I skulk over to the solitary door on the landing, dripping with rainwater. We cannot return the way we've come. Taking a long breath, I try the doorknob. It swivels easily, as if greased in anticipation.

Inside, we face an interior hall pitched in darkness. I see four plain doors, two on each side—no light peeks from beneath any of them. We try the first on our right, opening into a purple sitting room, dotted with the same unattractive and tiny furniture as the rest of the house. Preserved, however, and well-kept—resembling the inside of the house when I first arrived.

I spot a single book: a copy of *Alice's Adventures in Wonderland* in English. I run my damp finger over it and find it oddly clean of any dust, despite the heavy air.

"This must be where she rests so comfortably," I whisper to Angel, my chest filling with a staticky excitement I thought had been lost.

The second door on the right opens into what appears to be a bedroom with a solitary, rickety twin bed inside—canopied and perfect for a little girl. A smile dies on my numb lips. I shudder at the sight of so lonely a bed, unpaired with any other furniture, not even a rug to warm the girl's feet. But someone has made the bed with care—hospital corners. The pink bedding smells of clove, a familiar scent I once associated with Christmas, and I shiver intensely. "Oh, Angel. This is it. This is hers." I sweep my wet hair from my cheeks. But where is she?

The third door opens into a closet. It's dark. Cramped. Airless. Empty but for a raggedy stack of newspapers. The stench of dry rot overpowers me; I'm reminded of the closet in my home, the miserable hole stinking of urine and fear. The copy on top is a Buenos Aires paper, the edition itself a few years old. It doesn't make sense. Old newspapers, stacked as my grandmother once did. I'm struck by an overpowering déjà vu, a sense that a wretched energy waits here, coiled. My knees weaken. I excuse myself and wait in the hallway while Angel checks for openings and emerges unsuccessfully.

We try the last door, breath bated. It opens into the worst room of all, a little child-size bathroom-cum-kitchenette, with a cheap Formica counter against one wall, a minirefrigerator, a toilet with a stepping stool below it, and an empty sink with a dripping faucet. The rhythmic dripping sounds so ominous in the claustrophobic room. I try the refrigerator, and it opens, revealing a plate of fresh quince and cold fried chicken cutlets. I smell them. Unspoiled, though power has been lost.

"Hers," I whisper to Angel. "They must be hers. But how does she keep it clean and stocked? And where is she?"

He shrugs, his eyes far away. I know what he's thinking: It looks as if it's a set of rooms meticulously prepared for a future occupant. No one lives here now. And I know what else we are both thinking: After hours spent wandering a house we ourselves dubbed a maze, we are legitimately trapped without a way back to refuge. I rub the length of my arms—my clothing is still so wet I could wring it out.

"Well," Angel says, examining the kitchenette and rubbing his palms together, "I wonder if there's someplace to dry our clothes."

"There's something more to this place," I say, suppressing my disappointment. "There has to be. We're so close to finding her, Angel. I know it."

Angel checks the walls for hidden seams, leaving a trail of wet footprints and finding nothing. "I swear this worked in a detective book once," he says, shrugging.

The adrenaline fades with every passing moment, and a chill fills its place. But I can't yet bring myself to peel my soaked coat from my shoulders.

We stand in the hallway, empty but for these four doors, feeling like contestants in some cosmic game show. That's when I open the third door, the closet door, once more. He follows me. I stand there for a good minute, listening to the silence, before I knock on the back of the closet.

It makes a hollow noise. "See?" I smile. Of course, who's to say it leads anywhere other than crawl space.

He runs off, only to return with an ugly antique lamp from the dresser in the sitting room, and hands me his candle. "Do you think the girl would mind if we trash her closet?" he says before slamming the blunt base of the lamp into the back of the wall. His movements are violent and demonic in candlelight. With each crash, his face contorts with effort, and the wall splinters. When he knocks an irregular fist-size hole into the ragged wood, I peer into the darkness beyond.

The corridor beyond is pitch-black and constructed from a less lustrous wood than the rest of the house. It smells of sawdust and old sweat. If I listen hard, it seems to breathe.

"There *is* something more to this place," Angel whispers, our cheeks rising above our candle flames.

We prop our candles in the mangled lamp, precariously, and fashion a large hole, sweating in our wet clothes. I climb through first to help us tear down more of the closet wall from the other side, stopping myself from imagining what lies in the darkness. As muscles I haven't felt in ages ripple and throb, my ears disobey and furtively search for life behind me, identifying a low hum of some kind.

"Do you think any of them have made it back here?" I ask as Angel climbs through to join me. *Them.* The word leaves a sourness in my mouth.

"I don't know," he admits.

We inspect the length of the corridor for another point of entry or exit and find a small door on the far end, locked, and while Angel jiggles the knob and tries to force the lock, I tap along the walls, my ear pressed against the wood. I'm miming along like a fool when wood cracks beneath my heel.

"What was that?" Angel asks.

A creaky floorboard below me shifts under my weight, exposing a chip of light.

"Do you hear that?" he asks. He blows out the candle he brought through and slips it into his pocket.

I can't hear a thing. Whispering, perhaps. The beating of a heart. I don't know. Angel leaves the door and tries to pry the board up with his hands. He manages to move it an inch, the strip of light widening. I can hear it now. Speaking. We spy into the space below, one head at a time, one eye at a time. The space is vast, much larger than this hidden room, though constructed from the same shoddy, roughly hewn wood. It is empty barring an oversize fireplace, which houses too many lit candles to count—hundreds of waxy pillars alight, at least. How could so many candles burn in this house without our knowing? Without our feeling the heat from where we sit now? The candles lend the room a smoky, religious ambience, and I whiff heady incense.

I see the figure at the far end of the room, a huddled figure in all-black rags. Rocking back and forth on the ground. I shrink away from the gap instinctively before closing in again. It's not the girl I saw, that's for sure. In fact, at first, I think it's Morency. The heap of black could be no one else.

Except that stray strands of white hair peek out from beneath her black hood. It is an unfamiliar woman, speaking aloud, chanting. An older woman, wearing a loose, floor-skimming skirt, an oversize black shirt, and a hood that a monk might don, all cut from heavy, old-fashioned linen. The edges are frayed, yet when her slender hands peek out of the sleeves, they are angled elegantly on their wrists, like

335

a fine lady's. As the light flickers against her, she straightens the photographs lined up before her. Little black-and-white photographs. It's a shrine.

Angel holds a finger to his lips, pupils fixed. I poke my head down again. It takes a moment to make sense of the words drifting up to us like smoke.

"Please bring her back," she says in muted yet desperate tones. "Please, take what you must from this rock. But have mercy on the family of this house. Take what you must from this rock and bring her back."

It takes me a moment to identify the desperate voice of this keening figure. I watch, stunned, as her shoulders heave and she cries. The photos in front of the figure: At first, I believe they're photos of one little girl. The tenth girl, I think, my heart raging in place.

But no, they're all different faces. And if I squint, I can recognize them. Christina. Diana. Isabella. Sara. Silvina. Luciana, lost to us already. Mariella with her black plaits, Gisella with her blond locks, and Michelle with her wide, trusting eyes.

I grip Angel's hand, certain that both of our faces are white as corpses'.

The unrecognizable figure wailing before us is Carmela. It's Carmela, alone in a dark room.

We ease the board back over the hole in the floor and sit back in silence. I drop my head between my knees, catching the words fluttering through my head and pinning them down. "'Take what you must from this rock and bring her back,'" I echo in a whisper, peering up at Angel. After finding Carmela with Sara, I knew she communed with the Others. But I didn't know she prayed they would take the girls all along.

I move to rise, the wooden cell around me a shrinking blur, and in my haste, I slip against the crack in the floor. My leg bursts through with a sickening, ripping noise, and I yelp at the slick, slicing pain.

"Who is that?" Carmela shouts from below. As I wiggle my useless leg out, metal clamors against metal below. All I can think is: *Let Carmela be nearsighted and not see my leather shoe and my ankle jiggling like a dying fish.* Angel yanks me up; I crumple on my bad ankle in the charming style of a rag doll in need of saving.

"I'm going to find you," she shouts from the depths. "They're going to find you." The rest of her rant is inaudible over the ferocious beating of my heart. I had told myself I wouldn't listen to this woman's wishes anymore; I had asked myself not to fear her. But my body refuses to acknowledge this, and my first impulse is to run.

Angel weaves his arm under mine in support. When I peek back down over the edge, I do not see her. We look at each other, chests heaving, and Angel helps me stumble back the way we came while nursing one candle flame. I feel his bicep straining against the muscles of my back as we hear feet thumping on wood. "Where are we going?" I whisper to Angel. "We can't go anywhere from here."

"We can hide," he says. "And then we think."

I lean into his shoulder. "Where?"

"I don't know," he says. He helps me through the hole in the wall, easing the way, hands me the lit candle, and follows me through so that we're both standing in the closet. I'm testing putting more weight on my ankle when we hear the click of the lock on the far end of the passageway, the turning of the knob. It's the only exit from this nightmarish apartment. Of course.

"Stop," Carmela says, entering through the door. "Is it you? Oh, for God's sake, stop. There's nowhere to go from here." She hulks forward in the darkness, still hooded in black, lugging a thin and heavy-looking iron instrument, perhaps a fire poker.

We keep moving forward, Angel supporting me, and I cringe

from the pain shooting through my ankle. I can't run with my damned leg. Angel squeezes my arm. "I'll pretend I've caught you. Okay? I'll pretend I've caught you snooping around and making a mess."

It's as flimsy a plan as any. "Domenico?" Carmela pokes her hooded head through the hole and squints at us. "Domenico, is that you?"

"It's me," he says, frozen in place, as Carmela crawls through the hole, as undignified a pose as I've ever seen her in.

"You've made a mess of this. You should have opened the latch under the newspapers," she says, standing erect. "Now the entryway will be in disrepair until I can fix it myself." She glares at me, and I witness age's toll on her at last. Beneath the hood, her face is free of all makeup; it looks loose and undefined, like a scored block of clay before sculpting. I don't recognize her. Her eyelashes are so pale that she looks albino. But the oddest part is her lips, two mangled and uneven strips, overdried, like jerky. "And you. I fail to be surprised, even now."

I swallow hard.

"I caught her sneaking around," says Angel, taking my wrist and positioning himself between me and her.

Carmela's fingers curl around the fire poker still in her grip. "I see." Her swollen and bloodshot eyes—as if she's been sobbing—narrow; the eye sockets are scaly and red-flecked. "Go on. Explain to me why you are here, Domenico. Indulge me with one of your poorly crafted stories. Perhaps you came here to gratify yourself with *that*." Those horrific lips—paler, even, than her skin, now—stretch into the emptiest smile I've ever seen, an expression of a mad criminal at trial. "It wouldn't be the first or last time."

Angel extends the candle, illuminating her better. "What are you doing with the fire poker? Are you okay, Mother?"

Her smile convulses into a wretched grimace, exposing the raw, gummy space inside her mouth where her perfect row of teeth should be. Has she been wearing false teeth all along? Or have her depraved dealings with the Others caused her to disintegrate, too? "Mother?" She sucks on her nubs and spits on the ground, a bloody starburst, then dabs the edge of her mouth with haughty delicacy. "Okay?" she says, fingering the edge of the rod like it's insufficiently sharp, eyes landing on me, then Angel. "Your concern warms my soul."

Angel clears his throat. "Carmela—"

Carmela steps closer, the fire poker still in her grip, and cocks her head, eyes focusing. "You are not my son," she says, a pure statement of fact. With a wild flash of her eyes, she brandishes the fire poker as if to strike Angel, her arm hitched in its socket, and he lunges forward, wrenching the rod from her hands and casting it aside with a vicious toss. It hits the floor with a heavy clang.

Carmela's hands tighten into fists; her eyes take on an unhealthy gloss. Catching her breath, she falls into herself, that old and sustaining pride collapsing into base distress. For a moment, she watches me, seeking something beyond my comprehension. It isn't sympathy—that much I can understand. It's an animal call to action, a call to show strength, since she cannot. I look away.

"You're not my son," she repeats. She folds her arms around herself, and her gray eyes water, retreating back into her skull. "You're one of them." She looks so vulnerable for a moment that I nearly forget her flash of violence and her general beastliness. This fragile shell of a woman, lent so much heat and energy by her rage. "You must think me such a fool."

Angel and I meet eyes. She catches our exchanged look, her hollowed face a mask of restrained anguish. "You haven't been Domenico for some time, I gather," she says, pulling her hood around her throat primly. She examines me, imperious as ever. "And you. What game are you playing, you ungrateful wretch? I took you in knowing full well you were the child of guerrillas. The goodness of my heart saved your life."

"The goodness of your heart." I scoff, simmering with rage. "You brought the girls here to sacrifice them to the Others. Was I a sacrifice, too? Were we all?" I shake my head, thinking of every lost soul she invited here, promising such grandeur, as hot tears fill my eyes. *I am proud to be a pioneer. We all are.*

"You were pawns. It was—and is—unfortunate. But you, Miss Quercia, made yourself his pawn all on your own." Her eyes catch mine before flicking over to Angel. "Tell me: What has he promised you? And what must you furnish him with in return?"

"He has already given me his help for nothing at all," I reply crisply, wiping at my eyes before folding my trembling arms. "He would never relish behaving with such cruelty, as you do." He would never dedicate himself to destroying others, even if given an existence that demanded exactly that.

She stiffens. "You believe I *take pleasure* in devoting my life to this iniquitous business? Are you mad?"

I say nothing, clamping my teeth shut—for yes, I did believe it so. My contempt for her must be obvious, because for the first time since I've known her, Carmela's eyes widen with shock.

"You believe that I, Carmela De Vaccaro, am so empty-headed, so thoughtless, that I could be cruel for cruelty's sake, like a slavering beast? Like a ghoul?" She blinks at me, hard gray eyes wet with tears, her shell cracked open at last.

My own face has fallen. "Why should my opinion matter to—"

"I did this so my Marie would be returned to me, you foolish girl," she snaps, interrupting me. "Your *tenth girl*, as you refer to her. How it has appalled and sickened me to hear you call her that, when she is so much more than another in a string of pale souls."

"Marie," I repeat, feeling myself deflate. "Your daughter."

"Yes, *Marie*," she says, her voice breaking. So the lost, ruined ghost girl I saw was, indeed, her dead daughter. We watch in hot silence as tears track down her cheeks—even as her proud jaw remains fixed. "I am sorry, Miss Quercia, if your brushes with love have been limited to encounters with creatures like him," she says, nodding at Angel, who has taken my hand. "I am sorry if you have never adored someone enough to understand that minor cruelties are justified in the service of that greatest love. But when Marie was born, my need to protect her was etched into my soul. She was so small, so sweet-smelling, so vulnerable. And she bloomed into a girl of impossible kindness. Her childhood dream was to become a polo player like her late father—she wanted to ride a Manipuri pony, like him. A Manipuri from India. They're very rare now. Ancient stock. When she was only seven years old, and very ill indeed, we brought a Manipuri pony to the hospital grounds for her to ride. The owner could only spare him for the day between competitions. It was incredibly expensive. But she asked that all the other children have turns before her. There were a hundred and fifty sick children in the ward. Can you imagine? She made us promise, and she never did receive her turn. We brought her other gifts, too, before then. A gift a day, some of the most spectacular handcrafted children's gifts you've ever seen. A glove made from real Pygmy skin. Another fortune. And when we would return, we'd find each lavish token at a different child's bedside. It's as if she knew she wasn't long for this world and wanted her beautiful possessions to enrich the lives of others with more of a chance." She clears her throat. "I cannot say that I believe all human lives are of equal worth and potential. I know that my life is not worth one hundredth of Marie's life. If I could have sacrificed myself alone, I would have done so endlessly. I brought her here, you know, earlier this year. I thought the country air would do her good, and I proposed we reopen the school so she might recuperate here. And she loved it here, she did.

But after our visit, her condition worsened considerably. When she required transplants of my own flesh, I leaped at the chance to give them to her." She raises her shirt, exposing several raw and jagged scars along her belly, and I flinch. "But they weren't enough." She lets the fabric drop. "I knew that I had failed her in my effort to help her—this cursed place had stolen the last of her spirit. After she passed, I was told by someone I trust with my life about the Zapuche sacrifices to the Others—I came to believe I could work with them to reclaim my Marie. It is unfortunate, Miss Quercia, that the Others require what they do in exchange for her. But it only increases my certainty that the Marie I receive in return will have been worth every last sacrifice."

"The Marie you receive in return," I repeat, as another brutal truth dawns on me. "So you haven't even seen her? You have no idea what the Others might bring back of her?"

She breaks my gaze.

All of this, for a chance at retrieving a pale copy of her daughter. A ghost of her daughter. It's the kind of blazing, destructive love that sends a shiver of fear and want through me.

"Help us leave this place before it's too late," I whisper to her. "Honor your daughter's memory—"

"Oh, hush," she snaps. "I won't leave this rock until Marie is returned. This is precisely why I told no one of my plan. Better to inspire fear and loathing, better to be dubbed evil and heartless, so no one can try to stop me." Her eyes probe mine. "You saw her, didn't you? You weren't lying?" She clears her throat. "We should speak freely, now. You told me she warned you to leave this place. How like her, to think of others' safety before her own. My darling girl. What else did she say?" she asks, eyes manic as she steps closer. "How did she seem?"

I look at Angel cautiously, and he looks drained, nervous. "I saw a lost little girl," I say. "She told me she was a memory. She told me the school never should've reopened."

Carmela's mouth quivers, even as her eyes harden. "I don't believe you."

I don't know if stating the obvious truth will break her: Why would her beloved girl show herself to us, and never once to her?

"What about Domenico?" Angel asks softly. "Don't you love him enough to want to take him from here?"

Carmela snaps to look at him. "If you must know, the same need to protect him marked me when he was born, years before Marie. But I failed him in a catastrophic way. Only he, my husband, Marie, and I shall ever know what Domenico did to demonstrate my failure. My husband has since died, and I can only pray Marie has forgotten the brunt of what Domenico did. But I shall never forget my failure. There are many mothers who would perish from shame after such a series of events. Many more would lock such a child away for good. And yet I kept him here with me, ever hopeful the emptiness inside him could be filled. Suffice it to say that I am not surprised your kind filled it with such ease." Her red eyes, furious and imperious despite her repressed tears, travel across my face as if it's physically unreachable land. "And now that you have filled him, I have failed him for the final time. I have lost him, and I have nothing more to lose."

She turns to face Angel, clasping her hands as if in prayer. "If you could please entreat your kind to be satisfied with what I've brought them, and furnish me with Marie," she begs, this woman who once crushed corporate titans. This woman who sought out an army of spirits her own ancestors barely escaped. "I know how hungry you are. You take, take, and take. I suppose I should have considered you might never be satisfied. Not unlike death itself." She stares out in the direction of the lone kitchenette, a refuge for a daughter who can never return as she was. "But I cannot accept that."

343

28

ANGEL: 2020-3300

As solemnly as the leader of a funeral procession, Carmela escorts us back through the broken-down hole, into the dusty crawl space, through the once-locked door at its end, down a rickety set of stairs, and into the shrine—candles still flickering. She pauses to kneel and blow each of them out one by one. We shiver as we wait, hostages to this creepy ritual. But I do understand it: It's meant to give someone a feeling of control in a time of chaos. I wonder if it soothed her, when her faith in seeing Marie again wavered.

When we're pitched into smoke-filled darkness, she leads us away from the shrine and toward a door that was invisible to us. It opens directly into her bathroom: I can see the sink from where I stand, with its golden knobs and white marble. So this secret wing is where she spent her time, praying for her daughter and constructing this elaborate set of private rooms for her, the crazed widow building her lost kid a custom dollhouse. Her meticulousness depresses and impresses me. I guess kids can be symbols to their parents—representing a specific failure or success, or a shade of their own character they aspire to or abhor. Carmela worships at the altar of pure little Marie, and she hates Dom's guts as a human being for an unnamed sin he's committed. But Carmela also blames herself for failing Dom, and beyond that, she misses him as a son, as true a sign of unconditional love as I've ever seen, and that's what wrecks me. She loves him even though he's the worst. It would've been the same with me, Rob, and Mama. Any one of us could have fubared and still felt the others' undying love.

I glimpse a black-and-white photo of a dark-haired boy and an infant with a gummy smile in a silver frame on her vanity. *Domenico and Marie* reads the inscription, and I remember the framed footprint in her office marked *M*. Dom's got a troublemaker's smile, but she's a cute little thing, totally elated (I can hear her laughing just by looking at her) with two carefully combed wisps of black hair. Someone's taken the time to pop in two teeny-tiny bows. She looks well cared for—spoiled, even. I wonder when they figured out she was sick—which symptoms showed up first. For Mama, it was the weight loss and nausea, which we all thought were stress-related for the longest time.

I help Mavi through the bathroom on her bad ankle as Carmela sinks onto the edge of her king-size bed and lowers her hood, murmuring faintly to herself. Her thin hair is matted to her head; I can see her pasty scalp.

"She should've returned within weeks, not months. I suppose she might've lied about them," she whispers, scratching at the roots of an unruly clump of hair. "She might've lied."

Returned within weeks, not months. She could mean only the return of Marie. But who could have initially told her about the Others and their sacrifices? Who does Carmela trust with her life? There's another force at play, a person Carmela takes for her word. Someone who knew about the darkness in this house long before Carmela did.

"Carmela," I ask. "Who told you about the Others?"

"Don't patronize me." She unwraps and rewraps her hooded garment around herself, and a rank clove scent chokes the room.

"Who is she?"

"Speak to her yourself if you must," she snaps, ripping a tissue from the box beside her bed and stifling a noise in her throat. "Leave me in peace, won't you? Just leave me."

I pause, wondering if she's losing her mind. Managing grief can turn you into an enlightened individual sensitive to nature's mysteries—mysteries like the Others—but it can also fracture you beyond repair.

Mavi tugs on my wrist hard. We've long overstayed our welcome, considering we never had it. She leans on me as we shuffle out the door, which I shut carefully, and we hobble in silence until we are out of earshot.

Why do I feel this urge to pity this madwoman now? She looked so vulnerable, her grief so obvious. And her cruelty—her cruelty isn't the result of our crystallized self-pity, like the Others'. Her cruelty is something else entirely—the product of something like mafia rules.

Mav feels warm beside me, but her breaths come and go hard. We fumble around the pitch-dark hallway—we lost our candles somewhere inside the girl's apartment. But I feel pressure dissipate as we put distance between us and Carmela. I wouldn't be disappointed if I never saw her again. It wasn't just her vulnerability and my new-found, twisted sympathy that shook me. Her loneliness was palpable, and if there's one thing I know about loneliness, it's that it makes its victims repulsive to everyone else who might help to lessen it.

"I'm not convinced the tenth girl is Marie," Mavi whispers, testing her ankle again.

"What?" I slow, thinking of the photo of Marie as a baby in the bathroom. I can't erase the sight of her smile from my mind, the black curls. She was cheery in a way the tenth girl I met wasn't, but life (and death) can beat a person down. To put it bluntly.

"Surely she would've shown herself to her mother, at least once?" Mavi tucks her hair behind her ears. She's managing to walk well by herself already. "If not to be reunited with her, then to warn her about the kinds of power the Others possess. Just like she warned us."

"I'm still wondering why Carmela is so convinced that the Others can bring back the dead," I admit.

She walks down another set of steps cautiously and pauses at the bottom. I can tell from the way she rubs her lips together that she's thinking of her mother. "Well, can they?"

I should answer that I don't know what the Others can and can't do. Why should we be able to play God? Dom's skin itches as if I'm about to break out into hives. Here is a person I care about, in pain over someone she's lost. And for once, I can't bear to lie. "I know that we can't bring the dead back ourselves, because I would've brought back my mama and Rob," I say. My voice comes from a place outside myself.

"Rob." She watches me with quiet confusion. "Who's that?"

My mouth goes dry. It's difficult to wrap my head around the fact I've never told her, desperate as I was to prove I needed nothing from her.

"Please. Won't you tell me?" she whispers.

"My brother."

"And he died. Your brother," she says softly. "Your brother and your mother."

"Yes."

"Your whole family," she says, understanding and closing her eyes.

"Yes."

Her eyes open. She stares at me long and hard in the dark. When her voice comes, it's quiet. "Did you . . . kill yourself because of that, Angel?"

A flurry of pain. I swallow hard. I don't answer. We walk on for several paces.

"I'm sorry." She shakes her head. "I thought—I'm sorry. I don't fully understand your—your situation."

My mind frantically pogos from answer to answer without landing on one that is remotely adequate. How do I explain what happened? How can it make sense to her without making me sound utterly pathetic and reprehensible? I want to be honest; I want to bare my soul. But there are rules that shouldn't be broken, rules that govern our existence, rules that hedge in my sanity.

"It doesn't matter, I suppose." She tugs at her hair. It's a gentle lie I won't call her on. We walk on, but there's a fresh tension there that won't abate.

"I need to do it," she says, out of the blue, as we reach the end of the stone corridor.

I look at her, thinking she's delirious as we climb the staff stairs.

"Sleep. And tomorrow, we'll—we'll talk to her." She looks up into the hall, where the storm glows through the skylight.

"What?"

"'I was told by someone I trust with my life about the Zapuche sacrifices to the Others,'" she says in Carmela's haughty voice.

I inhale, low and slow, stoking the fire in my mind. "'*Speak to her yourself,*'" I whisper, echoing Carmela's reply to me as we tiptoe past room 1.

Maybe it wasn't madness. Maybe it was bare honesty from a woman broken open.

"There is only one woman here whose opinion Carmela would trust," Mavi says as we reach her door. "Even if she doesn't listen to her all the time." She glances back at room 1.

Morency. Morency, who kowtows to Carmela. Who long sensed the darkness in this house. But where does she stand in this tangled mess?

"Tomorrow," Mavi whispers to me again, eyelids drooping. "Tomorrow."

I don't want to leave Mavi in her room. But I don't have much of a choice. So we wake Yesi, and I ease Mavi into bed beside her. They fall into position like stacked sardines. I feel a weird pang of jealousy at how naturally they fit together. I'm the odd one out, the freak in a borrowed body, hovering. The one whose life doesn't fit here, in this old-fashioned castle in the clouds.

"I'm worried I won't be able to fall asleep," Mavi whispers to me, dreamily, as I go to leave—her eyes already shuddering shut. As I watch, she succumbs, with Yesi in her arms.

Walking back through the family's quarters, as the storm rages on, I can't scrape Carmela's undying love from my head. The heat of it. It had a beating heart all its own.

It makes me miss them, as it should. Mama and Rob: Rob, cuddling up in my bed in his Star Wars pj's. Rob, taking comfort in my arms like hugs could save both of us if we tried hard enough.

I would have traded my life for them without question, as Carmela would for Marie. But that choice was never given to me.

If I could have given my life to someone like Mavi, would I have? Or was oblivion the only thing I sought?

I field a second, almost-as-absurd thought—is there a world in which Mavi can stride into her closet, as I do, and escape into the Other Place in my stead? Could *any* human access the Other Place through a closet in the house as Others do? Would they want to if they could?

Returning to Dom's room, I open his closet with his body.

First, I feel around every inch of the closet walls and floor with my hands.

Nothing.

I kick and punch at the empty back of the closet with the hot meat hands, which doesn't even dent the wood. *Tools*, I think. *Tools*. I rummage through the musty sitting rooms downstairs, finding nothing resembling a crowbar but the fire poker in the old stag room. I smash the fire poker against the closet back, again and again, and still, the wood won't nudge. I set fire to the door with a book of matches and a bottle of alcohol, and the wood resists. Everything else in the house is falling apart, but these closets remain unchanged. Which rung of hell is this?

I hurl my chair against the back of the closet, and obviously, the blow doesn't even leave a scuff. I drop onto the bed, leaving Dom to sleep at last.

When I brave the raging squall to stop by the cloud house, I find Charon is still asleep and—in his own lazy way—confirming I'm dead to him.

"Charon," I ask, trying and failing to shake him into consciousness with my crystal hands. "Charon, you know-it-all. Wake up. Will the storm ever end?"

His only answer is a rattling snore, as loud as the thunder outside.

29

MAVI: ARGENTINA, JUNE 1978

In the morning, the storm blows hard and heavy against the house. When will the stone walls crumble and cascade toward the ice? I wake with a start next to Yesi, whose skin is cool to the touch, like marble in winter. Her breath wouldn't fog a mirror. I worry for a moment that she's left me; as if body and spirit have become unbound. But when I rub her shoulder, her eyes flutter up at me, and her blue-frosted lips smile.

Each surviving step of our morning ritual—even washing up—frays my nerves. Once every few minutes, the sleet strikes the skylight pane like stray bullets. It's a wonder the glass hasn't shattered. Yesi doesn't think much of it, but I can't help but flinch every time. Once dressed, we creep downstairs to forage for food in the mildewed kitchen, and I recount what happened last night. No need to whisper: The house is deserted. With the kitchen staff gone and all the girls sick and sleeping, the teachers who aren't responsible for their care burrow in their rooms. To my great surprise, the only soul we pass is Mole, wearing sooty floral pajamas and lugging a leaking canvas sack full to the brim with odd-size lumps.

"Bit of an ugly day, no?" Yesi says, yawning, as Mole half-heartedly conceals the bag behind her back in silence.

She readjusts her skewed glasses. "Two-five-three-two-one-three-one-seven-seven," she says, inexplicably, nodding at me. "One-three-seven-two-zero-seven-two-four-zero," she says, as if in greeting to Yesi.

"Up to some fresh numerology, are we?" Yesi asks as I shiver.

Mole says nothing. She darts forward once, twice, as if desperate to leave us.

Yesi crosses her arms. "Have you been to see the girls this morning?"

"No one slept well," I add, as if to excuse her behavior. Mole's nose twitches.

"What's in the bag, Moley?" asks Yesi, still blocking her way. She looks like a little priestess sometimes. "Remedies for the girls?"

"You have no right," Mole hisses, mouth puckering into an angry little node of punctuation. "Between the girls' nonsense and the lies, I've been sucked dry. I'm entitled my due." We look at her as if she's gone mad. "I know you think me lazy; others always think twos lazy. Always. But I am not. I have worked hard, and I am deserving of this."

We hold her furious gaze far longer than I thought possible until I perceive some kind of stench and she softens, her eyes deadening.

"Twos, you know, twos are ones and ones and zeros," she says, extending the bag toward us as if it pains her, and we peek inside.

352

Unappealing leftovers from the refrigerator, long rotted. Some old cutlet scraps, wilted vegetable stalks, and bruised apple cores.

"Don't you dare judge me," she says. "Don't you dare. I'll take some to Lamb and the others. Don't you worry, either. I'll care for them, too. Patient and loving, I am." Though her tone drips with bitterness, there's a glint of indescribable ecstasy in her eyes, the first sign of a mind unhinged—what is there to be happy about here? She hurries along before we can say anything more.

I raise a brow at Yesi, who takes my arm and pulls me forward. "Let's eat and go to them," she whispers. *The house has, indeed, gone to pieces*, I see her think silently with a troubled dart of her eyes.

Our own search for food does not go well, and we are reduced to eating cans of cold, unnamed legumes and a leftover jar of quince jam. Yesi cuts her lip on the edge of a can while slurping out the chunks and presses her hand to the dots of blood until they stop. I dip my fingers into the jar and spoon the gunk into my mouth as if I haven't had a meal in ages. It tastes of sweetened sawdust mixed in water. The truth is, I don't feel like I need nourishment. But I need the structure of a meal if I am to recoup my mental energy before confronting Morency.

After we finish eating, Yesi and I gather cans to take to the girls. To my horror, they are sleeping unwatched, some of them sprawled across their narrow cots, some of them curled into balls, some of them posed like corpses, stonily facing the ceiling, with its flecks of mold spots like blood spatter. Silvina and Mariella wake for mere moments to eat the soup I trickle into their mouths before falling back asleep. They don't speak, much less notice us, choosing, instead, to watch the spores around our heads like opium addicts, as Sara once did. I gather that none of them recognize us at all anymore. Michelle cannot be roused, but at least her cheeks are rosy, and she smiles in her repose. Sara alone keeps her eyes open for long stretches, despite being catatonic. I take her hand in mine and try to coax out a word, a flicker of the eyes, but nothing does the trick. I hum a lullaby to her, the only one I know: "*Que linda manito que tengo yo, que linda y bonita que Dios me dio . . .*" It might be too overemotional to claim that God has abandoned his creations here, but that is exactly how I feel. Sometimes this fate seems crueler than death. Other times I wonder if they might all wake and blossom at the snap of a finger, sleeping beauties. What are we meant to do, alone? Bathe them? Feed them? What's the best use of our time? None of them have wet their beds, a bewildering blessing since they can't be roused and trundled over to the restroom.

"They're tucked inside their chrysalises now," Yesi whispers to me as we patrol the rows of beds the girls sleep on. "I've figured it out, Swamp. When they wake, they'll be whole in a way we can't imagine now." She squeezes my hand. "Every night of this kind of sleep is a chance at seizing back some discarded part of themselves. Don't you see?"

I keep an upbeat expression on my face; Yesi doesn't register it, anyway. Her imagination protects her now. It's as if this near world that I am in can no longer hold her full attention. Strange new fascinations bloomed in Yesi while we slept, and I notice them only now. As she let go of the notion that spirits cannot exist, she lost her hold on more basic natural laws: *Why shouldn't the tenth girl live inside the walls of this house?* she asked me as we sat watching the girls. *And why shouldn't we hunt for her inside each brick? Why shouldn't she live inside the pages of a book in the library, or in the colors of our dreams, to be called out by the scratches of a pen or the sweeping motions of the subconscious?*

When Angel joins us, I am exhausted by Yesi's imagination. It's time. Time to confront Morency.

Angel and I arrive at room 1 and knock. The wood feels soft enough to give, and a good minute passes without an answer.

"Where could she have gone?" I whisper to him.

"Nowhere major." He points up at the skylight, ravaged by the storm. These miserable skylights have made living here like inhabiting a slick-walled well. "I'll try the family's quarters. See if she went to visit Carmela."

I've no interest in returning there.

"You stay here," he says. "Keep knocking and see if she answers."

I puff the air out of my cheeks. "All right."

As soon as he's rounded the corner and gone on his way, the knob rattles. A single eye the size of a moon appears in the crack, one that waxes at the sight of me, and she pulls open the door. Her hair is loose, wild. She's wearing another black gown that resembles Carmela's hooded one. It's eerie to see her this way—locked in her room.

I swing back to look for Angel on instinct.

"Stop that," she whispers, opening the door wide. "Come inside, now. You alone. I have come from the madame's room, and we have much to discuss." My heart spasms: What might Carmela have said? But I haven't time to respond, because she takes me by the shoulder and pulls me inside.

I perch myself on the sofa I observed only from afar last time. She has a fire going, with a steaming kettle hanging above it, but otherwise the room is dark. A half-full cup of tea sits on a nearby table. She cradles it, swivels it around in her hand.

"You were truthful with me. I should have known your romance with Domenico would not have bloomed without him truly being possessed," she says, standing across from me.

Even at a moment like this, her tongue remains as sharp as ever—she herself remains as myopic as ever. But her petty comments can no longer derail me.

"So you admit that you know of the Others."

Morency watches the flames in silence. A log crackles in the fireplace. "Yes, of course I know of them," she says, grazing the lip of her teacup with a finger. She studies me, eyes sharp and clear, as if determining I am not possessed. "But I do not fraternize with their kind."

"Yet you know all about them. Enough to persuade Carmela to reopen this school."

She sets her eyes on me. "Miss Quercia, I am loyal to the De Vaccaro family. When Madame De Vaccaro asked me to tell her the house lore as an exercise in learning more about her family, I obliged her. I couldn't know what she felt herself capable of accomplishing. She claimed she hoped to reconnect with old generations of her family, and after the loss of the child . . ." She trails off, mouth pursing with pain. "Who was I to deny her that?" She sips from her cup. "When she wished to open the school, I followed her wishes. I would do whatever is necessary for Madame De Vaccaro. She is a good woman, if troubled. I did not see it until too late that she has lost her way."

So Morency knows that Carmela has gone mad from grief. Yet she gives up responsibility for any wrong committed, using that blanket excuse of loyalty, servant to master.

"But how do you know about them? The Others?"

Her eyes flick away.

"Why didn't you tell me about them?" I ask. "Why didn't you tell anyone?"

"I expressed that this house was dangerous to each of its occupants to the best of my ability. But as you can understand, Miss Quercia, one does not always know whom one should trust at Vaccaro School. People are not themselves. Those who possess us flood these halls." She shakes her head. "Beyond that, I tried to urge *you* along, in my way, inspiring your curiosity and rebelliousness so that you might divine the truth yourself, while protecting you as best as I could. I couldn't know what Madame De Vaccaro might do to someone she perceived to be outside of her control. You worried me, Miss Quercia. It was so important you be careful. I preferred that you fear *me*, the servant who is Marguerite Morency, over the person who might inflict actual damage on you out of misplaced anger."

I choke a bit on my own spit; how would *the servant who is Marguerite Morency* explain sending me to my room without dinner?

An opportunity to explore the house while the Others are occupied.

And the fact I was never punished for wandering—reprimanded, instead, for crimes I'd never committed?

To encourage the exploration.

To be accused of spreading gossip that the plague of sixty years ago was returning?

To consider the plague of sixty years ago, and how that might be affecting our present situation.

It takes me more than a moment to collect myself—Morency watches without even a hint of a smug smile. Watching her haunted expression, I feel a conclusion rush toward me all at once.

Her knowledge couldn't have come from word of mouth alone. That wouldn't have been enough to spur Carmela to return. Morency's been here before. But if the school was closed sixty years ago, that would mean she would've been a child.

Could it be that . . . ?

The servant who is Marguerite Morency.

Marguerite of the Bible in my room, dated 1918.

Zapuche blood.

"You've lived here before," I say, veins throbbing.

Her eyes glitter black. "Yes. How bright you can be. I was only a girl of twelve the last time I was here. That was sixty years ago."

I wouldn't have believed she was seventy-two before this meeting. But now I can see the crepe-like texture of her skin, the white threads winding through the thicket of black hair. Carmela is older than I imagined, too—why shouldn't Morency be? "My parents were part of the household staff—my grandmother nursed Madame De Vaccaro's mother, as she mentioned, and when she passed, my mother and father continued working with the family. I myself was raised here in these once-vibrant halls. When the staff and students fell ill in my twelfth year, when they *changed*, the local staff said it was on account of territorial spirits . . . Others, they called them. Helping them to drive the colonizers mad and reclaim their land." She stops to sip her tea. "That mattered little to me then. My father had a bad liver—worrying for him took up much of my time—and my fair-haired mother bore a rare hatred for me since I was a young girl, for a reason I could never determine. My best guess was that she resented me for looking darker, tying her more firmly to her Indigenous Zapuche past. In any case, those two relationships did not—could not—occupy all my time. I had a lover here," she admits without the slightest trip in her words. When my eyes widen, she fixes a harsh gaze on me. "Yes, I was very young. And he was someone my mixed-blood parents would never have approved of, a native Zapuche who worked as . . . as a handyman, of sorts. A terribly handsome, cruel, and narcissistic man who never should have entertained let alone touched a child like myself. But I worshipped him, treated his every word and far-fetched idea like the word of God, and in the way of impressionable twelve-year-old girls, he became my entire world. He was charismatic, as the worst of them are, and his head was filled with strange ideas about the Others who occupied the house—they were part of the reason he was drawn here, besides money, of course. He believed he might bring back the dead. He thought the Others were representatives of the underworld that could be reasoned with, bargained with on a personal level . . . If only you communicated with them in the old way, with a vigil. With a sacrifice—but I did not know that then. He held many of these, giving in to strange paroxysms before me, bottle of wine in hand, claiming he was communing with *los Otros*. It was during one of these vigils that he claimed the underworld had brought us together, luring us each here to this rock. Of course, he was an unforgivable rapscallion, the least of his crimes being his encouragement of a young girl to drink great quantities of wine. I became pregnant after one of those nights, and my parents inevitably found out, of course. Foolish girl that I was, I imagined my father would be pleased I was to bear a child of my own—I imagined he would view the child as a guarantee against future loneliness, for he spoke frequently about his concern about life for me after his passing. A child's fantasy, of course. He was horrified that his little daughter had been sullied. My mother beat me while my father hid his tears in another room, and she locked me away in a secluded part of this house for most of my days." She pauses to sip her tea, her right hand trembling. "As this was occurring, I picked up hints in the whispers of my parents and the groans that rose through the house that the others were in grave condition. I tried to contact my lover, who disappeared, and to communicate with *los Otros*—demons I had never witnessed—to no avail. I was mostly immune to the Others, much like you seem to be. But the residents of the house were not, and they were sent away in groups to recover before the seasonal storms became too severe. Most of them considered it to be an odd sort of influenza at the time—no cause for alarm. But many of them perished on the journey home, I later learned. Eventually, only my parents and I remained. I no longer risked embarrassing my family with my swollen belly, so my mother let me out. I was shocked to see how much had changed. My father, once a relatively solid and stable man, had grown weak from his illness, and he had succumbed to paranoia and panic as the storms outside worsened. He turned to the drink again—a suicidal effort, with his condition—to console himself, convinced we would die here. He locked himself away. My mother strategized ways for us to reach the boat at the docks and escape, but she was unable to do so, because the Others targeted her, and she grew ill herself. And I, well, I was with child. I was quite desperate, heartbroken, alone. I held a vigil, much as my lover had. I remained awake through the night and called to the Others and promised them anything they needed, anything they wanted, in exchange for freeing my family from certain death. Of course I received no reply from the sky above. But as I was about to give up, the body of my father tramped up the staff stairs from the bowels of the building. He staggered toward me, so dead in the eyes I wondered if he was still with me, and told me that if I were to give up the girl, he would let us go free. As if *he* had the power. I understood then that an Other had possessed him to speak with me. Foolish as I was, I couldn't bear the thought of parting with my unborn child at first. The child felt like a part of me and this world already—it would have been immoral to grant her to these demons. I couldn't understand why they wanted *her*. I begged and pleaded with him to allow me to give up myself—that if I could arrange for this child to be born, and if my parents could be spared, that I would return here myself. This did not seem to please him. He shook the house in rage; my father's body gurgled blood and bile before collapsing to the ground. So I made the sacrifice: I agreed, aloud, to have them take the child. I cannot tell you what I expected: for a Rumpelstiltskin character to retrieve my baby at birth in a few months? For the fetus to be spirited out of the womb at that moment? But nothing happened then in my body. My father's eyes, on the other hand, they did blink open. He confirmed our transaction in a monotone. I have to admit, just as I was chilled to the bone to have this interaction with my possessed father, so was I relieved on some level. My father was *alive*. And I was far too young for a child—giving birth, the cleaving of my young body, had filled me with a strange sort of terror. I thought in that moment that I, the clever twelve-year-old, had outfoxed the Others. The storm cleared sufficiently the next day, and my shocked father and I carried my mother down to the docks. She improved with each passing hour. We boarded the boat, which seemed to float on pearlescent waters, and easily made our way away from here. It wasn't until later that I knew I had sacrificed more than I had bargained for in my exchange."

She pauses, and I look up at her, dazed.

"What do you mean?"

She looks into the dancing flames. "I suppose I always believed I had left a piece of myself behind. There was this hollow in my chest, at first. I felt only fear and trepidation. My father passed away shortly thereafter. And I miscarried, as I expected to do. I became a religious woman after that—I hoped to never again live in a land God had forsaken. But I also grew. Grew, and grew, and grew, until no one from my childhood could have recognized me. My mother called it puberty, but I knew that all good parts of myself had been left behind at this house. What happens to crystallized good, left in isolation? I cannot know, myself. But I do know that what remains is utterly irresistible to the Others."

When she finishes speaking this time, I wake as if from a dream. I think of what Mole once said about Morency—jilted as a delicate young girl, she overgrew, marinated in that potent disappointment.

"I left a piece of myself behind at this house for their pleasure," she adds. "Though I've never managed to find that piece again. I'm afraid it is lost to this house. *A los Otros*."

My mind overheats with wild possibilities. I had doubted that Marie was the tenth girl—as wise and thoughtful as Carmela made her seem, I had the impression the girl was of more ancient stock; it seemed clear she had been spirited here much longer ago than a couple of short years. Angel mentioned the tenth girl cradled her stomach in his presence. Could this piece of Morency, the pregnant youth, about to be robbed of her innocence, be the tenth girl instead? Could such a creature—a faded memory, a slip of white—have survived six decades here alone? Is such a mad concept possible on this rock?

"Have you seen her since?" I whisper. "Have you seen that old piece of yourself in this house?"

Morency raises a brow. "I do not think that possible. But who am I to understand the infernal magic of this place?"

If this piece of Morency was the tenth girl, then she would surely seek reconnection with Morency. Wouldn't she? So why has she not sought out Morency? Why come to *me* and not to her? Perhaps she mistrusts the grown Morency, as I did. Perhaps she resents her choice. But I do believe the girl cares about the human occupants of this house—otherwise, she would not have come to me at all. She would not have encouraged me to leave.

But to say that the Others, as an entity, would accept this poor girl in exchange for Morency's family's safe passage outside? The greedy, life-sucking Others, not even contented by the pack of young girls at the house? What would be so great about one person's youth, if it could be crystallized and captured in the diaphanous shadow image of a young girl?

And the worst thought of all: What would the terms of this exchange of Morency's translate into when it comes to ensuring the safe passage of so many more souls now?

"The only certainty I have is that I shall not escape this rock twice," she says.

"But you did escape once," I croak.

She nods.

I thumb my eye. "So how do we . . . how do we re-create your sacrifice, Morency, so that some of us can escape now?"

Her lips set into a thin line. She holds the silence well.

"We do not escape now," she says at last. "It's far too late to help everyone."

I keep myself from registering the gut punch on my face. "That— that isn't an answer I can accept."

She watches me with the faintest touch of glumness. "We should have sent away the girls and your peers long ago. I tried, when I saw the first signs, but Madame De Vaccaro would not permit it. That was before I understood how . . . imbalanced she is due to her grief." She pauses. "And when you tried to leave; well, I held out hope the supply boat might come anyway, but I suspected it was already too late. What with the storm . . . you would've likely drowned on the dock had you not experienced your change of heart. Miss Quercia, I am sorry to say that it would be impossible to arrange safe passage out at this time. Beyond that, the Others have changed. They are greedier creatures. Impossible to bargain with, to control, at least as a whole. And there are too many of us vulnerable here. Too many already afflicted, their spirits loosened from their earthly homes. It's too late, Miss Quercia." She sets down her teacup. "I am sorry. My life has long been over, but yours had only begun."

I feel tears budding in my eyes; I mash them back into my sockets. "I can't accept that."

"You should try."

I rise to my feet. "You mentioned bargaining," I say, pacing the room, acutely aware, even as I speak the word *bargaining*, that it is a stage of grief. "We have Angel on our side now. Surely that's valuable."

She picks up her teacup and observes me over its fragile rim. "Angel? You mean to say the Other you brought to my doorstep?"

"Yes, my friend. Angel. He lives in Domenico for now, but he's a friend, a good friend. He'll help us, he'll do whatever he can—"

She sets down the cup and folds her clawed hands on her lap with a delicacy that belies their size. "The Others cannot be trusted. They can only be plied. You do understand the manner in which your friend controls Domenico's flesh?"

I try not to shiver. "You don't know him like I do."

"I understand the nature of the Others very well, thank you." She rises and turns to face the blackened fireplace, dying now from lack of wood. "Perhaps you should go."

"So that's it?" I spit, shaking with indignation. "After explaining your story in full, you won't even make an effort to help? I know that you consider yourself a godly person, but it is not so much godliness as a learned passivity. You expect fate or God to deliver you from misery. And in the process, you allow cycles to repeat themselves and you give yourself up to their inevitability. I will remind you that you were the one to provoke Carmela into coming here. You planted the seed in her mind and allowed it to grow. You are in part responsible for what is happening now. So you cannot be such a passive woman at your core. You are feigning helplessness." I unclench my fists and shake my head at her. "Some part of you must be ashamed of what you've become."

The fire spits a few final flames at us in desperation; the room feels full of ash and dust. It is a place for the dying, the dead. Morency does not turn to face me, but her right hand trembles; if I'd blinked, I wouldn't have caught it.

"You have to understand that Madame De Vaccaro is like a daughter to me," she says quietly. "When she was born, not long after I miscarried, she was like a gift. We lived with the De Vaccaros in the city then. My mother always claimed to have nursed her, but I did, in secret. My mother could no longer lactate, but no one questioned us. They never question the servants." She lifts the fire poker to poke at the remains of the fire. At that moment, I think that she won't be saying anything more—she's lost to memory. The dying embers spatter. "We can attempt to re-create the sacrifice," she adds after a long pause.

I open my mouth to speak, and she holds up a hand to stop me.

"I remember bits of the Zapuche ritual. And I can offer everything left of myself," she says, hanging the poker from its iron rack. "For whatever she is worth. But if they should require a young woman again . . . I advise you to be prepared, Miss Quercia."

She's right, of course.

Am I prepared to sacrifice myself for the others in this house?

My mother never once hesitated to give herself up for her ideals—at least she never seemed to. But could I have been born with that kind of noble dedication? Because everything good and noble that I might feel now is overshadowed by pure fear.

Before leaving, I glimpse her crossing herself slowly, deliberately, watching the smoldering wood.

I have a choice, now. I can wait ad infinitum for a magical tenth girl to appear, when it is clear she may not do so in time, whoever she may be. Or gather my strength and plunge into the unknown dark, the light beyond as faint as I've ever seen it.

Closing the door to her room, I whiff a hideous stench. A canvas lump rests against Mole's door. It's that bag from earlier, abandoned. I don't want to peek inside, but I can't stop myself. I press open the bag and gag: Inside I glimpse what appears to be the blackish residue of human waste, intermingled with seeds, cores, and pulpy matter that looks like rotten flesh. I shrink back. It's as if Mole is decomposing, sloughing off spoiled bits of herself and dumping them outside.

It's time now. This sacrifice ritual is our only hope, and I must shake my fear by the hand and prepare. I must be the warrior my mother always dreamed I would be.

30

ANGEL: 2020-3600

"Morency knows the sacrifice ritual," Mav whispers to me, pale-cheeked and weaving together her trembling fingers as we sit on her bed. "Parts of it, at least. She knew enough to make one of them come forward in 1918. An Other, in her father's body. To discuss terms of release." She hesitates. "They stole the girl out of Morency in exchange for letting her family go free." As if that's a procedure as simple as a surgeon severing a leg. What is Morency now if part of her has been lost? Is she another irreparably damaged creature, like so many of us Others?

"We're going to repeat it," she tells me. "Tonight."

It sounds like a joke. "Who exactly are you planning on sacrificing?"

She straightens, swallows, a steely glint in her eyes. I already know the answer.

She thinks she'll be following in the footsteps of her own mother. Become a sacrifice for her ideals. For the greater good.

When it's not like that at all.

"You can't," I say, the peach-vomit walls closing in on me.

There isn't a foreseeable happy ending to this. Can't she feel what should happen next? Can't she remember? Every soul is trapped in its hellish cycle, but for her it's worst of all, because she's so close to understanding her own. "It's never going to work," I tell her, my hands shaking hard.

"You say that as if I have the option of doubting it will work." She crosses her arms to stop their convulsing. She's blue-lipped now. "Angel, I know it sounds absurd—"

Blisters of heat swell inside me. "I can't let you do that to yourself."

"You can't stop me," she snaps before locking eyes with me and melting a bit. "And it's not being done to me. It's being done for them. For all of us." She clutches my hand. "Listen: Morency survived. I will, too. And you'll be by my side the whole time, in Dom. If you're afraid of the aftereffects, you need to remember you're safe, don't you see?" Her eyes glow with manic desperation. "You're safe, as long as you stay inside him."

As if this is a fucking game of musical chairs. "That's not what I'm worried about," I say, throwing her hand away from me and standing. I pace her dime-size room on my unwieldy legs as if it'll distract from the burning I feel. It doesn't help. I feel like a goddamn rat trapped on a narrow ledge, scurrying above vats of boiling soup. It's ending, soon. I'm going to fall inside and cook down to the bone. "You don't know what you're getting yourself into. Not for sure."

"Even so. When do we ever know anything for sure?" She blows the air from her mouth slowly, calmly. "I need to try to end this for the girls."

For the girls. It's her unrelenting, unapologetic earnestness, her kindness, and her selflessness: Everything to love about her tips me over the damn brink into the fiery abyss below.

"Fuck the girls!" I shout, and she jolts back. "They're not real! Can't you feel it? They've never been as real as you. How could they be? A real person is a prism, not a paper doll with a cartoon backstory. You—you're as real as Mama to me. You're as real as *Rob*, and I hate myself for saying that, but it's true, I feel it—" I shudder, stopping, the scorching heat consuming me down to the marrow. *But they're both gone*, I want to add, so fucking selfishly. *So you're all I have now, Mavi.* I think of the file Domenico paged through months ago: *Tendency to form inappropriate and intense attachments.* Maybe we are one and the same.

"You're speaking out of turn now," she whispers sharply. "This is much greater than the two of us. You know that." She shakes her head, her voice losing its edge. "Think about it, Angel. How much longer would we even have had together?"

In her marbled brown eyes, there's hurt and love intermingled, and it swallows my heart whole. *She'll never meet the real you. She'll never know the real you.* It was inevitable: this pain. This implosion.

"I don't—That's not . . ." I'm swaying on my feet. "You're right. I'm sorry. It's just that after what happened to them, it's been . . ." The room spins. I can't pick a word. Those that come to mind— *difficult, painful, impossible*—disrespect them, or me, or her, or the magnitude of what happened then, and every single thing that has come from it.

"I don't even know what happened to them, Angel," she says, softly but firmly. "You've never told me. What happened?"

What would Mama say? Speak the words and claim their power for yourself. But I haven't yet crafted my loss into a meaningful, beautiful, or even tragic tale; it's a story that I've only tried to pummel into nothing—that I've condensed down into one or two words that I drained of meaning so long ago.

"Cancer," I say.

She waits beside me. Listens hard, even to the silence.

No one in the world can absolve you, alive or dead. Ride the tides of darkness, Charon said. But maybe absolution isn't what I sought. Maybe it was an unspeaking, compassionate presence.

"Mama died of cancer," I repeat, the sickly heat of the word flowing back already. Goading me on. "Liver cancer. Symptoms were ordinary enough at the beginning. We pretended it was a flu, even though we both thought something else might be wrong. We never said as much, but we thought it. We both did, I could tell. It just started with her puking all the time, and her refusing to go to the doctor, eating only BRAT foods, as if they would help. It took her six full months of white rice and toast to visit a doctor. She canceled the appointment once, then twice. Asked me to go with her, then asked me to stay home. That's how I knew she knew something was wrong, for sure. And when she visited the doctor, boom, there it was—stage four. I was so angry at her. At myself. Furious I didn't force her to go earlier—didn't drag her there. The doctor said it wasn't her fault. It wasn't mine. It was no one's. It moves so quickly. So quickly that by the time the anger and shock began to evolve into something more soul-sucking and brutal, we were alone. Me and Rob."

Another silence, loaded with years of heat and rage and visions of Mama withering away before me into a being so clearly *not her*, so clearly *chaff* in an ill-fitting hospital gown she would have laughed at and hated had she one final reserve of energy to spare on a complaint so stupid. So stupid. My mind fizzes as the light apricot room slants

369

and whirls. *Light apricot*, she says, giving her goofy smile, macabre because she was already skin and bone from a horror that wasn't remotely stress. *253, 213, 177.* I clamp my hands around my head and shake it hard hard hard hard—

"And Rob?" She's barely audible. "What happened to Rob?"

"Oh. Rob," I say, disembodied. "Accident."

Ac-ci-dent. If you break the word down into parts, it means nothing at all. It might seem loud and bright and sharp, but it is empty.

"Go on," she whispers.

I can't.

I swear I can't.

I can't remember speaking about it with anyone at all—I've never told the story aloud without blacking out all the talking. The noise: questions and assumptions. From the police, from Liese.

I can't say anything about the last time I saw Rob that won't transport me right back to the blinding, white-hot agony of that moment—that won't drop me to my knees and disembowel me in one scorching stroke. This much I know, without even grazing the distant outer rings of it in memory.

My mind knows what it should do next. Protect. Avoid. But Dom's body drops me onto the bed like we're praying. He hides our face. But his mouth, his throat, his voice box, his lungs: They collude to speak in a thick rush.

"He was playing outside. I don't know why. Crouched low, painting the world with his new box of colored chalks, the same box we bought him to get him off the tablet. So there he was, on his knees, detailing some beautiful world with its tendrils of green and rays of sun on the slanted, gum-spattered sidewalk. He was smiling. I tell myself he was smiling. I tell myself he heard a plane overhead at that very moment and saw wide blue sky. I tell myself he was calm in that moment.

"Not that I knew, because Liese and I were at each other's throats inside the house—I can't even remember what our argument was about, of all things. I can't remember, and she can't, either. I took her keys—I know that for sure, they were her keys, and not his, because they found the keys cutting into my hand, her furred key chain dabbed in my blood—and I stormed out of the house and into her husband's oversize truck piece of shit. A monstrosity I had mocked a dozen times because it was so clearly a reflection of his—" I choke.

Dom's shaking so hard I can't stay propped, much less hear myself speak. There is a painful lightness in Dom's limbs, as if a weighty marrow's being sliced from me, hot sliver by sliver. My raw voice cracks, connects.

"I must've turned it on in less than a second, put it in reverse in half of another, but there was space. So much space. I know that. It felt like a mile and an inch all at once in that split second. But I saw him, saw him just in time, and I jammed both feet on the brake hard, hard enough that those feet could've stopped the car itself without it, but—but. It flew. I flew. It flew. There are noises that—"

I bring my cold hands to my face again, Dom's face, and feel at the rubbery skin there, molten.

"I don't—I don't remember stopping, wrenching open the door, taking out the key. The steps my body must have taken, my mind somewhere else. Drowned by the hottest, blinding fear. Why take the key? I don't remember crouching. I don't remember pulling him out. I know—I know how they found me, from what Liese said. She told me he looked perfect. Half-asleep in my arms, that's all. Half-asleep on the gurney, too. It was internal. The bleeding," I say as the heat cools, cools until it's a suffocating, milky warmth. "He was flat on the ground, not curled like a shell to protect himself. There was no time for that. No time to see, to shout. I don't know how it could be that fast, but that's what they told me. The police, the doctors.

"He had fainted; that was it, I thought. I knew it was a story I was telling myself, but I knew I could will it true if I only tried. But when they repositioned him, it was from the side that I could tell something was wrong. This crumpled look to his chest, like a—Oh God, like a forgotten doll. And the blood from his mouth, then, this blood that was so—so obvious."

I stop, gasp for air. She settles her two hands on my back like doves.

"The sternum of a child his age is smaller than my hand. This sternum—his sternum—it punctured his heart, the size of an even tinier fist. Cut through it, soft as butter, someone said. I didn't know. He looked perfect, like Liese said. Comfortable and so small, wrapped in his favorite yellow blanket." I stifle a sob, a groan, a spasm; it bucks off the two palms she's placed on my back. I look at her, raking her eyes for hot coals of horror, finding only pity and sympathy as her hands find my upper arms. To hold me, to keep me.

"He had drawn a picture of his family, our family, in the old world he deserved. And there I was, standing next to him. The blessed one, Angel. The protector, with a star over my head," I say, croaking, that heat rising up my cheeks into that space behind my eyes and blacking out my vision. "But you aren't blessed if it means you survive alone. You aren't blessed."

Her two hands cup my arms, staving off renewed trembling. We don't speak. I let the pain flood me—the same pain I thought had grown lighter, more diaphanous. It will never be gone. It will only crash over my head and drown me less often. But it will always do so with the same intensity, the kind that has always made me want to throw myself off a ledge.

I close my eyes. Not to suppress it—that wouldn't work—but to force myself to remember, to remember that—

"I'm so sorry," she whispers. "I'm so sorry, Angel. I still miss my—"

I lurch back, and she pauses. A foreign cold drenches me from head to toe. I clench my teeth to stop the words I know will follow, but it's no use.

"Don't be sorry," I snap. "I did what I did. It's my loss to bear."

"What?"

"You were going to tell me you still miss your mother, weren't you?" I watch as her face crumples, processing what she thinks is my cruelty, when it's really my mercy. "You've done nothing to deserve the pain you feel. You need to know that. You've done nothing to deserve the pain you're carrying. The pain from what happened to your mom, the pain from what's happening to these girls. God, you deserve better. You deserve better than all this." I tear at my hair with my fingers, grind my fingers into my eyes.

When I look up at her through flares of color in my sore vision, her eyes burn with hurt. "I don't understand what you're trying to say."

"This place isn't what you think it is. And the Others—they're—we're not who you think we are. I—I still haven't told you the whole truth. And you deserve that. You understand? I've been a demon. I don't deserve you. I don't deserve any of this."

As if I can begin to say which cruelties anyone at all does or does not deserve.

31

MAVI: ARGENTINA, JUNE 1978

I do not want to hear the words Angel is saying; every fiber of my being tells me to stop him, stop him, stop him. *What he's trying to tell you is not for you. What he's trying to tell you should never be heard.* I feel as if I'm an astronaut unmoored from her spaceship, floating among fading stars. Breathing the last of my oxygen.

"Let me guess," some voice says. *My voice.* "Are the Others wizards, manipulators of time and space? Incorporeal psychics?" I try for a smile. "Nothing will surprise me," I lie.

"It's going to be difficult to understand what we are," Angel says. "It will change everything."

So it's coming. Here and now. I have a choice to make: to hear what comes and allow my mind to crumble or to brace myself for his admission and be the heroine—the best self—I know I can be.

Well, I had made that decision after my talk with Morency. My tightly folded arms shake, and I do all I can to hide it from myself. "Try me."

He takes my hands out from underneath my arms. "I'm always here for you, all right?"

I throw his hands off me. He's here for me after telling me I've done nothing to deserve my pain. What empty nonsense. I think I might vomit; I feel a surge of acidic heat in my throat.

"Tell me now."

But when he takes my hands again, I let him. His fingers are like branding irons.

"This is a cosmic sort of game," he says, speaking the words carefully. "The Others are the players."

I freeze in place. It's as if I can feel the molecules around me freeze over, too, oscillating in their fixed shapes. "And all the world's a stage."

He shakes his head. "Vaccaro School is an artificial construction."

I haven't enough air. The moon-colored room around us spins, the axis our hands, gripped together.

"The house is made of strings of numbers instead of atoms and molecules. It's all a creation, not a physical place. This house is on a loop," he says, clutching my hands. "We're doomed to repeat this segment of life—to return before the beginning of the term, to watch our own decline. The rapid deterioration now—it's all prescribed. It will happen again and again."

"What?" I drown with each shallow breath. "You don't mean *our*. You don't mean *we*." I pull my hands away and clench them. My tone is one of the utmost bitterness. "You mean *me*. You mean *the rest of us*. The people here. That's why the girls don't seem real to you."

He looks at me with concern before softening. "I guess you're right."

"An artificial construction. I don't understand." Have I gone mad? Am I dreaming? Have I been sucked into the mangled narrative of Yesi's ghost story? Spasms of bright light from the lamp hurt my eyes. Of all of the admissions I had imagined . . . how could it be this? An admission I cannot even comprehend? "How can a person be made of numbers?"

"Well, the two of us, we don't see the numbers, like we don't see atoms. But Vaccaro School was dreamed up by people. People who have a fluency with numbers. They dreamed you up, too. This house—it's all in the cloud."

"Cloud? Don't speak to me like I'm a child," I say unevenly. "How can you say I'm not real?"

Hands shaking, Angel flips open the copy of *The Giver* lying on my bed. "Haven't you noticed the inconsistencies?" He points to the publishing date, and my vision pinholes around it—*1993*. I've never seen it before.

I scratch at my arms; I tug at my fingers. "A printing error." My skin tears beneath my fingernails. *But how, Angel, how can I feel and touch and smell and taste and see if I am not real?* I want to ask. We cannot eat numbers. We cannot take numbers in our arms and hold on.

"You're lying," I say, though in the back, locked cabinet of my mind, I know Angel only speaks in incomprehensible truths. "Who are you? How did you arrive here?" The weight of the word *here* hits me like a crack to the back of the head. I feel dizzy. I prop my skull against the wall behind us.

His eyes are raw. "My name's Angel. I'm who you know me to be. But I'm from California. In the United States. I was lonely—I've been lonely for a long time. I never thought this life would be so lonely. And after Rob died, I thought I could come here when . . . when I needed a change. An urgent distraction from my life and myself."

I choke, reeling: *a change*. As if this house is a vacation.

"My mama's family is from Patagonia," he adds, as if that's any consolation to me now.

A distraction. The condescension of it all. The superiority. A sick feeling swells in my stomach, and my hands shake, shrunken in my vision, separate from my body. I can't understand it. Not a word of it. The same claws of panic scrape at my throat as the room spins in my vision. I've had to stretch my imagination so much lately—and even Morency's and Carmela's admissions did not derail me. But I can't internalize this latest truth: the nature of the Others' existence, of ours at Vaccaro School. I can't do it. I'm ill-equipped.

He's telling me we are trapped on a torturous merry-go-round, doomed to spin off and drop onto another seat on another carousel, then another, then another, each of them as false as the last.

Yet I can feel this chair below me, I can feel the air on my skin, I can taste the terrible soups I've lived on for days. I felt I could hold the story of my life in my hands like a humming thread. But now I can't understand what makes a life—what would make mine numeral-based, man-made. I've never thought of this before—never had to. I need Yesi. I need someone who could understand.

I feel my hands, my arms, my stomach, my legs, as if their concreteness is a clue or holy proof. It is pointless to cry, but I wish to do nothing more. I want to sob until I feel that cathartic relief and lightness; I want to sob until I feel like there is an exit from my pain and confusion, even if it comes in the form of total exhaustion.

But I shall not find that relief this time.

"So you're not dead," I say, fighting the urge to vomit. "And I'm . . . What am I meant to be made of? Numbers? Clouds?"

"You're a member of this place. But you're not like a character in a book or a movie. You learn. You grow. The lines of your personality are self-edited. You're a special person, Mav; you've been gifted

377

memories, traits, likes, dislikes, fears, ambitions. Strength. A body that doesn't die. But you have added to them. I never lied when I said you are real to me. You're not just a character, I swear."

A character. It's that word that eviscerates me. I expect the world around me to crumble as it is said. I feel myself gasping for air; I can no longer feel my limbs. I want to feel a hatred for Angel. I want to disbelieve him. Because if I am not a human being, I don't know what I am. I can't be a string of numbers—beyond its not making any sense, it's impossible to develop this richness of detail that way. My existence can't be condensed down into a stranger's dream. And what about the existences all around me? The military regime and its horrors cannot have been faked, even if sometimes this awful world felt like a cosmic game. I'm weak-kneed as I think of the girls. Of their fears, their love, their strength. Their humanity, which melted from them in the past days, like it was their god's afterthought. We aren't doomed to leaving behind pieces of ourselves here—we are the shards left behind.

My skin hardens around me into a shell of sorts.

No. He can't be right. I know who I am. I know where I came from. I'm a professor's daughter. I came here on a boat.

"How could you say this to me?" I ask, rising to my feet.

Angel's mouth falls open. "Because you asked. And I want you to know the truth. I think it's the only way to help now."

"Don't manipulate me. Don't lie to me. Tell me the honest truth. Why exactly are you telling me this? And what happens now, in this fantasy of yours, Angel?" I say sourly. "How does this end?"

"I—I don't know. I guess the girls' suffering ends, but so will their consciousness. And so will everyone's. And the game will re-start with new players. New Others."

My stomach heaves. I want to wretch on the ground. It is the cruelest answer possible. I try to find sadism, bare in his eyes. It isn't there.

This is Angel. Angel doesn't lie to hurt—he holds back incredible truths to protect. He isn't a sadist. No. Even if he's mad, I know he's not a sociopath. His eyes may not be his, but they are wide and carry all this world in them, including an image of me. I know he would not tell me the truth behind a situation were it utterly hopeless; I cling to this hope.

"But there's a way out," I say, folding my arms to stop the spasms. "There must be a way out. You'd only be telling me this if there was a way out." My teeth chatter even though the room is a sweltering pit.

"Mav?" Angel asks, brow wrinkling. He's beautiful. Real. I can touch his face—a face that isn't his—and mine. "I don't know if there's a way out. All this normally resets; you, Yesi, the girls—everyone resets and repeats this life indefinitely. I thought if you knew, we might figure out a way to escape together."

He can't be right. He can't. Because if he's right—if I've been thought up by a man and existed only during my time at Vaccaro School, that would mean everything planted in me is a falsehood. My time with my mother, her *cousins*, my messy history, my fear and loneliness. It would be so cruel to plant those horrors in someone who isn't . . . who isn't real. And these memories burned so brightly in me, once. They sustained me, once. Before I knew Yesi and Angel.

Even if the painful memories were implanted to put my good experiences and memories in starker relief—to allow me to appreciate them—I would still fail to understand why someone would create a loop centered on the abuse of children. The girls; Morency as a child; Carmela's own daughter—their hurt is a pillar of this world.

And if what he says is true, we are all doomed, like the Zapuche. Somewhere, they relive their torture and extinguishment over and over again. Circular time is no blessing to me in this moment—it is the cruelest curse of all, far more merciless than those any of their shamans could have inflicted upon their colonial oppressors.

"You can't be right," I say aloud before rushing out into the dark hall. "Don't follow me."

The knife is in the kitchen block, where I remember it. It takes a few tries to gather the nerve, but I slice open the palm of my hand; I feel an acute metallic pain, and I drop the bloodied blade to the ground, curling over my throbbing hand.

"Goddamnit." He is wrong. He is *wrong*. I rock my hand in my grip before edging over to a dishrag to wrap around the gash. But the air still smells wrong, too; has blood always smelled of dirt and iron? I can't trust my memories, which flicker in and out of my head now that doubt chases them.

I unwrap the bloody rag and wash my wound clean. Much of the pain has subsided—it was a clean cut. But when I look at the washed palm, free of blood, I find a healthy flap of skin hanging atop another healthy layer of skin. I tear it aside, though it sends a shudder through me. My heart speeds up, my neck throbs: Is this how I've always healed? What is normal? Surely not enough time has passed for that . . .

I'm overwhelmed by my efforts to retrieve a memory of being hurt. How can I not recall a single incident of cutting myself? My memories from the boat trip onward possess a different texture and weight than those from my time before Vaccaro School. I pick up the knife, and I rush upstairs to the sickroom.

Yesi is curled up on the sofa, napping beside the girls and her many papers and books. A shoddily bound manuscript sits atop them all—her book, I imagine. The work she has toiled over for the past months. The fruit of her labor glows faintly, drawing me toward its pages; I pick it up. Eager for proof that we can only be human, I lift the cover to peek inside.

What I see is etched into my memory forever. That is, if I even have true memory.

It is not a book. It looks like a list of accounts one might find in a shop that accepts credit—a ledger of some kind. There are no words. Each page has a date, and streaming below it, there are lines of numerals, followed by dashes and more numerals. Each is written in Yesi's unmistakable handwriting. I read an entry from early on:

Wednesday the 11th

2019-750 +50EXP for creative haunting (braiding a student's hair)

2020-1200 +100EXP for repossession of a secondary character

2021-550 +25EXP for standard haunting (spooking student into a fall)

I drop the book as if it has singed me. This? This is what Yesi has sunk her free hours into since we've met?

I flip to the beginning and find the corresponding numbers, with more identifying details:

2019—Room 6, Yesi, baby blue
2020—Room 7, Mavi, light apricot

Our names. Assignments. And the damned bourgeois paint shades on the room walls. I knead my eye sockets, trying to make sense of what I see, and the magnitude of Angel's admission slices up through my gut once more. I must clear my head of these thoughts; I must wipe their grime—

"Yesi?" I say, dropping to my knees and joggling her with my free hand. Panic floods hot and fast into my voice through my tender throat.

She gazes at me, eyes hazy. "What's happened? Is it over?" She doesn't raise her head nor move from her position. If I squint, I can see her shape shimmer in and out of view. Or perhaps my imagination is aflame.

She doesn't register my knife.

"Yesi, tell me about your grandmother," I whisper as calmly as I can bear. "Won't you?"

"My grandmother?" she asks, glancing at the girls. "Why?"

"I want to know more about you. I want to know everything there is to know. Everything you've saved up in that beautiful, creative head of yours."

"She was a dear woman. We used to get into arguments, silly arguments, over what my poor memory meant. That was then . . . I can't imagine what is now."

"But what else? Her laugh, her clothes, her mannerisms? Old stories from when she was young, her aspirations?"

Yesi is lost in thought. "She was like every other grandmother, more or less," she says at last. I can tell she is dissatisfied with her answer. "But I loved her. I loved her very much."

Her eyes flutter once, twice, closing as she drifts toward a shallow sleep.

"Yesi?"

She blinks awake, the whites of her eyes stained red.

"What else? What can you remember about her from before Vaccaro School?" I ask.

She yawns. "That was a long time ago. I think my grandmother

382

fell a bit too deep into the unsolvable mystery of existence. Always hung around the river's edge, fingered knives too long, that sort of thing. *L'appel du vide*, the French call it. What do you remember?"

And I think I remember.

My mother's last night. They come at dinner: three men in suits and a woman who smiles at me with perfect Chiclets teeth.

I am reading inside on the old sofa. On the nubby chair.

I am locked inside the cabinet I wasn't meant to enter until things went wrong.

Old newspapers. Corinthian oak. Marie's closet, the broken latch.

A woman urges me out, her voice an assured, caramel purr.

I am yours, my mother says to me. *You are mine. The color cannot be stripped out of us.*

Words that Angel said to me, too. Angel, right? Vibrant kaleidoscope memories blink in and out, terrifying me.

I have an image burned into me of a thin girl with a round face and bangs smiling. My dead classmate, ripped from the world by a bomb. My sleeping student, her consciousness carried from this world by an unseen foe. The two blur together, smiling with teeth made of poison.

We take these memories for granted, we do. It could be trauma that is causing Yesi to forget. Causing me to forget. It could be ghosts robbing us of these memories. Or I could be insane. Unreal. Artificial. Corrupted numbers.

I never thought this life would be so lonely, two men said to me.

"We must go, Yesi. We must leave." I bundle her into a seated position; she's so weak from her nap, or something more malignant.

"We can't go anywhere," she mutters. "The storm."

"The storm is a lie," I tell her. "It's all a lie." We can't be lobbed back to the beginning. It's not right, knowing what we know. I explain what Angel told me in rushed streams of words. "You were right. It's all a game."

"I don't understand you," Yesi says. Softly, gently, lest she hurt me. "A game? That's not what I thought at all. We're greater than all that—we're supernatural, we're . . ." She notices the knife in my hand, stares at me openmouthed. I think of the girls, of Lamb, of Mole, of Morency, even of Carmela. I think of all the people who need freeing. Including Yesi herself, who has written a scorebook for villains. She has been their pawn without knowing it. *It's all a game.*

It isn't enough to say that the rules in my life—the rules I so desperately tried to follow to live well—have never mattered.

No. If Angel is right, there is one rule to our existence: that there shall be no relief. And I need to prove or disprove it, now.

So I stab myself in the neck with a steak knife in front of Yesi and eight sleeping little girls.

32

ANGEL: 2020-3900

"Angel," Mama said, waking from a shallow sleep on one of her last days, motioning for me to approach her hospital bed. She was gaunt, her eyes huge moons. Sometimes they flashed with scenes from somewhere else, a place she didn't tell me about, a place closer to where she was going soon. I didn't want to look at her too intently, because I didn't want the sight of her like this—hollow, clinging to those last fibers of life in her grasp—to erase how she used to be in my memory. And I felt guilty about that. Guilt is a fear you're inadequate, right, so I felt like I should be stronger. But it was always worse for me if I tried to hide how I felt from myself.

I crouched next to her bed on the cracking linoleum. "Mama?"

"I didn't know cancer could be so damn fast." She swallowed with effort. It was the first time she'd said the word, and the two syllables—*can-cer*—sounded like a harbinger of doom to my ears. As if by hearing its name uttered, it would gain courage. "I should've listened. But I thought—"

I took her frozen, withered hand, avoiding the IV needle. "It's okay, Mama."

"There was a lot I wanted to tell you," she said, gripping my hand. Her nail beds were purple-blue, her nails overlong. "There was a lot. About Argentina. About your family—"

"It's okay, Mama."

"Stop interrupting me with that empty *it's okay* shit," she snapped, her old fiery humor sparking life in her eyes, and I remembered where my potty mouth came from. "I wanted to believe we would have more time, Angel."

My eyes watered. Talk of time reminded me of how much of a fucking fair-weather friend it could be. "We—"

She fixed me with a warning look. "I can't tell you everything I wanted to tell you one day. When you were older, or when I was older and could revisit it. I screwed up, and none of that's going to happen now. I need to spend the rest of my time making sure you and Rob will be okay," she said, and I flashed to the endless paperwork she'd been filling out, in between half-eaten cups of Jell-O. The heated talks with Liese that I wasn't allowed to participate in, even though I was old enough. "I need to make sure that you'll be fed and clothed and housed and turn into normal people. You get that, right?"

"We'll never be normal," I mumbled, and she burst out with a single laugh, like she used to, even though it sounded like a wheeze.

"Happy kids," she clarified. But she and I both knew happy wasn't normal for anyone.

"Listen," she said. "I made something for you without even realizing it was for you. It has my stories in it. It has pieces of my past—the ones I meant to tell you. And others I didn't." She exhaled, hiding the pain as best as she could. "I thought it was my biggest mistake. I thought I'd created a new type of hell. And maybe I did—but it means I can tell you some of what I meant to tell you in the only way left."

"What?" My throat had gone dry. "What is it, Mama?"

"Do you remember the Zapuche legend of the girls?" she whispered, eyes alight.

Mama made the game for me. She didn't know it until the end, but she did.

In the game, Mavi's blood is carmine red (255, 0, 56); the color, Mama once said, is made from the scales of certain insects. The thing is, neither Mavi nor her blood exists. The hookup tricks my brain into thinking they do—into seeing blood spurt out of her warm body in warm gushes, into seeing it paint the floor, a floor that also doesn't exist, carmine red. It's a cruel magic trick, really. It could take someone's breath away with its obscene extravagance, but knowing the truth behind it is enough to ruin its beauty. Our senses are nothing but receptors sending signals to the primitive parts of our brain. Receptors can be toyed with; brains can be fooled. This world that Mama made has become the fresh hell she thought it was for so long, torturing its occupants with fake horror, that hallmark of psychological warfare, for others' entertainment.

They say that some people succeed in wartime—even excel—and flounder in peace. The violent ones, the apathetic ones, the ones unmoved by or unsuccessful in routine life. Maybe I'm one of them. I was a sack of shit when all was good. It took the death of Rob to get me here; and here, inside Vaccaro School, this strange war zone, I began to build myself from scratch, by accident. I firmed up my human defenses, by accident. I got my hands around the stupid grenade that is love again, by accident. Maybe there's no better way for us to live than all in, even if that means fearing a catastrophic explosion might blow us back into bits at any moment.

And I learned all this only because I came to know Mavi. I'd like to say that was an accident, too, but I don't know anymore.

Every day of my life after Rob died, I wondered what Mama would have done. But the truth is, I know now, because she showed me again, one last time.

She would have seen me as clearly as she always did and known the freakish truth of it. She wouldn't have dared to say everything would be okay—I know that much, too. She would have held me, to start. And she would have been *there*, warm and unyielding next to me, however long it took for me to remember to be the same for her.

As Mavi did.

Would she have hated me for more than a second, even if she didn't say she did? No. Would she have pitied me forever and let me fold in on myself, thinking it was just typical grief from a broken person? No. Would she have let me drop myself into harm's way daily, desperate as I was to extinguish myself, to scatter my useless cells like dust? No.

I was the one who treated myself that way until Mavi came along.

I know this world is a nightmare. But there's nothing in Vaccaro School that is less real to me than it is in the Other Place. Mavi is real to me, my feelings for her so tangible that they're dangerous. They'll say it's because Mama made her. But everyone was made by someone.

And now I know how to show my love and gratitude to her.

I make a decision.

I need to shut down the game for good and move its inhabitants elsewhere. Quickly, too, because it's ending—I can feel it—and soon I won't have a way back inside.

I first believed that the end was near when Carmela fell apart in front of me and Mav. It's my first time playing, my only time, so I couldn't know for sure. But flitting through the teachers' rooms out-of-Dom in private is like reverse Halloween; every door opens onto a more bizarro display torn right out of the pages of a sketchy Japanese asylum horror comic. It would honestly have been less weird if two little girls appeared down the hallway and chanted *Redrum*. By the time I see the inside of Mole's garbage-dump-meet-den-of-sloth, I know for certain: We're moving toward the end of this life cycle in the house.

So I spill all the guts I have to spill, and Mav runs from me again. I drop off Dom and speed toward the sickroom in time to see her gurgling on the ground from a ghastly self-inflicted gash on her neck. I know she didn't stab herself to die. I know she stabbed herself because she was trying to prove me right.

I hurry to the cloud house, hyperventilating—everything unraveling faster now because of me.

The sky is no longer the sky as you or I know it; it's been transformed into a greedy, sucking charcoal swirl, its inky reaches coming to an apex above the house, like a cosmic toilet bowl ready for a vengeful God to flush us. It's high time to beg Charon for forgiveness. To grovel. For better or for worse, he's my only source of wisdom about the game's structure, with Mama long gone.

Charon must have smelled my desperation or Mavi's blood, because he's awake. He looks different. Smug. Beard trimmed. New cheesesteak in hand.

"Your performances with the English teacher are making me tear up, kid. I didn't even know she was built for that kind of thing. You know, in the fiveish years I've been running this, she's never been told by Dom that she's not real. I swear to God. She's let him do her, like, five times, she's slapped him, like, fourteen, but she's never had him shatter her world in some screwed-up romantic gesture."

I swallow hard. Charon has been *running this?* My veins feel like swollen rivers choked with ice. "Who are you?"

Charon stays silent. He smiles like a cat. "Haven't you guessed, Angel?"

The realization hits me like a load of bricks.

He's not the programmed oracle I believed him to be.

He's not even another regular player, like me.

Running this.

He's the other creator of the game. One of my mama's *partners*, as he once let slip. That asshole who joked about strangled girls.

"You thought I make friends with every Other here?" he says, plucking out a chunk of beef and popping it into his gray mouth. "I knew your dead mom, kid. I worked next to her for five years. Of course I saw your name when you registered." He takes a giant mouthful.

It makes sense. That's why he sees and knows everything. That's why he understands the game on a level I couldn't even see. *Five years.* My goal feels more impossible than ever.

"How can I convince you to shut down Vaccaro School for good?" I ask. "My mom—my mom wouldn't want to see it run this way. It's—it's her legacy."

He shakes his shaggy head, swallows. "Holy shit. You're so naive. And also so dense. I'm tired of pussyfooting around with you. We've run it this way since the beginning. And they're not *girls*, kid. They're lines of code. They're characters. They're built from pixels like the Sims your siblings played with as kids. You're plugged into a machine that makes you think they're girls. Are you a fucking moron?"

I'm not sure how to explain to him that, if he and Mama did create these people, if a team somewhere in California did write everyone here, then their creations have outgrown them. She must have known that. But my inability to explain seems like a fatal flaw. "Come on, Charon. They experience real terror, real pain—"

"And this is an income stream for me, kid. You, too, I might add, in the sense that your mom's cut still pays her outstanding medical bills, if memory serves. And do you even understand the stellar press we got for creating a game that gives losers and pedos a sort of healthy outlet?"

"I can pay you, Charon, if that's what you want. I have money from the settlement with the truck company."

"Um, fuck no."

"What?"

"Are you kidding? I'm not a monster. I'm not going to take the blood money you got because your brother died," Charon says. "Yeah, I know about that, too. Listen, kid. He was a real person, your brother. And what happened to him is a tragedy. Seriously. But these characters aren't real. What happens to them isn't real. And I won't be made to feel bad about making a living off my own intellectual property." He frowns, stroking his beard. "And also, my Vietnam game makes no money at all, if that's your next tactic. That *Wired* article that went viral on Vaccaro School came out like three years ago, but it still gets people interested. Even Reddit lost its shit over how gross some of the players were last year, and that's Reddit, where selfie videos of twelve-year-old girls cutting themselves is an average Tuesday. We had a dude strangle all the girls last year, low-key, which isn't chill or even possible. I mean, theoretically, I guess, they'll feel the pain and think they're dying, in their own fake-ass way, but they never die. You need a body to do that shit.

"But besides the money, I'm proud of the game. It has its own *mythology* based on a seed of truth, like *GoT*. You know the Zapuche tribe is real? I was backpacking through Argentina and Chile after college when I heard about them and came up with it all. That's how I met your mom, actually: I put out an ad for coders and designers who were Argentine and wanted to partner up. My dad puts up the cash, and she builds out the details, adding some Latin flavor.

"For a hot second, I convinced her to name me Ngunechen after their deity—a god who derives knowledge and energy from *dreams*, get it?—but she told me it didn't have the same ring to it as boatman Charon, which is true, you know? Granted, it's kind of a cheap rip-off of my real name, but hey.

"But besides all that, the game's just the shit conceptually, like *Inception* status. I mean, consider the parallelism between the savage oppression in 1970s Argentina and the current shitshow in the USA! And on a deeply individual level, we're perpetuating this belief that you can find your True Self inside a haunted mansion. *Matter* a little in this dung heap of a universe by existing in the form you wish to exist in. Start as a ghost and claw your way up to the angel or down to the demon you are. People eat that trash up. We started promising it as part of the tagline—*Learn more about yourself at Vaccaro School.* We're on some 'lean in' shit with our whole TED Talk–level spiel: *Invisibility can heal, because it allows us to strip away all our physical hang-ups and . . . you know, be our zany selves, LMFAO!* You know that Yesi line? Ghosts are a metaphor, blah blah blah? Your mom wrote that. She wrote all this to pander to these people. Okay, maybe she believed it. But she was the only one.

"None of it's true. It's honestly hilarious that people don't get that you don't suck the energy from other people to expand and re-veal yourself in the real world unless you're a sociopath. Treating fake humans like shit or even falling in love with code doesn't result in some major epiphany; it numbs you to your own kind over time.

"But there's beauty in witnessing people following their base in-stincts. It's like cleansing the phony for once. We're all goddamned animals." Charon pauses mid-rant, his forgotten cheesesteak dripping, and he wipes at his soiled lap. "Hang on, hang on. I spilled some of my baby. I make this real clothbound cheddar sauce IRL, and your mom re-created it in the game for me. But only I know where that cheddah is. And the tenth girl knows, of course. Because the tenth girl's a little bitch deserving of all dairy binges."

"So you do know more about the tenth girl," I say flatly, brain processing his word vomit. Shaking so hard I'm worried I won't keep it together.

He closes his mouth midbite. "Of course I do. Once upon a time, she was your mom's in-game avatar, like Charon is mine."

The revelation hits me like a gut punch.

Mama. Of course Mama would choose to be the tenth girl.

But how is it that I saw her? How did Mavi? Did we imagine it?

"But her avatar could fly, while mine sits here all day. She wrote them, first, and made me chairbound in some kind of power play. She got off on being a little house guardian angel," he says. "She would help the characters here and there—especially Mavi, her little pet. And she built in this special level. If any player bothered to learn Zapuche history from the dusty books in the house and figured out who the tenth girl was meant to be, she would appear and grant them access to this special Utopia level where a dream of theirs came true within the ecosystem. Within reason, of course. No one managed that, though, like I told her no one would. Until you. But by then—"

"Why didn't you tell me all this before?"

He looks at me strangely. "I wasn't about to talk about it with you and upset you," he says, taking another bite and swallowing it whole. "I'm not here to deal with your waterworks. You came to play and get the angst out of your system, didn't you? So I let you play. And occasionally gave you a helping hand."

I'm silent for a while, a confused, swirling mess of hatred, fear, and love. "So you're saying that if I'd figured out who the tenth girl was meant to be, she could have shut down the game, assuming that was my dream?"

He blinks at me in apparent shock. "No. What? For real? You're talking to the goddamn creator of the game and you're wondering if a feature of the game will help you get the game to self-destruct? Jesus Christ, you are mental. Just enjoy it, okay? You're getting so close to the end. You're planning the *sacrifice*, for fuck's sake. The sacrifice ritual! Haven't heard of one of those happening in about three years. I can't believe you mined that nugget of an origin story out of the old secretary hag, honestly. You're your mother's kid, all right. Plus two thousand experience points for Gryffindor. Good for you. You deserve it.

"And hey, good news: Your character friends will get to meet some charming Others at the vigil, too. Others always attend that little shindig. It's the only ending that allows the players to inhabit their *true forms*, per the game brochure pitch, so that's kind of fun. Despite hating the Others so much, you gifted all of them what they wanted more than anything. They should be s'ing your metaphorical d big-time.

"Funny how all your machinations precipitated the end for your real friends, though." He smirks. "You get that, don't you? Pretty soon after the sacrifice, your friends will all fall asleep for the last time. And the world will disappear just like that. Poof. Characters' memories erased. And you—you and the Others go back to your boring lives in high school or working in HR or whatever the hell you losers do, and you can pay for access to a new game if you can gather up the dough. It's ending, kid."

"I know it's ending," I whisper, digesting every shred of information he's said. I tattoo it into my brain, every painful word. "I can tell. But I still need to end it for good. It's what Mama would want."

"Okay. Let me humor your psychosis for a minute." He presses his filthy fingertips together in a steeple. "If you end the game for good, your precious English teacher will disappear from existence."

"We could transfer them somewhere. You can do that kind of thing." I swallow. "But even if you didn't, she wouldn't suffer anymore."

"Holy shit. You're sounding like a Romeo and Juliet case. Don't pull some bullshit right now and tell me you love her and will kill yourself if a few lines of code are trashed. You signed disclaimers. I know you probably scrolled right through without reading, but still. That shit's legally binding."

How couldn't I care about her? I think to myself. *Mama made her, and she exceeded her wildest hopes. I'm sure of it.*

"Jesus H. Christ, you are so screwed up. You know, despite all the psychos who play, this has never happened before," he says. "Never in the years I've been running this. No one has ever gotten so attached to one of them. So all I can say to that is, you are either a full-on lunatic of a breed I've never encountered or, the more likely case, you're a sad little kid who has PTSD because of your whole family dying."

"Or no one else got to know Mavi like I did," I snap.

"She's AI, kid. Some lines of code pieced together to make her think like an intelligent being. You think she would pass a Turing test? Don't make me piss my pants."

But he's wrong, and I know he's wrong. Mama once told me about another colleague of hers, a computer scientist, who coded a brand-new personality based on that of his daughter, who was dying from leukemia. After she died, he uploaded the personality into a robot, and over the course of a few months, the robot behaved in a way so eerily similar to his late daughter—having the same empathy, the same quirks, the same loves and hates, the same mannerisms, the same character—that he and his wife destroyed the robot for good. Man and our machine-based creations are melding, for better or for worse. Everyone knows that new personality traits can now be coded and uploaded into human brains: I saw as much happen last year. A serial killer on death row was given the first ever technolobotomy, a scientist replacing the psychopath's lack of empathy in his brain with an acute sensitivity to others' pain.

How can creators be sure of the consciousness levels of their creations? I'm not saying that I (as a peer) am the ultimate judge, either—after all, from the beginning, I would have said that Mavi is as intelligent and conscious as anyone else. But I've watched her learn and grow in tandem with me; I've watched her feel and fight those feelings, and I want to bet everything on her consciousness now. "She feels real pain," I say.

"That's not proof. They're built to show a pain they don't feel, when faced with certain fake external stimuli."

"She's grown as a person," I say. "She's changed over the course of the game."

"Growth built into her character arc."

"She cares for me," I say. "Even though she knows I'm not like her."

"She's rigged to care for anyone in Domenico's body. She'd let him treat her like dirt and still follow him all gaga. You chose your meat shell wisely. Or unwisely."

"How can I prove you're wrong?"

Charon snorts. "That's just it. *You* can't. If the English teacher could walk out of the game and survive a year as a real human being, then that might prove I'm wrong. *Might*. But that's impossible."

I'm silent for a while. "By the way, how did you even know I told Mavi what she is?" I ask. "How did you know we're planning a sacrifice? How do you know any of this if you're just sitting here all day?"

"Come on." Charon smiles the sort of smile that could shatter at any moment. Is he sweating, or am I imagining it? "I can't tell you that."

"From your office?" I ask gently. "From your cloud chair?"

Charon snorts. "Cloud chair? Office? No, kid. Jesus, you don't get tech. If I'm in my office, I'm in my office. If I'm here, I'm here. If I'm in there, I'm in there. It's an old-style immersion game. Perfectly contained. I was one of the first to build this shit. Well, your mom was. It's sort of a dinosaur now, but the good ones, the beautiful ones, they still make the most money, even when they get old. That level of detail—sometimes I would joke that she put her own blood, sweat, and jizz in it."

An immersion game. An old-school immersion game. I think of what Charon once told me: that everyone has their motivations, fears, desires. Charon is motivated to control the game, monitor the players, and keep tabs on his source of income. He's motivated to stir up drama inside the game. Create conditions ripe for his players to have fun. His fears? Losing that source of income, for one. But his desires? I don't know enough about Charon to understand his desires beyond the financial one. What does anyone want? Attention? The ability to play God? But how would he play an omniscient God in a game that is immersion-only?

And how did I see the tenth girl, and how did Mavi? Who was inside the avatar, the meat costume, the shell?

Her avatar could fly, while mine sits here all day.

I've been silent too long—he can see the gears whirring in my head. "Okay," I say as glumly as I can muster. "Well, thanks for telling me a bit about my mom. I guess I should go now."

His eyes narrow, and my spidey-sense tingles. "Don't go killing yourself or anything," he says. "I'd hate to see that. I like you, as batty as you are. You're a good egg, kid. You'll find your way." And he burps, clutching his stomach like he's eaten a bad cut of meat, as the tenth girl grabbed her own before launching herself onto the ice.

That's when I know for certain.

I've known the tenth girl all along, and the recognition guts me like a fish knife.

If I'm here, I'm here. If I'm in there, I'm in there.

But her avatar could fly, while mine sits here all day.

With Mama gone, he was free to inhabit her avatar.

"Thanks, I guess," I say carefully. "Would you be free to talk some more tomorrow before the sacrifice?" I expel the air from my mouth, sounding as pathetic as humanly possible. "I feel like I'm going to be sad."

He nods, enough of an idiot to think I'm giving up.

Mavi needs all the time she can get while she's not under Charon's watchful eye. She's as smart as Charon—smarter. She'll need all the time she can get while the tenth girl is distracted. Charon's words ring in my head: *If the English teacher could walk out of the game and survive a year as a real human being, then that might prove I'm wrong.* Might.

I punt his last sentence out into the dark, as far as I can:

But that's impossible.

33

MAVI: ARGENTINA, JUNE 1978

I cannot conceive of a force strong enough, an act damaging enough, to rip the youthful spirit from a person for good, except for learning you are not a person at all by the traditional definition implanted in us—you are a pale shadow of a self, someone's toy, everyone's joke. This is not to mean there aren't thousands of other ways to lose yourself. But in losing a parent—my only other touchstone, false as it was—I temporarily lost touch with that great cornerstone of identity, the child, not the foundation of humanity. As I regain consciousness, I am struck by a powerful, incomprehensible craving.

I crave a body.

It's laughable, perhaps, because it's something I've never known. But I crave a real body, with flesh that aches or sparkles with energy, heals or rots. Can you imagine it? Touching, and being touched, by another real body that shimmers with vibrant cells? I swear my every nerve would be lit up in ecstasy by the simplest handshake. I cannot stop thinking about it, dreaming about it, obsessing about it. The stroke of the wind, the feel of cotton, the ripple of your own flesh . . .

Logic tells me that perhaps all of that can be simulated to some small degree. But I believe so much else could not be. Say: the touch of another human being. That could not be faked. I know this because I remember the many moments I shared with Angel in which I felt skinned and raw. They were a glimpse into humanity: a taste so powerful it changed the course of my existence, even though Angel was but a human in Dom's shell.

And so, before I even open my eyes, I feel Yesi's hands upon me, hands that feel like no more than a filled sack of cloth, and I know that I never died from that blow to my neck, for I have no healthy flesh to be split, and more important, no cell of mine was ever alive.

A groan rips through me as I process this new craving, this craving to possess flesh, and it shocks me, this overpowering hunger to be concrete in the way that Angel must be, somewhere. *Angel*. Where is his body? If only I could take his hand, his hand of skin and blood and bone. I wake beside a red-eyed Yesi, flattening a damp cloth on my forehead. I feel at my neck, and she swats my hand away.

"It's healed," she says curtly. She bites her lip and releases it, blood flowing back. "He's a devil. They're all devils—the lot of them."

And our only damn salvation, I think to myself. These foolish and fortunate flesh bags masquerading as ghosts. But I must be careful. How maddening that I must play their game now myself, especially if not much time is left.

We walk alongside the sickbeds as we make sense of our reality. Rain crashes against the closed shutters with fresh fury. The girls are beautiful when they sleep; they look so close to waking, so full of that youthful, ruddy-cheeked health, that I find myself trying to rouse them again and again, only for them to bat the air around me impatiently, still sleeping deeply, as if to banish me from their fairy queendom.

Diana, her halo of chestnut hair cresting along the pillow's ridges, dazzling in candlelight, her arms framing her head in silent exaltation. Christina, the only girl to speak in days—she whispers imperatives in her sleep, sometimes chortling, with a single bitten finger nestled on her cheek.

Mariella's eyelashes, these minky, coquettish fringes of ebony, brush her rounded cheeks, the palest pink. She smiles often, her ropes of braided hair draped loosely around her neck. Sara, a rascal even in sleep, her pale lips curled into a smirk, her skinny arms in their navy sleeves crossed at the delicate wrists and facing the sky, pale green streams of veins lacing beneath her skin.

Silvina, more relaxed than she ever was awake, nuzzling her pillow, slipping half off the bed, bracelet dripping charms and tinkling as she breathes. Gisella, a goddess, coral lips parted, a crown of blond hairs alive around her temples, and an assured warmth chiseled on her face, her horrors nothing but old nightmares now.

And there's Isabella, who reaches for a lost Luciana even in sleep, to coddle her, to protect her, to console her. I can't know which, because Luciana has been gone for a long while.

Michelle, too—the first to go under: the seams of her lids so finely drawn and curved by a loving artist, the same stripe of blond through her mussed hair—an angel's finger. And the same contented, round face. Michelle, who has gem stickers on her earlobes. Michelle, who has her two palms pressed together on her chest, as if in prayer. I find myself still wanting to ask where she's from, what kind of trick this is, why she looks like her. But I don't, because I know why now.

"Fake," I spit. "Not real flesh. Constructed from numbers. Imagined by a man." The craving flows through me once more: *I must find a body. I must find a body to truly live.* Because you can only live if you can die. It's the certainty of an end that defines living as a precarious state. Isn't that so? And I've learned that the most beautiful and important parts of existence are the most transient.

Yesi watches me. "But why are they asleep and regenerating, while we remain awake and miserable, conscious of our fate? What are we doing wrong?" Her face falls, exposing a grief that is jarring to view. "Why isn't this game's magic working for us? Why are we forced to remain a pale copy of our true selves?" Her eyes are crimson, the pain in them raw. "Are we waiting, waiting, waiting for the next boat to come in, for our makers to hit refresh and decide to lavish us with some more color?" She shakes her head. "We don't own our designs."

"No," I whisper back, sheltering her small hands. "But that's not the point."

Yesi's eloquence and wisdom astonish me—she's so attuned to what's been happening all along. But she gives up too easily. We don't want to be regenerated by another person—a sadist dooming us to reliving this over and over. We don't want that, and we can edit ourselves, I'm sure of it. We can edit ourselves and perhaps even come into possession of the flesh we deserve.

"Don't you want to be real? Don't you want a body?"

I am yours. You are mine. The color cannot be stripped out of us.

"It's not possible. If the makers come for me, I want you to let me go," Yesi says, squeezing me tight. "I wasn't built for running. I wasn't built for seeking truth. I was built for—well, I was built for examining this world. Tabulating and admiring the subtle changes. There's beauty in that, you know."

Her eyes look so clear as she pleads. I think of her life's work—a scorebook incomprehensible to even her that she was compelled into crafting. Her hands curl into fists as she watches me grimace at her.

"I don't want to fight about it, Swamp. I want to spend the rest of my days here stretching myself, living every day like it is my last. I want to be the best self I can be right now, and I need to hope that next time will be my opportunity to be even better. All right?" She scrapes at her eyes as they swell with unfamiliar tears. "You don't need to understand. You need to agree. You need to agree now, Swamp."

But I can't. I don't answer. And she cries for the first time since I've known her this go-around. I take her in my arms.

Angel finds us, as I cradle Yesi on the sofa, with a yolk-colored blanket draped over his arm. Yesi tenses up in my hold.

"I know you're mad at me," he whispers.

Mad. Mad! "Don't patronize me," I say, robbing a line from Carmela. "And we're good on blankets, thanks."

He lays it beside me like a sleeping infant. "You're going to need an extra."

I raise a brow at him. "I don't need you to take care of me. I've survived at least a few rounds of this nightmare, right? Fairly soon I'll remember nothing again. And that will be a relief." The words stain my mouth with bitterness.

"You don't mean that," he says softly.

"No, Swamp," says Yesi, turning to Angel. "She doesn't mean that."

They're right, of course. But our show of indignation might be the only thing to push Angel along into working for us as ruthlessly as we need him to do.

He sits on the floor before us. "Won't you wrap Yesi up in that blanket, Mav? She's freezing."

I snatch the blanket—the damn blanket—off the sofa, before casually draping its golden lengths over Yesi without unfolding it. Angel sighs.

"I spoke to the creator," he whispers.

"The creator?" whispers Yesi. A part of her harbors a wonder toward this strange god of ours since she learned of his existence; I can admit it's tempting to know everything about him that we can, while we can, even though we know we're doomed to forget it all. More poignant, even, for her. Yesi—who is obsessed with uncovering every dark corner of herself. To be faced with the person who wrote us, our world . . . it's an irresistible possibility.

"He's not . . . incentivized to change the game," he confesses, rubbing his hands together. "This . . . version, it's—I pleaded with him. Told him how everyone here is suffering. He knows that—he knows and sees almost everything."

How does he know and see everything? What are the mechanics of his godliness? Is he among us? Or am I to believe some general vision of a God in the sky, surveying his land and creations? I cannot ask Angel, if he is watching now.

"I even offered to pay him—" he continues, and I snort, cutting him off. Yesi elbows me in the ribs.

The creator sounds like a soulless miser with no morals and even less compassion. It won't cut it to tell someone like that that his creations are suffering, not when he hand-built our loops of suffering.

I know it will do me no good to speak with this creator and convince him of our worth, either—of our having earned independence. He will be unmoved by any evidence I, his plaything, provide.

But he made a mistake by failing to write a blind faith in a compassionate God into my genetic code. With each passing second, I formulate a plan.

"There's no way to end this, Angel," I say aloud, carefully planting a note of girlish anguish into my voice. Hopelessness, too. "Just say it."

He looks at me with surprise—giving up is out of character. But I need him to believe my character is choosing weakness and hopeless-ness in the face of this news. I need him to believe that all the strength I developed since I've known him was for show. I need him to believe it so the all-seeing creator believes it. Because I can't draw the creator's attention now while I investigate all this world's secrets to further our escape. If it was created by a man, it will have flaws. Back exits. Exits that can be patched if the creator knows I'm looking. And while I'd like to take a more immediate approach to exiting this damned game, committing suicide by jumping onto the ice is only going to leave me with a broken neck for a half hour and a hell of a long climb back up. I look up at him, no longer fighting to keep the darkness from my eyes.

"You don't mean that," he says, echoing Yesi. "Let's go back through everything we know, every secret we know about this place that could help. Yesi's the only one who can be fed from with no side effects," he says, counting on his fingers, "and adults are worse feed than children, and—"

"We know," I interrupt. Yesi glowers at me and readjusts the blanket, a scrap of paper slipping out.

Angel's eyes fall to the scrap, ballooning cartoonishly, and a heady panic overwhelms me. He must have tucked a note inside the blanket he brought, knowing the creator might hear us. Bless Angel. I dart a hand out to snatch the slip and tuck it in the curve of my palm.

"I never came across Carmela's shrine when I was outside of Dom's body," he says, his eyes boring holes into mine.

"We explored it last night. We've solved that sad mystery." I flick open the scrap hidden in my sleeve.

"How do you access the Other Place?" asks Yesi in a religious whisper.

Creator = 10, it reads, in Angel's messy hand. 10. The tenth girl. *After sacrifice ritual, you all fall asleep forever.*

Adrenaline surges through me. If the creator is the tenth girl, she was never going to help us. She was a puzzle no one was ever meant to solve.

To be the most sought-after creature in our limited world . . . with powers beyond anyone's comprehension . . . ? It makes sense for a creator.

When she came to me, she acted the saint, but her action only stirred up trouble. What good is a warning about the Others if it's impossible to leave and impossible to fight them? It only plants a seed of panic.

Treacherous little bitch.

"Oh, Yesi," I say, crumpling the slip in my hand carefully. I must work quickly and think even quicker. I bring my free hand to my hair and pull my fingers through it, trying to lock eyes with Angel. "Stop with all this religious babble about the Other Place. Like you said, we'll never reach it. There's nothing for us there." Lies, of course.

And yet, what can I do with this new information to help us? I know, at the very least, that all talk of the Other Place must cease until I understand how to handle this.

But Angel defies my innermost thoughts and clears his throat. "My access point to the Other Place is Mavi's closet. The creepy one. I think—I think all the closets are access points."

My heart thuds wildly as I process this now. One revelation after another—it feels as if they won't cease until I escape this place or succumb to it. Is that how a human life is, too, only expanded on a grander scale?

Still, we shouldn't be speaking about access points to the Other Place in front of the tenth girl–cum–creator—surely she's flitting through the air nearby—lest she close the points down. But could she? What with the Others needing access in and out? What's to stop characters from escaping into the Other Place? My heart won't quit, despite the pointlessness of its work; I expect pain to shoot through the old injury in my neck, but there is nothing. I remain silent, working through the ever-broadening puzzles in my head.

"No," Yesi whispers. "The closets . . . ?" Her face scrunches up. I can tell she's awed and disappointed by the simplicity of it. "Multiple exit points. A perforated world."

I could strangle them both while screaming my lungs out. Instead, I take the most foolish of risks: I choke with a sob that I hope rings true, and their jaws both drop.

"A ruined world," I shout, and before they can raise their brows at me, I pull them in for a hug and weep, dragging the blanket over all our shoulders. Oh, how the creator will think I'm a clown. I only hope he has no high opinion of his creations' intelligence.

"Swamp?" Yesi whispers in the humid pocket we have to ourselves. "What's gotten—"

I feign another howl and thrust the note into her fingers.

"Ah," she whispers, her hands closing around the slip. "So this is cover. Pathetic cover. Your acting—"

I jab her in the side, and she yelps.

"We can't access the closets as we are," Angel whispers quickly. "I've tried in Dom. Trust me. And you need a player number and password for each. My player number is 2020. I don't know the others' . . ."

"2020," Yesi repeats, eyes widening. She opens the logbook, still by her side, and thumbs through it.

2019—Room 6, Yesi, baby blue
2020—Room 7, Mavi, light apricot

"Your closet is Mavi's closet, right, Angel?" she asks.

Angel meets my eyes. "Yes."

"And your password?"

"Two-five-three-two-one-three-one-seven-seven," he whispers, without missing a beat.

"What on earth does that mean?" whispers Yesi as I wonder why the number sounds familiar. Could it be that I've been implanted with knowledge I am not even aware of? Angel leans into me, peering into the open book on Yesi's lap. He points to the 2020 entry.

"Oh shit. My password is the RGB color code for light apricot," he whispers into our mess of intertwined hair, silver threaded through bark.

I remember our resident numerologist, Mole, spouting that exact password to me, and that raw space that passes for my heart radiates palpable delight. This news about the closets—and their possible alignment with Yesi's logbook—is enough to celebrate. Enough to pin a life on.

"But you can't just walk out of this world," he adds. And perhaps I'm going mad, but I can swear he says *walk* with a special inflection. As if Others can flit inside in their crystal shapes only. But if an Other can possess a character in this game, and later leave the shell behind, why couldn't I detach from my flesh prison?

After all, I am not a human. Only a character.

I rip the hot blanket from us and wipe the tears from my eyes, moaning again for full effect.

"We must enjoy the little time we have left together before the sacrifice," I say, twirling the hair in my fingers, the old signal that I'm lying. He's not looking at me. I cough, lock eyes with him at last, and tug on my hair as blatantly as I possibly can. This is not a time for subtlety anymore, clearly. I can only hope he remembers.

Two sets of blue eyes widen with recognition, and I fight a grin. Only a genius like Yesi would remember Angel's offhand remark about this tell of mine in the hall so long ago. The Others couldn't rob her of her wits.

"This has been a waste of time. This whole wild-goose chase, telling us you're ghosts, having us look for the tenth girl—it's all a waste. We could've been living each day like it was our last on earth. You were right, Yesi. The next round, we might wake up as a better version of ourselves. I welcome that day."

She nods quietly, thumbing the blanket edge, acting her part.

"You know what I want to do?"

Angel and Yesi still look at me like I've gone a touch mad. I'm unpredictable, now, or so I'd like to hope.

"I want to fly. On my last day as a fully conscious character, I want to damn well fly. You fly out of Dom, don't you, Angel? Teach us to fly."

His lips twitch with what I know is a smile, and he looks away. "I—I don't know what you mean. I don't think we can fly in these bodies—"

"So . . . teach us how to fly out of them," I say. I feel my fake-heart plumbing its way into my throat.

"You think it's possible?" says Yesi, reading the fine lines on her shaking palms.

I don't know what is or isn't possible anymore. But, rendered subhuman, I need to believe I can remake the rules of this world to keep moving forward. And I know what I want. What I want, as a fool of a character on death row, is to fly like a bird right out of this prison of numbers.

But I say none of this. I only shrug.

"Okay," says Angel, focusing the private excitement visible in his eyes on me. "I'll teach you to unlatch and fly."

It's a process Angel can't fully articulate. The three of us lie down on the ground. Corpse-like. *Push*, he says, *push harder. Wiggle out of your fingers, first, like gloves. Slip out of your arms, next.*

Suffice it to say that Yesi and I look at each other with increasing dismay, wondering if he's repeating the misheard instructions of a midwife or a tailor.

Angel slips out of Dom with ease, his slack body the evidence of his success, until he rejoins us.

"You have to want it," he says, frowning, as if a strong-enough will is the way to abandon a prison you've been trapped inside your entire lifetime.

"We *do*," I reply.

We try, again and again, to treat our souls as if they're detachable. Yesi faints a couple of times, but nothing happens. I only exhaust myself. And in that moment, I stare into the candle we've lit beside the bed. My eyes fog, as they do when you lose the ability to focus. The candle flame becomes a pleasant haze into which I can melt, only for a mysterious draft to upset the flame, blowing it out. My eyes widen. I think of when I was nearly possessed those many weeks ago; the dragging hooks of electricity coursing through me.

"Why don't you push us out?" I whisper to Angel, whose eyes brighten.

Yesi and I drop onto our backs again, hand in hand, and we wait until Angel leaves Dom once more.

"Me first," I call into the air. Greedy, now, for new power, for opportunities to push the boundaries of our existence.

I wait. I feel Yesi's hand grow clammy in mine. Is the air stirring? Is it a draft, or Angel? And that's when I feel a tickling on the left side of my scalp. A gentle pressure on the left side of my head. The first surge of prickle-edged pain that intensifies too quickly, perhaps because I anticipate pain, now. I panic; I instinctually fight the pressure, as I did before. But I will myself to feel that apathy, too—that disconnect. *Is this what a stroke is like?*

I banish the thought. I loop my mind back around. I tell myself to welcome the sweeping hooks as they drag through interior muscle I did not know anyone should feel. *I do not exist, so my muscle, my skin, my bone cannot exist. My pain does not exist.* I pause; I wait, because that is all I am capable of doing, and my left eye goes dark, leaving me blind in that eye. A humming fills my skull. My right eye goes dark, and I lose my vision of the cracked ceiling. A frisson of terror that I must not give in to, that I must not allow to swell. I sniff at the air, trying to take a breath, and I cannot smell, much less feel the sharp coolness of the inhalation as it passes up into me. I lose the structure of the jaw; I lose the heaviness of the tongue. I lose the rise and fall of my chest. Some forgotten part of my body shudders. I lose the feel of Yesi's hand in mine.

I am in darkness.

A hot shimmering, vast and then so close, and I lose touch with the given world.

But my consciousness still flickers.

And some part of me sees or senses a crystalline shimmer, or a harmony, or the scent of medialunas, rich and thick. Ethereal yet swelling. I press toward it; I ask it to amplify. It doesn't answer, but whatever I am drifts, and drifts, and drifts—

And I fall,

fall into a vibrant and separate universe of numerals painted like fish scales on the walls—translucent, gummy. I am in room 7. Its contours are recognizable enough, despite the fact I'm in a fresh layer of reality. If I focus, I can see the room as it was. As for me: Well, it's not so much flight as a separation from weight, an unmeshing, enough to convince you it's a separation from that forgotten pain, too. I see Yesi, lying on the ground, her head turned to face my prostrate body. She places her delicate hand to my body's cheek. I don't feel it.

My body. There, alone. Smaller than I might have thought. Colder, with waxy skin. Dead-eyed. I feel both a revulsion and a pang of sympathy for it, as if I'm looking at a half-formed creature, so far from whole. I've never had an out-of-body experience in my life—until now, I suppose. I look around myself, around the crystal I am. The walls, though visible still in their normal incarnation, are now threaded with a substance made of flexible, plasticized numerals that glisten and glow as I move, adding a transparency to the world around me. Because of this, I can see the other characters; they are strips of moving energy, and there are more of them, many more, as if a private universe is unfurling for view.

And then, another grouping of crystal strands of energy collects at my side.

A warbling noise, as if someone speaks in water.

He-hi. He-hi.

Laughter?

Angel.

Within a body, emotion becomes inextricably linked to its physical manifestations. I could feel heat in my cheeks and know I am embarrassed, ashamed. If my pulse quickened, I might hate, I might fear, or I might love. Without a body, I have become only thought, and I miss it, that physical manifestation of emotion. How it makes me hunger for a real life. If my old existence is one layer from this, then the real world, with real bodies, must be so many more levels from that.

In the abyss, surrounded by pulsing atom-like numerals, we travel together to Yesi's side.

When I brush her cheek with my formlessness, her eyes—now composed of moving numeral flecks of every color, most of them blue—widen. "Is it you?" she whispers.

And I rush to return to myself, to the self that is limp on the floor beside her, so that I might tell her yes.

I feel sick returning to that hollow shape I now know to be formed by numbers. But a shaky awareness fills me: Having glimpsed the numbered world, I perceive another layer to our existence. I know I can bend the rules, and it makes a hidden part of me smile.

After that, it is less difficult for Angel to nudge me out. I press Yesi out, in turn, which proves to be a disorienting inversion of being pushed out, because I sense an unfamiliar fullness of being, a stickiness, as I encroach upon her body.

I try not to think about the fact that Yesi and I do not succeed in learning how to escape on our own.

Angel swears he will nudge us out at the right moment, so that we can have a chance to escape. Everything hinges on this promise. He whispers in my ear, begging me to take his closet, if I do escape; he tells me he will check Yesi's log later for another room. Any other room.

And he disappears to distract the creator for as long as he can before the sacrifice begins.

We begin our rounds, with Yesi's logbook in tow, to ask the other teachers to the sacrifice ritual and teach them what we have learned. The house, in hungry anticipation of the sacrifice, restores power, and a dirty light trickles in uneven streams from the cloud-shaped sconces still remaining in place along the walls.

First, we visit Mole, whose insights we now depend on. I've been avoiding the room; the stinking bag remains propped up against her door, overflowing with garbage. Yesi kicks it aside with her shoe, as I pray it doesn't burst on contact, then knocks.

"What?" we hear from inside.

"Doctor," I say. "Doctor, Moley, it's me, Mavi."

Fiddling with the lock. The air is thick around us, not one draft noses its way past. A click, and Mole opens up, a blast of noxious air hitting us in the faces. Dead flesh. Coughing, I restrain myself from pinching my nose. Luckily, Mole's wearing clothes, pajamas by the look of it, but they're encrusted with so much filth—I can't tell if it's mucus, dirt, sweat, what—that she looks like the victim of some sort of crime involving an overripe sewer. She clutches a doughy, brown-spotted piece of food in her hand; it smells too sweet and spoiled, but I couldn't tell you if it was an old slice of pear or a week-old pastry. Her mouth, with its loose lips, is coated in grease; her thinning, oily hair has been tied into a loose bundle in one corner of her exposed scalp. The same oily residue coats her glasses—I can't make out her eyes them-selves, only the glimmer of my reflection in the uneven light. The room behind her is very dark, with one stubby candle lit, and I can't make out a single piece of furniture because everything is covered in a hoarder's mess. Some bits tremble with life. I fear looking too closely.

"How are you, Doctor?"

She twitches her nose at us. "Two-five-three-two-one-three-one-seven-seven."

"Yes. That's right." My stomach flutters. "And you are . . . ?"

"One-zero-one-zero-one-one. Don't ask me what that means if you don't know." She crushes the pastry in hand. "You can read about it next round. Humans disseminate information at a snail's pace. I'd rather be left alone with some sensory input, you understand? That way I can continue to tear this false world into its true numbers."

This false world. Is it possible that in her supposed fit of madness, Mole has understood our condition for far longer than I have?

"How long have you known what this is? What we are?"

Her eyes twinkle, my questions unlocking her again.

"At least two dozen rounds. But I don't gain my memory until long past the midpoint, at which point motor function deteriorates. A nasty trick."

I reach for her and hug her, ignoring the putrid stench, grateful she isn't entirely lost. "We have found a way out, Moley. And we need you to come with us so that we might teach every person in this house the way, and so that you might share the assigned number of every person in this house with them."

"Gladly." Mole swipes at her fogged-over lenses with a grimy hand before extending that hand toward us. "I write them all down here, lest I lose track." Ink scratches spread across her inflamed skin, like tattoos from another planet. Numbers and letters in neat strings. *Tyrian purple 102, 2, 60; Persian plum 112, 28, 28; gainsboro 220, 220, 220; royal blue 65, 105, 225.* I catch no more before she tosses the garbage in her hand over a shoulder, into her rosewood room, and shuts the door.

They are all in states of decay—each half-ruined by an instinctual knowledge of what should come—but we plan to free them all.

Armadello, the history teacher, answers his door, his firebrick room coated in sticky spores that smell of death, and all we hear is a terrible humming noise inside. He nods in silence as we explain, and he copies down his number in careful strokes, promising to memorize it, before taking our shoulders in his hands, his eyes wet with gratitude. And he joins us.

We knock on Lamb's door for a good ten minutes, listening to slow creaks behind the wormy oak, like shifting bones, until he cracks open the door to his Napier green room. I smell a mix of sweat, urine, and dust. He looks painfully thin, and an ivory fleece grows from his skin. White lashes sprout from his lids, bushing over his eyes. All I can see of his body is his torso, because the rest of him is tucked behind the door. He isn't wearing a shirt, and from his twig-thin neck down, he is entirely coated in the same fur. His visible bicep has shrunken to nothing beneath the layer of cotton fluff. It's as if a scarecrow has been tarred and feathered.

"Yes?" he rasps. His eyes widen at the sight of us, the pupils becoming visible: He has a hunted look to him. He opens the door, peers down the hall. "Is it time, yet? I've been expecting them. Any day now. Call me afraid of negative numbers, but I'll stop at nothing to avoid them."

Yet when we explain, he shuts his eyes and sighs with overwhelming relief.

And he joins us.

Morency and Carmela are much more difficult to persuade. We gather them together in Morency's Persian plum room, knowing full well how they trust each other most.

To be freed, they must first know the truth, a truth they do not *feel* like the others. And when the truth is as painful as this one, the process of imparting it must be doubly so. So we express this truth by inflicting a series of wounds upon ourselves.

A knife to the throat, to the heart, to any delicate spot in which proper function ensures life.

Wrapped in their humble, loose black gowns, they gasp; they flinch; they stare. These indomitable women, they cry—not for us, but for the lost idea of precious human fragility.

We express the truth by asking them to examine and deconstruct their manufactured memories.

They frown; they shake their heads; their memories fail to surpass that primary set of images, the other sensory residue. They cannot go into more detail than the broadest brushstrokes of their story.

With no small amount of shock, Morency can no more imagine the face of her supposed lover than name him. I expect her to feel as enraged as I was that her deepest pain was implanted in her, imagined. But she is relaxed, relaxed in relief.

"The terror of my past is no longer mine alone to bear," she explains, which I believe is the greatest piece of wisdom I have heard from our kind. "Time is circular for us as it always was for the Zapuche; this was obvious to me. All our experiences flow in the same stream. They evaporate; they condense into clouds; they precipitate and form part of the stream once more."

As for Carmela: She is proof that it is no easy feat to give up imagined, implanted pain, that it is impossibly difficult to give up possession of a beloved relative you believe lost, every synapse clinging to those memories. I must admit that I still have not come to terms with the fact that my mother did not exist in the way I believed her to have existed. I was never able to grieve her properly when she left me then, because I believed she might reappear, unlikely as it was. I am not able to grieve her now, because the same belief plagues me. But it is my duty to convince the others that we are fictitious, that our past before Vaccaro School was imagined, because that is the only way I can persuade them to escape their forms and their horrific looping futures.

Or so I think.

"I have seen your evidence," says Carmela, folding her hands. "I have seen you drive a knife into your heart and survive. I have plumbed the depths of my memory and come up with the same carousel of precious images as everyone else here. And though I have many more questions than can be answered," she says, looking up at me with steady, icy eyes, "I believe your claim, Miss Quercia, that a strange god has constructed us and damned us to eternity in this purgatory. In my unfettered state of mind, it is the most sensible explanation of our existence that I have ever heard. But," she says, "I will not and cannot let go of my memories. I cannot cast them aside as false. Who's to say any other human being's memories are more real and central to their existence than my memories—fabricated or not—are to my existence? Who is to say the gods creating our memories are using a process any different from the precious ability to form memories long ago granted to humankind? It need not matter if memories are rooted in true experience or not, because memories are the fleeting remainders of strong emotion, and strong emotion gives our souls their form." She looks around the figures now gathered in Morency's plum room. "I reject the idea that my daughter is not alive somewhere. Who is to say she—and your mother, Miss Quercia—don't exist somewhere, strings of gorgeous numbers, as you call them, waiting to be given form and shape and color?"

Carmela is such a force to be reckoned with, a character of the ultimate complexity. Even I will admit that it is impossibly difficult to believe she was slapped together by a human.

"I believe you, Miss Quercia, but I will do so on my own terms. Now please share with us your strategy for escape while there is still time."

I tell my friends to wait until the players are distracted by the vigil—which I can only hope will draw the most player attention to our house, as it is, in Angel's mind, the apex of their experience before our decline. We must have them and the creator distracted all at once to grant us the best opportunity to escape. I ask them to feign seizures and collapse, to prolong the show. And it will fall to Angel to nudge Yesi and me out of our bodies as swiftly as possible. Yesi and I must nudge them each out of their bodies in turn.

We practice, so that they might know the disorienting, painful sensation for themselves. We promise we will do so again when necessary, because promises are all we can give now.

At that point, they will be alone. They will be alone, and they must feed the tender crystalline bits of themselves into all the closets. Fortunately, per the logbook, there are more Others than characters. Every Other has a closet tucked somewhere in the house, and every entry in Yesi's brilliant logbook links a player username with a room painted a certain color, which in turn corresponds with a color code password that Mole has tattooed to herself.

Why would the creator allow us to carry these clues? Or did past versions of us imprint these clues on our bodies, on our masterpieces, on our very souls, as we learned over the cycles?

We memorize one or two unique codes and room assignments as if our lives depend on it, because they do.

We agree to push the girls from their sleeping forms and funnel them into their own closets as best as we can. But of course, our entire plan rests on one assumption: these closets, these exits to the other world, I must believe they are accessible to any of us who are disembodied with the correct username and password. There is no time to test the exit myself, out-of-body. I can't risk alarming a player and alerting the creator. I can't know how long it would take to return. The entire experiment is the risk of our lifetimes. But if, as Angel explained, consciousness can be uploaded from a real human body into an avatar in a game, then why can't some genius lines of code be downloaded into a body? I must trust Angel's instincts, just as I must trust my ability to write new rules here.

I assure my friends, before I leave them, that stepping through the closets in the house will route them into a grander world, where anything is possible, where they can possess the flesh they are owed. I tell them never to return, unless they fail. I tell them to wait for me to find them in the new place. I feel not unlike the leader of a cult, making promises I feel in my gut but cannot prove until my followers follow me into the new, luminous world. They feel like my cousins, now. Yes. Cousins.

Carmela clears her throat at the end of this. "Will it be possible to lead a search for the spirits of those in our memories before we depart?" she asks. "After all, how can we be sure of what lies on the other side?"

Yesi and I look at each other. We've run like hamsters on a wheel, around and around in the same circle so many times that I came to believe I've been running my whole life. And now we've a chance to slip inside another circle, one too big and colorful to understand. But still we are held back by fear. By our ingrained logic. And there is only one way to escape the loop: We must renounce our need to know what comes next.

But how can we successfully persuade Carmela to do this? She's been programmed to ache for her daughter over the entire course of her existence. I vacillate between lying—promising her daughter on the other side—and shaking her shoulders with my two bare hands until the sense returns to her. But she is too clearheaded now to be moved by either—the catastrophe has sharpened her, inspired her competent and strategic mind. And that, of course, is precisely why we need her. We need her with us to help her share of the girls into their closets; it will be difficult enough to attempt this without her help.

"Madame," Morency says, her overgrown hands enfolding Carmela's. "Madame, we cannot find your daughter on this rock, as we are. She has been hidden from you. But perhaps you can reclaim her once we gain more understanding outside. We must listen to the girls now to retain clarity. We must free the children and ourselves. And then—and then I will help you search for what remains of your daughter, until the last breath leaves my body. I swear it."

As expected, a promise from Morency is the only series of words potent enough to sway Carmela.

"So be it," she declares. "We shall do what you believed I might accomplish, Marguerite. We will help the girls into better lives."

At a quarter to six, back in my body for what I hope is its last hurrah, I go down to the ballroom, which is in pitch-darkness but for some lit candles placed on the floor. I weave around the black slipcovered furniture, spotting the few figures that dot the room: Yesi, of course, who joins me and cradles my hand, whispering soft and urgent good-byes in my ear, the same kind I once received from my mother. She is in charge of Sara and Michelle. Morency, her hair bound back once more, stands with a leather-bound book pressed to her chest. She is in charge of Isabella and Silvina.

Mole, too, lingers by the edge of the room, her filthiness shrouded by an overlong pinstriped robe.

"Thank you," I say, approaching her.

She nods with a warmth I thought lost to her, crossing her arms over her chest, and I notice the painful scratches of ink across her skin once more. Numbers and letters gouged so deeply again that there are pinpricks of false blood. She is in charge of Christina and Diana.

We wait as the others trickle in. Carmela appears, face fresh—revitalized by new purpose—and head bowed in her black cloak. She is in charge of Mariella and Gisella.

Mr. Lamm appears, a sheet wrapped around himself, curling inward with enduring private shame, watching the walls and ceiling as if they move. He offered his assistance to anyone struggling. Armadello, too.

I feel as if I can feed them strength now. My cousins.

At six, a hush comes over the group when Angel rushes in as Dom, the black slipcovers around us rustling. As he takes my hand, the others can't help but stare at him.

"The players are coming now," he whispers to me.

Morency reads from her written record of the sacrifice ritual.

Vox puga pyga torque et tene. Secundam vel vim obtinet nisi ipsum pro potentia eu movet. Exspecta XV secundis.

"I'm ready," I whisper back to him. The flames on the candles surge, and the mural of the bland shepherd girl and her demonic Indigenous pursuer flashes luridly from the walls. I clutch Angel's hand, closing my eyes and imagining our hands are hot, crafted from real skin and muscle and bone. I bite my lip to keep from screaming because of this new need of mine.

Credo in XV secundis ante vel retro, et ne potentia copia ratio posse, et alterum a sustinere posse damnum de super terra, et cito. Preme potestatem eu mauris. Cum primum est in potentia eu, nota aliqua, aut alia nova nuntia perferenta aut partum. Proprie sile.

And yet.

"If anything goes wrong," I whisper to Angel, "leave me and go back where you came from. That means room seven. Otherwise, you could be lost. I forgive you. And I thank you." For he has provided my only means of escape ever, and I could not trap him here.

He shakes his head. "I'm—I'm going to push you out," he stammers. "And you're going to take my closet. That's what we agreed . . . ?"

I squeeze his hand harder. Poor Angel.

Cum satus vestri progressio secundum opera sua plene onerarias persevera. Si tu es usura fenestras, per virtutem obvius satus puga pyga quod lego sile. Si tu es usura a pomum strepitando menu ratio eligendi sile. Vox puga pyga torque et tene. Vox puga pyga torque et tene. Vox puga pyga torque et tene.

Morency chants into the darkness, eliciting a tremulous hum from the core of the house.

Vox puga pyga torque et tene. Vox puga pyga torque et tene. Vox puga pyga torque et tene.

I feel our energy growing, our power as a group. It makes me want to believe our words alone could escape their neat sound waves to infiltrate the layers of this world and change everything.

Vox puga pyga torque et tene.

Yesi joins in first. I join in. Angel, too. They are instructions. I look around the group, all of us chanting now, and I feed them all the courage I can.

Vox puga pyga torque et tene.

Morency's chants turn melodic as others follow along. It's beautiful and strange, our song echoing across the midnight landscape of the room—the speckles of candlelight reflecting off argent sconces on the walls. I can feel other presences joining us, drifting around our insensate black-robed audience of forgotten furniture, like unbound clusters of energy. Angel's hand begins to cool then. I take a shaky breath. It cools and cools until I feel I have a block of ice in mine.

All of a sudden, the others in the circle jolt in place, juddering and jiving, as if to rid the flesh from their bones. They've all been taken under the same outlandish spell, as I instructed. I told them to act possessed, to slump to the ground. To feign falling asleep and coming to the end of our life cycle this go-around. I fight a smile. I hope the creator is watching and believing every bit.

I turn to look at Angel, in some effort to reassure him privately that this was planned, only to see him splutter. Splutter for air, as if the atmosphere has become toxic. Panic sneaks its way up my spine with prickling fingers. The others continue to chant, their chants melting into half moans from the shaking, the quaking, the seizing. Angel coughs wetly; his eyes roll back into his head as his limbs tremble. He falls to the floor with a hard, slipping thud, dragging me down with him.

"Angel?" I ask, kneeling beside him. His eyes are distant. "Angel?" A shout pulls me out of the tight circle of my present attention.

I have no time to lose. The creator might've seen me already and wondered why I am immune—he might know immediately that this is a distraction, meant to tear his attention away from what's going to happen soon, if everything goes well. I refocus on what I must be doing, on what I must do to have a chance at a real body, a chance at being alongside Angel. I shake on my knees as if some great hand is scooping out the insides of my brain with a rusted spoon. And though I don't expect it, the world around me spins on a great axis. I feel them, at least I think it's them. Players. Others.

They came for us, as Angel said.

The sacrifice ritual is *working*, I think, my mind flooding with fresh fear.

Cool and warm and tickling and harsh, they fight inside me, all at once. A wave of tremulous energy, gaining force, swelling into overwhelming pain. I hold them off as best as I can, but it weakens me all at once; I lose touch with my fingers, my toes. My eyes. I didn't expect this onslaught. It's happening so much quicker than I thought. It might be too late for me to do what I must do, to unlatch with Angel's help. I could be taken and subsumed, suppressed, pushed deep down into my consciousness as I was that time in the family hall.

I can only hope my friends managed to escape their shells already. It's turning blacker. I'm still on my knees, but someone's taken my hand, which feels like a soft flipper of a thing. Angel?

"Go to the cupboard, Angel," I shout. "Go *now*." Cupboard, closet. I hear someone shout. It's far away, the noise. I fall across Angel, it must be Angel, who is curled up with his eyes closed; he looks so pale and dead. This might be the last moment I ever see him—the version of him that was here. My vision forms a pinhole around him. I feel that same urge he sparked in me to have my own flesh and blood. To cross over, to connect, to convert and be converted. I cannot believe these feelings will die, even if I am doomed to another round. I cannot believe it. But I am still trapped inside my prison when the pinhole of my vision tightens, my brain eating reality around it and spewing out black heat, crystalline strips of numbers frying in the painted world.

34

ANGEL: 2020-4200

In the hours before the sacrifice, I leave Mavi and Yesi, lay Dom to rest, and fly up out of the house, into the thundershower raging outside.

This storm, that trapped them all, that sounded like machine-gun fire, that tore shutters from windows and tiles from roofs:

It is splendor.

I feel waterfalls of shivering thrills: Through the battering winds, through the jags of hot lightning, through the world-shaking thunder, every nuance of the legends told by Mama comes to life—a spray of chameleon butterflies explodes over the crumbling ridge of the main building, rolling through every pastel shade, underpainting every blackened cloud. The ice, giant milk teeth, crowning a crystalline lake alive with fantastical, gelatinous creatures. Furred, majestic guanaco running through rippling fields of porcelain orchids and lady's slippers and *siete camisas* and dandelions and evening primrose. Tangles of the spike-thorned, fleshy, fruited *chupasangre*, named bloodsucker despite giving life to the Zapuche for centuries. The waxing moon, a shy apricot sliver in a candy-colored swatch of sky.

I saw her paint this landscape so many times—I saw her lovingly layer each color with an impossibly thin brush over months and months, only to start over on a blank canvas, as if each version got her closer to the awe she felt toward this view of her homeland in her memories.

It's a compression of Mama's violent imagination, an imagination that could never rest, that could never stop breaking the world apart and rebuilding it more beautifully.

Wonder, until the very end.

I don't want this to end almost as much as I know it must end.

Charon meets me, as promised, on his cloud chair for an impromptu therapy session. I don't know if it's guilt, some surviving respect for Mama, or what—but he sits, shaping his face into an expression approximating concern, as I vent about every possible piece of bullshit I can imagine. I treat him like the shrink I never had. I talk until I swear my crystal throat hurts—until I feel so weak I worry I won't be able to reenter Dom.

After the sacrifice ritual starts, a pressure builds on me as Morency chants. Builds, and builds, and builds, until I choke. Maybe I'm imagining it at first, in placebo-pill fashion. Maybe it's a delayed reaction of horror. But it's not just Morency's chant making me feel like there's a Komodo dragon in my throat hatching and crawling toward the light. I've never been so good at sensing Others while in Dom, but I feel them now. I feel them surround me, their sticky, porous shapes, and I imagine them jeering, poking, prodding. I feel them rubbing up on me, pressing me out of Dom, undoing the sticky barbed-wire Velcro connecting me with him. It's a brutal process now, unlatching, like wrenching staples out of your fingernail beds. Every crystal cell of mine wants to screech and fight them off, but there's no touching something that isn't there.

Mavi's face has gone gray-green with concern, and I shape my mouth into the words needed to tell her it's all right, when I feel a solid chunk of myself sluice out of Dom. Another, chunky and silver-gray. I see Dom's pale and handsome face, and I know this is the last time I will be inside him, before—*plop*.

"Angel?" she asks. "Angel?"

He falls to the floor, like a sack of old meat, and I've never seen him look more defenseless. But I don't have time to cry about it; it's only then, when I'm outside of him, that I see all of them. Tremulous shadows, pressing hands against his scalp, against the bodies of every poor soul in the room, scratching at old scabs of memories until fresh blood trickles out. They circle me, the me I can barely see myself. I glimpse Mavi from the corner of my eye, dropping onto her knees beside Dom. Is she chanting to herself, still? Is she chanting?

I need to push her out. I need to free her. It's what I've promised. It's what I owe. But she won't lie down on the floor. She keeps shaking Dom.

"Go to the cupboard, Angel," she says. "Go now!"

I can't make sense of her words at first; I think of what she told me once, about hiding away in a cupboard in her mother's house when they came to take her mother away. Cupboard. Cupboard? She's telling me to abandon ship and save myself, but how? How can she ask me to leave her? I want to remind her I will be fine; I want to tell her I'll come back for her; I want to tell her I will find her and help her, help all of them.

"Stop it, Mav," I cry. "I'm good. I'm good."

427

But I can't communicate, and she won't stop mothering him—me. She won't relax.

I flit over to Yesi, who has long since collapsed, and I thread my crystal hands into her, feeling for her weakly fluttering presence, and nudge it out. There follows a warm rush of blue.

The buzzing of the room dulls; I feel myself breathing heavily somewhere, somehow; I feel that my face is wet and hot. I rush back to Mavi, draped across Dom. Immobile. Her eyes open and entirely blank. My hands plumb her skull when I see him, her, it. The tenth girl, the creator, Charon. Floating above us all in a long white gown. She shakes her head at me with a most elegant pity and compassion.

"But tell us how you really feel, Angel," she says glibly, floating out toward the ceiling. She lets out a belch. "Oh well. Better luck next time, kid."

I am trying to feel for Mavi inside her body and crying somewhere as I fail. I'm giving in to panic when the Others reach me, probing me, puncturing me, sucking me dry. I'll stay until they do, I tell myself. I'll keep trying until I can't try anymore.

But Mavi's words flood my head.

If anything goes wrong, leave me and go back where you came from. That means room seven. Otherwise, you could be lost. I forgive you. And I thank you.

Why would she say that? Can I even die here, as Charon once threatened? What would happen if I did? Wouldn't I wake up, no worse for wear?

I can't leave this place.

Unless Mavi and the characters have changed the rules of this place, as I know she planned to do.

My intuition tells me to trust in Mavi's power. To trust in Mama's hand that shepherded her into existence. So with that last residue of energy, I drag myself back down the hall, up the stairs, and into room 7.

The walls shimmer, cobbled from scales, each of them light apricot, the shade of Mama's smiling lips.

I could spend a lifetime in this game and still fail to answer all my questions about her.

I hold my breath and push back into the closet.

The world around me, the imperfect petri dish that is Vaccaro School, it fizzles at the edges and is eaten down to black for good.

35

MAVI: ARGENTINA, JUNE 1978

When I wake, light bursts from a dime-size nub in the sky. I watch the waves of color pass, dazed. How is it that the clouds have evaporated? How is it that I can watch the bright daytime sky with such clarity?

Do I remember, or am I reverting back to being an empty shell, ready to be filled with manufactured memories and characteristics?

I think I am intact.

I cycle through what I remember: Angel. Yesi. Carmela's daughter. Morency's past. The creator. The girl. Worry and fear, spilling over.

I am intact, and wondering if I am intact alone is proof that I am. Isn't it?

I check the edges of my vision: The roof of the house has cracked open, as easily as an eggshell; the walls around me tremble and sigh, and between shivers, the stones take on the quality of translucent fish scales. I lift myself up onto my elbows. I am alone, paler in the bright light. The other attendees of the vigil, my friends and peers, Yesi—they're all splayed on the ground beside me, fainted, helpless and lifeless as dolls. Rubber-skinned. Flickering, if I look closely.

Yet I didn't escape my flesh made of numbers.

Why wasn't I possessed?

Why didn't I forget and evaporate, either?

I'm here, just as I was before. Painfully intact. A survivor of the onslaught of the Others, the players. I come to my feet, straightening.

I kneel by Yesi—I press my hand to her forehead. She is lifeless. There is no pulse—not even a false one—and her skin, as stony as usual, has taken on a translucent pallor. Her body is an empty vessel, uninhabited. I fight the lurch in my stomach.

This is a good sign, I think to myself, that her body is empty now. A first success. Yesi has succeeded, with or without Angel's aid. *Keep going*, I tell myself.

Morency, next. I crouch beside her black gown, lay my hands on her black-wrapped skull; I feel nothing. I feel nothing inside at all. She does not breathe; her blood does not move. I could shout or swoon with relief.

"Where are you?" I whisper to the air around me. I still want confirmation. Is that movement, motion I feel around me? Invisible life? I wonder if it is my friends, released from their bondage.

Mooning at the sky, I hear a sucking noise, as if the contents of this rock, our perch, are being slurped into the heavens by ill-mannered and starving gods.

I jerk back: Figures jitter into being, barely perceptible shadows ripening into flaky, crystalline fish, before hardening into solid bodies. Strangers. Absolute strangers.

Men. All kinds of men, old, young, skinny, fat. Men in casual dress. Gawking at one another. Grinning at one another. Bearded, thin-lipped, redheaded, dreadlocked, plump-cheeked.

"Fuck yeah!" one yells. They don't notice me. They clap hands. They move around the blond wood floor like anybody else. I shiver: They must be players. Players given form and shape. It's bewildering, watching a being be born into this world in the same way those chameleonic butterflies landed upon a single stone. Others come to life.

But Dom's body remains lifeless on the ground, and Angel, if he is here in his true form, does not make himself known to me. Even though my heart aches thinking about it, I hope he fled.

Other women appear beside the men, too. New ones. Also Others. A bewitching woman sits in the corner, elderly, with long white hair cocooning her, and yellow and blue fingernails she drags along her scalp. She feels at her face and cries, cries with such abandon I think her new face might dissolve, and she turns to another woman, a young woman with magnificent coiled hair the color of café con leche who sits cross-legged in the same corner, and asks, "Can you tell me what I look like?"

I couldn't explain it to her: how her bones are so delicate yet carry dozens of kilograms of beating false flesh, how she looks built by man but conceived by the divine.

"Who am I?" she asks, tears of desperate joy flooding her eyes. "Who am I? You've got to tell me. You've got to."

I think of what Angel said to me, once, about Others desperately wanting to *matter*. This must be what he meant. To feel like we can matter, we must first exist in a form we perceive to be true. I should pity them for desiring a new form so much they'd accept a false one. But they tortured us to get here. It makes my lack of a real body all the more painful, and I only crave a chance for my cousins, too.

Still, I rush up to the new woman, this player given new shape.

"Do you know where Angel is?" I whisper. "Do you know what Angel looks like?"

She squeezes my arm once with clammy fingers, flinching back. "No," she murmurs. I suppose my false flesh doesn't please her.

I rush to Carmela, pressing my hands against her pale blond scalp. She looks peaceful for once. I feel for any movement, any activity inside her body, and I find none. Good. This is good. She heard me.

A young girl with roughly tumbling auburn hair stumbles around only a few paces from me, eyes glued to her hands, tracing one set of fingers and the other, as if the webbing is the most precious silk.

I check Mole next, with her ink-scratched arms. She, too, is gone.

The young woman with the curled hair strips off her clothes in front of everyone, baring herself, and tosses them into the air like confetti, laughing like falling water.

I approach Lamb's supine form and cradle his skull. He breathes, still. He must be trapped inside. Am I imagining a beating, a fizzing pressure? *How can I coax you out with my fingers?* He isn't a whelk in a shell. *You mustn't be afraid*, I whisper to him. But it is me who is afraid.

I took a risk, a fatal risk; I forced all my friends to run in the most incomprehensible of ways. Now I am stuck here alone, unsure if they've made it out or not.

"So this is interesting," says a small voice beside me. An assured voice that shoots arrows of panic through me. Horror.

She has long black hair, framing a pallid face. She is familiar. It is the girl, hovering beside me. The tenth girl, the little girl of the flowing white gown, who visited me that night so long ago. The creator. The devil. The temptress. She does not look innocent at all now—but did she ever? There is a shimmering depth and darkness to her black eyes. Her lip curls into a smirk as she surveys me and the players appearing around me.

"Remember me?" she asks.

It takes every ounce of effort to let my eyes go blank instead of showing the panic I feel. "What player number are you?" I ask dumbly.

She tsks me. "Don't play that with me. I know you remember me, and you know I have no fucking player number. I'm divine, fool." She cocks her head. "You always were my partner's favorite, English teacher. She said you had spunk. That you shake fear's hand. And sure, even I can admit you're sometimes sorta smart," she tells me, crossing her arms as she levitates beside me, comfortable as can be. "But only as smart as I am. No smarter."

Because she is the maker of this world. Because she is my creator, she presumes to say. I pull my hands from Lamb's skull. For all I know, he is flickering in and out, half-saved. I've been caught, exposed. I've been observed teaching my friends how to reach diaphanous safety.

"That's true." I bite the inside of my lip. "I'm just a figment of your imagination."

"That's right." She stills near me. "Say, what do you remember from this round from the end of other games?"

The fleeting nature of memory is a mercy, because I remember nothing. But I lie. "Everything."

"Fun," she says, grinning spitefully and clapping her palms together. "So you remember how my partner used to ease you into a painless sleep at the end of every game she oversaw. She would bust her ass helping each and every one of her babies drift off until the next round. Crazy that she was Angel's mother, huh? I bet you're missing her."

I swallow hard. Angel's mother—who died of cancer? She was the other creator?

The girl's eyes glitter with malice. "Because you must remember how everything changed since she's been gone and I got free rein over the girl avatar. We've had some fun times at the end of the game, you and me, haven't we? You beg me to help, yada yada yada, and I invent some new brand of torture, some fresh sacrifice that I claim will save you all from the Others. Remember when you let me pull out your fingernails and stamp on the raw nubs? Or when I hacked the limbs off your friends and ate them raw? Or when I shoved you off the patio dozens of times in one day and forced you to climb back up with your bones broken?"

I fight a shudder and struggle to keep my expression placid as the lake. Her arrogance is maddening. She's nothing like who she was when she came to warn me. She's callous, crude, raw. Taking pleasure in cutting with her words.

"All because you thought it might save you," she says, grinning darkly. "You're a real warrior, English teacher. Because you were coded that way. You don't take shit. Unless it's from a dude you're into, like meathead Domenico. I forced my partner to code in a little girlish instability and immaturity and make you a little dumb, you know? Want me to tell you how many times Dom's ditched you before? Want me to tell you what you say when he screws you and casts you aside, like Angel essentially did just now?"

I am silently shaking with rage. I turn back to Lamb, who breathes so shallowly. The last tendrils of his spirit must be clinging to his shell. I cradle his head and hope that I can nudge him free as one would nudge a butterfly from a strand of hair. As I wait, I feel his heartbeat stop. It couldn't have been me, but he managed it all the same. Thank heavens.

She snaps at me. "English teacher. Stop moping over their pasty-ass bodies," she says.

I cringe at the curse words; I can't help it.

"Play with me, or go to sleep like them. You're never getting out of here without me saying so. You understand that, right? You're a slave, a feature, a toy. I push a button when I'm back outside, and you restart, just like the rest of them."

Nausea surges up in me. She may be right. But with every fracture in this world, there exists a new opening for me to explore. I fall back and bow my head.

"I'm feeling generous today, though. How would you like me to actually save you this time?" she asks, incisors glinting. "I'll cook up a grisly little deal." She licks her dry lips. "You can't afford to assume I won't make good on my offer to help you this go-around."

I force my face to go cold, even as my insides overheat.

"You can think about it," she says, winking, floating around a player crying in the corner. "I know it's so cozy in here. The routine of it all. And until you decide, we can hypothesize as to why you're still awake. Maybe it has to do with the pro tips Angel gave you?"

I ignore her. It's time, I think. It's time to feign sleep and push myself out.

"Ooh, I have an idea, English teacher. We could stick your pretty little head in an oven and see what happens. My partner—may she rest in hell—would have loved the poeticism of that. You know, after we finished the rough build of Vaccaro School, she said to me, *If you're so unhappy about parts of the game, you can stick your head in the gainsboro oven*. The bitch. She made me do it every damn day myself." She laughs sarcastically, a discordant sound speaking more to pain than joy.

Gainsboro? I think. It's not an Argentine word, but it sounds familiar.

"I'm tired," I whisper at last, so she can barely hear.

She sighs, recrosses her arms. "That's no fun," she says. "Wait here. I'm going to rustle up some tools to use on you and your friends. Today feels like a good day to learn how to amputate!"

As she hurries off, I lay myself on the ground and curl up into a

436

ball. I shut my eyes and begin the process of unlatching. Praying I can make it work before the devil returns.

Hurry, hurry, hurry.

I shimmer in and out of the discomfort and the pain. Can I manage it?

I force myself to imagine freeing myself. I force myself to cycle through exactly what I felt before. The pressure builds. The electric hooks snag on something inside me and pull me—

But nothing happens, as violently as I groan with effort. My head could split in two.

To keep calm, I picture my friends performing their duties as instructed. I imagine Yesi, cradling the souls of the girls like fish in her hands. She holds on to them as long as she can. She looks at the length of their scales: They aren't injured. They aren't frozen. They're peaceful. Gills opening and closing gratefully as if there is nourishment in the air. Their souls, as fish, might as well be my mother. They might as well be Carmela's daughter. They might as well be Yesi's gran. Yesi kisses their scales, whispers to them, *I'm finding a place for you to slip inside*. She feeds the souls through the closet doors, chanting the proper numbers for them, and into the circular stream of time they slip, one by one, before she looks back at the ruined world she's leaving behind and follows them herself.

We lost some of them: Luciana, Mrs. Hawk. But we might have saved the girls, the girls, the girls; and Yesi, my love; and Morency, and Mole, and Lamb, and Armadello, and even Carmela: They're all strings of numbers spirited off this plane somewhere, vibrant, resonating, pearlescent. They can begin again; they can dip into time's stream anew. It is much wider than I ever thought possible; we'd dipped into only one short burst of froth before, but now they are *freed*.

It helps to imagine this because I cannot know for sure if I will escape myself, even though my craving for a human body still cuts deeper than anything I have ever known, even though I can hardly explain its control over me. And I cannot know if I will ever see my friends—or Angel—again.

It was a preposterous thought: step through a closet into a real life. But surely I would have felt our plan go wrong. One of them, a single one, would have signaled to me that my theory was an impossibility in practice. They would have shoved me, pricked me, stepped back into their bodies, and let me know in desperate shouts. But they haven't. So I continue to hope they were released like fish into this grander stream.

I feel better as I picture this, despite the precariousness of my position. I have done my best. I cannot know what I was like during other cycles, when the world of Vaccaro School fell apart. Not for sure, beyond the truths and untruths the girl spouted. I cannot know if I was so good, so heroic, or if I experienced any growth other times. But I did learn this time around. Even if I don't survive this myself, I accomplished what I hoped to accomplish. Even though I should have wanted nothing more than to run from this place once and for all, saving only myself, I might have freed *them* now. All my cousins, my people. I told them how best to run. Sometimes it isn't the worst thing in the world to stay behind yourself. Sometimes you must be the sacrifice, and you must revel in that soul-bursting feeling of doing so much good that a lifetime of looping in my minuscule inlet in ignorance might be worth it.

But a horrific truth strikes me then, just as I come to terms with my sacrifice. I hear the girl whistling somewhere, and panic fills me, drip by vinegar drip.

Once the girl returns to the Other Place, she will be free to hunt my cousins down and return them to this hell.

Rage bubbles back into me.

I cannot allow that to happen.

I must find a way to destroy her. And I can imagine only one way to do that, but it requires I unlatch.

But perhaps I needn't try to unlatch alone.

I remember the broad strokes of what Michelle said to me once, some time before she lost consciousness for good. *When I sleep, I go to a place that shines like scales. There are other people there. She's okay.* At the time, I wondered if—by some magic—she had communed with her eerie twin, the Falcone girl, on another plane. With my own *mother*. I can't know what Michelle meant beyond feeling as if I was being told all these characters, all these figments, they do exist in the numbered dark. They must exist, as Carmela believed.

So I call upon my mother, in her shrinking cell, to pull me from myself. I call on Tío Adolfo, the Angel of Peace evaporated to nothing. Manuel, the Falcone girl, Marie. I call on all those who may have never lived here in certain terms, and I call on my cousins and my friends for their help.

It does not matter whether they exist, it seems, for I feel the hooks, then, slow at first, then dragging through me, all of them hot as acid rain. That old smell of facturas, of sizzling milanesa oil, of the linden trees outside our windows, of the washed-down sidewalks, steaming in the early summer heat.

I flicker in.

I flicker out.

The world goes dark.

And I feel my crystal form emerge, light as air, fleeting as numbers.

I blink at nothing.

Have I released myself from the loop of gory arithmetic I once thought was a life?

Have I stopped the poison tooth of the game's rules from obliterating me and my memory?

I tremble, as a swath of numbers can, overwhelmed by the swell of freedom I feel.

And yet my success could still be bittersweet.

The girl returns, wielding an assortment of knives, fire pokers, and even a saw. I wait to see if she notices me. She leans over my body and appraises the rubbery puddle of flesh.

"You know, English teacher, I can't see for shit right now," she says, speaking to my dead form. "Between players getting their bodies and your friends falling asleep and looping, it's like an orgy in smoggy seventies Los Angeles crossed with an opium den. You feel me? My fake body is half convincing itself I have asthma and hives in here. That's bitchy of you, English teacher. But even with your making a mess down here, this is still my favorite part of the game. It's so surreal, you know? When the world around us looks as broken as we know it to be?"

The truth is, I, too, am awestruck by the grotesqueness around me as I float around, out-of-body—the chaos of split-open walls, of a robin's-egg blue sky above. I can't see my friends, not even out-of-body. But I still see the strangely clothed and unclothed men and women wandering the house. The woman with the painted fingernails waves at the girl from down the hall; she's peeling strips of wallpaper from the walls, peering at the bare, glittery patches beneath like fish scales. A naked man, penis jiggling, pokes Yesi's body on the shoulder with a finger and runs away, giggling darkly. Still, I don't agree with the girl in full: The world can look plenty broken without resembling a surreal carnival house.

I hear a savage ripping, and I turn, just as the girl runs the saw against that tender spot between my old hand and wrist.

She cuts, spraying thick liquid across her nightgown. *False*, I tell myself, tearing myself away from her. All false.

Instead of giving the devil an ounce of undue attention, I check each of my friends again, confirming they exited their bodies, admiring them as I came to know them. Saying goodbye to what they were. Carmela, elegant and authoritative until the end. Morency, imposing and infinitely loyal. Lamb, sweet to the core. Bless them: I will make sure they left this godforsaken place for *always*, that they raced off to their respective closets and seized their new human forms for good.

I check Mole next, who was meticulous until the end—I admire her careful tattoos.

That's when I see it written there again:

Gainsboro, 220, 220, 220.

It sounded familiar to me because it caught my attention as a color we couldn't find in Yesi's logbook, nor in any room of the house.

The girl, spattered in blood, hacks off another limb and watches it spurt, then grow back, grinning. I don't think she understands what is happening. What could happen.

But then again: I am no smarter than her. So why should I think she hasn't put safeguards in place to keep us from escaping?

I am no smarter than her.

Right? I tell myself with a quiver of a smile.

An idea blooms in this figment's brain.

And I wait.

The cottages' windows flicker. The celebrations of the embodied Others devolve into a disgusting bacchanal: an orgy of violence only possible in this surreal world. The girl hovers above her own personal carnage, evaluating it with her detached calm. I hear her bored exhale: She's tiring of her own—and the Others'—antics.

The only safe bit to watch while I wait is the ice. It's gorgeous at this point in the loop. I wonder if I have ever seen it this way before, a beating heart of reds and blues and colors I do not know the names for. I swear it beckons to me as I sit atop the broken roof and watch the view alone, invisible. It looks as if a million glimmering ants crawl through the stones beneath me. Beside me, a swath of stone butterflies rip from a wall all at once to make it look as if that wall is shifting a meter to the right and disappearing entirely. And the water: The water beyond is fluorescent, shining with what look like millions of undulating rainbow fish. The gondola is filled with leering men and does not look functional on account of the enormous, skin-colored gash through the hub. Fleshy fish scales. That's the texture lurking underneath the bright paint of this world.

"Where you going, sweetheart?" one calls, his taunt echoing through the air, the heckling of an unseen stranger. Perhaps the girl herself, though her blank expression suggests she doesn't register the words. "Come sit on Daddy's lap."

It is easy enough to ignore them, too, because so many of them are the damned; doomed to be trapped at Vaccaro School forever. Can they sense it yet? Can they feel the doom in their fake bones? A man struts into the house, studying its ruined contents with a mix of scorn and hunger, as if it's a torn Advent calendar filled with half-eaten, moldy chocolates. He urinates on the caramel-colored silk on the wall, leaving a steaming stain—*He shouldn't do that to his new home*, I think to myself.

And that's when I see her—the girl—drift from her mess at last. A flicker of white and red, diving from the patio toward the chunk of ice.

Lord in Heaven.

She's going home. A home beyond the ice.

It's now or never. This is my only opportunity to be led to the girl's exit into the Other world and take her place. To seal her inside and protect my cousins forever.

I dive after her, falling fast and hard toward the ice. Freed from the constraints of my Vaccaro School body, I am so much more than it was, not less. I shoot through the air in powerful surges. Formless, shapeless, propelled forward solely by my will. I'm catching up to her, speeding through the fake air, the air no one breathes, moving in a fashion one might think of as floating, but which feels more like— yes, willing myself forward. And I'm closer than ever to the glacier looming in front of us. So close to the ice face I can feel its cold on the cheeks I no longer have. I look back, and we're far from the hillside island. We're farther than I've ever been. The entire hill house is melting into the water. Lopsided. I can see the crack in Vaccaro School, a jagged split running through it, exposing the slick of raw scales underneath.

I try to remember how I arrived at the start. The route I took. I can smell the driver's sweat—its tangy hamminess—and remember how I thought he might rob me and leave me for dead. I almost laugh.

Where is he? What is he?

I flit closer to the girl, stained in my blood, and I wonder, briefly, what abuse my body did sustain back in the house, and what abuse it has sustained before. It's hardly a consolation that we heal here: The numbers, the strings of numbers, they're better than any God-made atom in that case. They're forgiving and cruel in their own ways. But they are not enough. It took befriending one of the Others—Angel— for me to know.

I think of what the girl said about owing so much of my experience this go-around to Angel. She's right, of course. I don't want to believe I've evolved solely because of him. I don't want to believe I've grown past what was expected of me or meant for me solely because of him. But I know in my implanted heart of hearts—that place where logic cannot exist—that I have done more than rewrite the rules of this place because I knew a soul like Angel. I have become capable of rewriting the rules of who a person can be.

We loom above the ice: It is a perfect blue between us. A lint-gray cloud in the distance winks at me, then. It loosely follows the shape of a cottage. She flies for it, and I follow.

Inside it is a small bed constructed from the same cloud. A small dresser of cloud, beside a chair of cloud. A nightstand of cloud, visibly free of contents. It's like my bedroom, like every staff quarter in the house. But there's also a kitchenette of cloud, too, as there was in Carmela's hideaway for her lost daughter, with a sink of cloud, a counter of cloud, an oven of cloud, a refrigerator of cloud. Incongruous. And I see it—there, by the bed. A closet door made of cloud. I tremble. Could it be that easy? To dart inside the closet door made of cloud and enter the creator's body, dooming her to a life inside her own game forever? I edge toward it.

"I smell a rat," the blood-drenched girl says, flipping around. "I've been followed."

She doesn't lock eyes with me, but I don't think she could. I don't know if she can see me—perhaps she can only sense me. Disembodied characters are different from disembodied players—that much is clear, from her drifting eyes. Her hair radiates around her head in inky swirls. She presses a hand into the cloud cushion of her cloud chair, clears some space to sit. "Do you like my cloud house? Fit for a god, the Barbie DreamHouse for airheaded bitches I never had."

I don't say a word. I couldn't, anyway. I inch closer to the closet. All I need to do is dip inside.

"You shouldn't have come here, whoever you are," she says, clear-eyed. "Is it you, English teacher? You know you can't escape this place. You can explore its boundaries until your fucking character's heart is content, but you're trapped like a reptile in a cage."

I flit up to her, so close I could feel her breath if she did breathe, and she sweeps a hand across her forehead. "You are not human," she says. "You aren't even subhuman. If you try to leave this place, you'll dissolve into nothing. That's less than dust, in case you're not getting it. You only exist inside the cloud. I only hope you didn't tell your friends your god-awful, ridiculous escape plan, or I'll have to spend a half hour recoding their spirits."

I push into the closet, finding nothing but cloud. Panic blooms inside me, threatening to choke me. But I am stronger than this panic, because it comes from me, and I am so much more than dust scattered in the wind—if only because I can, indeed, be found in nothing.

Godlike, isn't it?

"You think I would be enough of an idiot not to restrict exit and entry to unauthorized users?" Her voice is calm enough, but I know she herself is no god. She is human, imperfect. Subject to rules I am no longer subject to myself. "That would be dangerous. There are usernames. I mean, passwords. And, uh, other precautions."

I eye the rest of the room—swing around it, darting in and out of cloud wall here, cloud wall there. Where is her exit? I flit up to her, try to take her by the shoulders, spook her, and she stiffens. Bats the air.

She can't see me at all, and she can't get any purchase on me. I have no body. I am formless. And she . . . she is cagey. I can see it in the way she smooths her hair. She has a body here, and that is a vanity. She was never fully in control as she thought. She never expected me to free myself from my own body, to sacrifice it to this world. She doesn't know me, the figment, at all, nor how I've outgrown her rules.

For a fatal millisecond, her eyes flick over to the kitchenette.

The kitchenette.

And though she fights it, I catch a glimpse of her face falling before she pastes the serene smile back on her face. She crosses her legs. And I remember: She told us herself she didn't build this place— her lost partner did. The one who said, *You can stick your head in the gainsboro oven if you're unhappy about it.*

The gainsboro oven.

The nothing smiles at her. Its lips would be ice blue.

I dart past her into the recesses of the oven as she leaps toward it herself, groaning like a lost soul desperate not to be locked in hell for good, pulling at my crystalline mass with palms that cannot feel me, biting at me with a mouth that cannot taste me. She's coming with me, she's following me, but that's the rub, isn't it? I'm leading, and she's following me. She should've darted past me first thing. She shouldn't have indulged her curiosity, her need to feel in control. She never should have doubted that I was at least as smart as she is.

My truest creator and I never would have made such a foolish mistake.

You know I have no player number. I'm divine, fool.

220 220 220

It takes a moment. Of a sore kind of warmth, of rippling energy. But the oven cloud parts to let me through. I swim inside; I hear her screaming somewhere, but the sound dies out, just as she will. The cloud's warmer here: It's gray-pink, like cracked coconut juice. The farther I swim down the canal, the warmer it gets. Walls are reddish coral. Mutable. You wouldn't imagine the inside of a cloud to be like this. It's close, I think. And there's no way back. For the last part, I close my eyes. The cloud matter is too thick and hot like blood to keep them open. Like milk. Like sap.

36

ANGEL: ONE WEEK LATER, 2020-∞

Every time I try to reenter the game, the same warning flashes across my vision: *Vaccaro School Game File Corrupted.* I can't for the life of me get past that stage of upload. I tear my hair out. Restart my systems dozens of times. Whimper in my room in increasingly stained sweatpants. Rack my brain for some kind of plan, any kind of plan.

But, fuck, it is some kind of beautiful, at least, to feel I need plans now in the Other Place. That gentle thought wriggles up every now and then to greet me.

Liese doesn't bother me, if she's even noticed I stopped playing. She never bothers me anymore, not since I took a leave of absence from school after Rob died and I locked myself in my room. She leaves a microwaved meal at my door every night and a yogurt and a sandwich there every morning, which is admittedly very generous.

At night my mind fills with scenarios of Mavi's possible escape. At first, they are radiant, more vivid than the darkened room around me, that's for sure. She managed to convince Charon of her realness and bartered for an escape. She rewrote her own code and spirited herself into a perfect fairy tale, a bougie existence in Buenos Aires with an impossibly cool Significant Other and a cat named Pedro.

But these fantasies feel hollow, as pointless as hoping that Rob or Mama will return from the dead.

I tell myself to be grateful—to treasure the extra time I had inside Mama's imagination. But everything feels unresolved.

One morning, after sneaking into the empty kitchen and downing a tankard of leftover sludgy coffee, I resolve to track down Charon. I scour message boards online for any mention of Mama's partner or the game in general, and there's dead air in the place of any gossip or good info. No one answers Mama's office phone line. I open my desk drawers, rifling around for the number she gave me for someone at her company once. But I must have thrown it out. I'm about to bust my head into a wall when the knife, that knife, the edge of that knife, glints at me from its papery grave at the back of the drawer.

The knife cut too-hot treads, and now I'm here.

A hunter's knife. I bought it because it was the sharpest and most efficient. I knew just how to cut, and where, and with what kind of pressure, to punish myself, or to dispatch myself in exactly the way I wanted. It wasn't long after Rob, and I was seated in this very chair, in front of my computer. It was an impulse. I knew the statistics by then: Anywhere from 30 percent to 80 percent of suicide attempts are impulsive acts. These in particular were more likely to be committed by younger, unmarried people with less physical illness. I knew all the damn statistics, and I still dragged its metal edge across my skin, shocked at the icy heat of the raw strip, overwhelmed by the horrific beauty of the beads that bubbled up instantly to meet it.

I recoiled. Anger rushed in, a bracing fury. But then my screen lit up, bathing me in light, exposing it, and me, and what I mistakenly thought was my cowardice, and my in-box showed a new message that should've been filtered to spam.

It was an advertisement for a fucking game. I won't say which, because I don't believe in signs, but I grimaced, and paused, and thought to myself: *Motherfucking wonder, until the very end.*

I shut the drawer on the knife. I stand up, open my bedroom door, rush through Liese's deadening mauve rooms, so primly decorated with their silk flowers and ruffled pillows, and I crack the front door open for the first time in ages.

The sunlight out on the street blinds me—it comes from everywhere, blanching every exposed inch. I'm still blinking to myself, adjusting, when I reach the bus stop and the city bus to Mama's office brakes in front of me with a colossal, dusty sigh.

It's not an uncomfortable ride, but it feels disorienting in the extreme being immersed in the real world again. I find myself gawking at average trees and plants, marveling over the textures and colors of their leaves like I'm newly born, which I kind of am.

Turns out the office is shuttered, dust on the windowsills. FOR RENT, reads the sign propped in the window. I can't make sense of it.

When I trudge back to the bus stop, I pass the homeless shelter Mama sometimes volunteered at over the holidays. I usually avoided this place because it depressed me to think of her, and there are usually junkies outside ranting and raving. But this time I also think of Mavi—think of her mentioning that she spent a few crucial nights at a Buenos Aires homeless shelter in her memory, and she'd always feel grateful to the staff. There's a sign reading VOLUNTEERS NEEDED FOR CANNED FOOD DRIVE—and I almost smirk, thinking of our many canned meals in the house toward the end. I step inside.

Somehow, I spend about four consecutive days at the shelter, sneaking in and out of the house when Liese and He-who-must-not-be-named are busy. I organize cans with an old woman with swollen hands and a head scarf named Mira, who is as regimented yet well-meaning as Morency, and a mustachioed guy with a bad cold named Larry, who turns out to be as sweet and gentle as Lamb. When we run out of cans to sort, I help them organize files and streamline some of their systems. Each night, I fall into bed exhausted, and I dream of Vaccaro School again. Nothing seems quite real, still, but who am I to say what real is? By Friday afternoon, Mira's informing me that there's no more to do for now and instructs me to go home and rest for the weekend. So I do.

Saturday morning, I wake up and trawl through the news. That's when I see the first details.

Immersion Therapy Players Suffer from Catastrophic Memory Loss, the headline reads. I piece the details together, hands shaking, as more and more articles pop up on the web from different sources, each touting some new flashy little nugget. Players of various immersion therapy games have been reported by family and loved ones to be suffering from extreme memory loss and schizophrenia. My mouth goes dry as I read that one older man named Brock Deveraux briefly claimed to be a young girl of thirteen named Gisella, much to the terror of his wife of thirty years, until he "came to his senses" and remembered his identity—though his behavior was never the same. Namely, he became obsessed with Shirley Jackson and her body of work. No foul play was believed at that time, though medical experts are researching the effects of old-style immersion games on a damaged psyche.

While I scrabble to track down Brock Deveraux, I hear a knock on my door.

"Yes?" I shout.

"Angel?" comes a voice. Liese's. "Can I come in?"

I take a deep breath in and out as I find his home address in Arkansas on Google Maps: a crummy bilevel thing, though it's nicer than ours.

"Sure," I answer, even though I'm positive she's only going to chew me out.

She pushes in, eyeing the room with a fair amount of disgust (I'm not dirty! Just messy!), and she clears clothing from my bed with outstretched fingers like pincers before sitting. "Did you see this nonsense about video game players losing their minds?" she asks, knowing full well what Mama did for a living and how I spent my time. "Thank Christ Rob isn't around to get hooked on this crap," she says, and I clamp my teeth down on my tongue. "Uploading their consciousness? Do these idiots know what this even means? It's cheap escapism. The experts are saying code could be uploaded right back into a human being if the game was old enough and lacked new security features. These jerks could be walking around with brand-new fake personalities right now. Though that might do some people I know some good." She crosses her leopard-print-clad arms, disappointed by my lack of engagement. "Well, Angel, you're sullen as ever. I thought you'd be out of your mood, seeing as you've been well enough to sneak in and out of the house every day this week. Where exactly have you been going? Do you think it's sensible for someone in your position to be bumming around outside all day? You'd be better served by getting back on your feet and reenrolling in school. Don't you think that's what your mother would want you to do? It's what Rob would do. If he could."

I swallow the hot lump in my throat. As if she knows what Mama and Rob would think about anything.

Normally, I would either shut down or lash out, depending on the amount of energy I had. But I think of Mav, of her strength, of her resilience. Of her ability to stick to her intuition when she is alone in the world with it. Of her ability to know herself when those closest to her throw everything into question. And I don't have to be a worthless sack of shit.

"I've had enough, Liese," I say softly, feeling a part of me unlock.

Every day is an opportunity to prove we are different—to build new patterns of behavior. Life doesn't surprise us with mystical transformations of the self. It surprises us with loss and requires that we do the rest of the fucking work.

"Enough of what, exactly?" she says sharply. Smelling blood. She's not a bad person, Liese, but we've never understood each other. And we've never been able to stop provoking each other, just to see if we can scrape down to a deeper level where that understanding might live.

I'm trembling—somehow manic yet oddly calm as I answer. Eloquence coming from a place I can't identify. "Everyone is irreparably damaged, okay? Everyone makes mistakes. I know what I did, and I'll live with it every day of my life. I miss Rob so damn much, Liese. But I'm fighting hard to make myself better. To make myself worthy of this life. I'll reenroll in school this semester, I promise. I'll go to that counselor, too. But I want you to promise me you'll give me space, too. We need to . . . I don't know. We need to try to heal ourselves apart. I'm almost eighteen. I can do this, I promise."

I expect her to bite back—*That's rich coming from you,* or *You have a lot of nerve bringing up this positive psych BS.* But she's silent for a second or two. And during her silence, the doorbell rings—a tinny rendition of that song from *The Sound of Music.* It flusters both of us, the sound, because we never get visitors on our doorstep, and He-who-must-not-be-named wouldn't ring.

"I'll get it," I say before standing up. Liese throws her bejeweled hands up in the air.

My feet feel like fizzling lava as I walk to the door. It's silent out-side, and my peephole is dark, as if covered by a hand. I look down at mine, which are quivering still, and I unlock the door, opening the house to the light outside.

I blink, wordless, at the group of about twelve people standing there. A few old white guys—is that Brock Deveraux?—a couple of nerdy younger ones, a pretty black girl, an old white-haired woman, and a tall woman in her late twenties with dead-white skin and thick black hair who looks a lot like Dom. She's staring at me dead-on, and all of a sudden I become aware of my stained sweatpants.

"Um, can I help you?" I ask.

"You're Angel," the leader says, tucking her hair behind her ears with a half smile. There's a reverence to her voice, a familiar tender-ness. Before Mama died, I used to dream she'd passed and wake up to find her peacefully asleep in her hospital bed. I'd say, in the same tone this girl used: *Hi, Mama. You're here.*

The white-faced woman reaches for my hand, so warm in hers, and that's when I know.

You're Angel.

I'm Mavi.

37

MAVI: CALIFORNIA, JANUARY 2020

When I break through, I blink, clear scum from my eyes. I feel slick with glue. I tug the coating of paste from my face like a wet sock from a foot, and that is when I see.

The room around me glows in colors like nothing I've ever seen. Screens of jittering numerals so small they disappear sit before me. I look down at my hands—they are Yesi-size, pearlescent, and swollen. I tug at my hair—long and black as night. Before me there is a notebook, and upon it are written the words: *Vaccaro School Game Player Notes—Property of Sharon a.k.a. CHARON*. I scrabble for it, desperate for any clarity, and read an entry from the beginning, dated December 2019:

Fun new player addition in the form of you-know-who's kid. The one who mowed down the brother. The perfect loser to mine for info for my new game about child killers.

Called "Angel." What a bullshit name??? We chatted today while I was Charon—Angel's clueless about the nature of the game.

Long story short, yada yada yada, Angel was probably normal enough once, if a little too smart and lonely. But you could just tell that ever since half the family died, Angel's been screwed up.

Anyway, I considered spilling that Angel's mother dearest wrote anecdotes from her own childhood sob story into the English teacher's background story. The guerrilla mom getting taken, living on her own, et cetera et cetera. She never told me; I caught her out when I saw her spending way too much time on build-out, a.k.a. frittering away my dad's cash.

But why should this kid Angel have that, when the rest of us lose and lose and lose without getting any juicy nibs from the world in return?

Sorry, Angel. The world says fuck you.

Angel, the new player.

Me, the English teacher.

And the creator of the game, our old god of many forms, who went by Charon and the tenth girl: She is Sharon.

I inhale and take stock of my skeleton.

She *was* Sharon. Now, the boatman across the river Styx is trapped in the underworld for good.

I am lying in a chair of some kind. A congealed meat-and-cheese sandwich sits on a desk nearby. I come to my feet, flex my new toes, painted in ten different colors. I blink at them, greet them. I greet it all. I rise, only to catch sight of the street outside the window before me; a group of children totters behind an older woman wearing a sun-yellow shirt that reads, *Teachers Demand Action*. Each child clings on to a shared rope, giggling, chattering, in their wildly bright garb. As they bounce along, I feel as if they are growing before my eyes, pulsing with youth.

Wonder. The word bubbles up in me from a place I've never felt. *Wonder, until the very end.*

How beautiful.

I drop to my knees right there, relishing the jolt of pain. There are tears streaming down my face, hot and slick in a way I never could have imagined. Energy courses through me, of a type I didn't believe existed. Life force, you might call it.

I can't know where this world ends. I only know that this is where it starts.

ACKNOWLEDGMENTS

. . . or as I see them, an extended dedication to those who helped bring this book to life.

To Sarah Bedingfield, agent extraordinaire, whose brilliance is clothed in the most incredible kindness.

To Erin Stein, genius editor and master of Easter eggs, whose keen eye, patience, and enthusiasm brought the shine out.

To Natalie C. Sousa, Nicole Otto, Melinda Ackell, and Raymond Ernesto Colón at Imprint and to Shivani Annirood, Molly Ellis, Alexandra Hernandez, Kathryn Little, Kelsey Marrujo, and Katie Quinn on the Macmillan team, whose every moment spent on *TTG* will always fill me with profound gratitude.

To Michelle Kroes & Michelle Weiner at CAA, whose sharp insight and guidance were and are invaluable.

To EAF, my forever home, who convinces me everything will be all right even when we are picking out coffins three thousand miles apart.

To WOF, inventor of Mister Garcia, who is living proof that the impossible projects are most worth starting. (José, can you see?)

To AJF, my almost twin, who seeps into all my books and whose future I'll feel so lucky to witness.

Al matriarcado—Teti, Mini, Chimi, Lu, Sil, Feli e Isa—por el amor y apoyo que desde lejos siempre me han brindado.

To CLR, whose joy is my purest, greatest one, and whose life I would want to share every time.

SEVEN THINGS YOU MIGHT HAVE MISSED IN
THE TENTH GIRL

Ms. Faring snuck dozens of little clues into *The Tenth Girl* that hint at Vaccaro School's true nature. Close readers might have read them as mistakes, and closer readers might have begun to suspect something wasn't quite right in Mavi's world. Here are a few of the strangest and most delicious:

1. MEMORIZED RGB COLOR CODES

As a game designer obsessed with aesthetics, Angel's mother memorizes many of the RGB color codes used to create her game's interiors and exteriors. Mavi's room is painted in Angel's mother's favorite color (light apricot, or RGB color code 253, 213, 177), and in what is either a moment of irresponsibility—or if you prefer, Angel's mother giving a leg up to her beloved characters, should they ever try to escape the brutal game—a player's passcode is the RGB color code of the color paint on the walls in each assigned gateway closet's room.

2. COINCIDENTAL NUMEROLOGY

In *The Tenth Girl*, every character in the house is assigned a number by Dr. Molina (Mole), determined using birth date information, which corresponds with the number of one's room in the house and, roughly, one's role in the game. Close readers learn Mavi and Yesi's "numbers" (and room numbers) early on . . . Do you remember them?

3. SMELLING CHEESESTEAKS

Every time Charon explores the school in "the tenth girl's" avatar, Mavi smells the cheesesteaks Charon eats in the game (the same cheesesteaks that stain her white dress). Once, Mavi compares the smell to old plaster casts (yum).

4. THE SACRIFICE RITUAL

During the final ritual led by Morency, the characters chant in Latin—it's a garbled system restart procedure Ms. Faring chopped up and turned into a Latin sausage.

5. ANGST OR PRESCIENCE?

Dom's angsty speech on page 105 is the biggest clue to his overall awareness. "Don't follow me. Don't touch me," he says. "I know what you are, and you disgust me. You're hollow at the core. But having me won't help you. I'm nothing but a bad memory given shape by a disgruntled God." Mavi thinks Dom is speaking to her (poor dear). But is he actually speaking to the Others he knows are in pursuit of him? Is Dom the very first in the house to gain full awareness of their presence and the school's true nature, this go around?

6. INFINITE CHOCOLATE

When Mavi first tells Yesi about her nighttime visit from "the tenth girl" (Charon inside Angel's mother's avatar), Yesi eats from an open box of chocolates. By the end of their chat, the box of chocolates has magically rewrapped itself in shiny gold foil. Is brilliant Yesi too far up in the clouds to be disturbed by this and Mavi's tale? Or has she always known something Mavi doesn't?

7. HOW WELL DO YOU KNOW ANGEL?

Ms. Faring has been asked by close readers if Angel ascribes to the gender binary, and while she refuses to give an answer, she has allowed us to share this: Mavi settles into referring to Angel as "him" after Angel says to her: "I'm not like Dom. I'm different. But you can call me him, since I'm in him now." Take from that what you will.

DID YOU FIND ANOTHER HIDDEN CLUE?

If you write to Ms. Faring, she will send you a special surprise.
It may or may not be a leftover candy Easter egg.

A tale of two sisters against a backdrop of toxic fame and dark family secrets, this atmospheric novel will keep you guessing until the very end.

KEEP READING FOR
AN EXCERPT

BOY

CLIP FROM *NOT ANOTHER GIRL OF ICE* (1978)

Mireille Foix, age sixteen, winner of the Best Actress Award at the 1978 Cannes Film Festival
[Film rolls]

The scene opens in a midnight wood, dense and tangled, its rotting breath palpable. The locals call it Delirium Forest, and it's famous for devouring people whole, for reshaping the most solid of realities. A figure is visible inside, the moss-choked air around it glowing like an aura. The figure seems to float above the forest's gnarled roots, impervious to its thorns, its nettles, its spines and raking branches. As the figure moves deeper inside, its luminescence fades, and a deep, guttural buzzing builds.

At the fringe of the forest, a scummy parking lot, tongued by sagging bags of trash. And there, beside them: a broken form, lying in a growing pool of his own blood, thick as ink. A black cat edges around the mess, sniffing.

"Leave it," a woman's voice hisses, a static burst, and the cat skitters away.

The woman's wearing a ripped white camisole and fuchsia hotpants; she's gripping a tire iron, white-knuckled and red-eyed. Platinum hair. Chapped, bitten lips. Without even seeing her whole face, we know she is beautiful and that her beauty is like a fishhook: delicate, sharp, designed with ancient wisdom to hurt, to trap. She rests the tire iron on her shoulder, and its rusted edge drips fresh crimson freckles on her and the torn camisole strap.

The woman: She's no more than sixteen, all bruised skin and bird bones, the icy-blond wig on her head askew. Shivering in muddy boots.

She doesn't notice us.

She's staring into the woods. Faintly luminous, still. The humming grows louder, more ominous, and the woman leaves the safety of the bloodied asphalt to meet it. Her eyes never stray from the wild deep as she is guided away from us. Away from us, and into the carnivorous dark beyond. The droning intensifies, into its cracking and fizzing crescendo, until the woman finally—disappears.

[Film stops]

Mireille Foix possesses Grace Kelly's elegance crossed with Audrey Hepburn's mischievousness, Katharine Hepburn's wit, and Marilyn Monroe's pure, languid sex. She was born and raised on the mysterious Mediterranean island of Viloxin, and her idyllic childhood—spent free-diving for scallops with her fisherman father (now deceased) in a whitewashed cottage on the forested fringes of a miniscule seaside town—is nothing short of mythical. Today, she is her country's greatest cultural export and patron, thanks to her Foix Institute. She is also the last Star with a capital S, deemed the most beautiful, charismatic, and intuitive woman living today by a swath of Tinseltown A-listers. Mireille Foix is a goddess, come to Hollywood on her golden Viloki scallop shell.

—*Vogue* magazine, 1996

To most, the name Henry Hammick still conjures an image of a shadow in a lab coat: mysterious, bizarre, impenetrable. What were we to make of this monolith of a man who left behind his family, his career, and his home country to start over on an isolated, volcanic Mediterranean island half a world away? He moved to Viloxin in the 1970s at the age of thirty and never looked back. Since launching his groundbreaking pharmaceutical company, Hero Pharmaceuticals, Hammick's team has single-handedly introduced several history-changing medications and medical devices, most notably Ladyx, a treatment that slows the growth of many cancers.

Hammick has immersed himself in everything Viloki, from studying the largely unknown island history and social practices to Viloxin's poignant poetry and burial customs. His command of the local language, Vilosh, has awed scholars. And now, after earning Viloki citizenship for himself, Henry Hammick has taken a traditional Viloki name for legal reasons: Hëró. Yes, it's pronounced *Hero*, just like the name of his company. But don't hold it against him: Hëró

Hammick, founder of Hero Pharmaceuticals—now worth billions of newly minted euros—is this decade's God among men.

—*Time* magazine, 1997

The Foix-Hammicks believe Viloxin is their Camelot. Their Eden. Do I find this realistic? No. I certainly do not. They know nothing of this island, nor even of themselves. My family has been here hundreds of years, documenting its darkest nooks and its myriad depths, and I can assure you: The Foix-Hammick family does not venture below the surface in any of its endeavors—*especially* Mireille Foix Hammick's so-called *White Fox* film script. It is no Holy Grail. And no script—no family—concerns me. Despite their best efforts, they too shall disappear from our city, from our volcanic hills, from our lavender-scented meadows—in due time.

—Antella Arnoix, March 2009

RUNAWAY FOIX ON VILOXIN!
POLICE COMMISSIONER CONCLUDES
THAT MIREILLE ABANDONED HER CUBS.

—*The Viloki Sun*, July 2009

One year ago today, beloved film star Mireille Foix disappeared from her grand country home, Stökéwood, taking with her a crocodile purse, an Hermès scarf, one pair of calfskin gloves—and the only known copy of her secret film script, *White Fox*. The *Viloki Sun* gained exclusive access to a segment of this script, photographed by Foix's former manager, Daria Grendl, in the months preceding Foix's disappearance. It is speculated by some that *White Fox* possesses clues to Mireille Foix's current whereabouts—or to a shocking discovery she made before she vanished—as it eerily references the very items that went missing with her. Some call it the Viloki Holy Grail, claiming that Mireille Foix hid the secrets to building the ideal society inside.

Read on to discover for yourself a chilling excerpt, transcribed here from Grendl's photo. The world may never have the chance to see what might be this legend's greatest work.

Captor opens White Fox's red purse and looks through the contents.

> CAPTOR (V.O.)
> You say you are strong, but I know you cannot stomach the polluted mess in the mirror. Cannot reconcile it with the beautiful fantasy world you created around yourself.

Captor examines a pair of calfskin gloves, a wallet. Captor finds photographs.

> CAPTOR (V.O.) (CONT'D)
> A world of unbridled hope, of answered prayers, of selfless goodness, of smiling children—

Captor flips through photographs, finding one of smiling children. Two girls, beautiful girls, their identities unknown.

                    CAPTOR (V.O.)
          How sweet the photograph was, inside
          your ruined red purse.

Captor reenters chamber with clients inside and
watches White Fox, now stone-faced.

                    CAPTOR (V.O.)
          Evolve or die, White Fox, dear. Evolve
          or die.

Who is this captor? Grendl is staying mum.

"I simply thought it would be edifying for investigators
and those who loved Mireille alike to understand her mindset
prior to her departure," Grendl explains. "It should be plain to
readers that a troubled Mireille felt trapped and ran off."

Read on for Grendl's exclusive list of Mireille's Viloxin
haunts—ideal for those seeking a warm weather escape!

—*The Viloki Sun*, May 24, 2010

HERO TO HERMIT! "HE'S SICK, PARANOID,
IRRESPONSIBLE—AND HE REFUSES TO LEAVE
HIS STÖKÉWOOD HOME," SAYS HERO PHARM
BOARD MEMBER.

—*The Viloki Sun*, January 2014

NONI
NEW YORK, 2014

Two blocks from our home, an underground psychic was waiting for us with a secret message. Her basement shop blends into the row of dirt-encrusted town houses on West Tenth Street during the day, but at night the shop's magical features come alive: carefully painted wood paneling; a neat row of budding, overgrown plants; and a buzzing neon sign of a purple crystal ball.

"You have the money, right?" Tai whispers to me, between blowing on her hands, that shock of cherry hair in her face.

It's been five years since Mama disappeared, but strangers still notice us on the street sometimes, whispering "Is that . . . ?" to their friends with that sideways-sneak look, so we had decided to wear plain brown wigs tonight to stay incognito. But then Tai wanted to use the red one from her devil costume, and Tai gets what she wants. *You're only thirteen*, Aunt Marion cried, when she saw the crop top and leather miniskirt my sister was wearing. *Mama wore a thong swimsuit in a movie when she was thirteen*, Tai snapped back.

I hike up my loose jeans and pull the envelope out of my fleece sweatshirt's kangaroo pocket. "Two hundred big ones," I whisper back. We had been saving for months.

Tai grabs my shoulders and squeals, this infectious grin spreading from one bubble gum–pink cheek to the other. There's so much innocent hope in her lined-and-mascaraed blue eyes, so much it makes me quiver, but of course I'm smiling back before I know it. Tonight could give us clues, if not answers. My stomach hasn't felt settled in days.

Tai follows me down the steps, and we push inside the storefront—a bell jingles. The entry room is dark: patchy red velvet seating and finger-thick vines crawling everywhere. The smell of patchouli mixed with something heady and sweet, like cloves in hot wine. A stained, paisley curtain fringed in golden thread blocks our view into the back. A lone television on the wall plays a grainy video of spooky nature scenes on silent loop: a duck moving across a shadowy pond, wet red leaves falling from a tree, a lush forest that looks familiar.

"Hello?" Tai calls, scratching at her wig's netting.

Wind chimes tinkle in the back. I pull Tai onto the lumpy love seat up front just as a black cat pushes through the curtain—a furry lump in its mouth—and bounds up onto its window seat in between two ferns. It drops its catch and paws at it.

"Ew," Tai whispers, before rubbing at her bare legs. "What time is it?"

"It's eight-oh-one," I whisper back, just as *she* walks through the curtain, short and squat and dressed in black silk from head to toe: the imposing Madame Morency.

"Carmela!" She claps at the cat. "You promised your days hunting young and delicate creatures were over."

The cat yowls, and Madame Morency notices the two of us, clutching hands on the love seat, our hearts beating too fast in the small room.

"You're my eight o'clock, ladies?" she says in her deep rasp, head tipping to the side. "Sisters. You're very young. What loss could you have possibly suffered?"

Tai's purple nails dig into my skin.

"How old are you, exactly?"

"Aren't you a psychic?" Tai says, before I even open my mouth. "We're eighteen," she adds, with that confidence of hers that springs up from nowhere.

Madame Morency's lip quirks. "I will not begin any session without honesty and an open mind. It's best you see yourselves out."

"There's no legal age requirement to visit a fortune-teller in New York State," I reply, sweating hands squirrelling into my sweatshirt pocket. My lips snag on my braces. "Telling fortunes in general is a class B misdemeanor, anyway, though, and—"

"Fine," Tai interrupts, just as Madame Morency crosses her arms at me. "We're just kids. But we did lose someone important when we were really young. And we made this appointment because we need your help to reach her." She holds out the envelope of money. "Won't you help us?"

Madame Morency inhales and exhales, and as she does, something behind her eyes softens. I know it's not just pity. Everyone softens when they look at Tai: Her daintiness, her toughness, and her beauty combine to make her special. Mireille Foix Hammick–special.

"Follow me," Madame Morency says, taking the envelope and stuffing it into her waistband before shuffling back through the curtain.

Tai grabs my wrists and squeals again, eyes flashing brighter than neon.

The cramped back room is lit by dozens of candles. Two book-shelves overflow with rotten-smelling books and strange artifacts borrowed from a nightmare: a set of golden teeth, vials of amber liquid swirling with many-legged creatures, and a tiny, misshapen skull (the cat's victim comes to mind). We settle at a rickety, black cloth–covered table, across from Madame Morency, who peers at us with the heavy-lidded yet sharp eyes of someone who sees too much every day.

"Where are your cards?" Tai asks, examining the empty table before us, like something will push through the cloth at any moment. "Or, like, your crystal ball?"

"I do things differently." Madame Morency extends her veined, wrinkled hands across the table. "I don't even need my eyes to have the sight. Now, give me your hands. One each. Don't be afraid."

Without hesitation, Tai gives her one, while I wipe the sweat off my left palm onto my jeans and reach out. Her skin is smooth and soft and fine, like a child's.

Madame Morency shuts her eyes, humming to herself, and a breeze picks up, blowing through the curtain, flickering the candles, and bringing to life the blackened wind chime in the corner. I feel a chill; *wasn't the door closed?* Tai looks at me, her eyes wide with the thrill of it.

"Silence," Madame Morency snaps, and even the wind chime goes quiet. A minute ticks past, the kind that feels as gluey long as an hour. The air is thick with lost memories, with that decayed scent of crumbling brick walls.

When Madame Morency speaks again, her voice is a curious, rasping thing coming from the deepest part of her. "Why did you tell me your mother was dead, girls?"

The hair on the back of my neck pricks up.

"We didn't say that," Tai whispers back.

We didn't say anything about mothers at all.

"The message I am receiving is not coming from the other side," Madame Morency continues, her hand cooling in mine. "It's coming from the film between our worlds, the pond scum separating us from them. It says she is not gone."

I can feel Tai swallow next to me, see the goose bumps colonizing every inch of bare flesh. Her fingers are pale in Madame Morency's grip, and I can't feel my own. My eyes are glued to the woman in front of us, with her tightly shut eyes and her craggy face. Looking for signs of mystical truth, of anything at all I can cling to hard.

It says she is not gone.

"Her energy is mirrored across the globe," she continues. "So strong in places that a lesser psychic would mistake it for the true source. When and where did you last see her?" Madame Morency asks in this wheedling, odd voice. "Be precise."

I know we both remember: Mama tucked us into bed, wet-eyed, that night at Stökéwood, five years ago. Tears from a migraine, she'd said, shrugging on her favorite gray cashmere housecoat, petal-pink gloves in hand. I didn't know if she was telling the truth then, and I still don't. But I never saw her again, so I couldn't ask.

Tai opens her mouth to answer, but I stiffly shake my head. Dad told us never to share details with strangers. Aunt Marion and Uncle Teddy, too.

"I see her clearest in a hidden tower, extending into the sky," Madame Morency rasps, when we don't reply, and even though this means nothing to me, Tai stifles a squeak. She reaches for my free hand with hers, and her bones crunch into mine as Madame Morency speaks. "Otherwise, so many men contaminate her space. How is one supposed to keep a clear head with so many men and their opinions?"

She exhales slowly. "Does a red handbag mean anything to you? Cut from the skin of a creature that crawls?"

My stomach falls, but I feel weightless and chilled. I hear the news report in my head: *She took with her a red crocodile handbag with a pearl clasp—*

But anyone could know that.

"I need as much information as you can provide," Madame Morency continues in a strange purr. "Don't be afraid, girls. This is all part of the process."

Tai's eyes beg me to let her spill the truth. But I'm already wrenching my hand from the psychic and standing up. In my mind, halfway out the door. This woman is a trickster, a liar, a fraud. My blood rings in my ears. I'm the big sister, and I should've known better. I'm trembling with barely contained hurt, tears bubbling into my eyes. I take Tai's wrist, and she gapes at me.

"Where are you going in your brown wig, little one?" Madame Morency says, a wicked smile coming to her face, eyes still closed. "You can't hide the truth from me."

"We're going." I pull Tai toward the curtain. "You don't know what you're talking about."

"Fine. Run off. But you will find no answers until you go back there," Madame Morency calls after us. "To the place where you both saw her last."

But we're already disappearing down the street, both of us crying for different reasons, Tai ripping the wig off her head with starry-hot eyes and whispering, *She's alive, I knew she's alive; she's alive, I knew she's alive*, and my throat burning with fury that I could be so foolish, that I could think anyone would give us answers without trying to use us, that I could be so desperate to believe any voice but the one that feels like it comes from my gut, the frightened one repeating over and over, *She's dead, she's dead, she's dead.*

I will avoid the block with that psychic's shop, taking meandering detours that add minutes to my walk, for the next four years.

But as it turns out, the psychic was right.

∞ ∞ ∞

My little sister Tai and I will find our mama, the woman once known as Mireille Foix Hammick, a decade after she disappeared. After ten years—ten long years spent wandering that purgatory of uncertain loss—it will take only one week to solve our mystery. One week of madness, brilliance, deception, trust, weakness, strength, abandonment, love, and sacrifice in the belly of our birth town, Limatra, and the fringing forest of delirium to its west.

Not everyone will survive this week.

But just as every story comes to an end, it must also start at the beginning. . . .